PETER WATTS

BALLANTINE BOOKS **DEL REY** NEW YORK

This novel adaptation is based upon the original story treatment of Crysis 2. Various elements have been added and/or expanded upon to provide a fuller prose fiction experience. You may therefore notice some variation from game play. Enjoy.

Cevat Yerli and the Crysis 2 team

A Del Rey Trade Paperback Original

Published in the United States by Del Rey, an imprint of The Random House Publishing Group, a division of Random House, Inc., New York.

ISBN 978-0-345-52678-6
eBook ISBN 978-0-440-42359-1

www.delreybooks.com

Book design by Elizabeth A. D. Eno

146028962

The following document is derived from voice recordings and technical reports provided anonymously to MacroNet. It is therefore difficult to corroborate many of the allegations contained herein. Official responses from the corporate and political entities involved—the United Nations, the Pentagon, CryNet and their parent megacorp Hargreave-Rasch—have ranged from no-comment to outright denial. Both MacroNet and Del Rey have been served with numerous subpoenas compelling us to reveal our sources. We have also been threatened with a variety of civil and criminal charges, ranging from industrial espionage to treason, should we proceed with publication.

We have decided to proceed regardless. The subpoenas are moot, since we do not know the identity of our sources. Whoever provided these materials went to great lengths to protect their anonymity, including (by all accounts) the destruction of Google's OPG server farm off the coast of Catalina. Even if we wanted to cooperate with the authorities, we would have nothing to offer them.

As for potential counts of treason and other national-security-related charges, we have been advised that—while we may technically be in violation of written statutes—chances of actual prosecution are negligible. The current administration is fully occupied trying to deal with the very threats described in this volume. New York City lies in ruins, and any number of other major cities are at risk of a similar fate; if even half the allegations contained in this document are true, the entire planet is under immediate threat. Should the authorities wish to waste valuable resources on doomed attempts at censorship under these circumstances, that is their choice.

Besides, if they could have spared the guns to take us out, they would have done so by now.

—Tricia Pasternak
Senior DHS Communications Liaison, Del Rey

War would end if the dead could return.
—Stanley Baldwin

Son, you seem to think this is some kind of game.
—Jacob Hargreave

The thing is, I thought it was all our fault.

It's not that far off from what the Greens have been whining about since the last goddamn century. Global warm—sorry, *anthropogenic climate change*. Tidal waves, rising sea levels, half the planet's population wandering around looking for a place to crash since their homes got flooded out. There's malaria in the Baltic now, did you know that? A tropical disease. In the fucking *Baltic*. And somehow South America turned into bloody Siberia when no one was looking, something about melting icepacks short-circuiting the ocean currents. The whole world's fighting over fresh water like a pack of starving dogs with one stripped bone among them, and then Brazil started shooting all those sulfates into the stratosphere and—well, it was turning out just like the environazis said, only way worse and *way* fucking faster. None of the really nasty stuff was supposed to happen for another forty or fifty years, right?

So we're fucked, and it looks like we fucked ourselves, and all the alarmist whitecoats we shat on before are telling us it's too late now, it's all *planetary thermal inertia* and *unstable break-points* and *big ships turn slowly*. There's no way to keep the place from blowing up but maybe we can at least contain the explosion a bit, you know? Try to keep the peace, share whatever's left of the loaves and fishes, keep the worst of the riots from hitting the good ol' US of A. Maintain some kind of order.

That's why I signed up. That's why *all* of us did. We'd fucked things up by snarfing pork rinds and playing video games while the world turned to shit, and joining the marines was—I don't know. Penance. A chance to make amends.

Except it wasn't us after all, not really, not yet. It was these fuckers from outer space, it was that bloody cryo weapon of theirs, that secret run-in way over in fucking *China*. We may have primed the avalanche, but Ling Shan was the snowball that started it rolling. And that was just a *skirmish*, that was so small they even managed to cover it up. A presidential directive or two, a few strategic pulse bombs to fry seismo and satcam, maybe a handful of surgical kills to take care of any Koreans out fishing in the wrong place at the wrong time. All you're left with is a few fuzzy rumors so whacked that not even Fox News would stoop low enough to run with them. Then when the whole world starts listing to starboard a couple of months down the road, you blame it all on greedy shortsighted humans and their damn fossil-fuel economy.

But it was just a *skirmish*, Roger, and you know what?

So's this.

—N2-2 Alcatraz/Prophet (tentative desig.—awaiting update),
excerpted from Manhattan Incursion Debrief
27/08/2023

PROPHECY

Voice-mike intercept, Forensic Debrief, Manhattan Incursion
Subject ID: Unknown (code name *Alcatraz*)
27/08/2023

Laurence Barnes, I think. Prophet.

Alcatraz, then. Whatever. It doesn't matter. Of *course* I know the stats: I'm dead, not senile. Name, rank, serial number. Doesn't mean shit. That's not who I am anymore.

I'm the guy being debriefed by a low-level functionary because his bosses are too chickenshit to risk being in the same room, that's who. You expect me to think you *volunteered* for this gig? You think the higher-ups *wanted* to bring you into the loop, you think they wouldn't be in here themselves if they weren't afraid I might go off the reservation again given half a chance?

You're lying.

No, that's an empirical fact. Your skin conductivity just went up 13 percent. Your eye saccades increased by 24. And you don't want to get into your vocal stress harmonics. You may think you sound pretty solid, but believe me: In the upper registers you're squealing like a little girl.

I can tell stuff like that now. It's not the augments—it's not *just* the augments. I'm not reading numbers off a tactical overlay or anything, it's more—integrated. I just *know* this shit. I know a lot of things I'm not supposed to.

But you've got nothing to worry about. Really. If I had any

interest in killing you, you'd have been dead before you got through the door. You must realize that.

Doesn't help much, does it?

How do you want to do this?

From the top, then: They put us out to sea the moment the media blackout came down. I mean the *moment*—Chino was watching *Body-Swap Boxing* when the Emergency Broadcast Signal cut in. One minute after that MacroNet starts talking about some kind of massive explosion in New York, and literally three minutes after *that* we're hauling ass down to the water. There's a Swordfish surfacing off the dock, hasn't even finished blowing its tanks before we're piling inside. Haven't even checked our gear. We are *mobilized,* man, we're moving just this side of outright panic and we don't even know why. They barely get the hatch closed before we're back underwater.

We strap in. You can hear the screws turning through the hull. The Swordfish is basically a troop carrier with a big drive and a few missile tubes thrown in so it won't feel like such a pussy around the hunter-seekers, but even a Sword has the usual stealth options so you can get in and out without a fuss. They're not engaged. Wherever we're going, apparently we can't even afford a lousy 6 percent cloaking deficit.

Then it's a classic case of hurry up and wait. For *eighteen hours.* Nobody tells us shit, and the shit they do tell us keeps changing. First we're going to be docking with one of those big inflatable jellyfish down in the mesopelagic, keep us safely off the game board until we're needed. I'm thinking that's okay, at least there's decent headroom in those things, at least they're big enough to let you get away from the—but no, now suddenly we're heading back inshore. And then we're circling off Christ-knows-where for fuck-knows-how-long. Some of the guys try to catch a few winks but the CO handed out the usual stims at the six-hour mark so everyone's boosted on GABA and tricyclics and that supernephrin stuff that makes your joints ache for two fucking weeks post-engagement. I keep a forty of tequila in my kit—you know, strictly for medicinal purposes—and I crack it to take the edge off. Offer it around but nobody else wants any. They say it makes a bad mix with all the neurotropes. Pussies.

Anyway, we're strapped in, we're wired, we're climbing the walls. And suddenly the whine of the screws picks up, the night-lights kick in, and the whole compartment turns bloody red, like one of those Asian necro parlors where they use longwave to make the corpses look prettier. It doesn't take an AI to figure out we're deploying to New York but the CO won't even give up that much. Says we'll get briefed on-site. So we're sitting there in our camo, cheek-to-jowl, and everybody's making up these fairy tales to fill in the gaps. Syntheviral attack, moho nukes tunneling up under Broadway, some kind of coup at CENTCOM. Leavenworth—you know Leavenworth? No, of course you don't—Leavenworth weighs in with his usual crazy-ass theories, says he heard some Venter Biomorphs went all Skynet and turned on their masters, and he won't listen to half the squad pointing out that the Venter labs are way the hell over in California and if we're really heading into the replicant wars don't you think they might, you know, *airlift* us instead of taking a submarine through the Northwest fucking Passage?

I don't think Leavenworth believed that shit half the time himself. I think he just liked yanking our chains. I'm really going to miss him, if I ever get that part of my brain back.

Every now and then you can hear chatter drifting back through the forward hatch; turns out there's at least six other boats deployed, under orders of some Colonel Barclay I've never heard of. And yeah, big surprise, we're all headed up the East River for Upper Manhattan. Except suddenly *we* aren't. Suddenly we're detached from the main group and diverting to Battery Park. Secret rendezvous, CO tells us. Maybe a rescue mission. I don't know if he's giving it up or making it up.

So everybody's making these wild-ass guesses and Chino even starts a *pool* for chrissake, right there in the sub, and I'm sitting there and all I can think about is—

You know I was afraid of water, right?

I mean, of course I didn't *tell* anybody—I worked through it like you're supposed to, even came in third in the open-water trials last year. It's not a problem. But I almost drowned back when I was eight. Kinda stuck with me. You *must* have known. There were all these tests. You must have sniffed it out during the psych workup.

Thought so.

So everybody's jammed in there with their theories and Chino's got his pool going, and it's been eighteen hours now and I've been white-knuckling the bench for at least ten of 'em. Parchman figures I'm hungover but all I can think about is: a measly seven centimeters of biosteel between me and the whole Atlantic Ocean and I don't care how strong they say it is, a bunch of threads squeezed out of some gengineered spider's ass is not gonna keep an ocean out forever.

Probably the last time I was right about anything in this whole shitstorm.

Finally some voice comes over the comm, tells us it's time to saddle up. And that's when we hear a *ping*—not sonar, not *our* sonar anyway, just a single, solid beat resonating throughout the hull. Everybody falls silent for just a second, and Behrendt looks around and says, "Anybody hear that?"—

And something kicks us hard in the side.

No alarms, nothing coming over the comm link, just one *ping* and a giant *boom* and the whole boat's rolling to port. We don't even have time to scream; there's one microscopic *whatthefuck* moment and the hull opens up like some giant took a can opener to us. The far side of the compartment just *crumples:* snaps Behrendt's back like a toothpick, turns her into a rag doll right before my eyes, and then a crossbeam or bracket or some fucking thing tears free of the forward bulkhead and squashes Beaudry like a bug.

We're going down, now—the deck's at some crazy-ass angle, there's water flooding in from the bow, the whole damn hull's groaning like a humpback whale. *Now* the alarms kick in. Or maybe it's just everybody screaming. There's blood everywhere and you'd think it would blend in with the night-vision redlight but it doesn't, it jumps right out at you, it's solid shiny black. By now the water's not even *gushing* in, it's *rising*—like a tide, like a liquid floor sliding up to crush us all against the ceiling. Except the ceiling's a wall, and the rear bulkhead is the roof, and—

And—

Look, you—you *know* this shit. The sub went down. Period. Why do you need the details? You're not making a fucking documentary.

I know, it's just that—

Fine.

So it's every man for himself. I barely even have a chance to take a breath before the ocean closes over my head and I'm diving down, pushing buddies and body parts out of the way, and I'm fucking *scared,* man, I can't see anything except bloody backlight and blue sparks as the electronics short out. The sub's still groaning around me, it's crumpling into a paper ball and at least the screams stop underwater but you can hear metal grinding on metal as though it were right inside your fucking head. We get through the forward hatch, it's still black and blue and red everywhere except there's this jagged tear off to the side, this blue-black crevice seething with bubbles. I push through. I look up and there's pale dim light, and I look down and there's this great dark wall of metal sliding past, gashed to shit and bleeding rivers of air. Somewhere down there the bow's already hit bottom because there's a big honking cloud of black mud boiling up from below, engulfing the hull like something live. Like something *starving*.

And all that matters, in that moment, is that I get to the surface.

There's no *Semper*-fucking-*fi* down there in the deeps, let me tell you. Maybe if I'd had my rebreather on. Maybe if I'd had more than one lousy lungful of air to get me thirty meters to the surface. Maybe if I wasn't fighting off flashbacks from fifteen years ago. But no: I don't try to free the trapped or assist the wounded or carry the unconscious to safety on my back. I don't even think about it. There are things in my way: Some are sharp and hard and some are soft and gooshy and I don't fucking *care*, man, I bull through them all without prejudice or favoritism. I'm an eight-year-old kid again, and I'm *dying,* and I know what that feels like. Not again. God, not again.

So I'm fighting my way to the surface. Didn't even have the presence of mind to grab a pair of fins, you know, I'm just kicking at the ocean with these stupid little ape feet and all I know is it's dark in one direction and a little less dark in the other and my chest is so tight it feels like it's going to burst, like somehow I've got a whole roomful of air jammed in there ready to explode. And it almost does, I almost suffer a fucking embolism before I remember that that last gulp of air I took, it was under *pressure:* the closer I get to the surface the more it expands, the harder it pushes to get out. So I open my mouth. I open my mouth and I vomit all that precious air into the sea and I follow the bubbles as fast as I can, I pray to God the air doesn't bleed out of me faster than it swells up inside. I'm kicking and clawing at the water and suddenly the light overhead has *texture* somehow, that dull greenish glow resolves into distinct shafts of light and they're *dancing,* I swear to God they're dancing. Suddenly there's a roof over my head, like a writhing mirror, like mercury, and I break through and I feel like I could swallow the whole fucking sky and I'm so glad to be alive, man, you have no idea. I couldn't care less about Behrendt or Chino or even poor old conspiracy-crackpot Leavenworth. I'm so glad to be alive I don't even notice the hellscape I've dragged myself into—

Oh, that.

Yeah, I *am* a bit more eloquent than I used to be. Sometimes. *Writhing mirrors* and *dancing lights.* Never used to talk like that before. Now I just, you know. Switch back and forth. Don't even notice it half the time.

But you know that story, don't you? Improved vocabulary's just a side effect. Just another reminder that I'm never alone in here.

What I am, and what I was, and whatever this damn armor thinks it is.

Heh.

We are legion.

To: Site Commander D. Lockhart, Manhattan Crisis Zone
From: CELL Oversight Secretariat
Date: 21/08/2023
Cc: CryNet Executive Board

Commander Lockhart,

Following this morning's Supreme Court emergency session ruling, and pending a formal announcement by the president, US Marines are to begin deploying in the Manhattan Midtown area under Colonel Sherman Barclay. Their mission is described as humanitarian intervention, but they have been briefed for other combat eventualities as well.

The constitutional outrage of these measures
notwithstanding, you are to cooperate with Colonel
Barclay's force and afford him any assistance he may
require, *so long as it does not conflict with your existing
mandate.*

Let us be clear in this; the decision to deploy US military
forces on American soil is considered by the board, as by
many of our friends in Congress, to be an extraordinary
lapse of judgment by a president too weak to follow
through on the legislative innovation of his predecessor.
We fully expect this measure to be revoked within a
short time.

In the meantime, we hope we have made clear the
operating latitudes you are afforded, and we have the
fullest confidence in your ability to manage the situation
as befits a senior officer and shareholder of our company.

I'm born again into dead of night. About a dozen others are on
the surface ahead of me, looking around while I'm still frenching
the atmosphere. A few more pop up like Whac-A-Moles as I get
my bearings. There's oil everywhere, streams and patches of it
mottling the surface.

Oil on the water, but it's the sky that's on fire.

New York stretches around us like a big dark tumor. Most
of the skyline's blacked out; ten dark buildings for every one or
two that still have power. You can still make stuff out, though; a
smudge of moonlight through the clouds, and the overcast flickers with something like orange heat lightning. If that's reflected
firelight, whole city blocks must be on fire in there. I can actually
see an apartment building burning in the distance; it looks insig-

nificant from out here, like a matchbox crawling with orange fire-flies. Closer to the waterfront a whole office tower has just given up and slumped into the next building over. Black oily smoke crawls into the sky from a hundred spots we can't begin to make out from the waterline but there's no missing the great dark blanket they feed into, hanging over the skyline: It's so heavy I wonder why it doesn't crash down and flatten everything that's still standing.

"Holy fuck," someone says. "What happened here?"

Leavenworth. You made it out, man. You made it out.

I turn, tracking his voice, but the thing that bobs into view is not Leavenworth, not military, not alive. It barely even looks *human* anymore; it looks back at me with clumps of pulpy gray tumors where its eyes should be. A network of, of—veins, or tendons, or *something* like that runs down its cheek and roots in the shoulder, like, like—

You know those big industrial meat grinders in the supermarkets? You feed all the leftover chunks and waste cuts and bits of bone into that hopper at the top and there's this kind of grille at the bottom where the hamburger oozes out like a twisted cable of limp red worms?

Something like that.

And I see now that the whole harbor's dotted with these rotted floating things, that half the people I took for brothers-in-arms are dead civilians turned monstrous. So now I'm barely keeping my lunch down and I'm wondering if *everyone* was right, if it was a syntheviral *and* a nuclear strike *and* a coup d'état—hell, why not throw in Leavenworth's rogue biomorphs while you're at it? Maybe someone's launched the mother of all out-and-out assaults, maybe it's all of those things at once.

Man, what I wouldn't give now, if that's all it had been.

And just then someone cries out and I turn to *that* sound expecting more death and corruption but instead I see a big patch of bubbles boiling on the surface. At first I think it's the dying breath of the *Swordfish*, belched up from the bottom of the Hudson; but the water keeps churning and I actually feel a flash of hope that one of the other subs has come to the rescue, that the cavalry's breaching at our backs. I can see something dark and metallic just under the surface, red light rising from below, although some part of me says in a very small voice it doesn't look like any conning tower *I've* ever seen.

And then it rises above the waterline, and it *keeps on rising* until there's no water holding it up anymore and it's *still* rising, big as a fucking house, it's got its own personal storm front underneath where the water's streaming back off its sides. I can't make out jack shit except for two glowing orange hoops the size of merry-go-rounds and a black shape between them. But it's pretty obvious that whatever this is, it's not from anywhere around here.

And even *that* doesn't get as much time to sink in as I'd like, because in the next second it clicks on its high beams and starts shooting.

My reflexes kick in. All it takes is the sight of that little line of splashes stitching across the water toward me. You can hear them below the surface, too, rapid-fire *thwip-thwip-thwip*s getting louder, fading away, coming back the moment you break the surface to grab a breath and a gamble. You can't get a bearing, of course. No time for that. You breach and breathe and catch the quickest glimpse of those lethal little tracers streaking down from somewhere overhead. Maybe you hear someone scream as they lose their own particular throw of the dice but then you're back under again, hoping you don't roll snake-eyes before you make shore—because, sure, you'll be exposed on land but at least you've got solid ground under you, right? At least you can *run* for cover instead of floundering like wounded bait waiting for the sharks.

You let your brain stem take over, let your muscles decide for themselves when to zig and when to zag. Don't think about what it *is*, that's too big and there's no time; think about what it's *doing*. It's using *ballistics*. Not phasers, not death rays. No infallible super-targeting computers, or you'd be dead already. It's shooting *projectiles*. It's spitting out lines of *bullets*, like it ordered its ammo from Ordnance "R" Us. Conventional weapons.

Of course, conventional weapons do just fine when your target is unarmed hamburger flailing around in open water. I hear the screams between the bullets and the bubbles. I can hear that airborne motherfucker mowing us down like dogs. But I keep rolling the dice, man, I keep breathing and diving and zigging and zagging, and they don't get me. I make it all the way to the shore. I nearly kill myself on the debris slope, I'm stroking so hard I don't see the rocks coming and a piece of half-buried driftwood just under the surface nearly takes out my eye but suddenly my feet are on the bottom, the rocks are slimy but they're *solid*, and I'm scrambling uphill and I run smack into a sheer concrete seawall. In one split second I realize there's no *way* I can scale it without grapplers or gecko gloves, and in the next I'm slipping on the slime and I go over backward as a line of divots explodes across the concrete right about where my head used to be.

I'm back in the water and those lights in the sky, those glowing eyes are sweeping off across the water in search of other targets. Someone's yelling off to my left and it's *Leavenworth*, man, you just can't keep him down, we've obviously found us a niche where being a paranoid conspiracy freak actually pays off. And Leavenworth is waving and gesturing, something's blown a hole in the seawall just a few meters along and he's already diving into that breach and I'm right there behind him. We crawl through a little canyon of smashed concrete and tangled rebar that tries to gut you like a fish every time you move. There's this stink in the air, not just the oil and the bodies and the shit in the harbor, something else, something—acrid. That's the word. Like ammonia.

We come out in the middle of something that used to be a road, hunker down under a slab of upended asphalt like kids camping in a lean-to. But the Eyes in the Sky are swinging around for another pass, and they've got a clear shot at us from their current angle of approach. Leavenworth breaks cover and starts running for the only other piece of cover in sight, old wreck of a building past fifty meters of parking lot. I'm right behind him, got my eyes on the ground but it doesn't help, I still see Leavenworth blow apart like a water balloon right in front of me. The ballistics are a fucking *hailstorm* now and we've just been massacred and suddenly there's this stupid giddy voice in my head that won't shut up, keeps saying *Well at least Leavenworth died happy—vindicated at last, blown up by space aliens . . .* and—

—And then there's this, this kind of a *thump*, a *tugging* sensation, and I'm not running anywhere anymore. I can't feel my legs. I'm facedown in gravel and there's blood everywhere, it's got to be mine because I can *feel* myself bleeding out, but—

But it doesn't hurt. I don't know if it's shock or a severed spinal cord or if the pain just hasn't crawled upstream yet but that's it, man, I'm dying, I *know* I'm dying. And it doesn't hurt at all.

I can still move my arms, though. And someone's still screaming somewhere so I'm not completely alone, not yet, not yet. I heave over onto my back—vision's shaky now, eyes swarming with floaters and there's a red mist over everything, but if this is *it* then I want to at least go out looking my enemy in the eye, you know? And there it is, big as death, Armageddon in an airfoil and I still can't see anything but a black shape behind blinding light but in my mind's eye it's got a hundred muzzles twitching and tracking, locking on, the fucker's looking right at me and in the next instant a sonic boom goes off in my head.

And the Eyes *stagger* in midair, like something just kicked them in the face.

For a second I think *That's the weirdest recoil I've ever seen,* but then I realize it's the *gunship* that's been hit. And whatever that ship uses for a pilot has just realized the same thing, it's forgotten all about me and it's spinning in midair, looking for whatever arrogant motherfucker had the audacity to fight back.

And there it is, pinned in the spotlight like a rock star.

It's some kind of battlefield robot. It's a cyclops with no face, no *room* for a face because that big bloody eye wraps halfway around its head. It's like someone flayed one of those big Greek statues down to the muscles—because that's all you can see, man, these bunched cords of muscle, gunmetal gray, almost oily in the searchlight, wrapped around a gleaming skeleton that pokes through here and there. You can see a spine. Something like a skull. There are knuckles and elbows and kneecaps and they gleam like chrome but you just know they have to be a thousand times stronger.

I swear in that moment it's ten meters tall. It comes striding across the wreckage like a great fucking golem, holding a cannon in one hand like it weighs a hundred grams, like it weighs nothing at all. The muscles flex and slide across one another with every step; they seem almost organic, but I've never seen anything live move quite like that.

It looks like it can take down that ship with a single shot.

It doesn't, though. The gunship gets its licks in, fires back, hits the golem dead in the chest and not a word of a lie I swear that fucker *stays standing.* He staggers, rocks back on his heels, almost goes over. But he doesn't. He keeps his footing, and he brings up that cannon again—I can see now it's some kind of tricked-out miligun, way too big for mere mortals. He must've swiped it off a Taranis or something but he's throwing it around like it's a paperweight and the sound it makes, that beautiful sound, gotta be three thousand rounds a minute and the ammo belt's flapping and slithering through that gun like .30-caliber tickertape.

I'm laughing like the Joker, I'm cheering him on so hard I almost forget I'm dying. He's my guardian angel, he's Gabriel blowing his horn against the heavens and that hellship is dipping and weaving and looking for an opening but it's on fire now, it's shitting smoke and listing to starboard and it can't even seem to get a target lock anymore, all that devastating firepower just spraying in these wild arcs through the whole 360, hitting nothing but sea and sky.

Doesn't blow up a moment too soon, though, because two seconds after it goes down my savior's cannon is spinning on empty.

I'm kind of laughed out by now. Actually, I'm having a hard time even breathing. Blood pools at the back of my throat. I can barely cough it back up. But Gabriel hears me, even over the roaring of the flames. He sees me, and he comes to me through the smoke and the wreckage with that miligun still spinning in his hand, nothing to chew on anymore but sheer inertia. He seems to notice that after a second, throws the gun away without a second glance, kneels down at my side and stares at me.

I stare back. Dark coppery visor, shiny and opaque; stubby metal snout underneath, some kind of integrated gasmask-respirator thingy. More of that corded gray muscle-armor across the cheeks, held anchored by metal strips running along the edge of the jaw; they meet up like mandibles where the mouth should be.

It's like being face-to-face with a praying mantis.

He doesn't say a damn thing for the longest time. *I* try to—*thank you,* or *nice shooting,* or even *what the fuck*—but those parts don't seem to work anymore. Finally I hear an electrical hum and a voice comes out.

"Let me guess. You're my ride out of here."

Golem. Angel. Cyclops. Robot. Still not sure *what* he is. It's surreal. I think maybe I'm hallucinating. I think I'm having a near-death experience.

Looking back, that's exactly what it was.

He saves me. I don't know how long it takes. I'm not there for most of it.

I remember movement; I remember being lifted up to Heaven, slung over my hero's shoulder like a sack of potatoes. I remember the feel of great bundled cables ratcheting back and forth, biting into my gut. I remember it *hurting*, at long last. I'm in agony now, I'm flayed nerves and broken bones and guts fed through a wood chipper. I faint from the pain, and the pain shocks me back awake, and then I faint again.

But I'm almost relieved, you know? Almost happy. I'm not dead yet, not yet. I'm still in the world. I can still *hurt*.

Still can't scream, though. Can't make a sound.

I hear *him* talking. Through the helmet. A voice, filtered through some kind of vocoder; there's an electronic buzz to it, a machine quality, but it sounds like there's a real man inside trying to get out. He raises his voice. He rants. He falls silent now and then, like he's listening. I listen, too, but I never hear anyone answer.

"This is what it was for, then. This is your Master Plan. You always have one, don't you?

"Yeah, right. Not the clay's place to question the potter. Except *your* feet are made out of the stuff just as much as mine, aren't they? *Aren't they?*

"You're not above it, you fucker. You're no higher than I am. You may be *in* me, but you're not above me.

"Goddamn you. You monster, you parasite. Goddamn you."

I don't know if he's swearing or praying.

Something's screaming the next time I come to. It's still not me; I try, believe me. I can barely manage a gurgle. But *something's* screaming, and that sound bounces off walls and ceilings and hits me from all sides, tinged with metal.

My hope and my salvation. He's brought me indoors.

I open my eyes, try to focus, can't. But the flames are still with us; giant flickering shadows writhe on a wall, and the backlight is orange—except just off to my right, where it's—wrong, somehow. Artificial. I turn my head just far enough to see the golem playing with a tiny blue sun dancing in his hand. *Laser,* I realize, and pass out again.

"Wake up."

Not dead yet. Still not dead.

"Wake up, soldier. Now."

Same place, different time. Bright dirty sunlight pools on the floor from barred windows high overhead.

I actually feel a bit better now. The pain's more—distant. That's good; it means all those nerves sending back reports from my broken fucked-up body have finally cashed it in. It means that maybe I can die in peace.

"Wake *the fuck UP!*"

Something big and dark and flaccid hangs in front of me. I force my eyes to squint, force my brain to interpret: a skinned carcass, a flayed—

—golem—

Instant focus.

My savior's been gutted like a fish. It hangs deflated from an overhead beam, split down the middle and scooped clean of its insides. All those high-tech gunmetal muscles dangle limp and unmoving; the interior glistens red as raw meat. Are my eyes fucking up again, or is that butchered carcass *bleeding*?

"Down here."

Big black dude. Shaved head, some kind of skintight black body stocking pimped out with white veins. Like a wet suit with a circulatory system. Dirt and blood smeared across his face and for one crazy surreal second I think he has *gills,* but no; it's just a bloody gash, still oozing, along the line of his jaw. I concentrate on his shoulder flash until it stops jumping around: AIRBORNE.

He's got some kind of hypo in one hand. I can feel the tingle, now; he's just emptied it into my arm.

"Don't try to talk," he says. (I almost laugh, but the pain surges back when I try.) "Just let it take hold. You're gonna make it. You're gonna make it."

It sounds like an apology.

He's not doing so well himself, you know. There's a trickle of blood threading out of his nose, he's swaying on his feet, his face is as gray as that wall behind you. One of his eyes is bloodshot, like every capillary ruptured at once. His hands are shaking. His eyes dart around like a bird's, like there aren't enough shadows in this place to hold all the monsters he sees—and there are *still* a lot of shadows here, that dirty daylight doesn't kill the darkness so much as just . . . throw it into high contrast. He doesn't seem to be seriously injured, physically—no bones broken that I can see, no major wounds—but it's obvious he's way past your garden-variety thousand-yard stare. I've seen some pretty horrific shit over the past couple of hours, and I'm looking my own death in the face, and even so I can tell he's *far* farther into hell than I am.

Something lands on the roof; metal clangs against metal. Airborne glances up at the sound and his face lights up. I mean, literally *lights up;* I could swear that dark skin *brightened* for just a second, but I blink and it's gone. I hear scuttling sounds, but it's dark up there; I can't see anything but the ghostly dim shapes of rafters.

"Don't worry about that." He jerks his chin at the ceiling. "That's the least of your problems."

More sounds from overhead; a soft gritty patter of displaced dust drizzles down on us. Those rafters look like a rib cage. I flash back to a half-remembered Bible story from the Vision channel, something about gods and whales. I wonder for a moment if some alien monster hasn't swallowed us whole.

"You are so fucked," Airborne says, and his voice is—empty. Transparent. As if the man has already gone away, and left some kind of autopilot in charge.

"There's no time," it says, and I can see I was wrong; the man hasn't gone away, not yet. He's still trapped in those eyes, one red, one white, jerking back and forth in panicked little arcs while the chassis short-circuits around them. But whatever's running the voice is still online, and it's got priority now. "It's up to you now, soldier. I can't do this anymore."

Suddenly those red-and-white eyes lock onto mine. They drill into me like restraining bolts, like spikes through my head. I really don't like what I see in there and I try to look away, but no dice; I just about pass out from the effort. And he's starting to *glow* again, there's a kind of *mesh* lighting up his cheeks from inside, like honeycomb. Dude has one of those bioluminescent tattoos, you know, the ones where they inject the glowing bacteria? The more excited you get the more they light up—it's a blood-flow thing, dissolved oxygen and whatnot—and this dude must be *very* fucking excited because that honeycomb is just about incandescent in his face, man, like those old lightbulbs with the filaments.

But I'm fading again. I can't hold focus, I can feel myself passing out. I might as well have snowglobes for eyeballs, there's so many floaters swirling around in there. The whole damn world disappears down a spinning tunnel, into a vortex of static with those wild wild eyes at the center, and that sad dead voice behind them saying *This is the best I can do . . .*

And something *engulfs* me from behind.

It's like being devoured by an oil slick. Something warm and slippery wraps around my arms and legs and chest and at first it hurts holy *fuck* it hurts, but then the pain recedes and whatever steps up to take its place is *really* nice. Way better than morphine; it takes the edge off the pain but it doesn't make you the least bit stupid.

My head clears. I experience new thoughts, I experience *old* thoughts in a whole new way. It's unprecedented. (I can even roll worlds like *unprecedented* around in my head without feeling like an asshole, although I'm not sure how I feel about that.)

But it's not just that my brain is firing on all cylinders again; like I said, it feels *good*. I figure it must be one of those new dopamine analogs you hear about, and then I remember *where* I heard about it: It was a MacroNet puff piece I caught out the corner of my eye for fifteen seconds *two years* ago. Either I really am dying and the whole life-before-your-eyes thing is *way* overrated, or this giant alien slug has just amped up my memory somehow.

My vision fuzzes and clicks into a kind of high-def crystalline focus that doesn't quite seem real, you know that ultra-high rez you find in raw tactical sims and cheap video games. Alphanumerics start scrolling up across my field of view, boot sequences and tactical overlays, but they're *inside* me somehow, you know? It looks subjectively like a head-up display but we're not talking about your usual HUD: Something's planting these glyphics *directly into my head*. More of a, a Brain-Up Display I guess. A BUD.

I've got my legs back, I'm upright, I can move again. I bring up my arm and there it is, the muscle suit, crawling around my forearm like an octopus as I clench my fist, flexing and tightening and accommodating every movement. It *flickers* as I watch; waves of light and darkness chase each other across my arm like storm clouds on fast-forward. Colors bleed along their edges— deep-sea green, stratospheric cerulean, who knows what the marketing boys are calling those parts of the spectrum these days. Suddenly my arm *disappears,* turns into liquid glass and just *fades.* A progress bar grows across my eyeball; a readout underneath tells me that CHROMATOPHORE INITIALIZATION SEQUENCE is 87 percent complete. When it hits 100 my arm fades back into view—just boring utilitarian gray again, laced through with a faint hexagonal mesh that looks a lot like Airborne's tattoo (I guess ol' Airborne doesn't have a lot of imagination when it comes to accessorizing). Tactical says CLOAK OK.

I am Gabriel. I am Golem Boy, I am my own hope and my salvation. And even though I must still be a pile of shattered bones and torn-up viscera inside this magic armor, somehow I feel just fucking *awesome.* Even wild-eyed Officer Airborne kneels before me, hands raised in supplication.

Except that's not what he's doing at all, of course. He's bolting me into this suit of his, tightening the last couple of lug nuts on my sternum. "Feels good, doesn't it? I bet it does. Gets old fast, though. Believe me."

Something's changed about him. The spasms haven't stopped, the tremors are as bad as ever, but that demon in his eyes, that panic—it's gone, somehow. His face is dark; the tattoo's gone back to sleep. The right eye is completely opaque now—a solid ball of scarlet, you can't see anything in there anymore—but the left is almost peaceful. He fixes me with this sad, steady stare, and he says, "It's alive, you know. Obsessed, you might say. It won't move on until I do, it's . . . viral. But it means well. Keep that in mind and you just might pull this off."

Pull WHAT off, I try to say.

He answers as if I've succeeded. "Find Gould. Nathan Gould. It's all I can do now, *you're* all I can do. I'm sorry, man. I'm so fucking sorry. It's all on you now."

He can barely stand, he's shaking so hard. There's a rattle in his chest I've heard too many times before. He staggers, turns, takes in the filth and the dereliction looming on all sides. "Look at this fucking place," he whispers, and even above the crackling of flames and the groaning of distant wreckage and all the faint faraway screaming, I can hear him perfectly. I swear I can even hear the beating of his heart.

"They used to call me Prophet," he says. "Remember me."

And puts a service pistol under his chin and blows his own head off.

ASSAULT AND BATTERY

Holy *shit*.

What do I, what just—

Fuck fuck *fuck*.

A cheery little overlay pops up while Prophet's blood and gray matter trickle down my faceplate: CN COMBAT SOLUTIONS. NANOSUIT 2.0. Suddenly I can't move. I'm in the middle of some kind of war zone, my entire squad has been massacred by a flying saucer from Zeta fucking Reticuli (there: I said it), the one guy who might have been able to give me some answers now ends at the mandible, and my magical new dream suit has stuck me in place like an ant in amber. Something's stomping around on the roof, acting in no way scared or cautious or the least bit worried about being discovered. Which only goes to emphasize how very much *I* should be feeling all those things.

On the plus side—if you can call it that—I'm not dead. And according to the medical diagnostics racing across my field of view, I should be. My back is broken in three places. My larynx is crushed. My femoral artery is torn. There's more blood in my lungs than air. The list goes on. Nanosuit 2.0's rattling off diagnostic and wet-repair capabilities like I've never seen outside a full-blown VA hospital—and while it's got me rooted in place like a garden gnome, it's also pumping me full of antibodies and autocatalytic fibrinogen and a dozen kinds of engineered osteoblasts to knit my bones back together. All things considered, immobilized in a custom-fitted body cast is not a bad place to be right now.

Just as long as I'm not immobilized when the bad guys come calling.

Eventually the biotelemetry slows to a drizzle. Scenery peeks out from behind the stats; the BUD gives up all the visual real estate except for a dusting of ice-green icons scattered around the edge of vision. Nanosuit 2.0 reports that it has INTEGRATED NEW DNA PROFILE, and unlocks.

I can move again.

And something up on the roof is just *waiting* for me to do that. Every now and then it stomps on the iron sheeting just in case I've forgotten, like the bogeyman who pushes just a little bit harder on that one squeaky stair outside your bedroom door. He *wants* you to know he's out there.

I *know*, already. I step over what's left of Prophet—roaches scuttle away from my shadow, the place is infested with them—and scoop up his pistol. BUD snaps a tactical silhouette around its edges, serves up an ID: M12 NOVA AUTO LIGHT PISTOL.

Empty. I fucking *hate* it when people use the car and return it without any gas.

Stomp. Clatter. More dust settles from the rafters.

"Welcome to the end of the world, marine."

It's just a chip voice buzzing in my ear, but I jump anyway. I run my eyes over tactical, looking for some kind of comm link. Each icon brightens in turn as I focus on it. Saccadal interface. Cool.

"Everything's online," the voice tells me. "The N2 is functioning within normal parameters."

Not comm. Suit AI. A bit of fuzz in the upper registers. Damaged speaker, maybe.

It sounds like Prophet.

"There's been some minor structural damage to the intercostals and the Ballard-stack couplings; estimated time to suit repair is twenty-six minutes. Estimated time to host repair is unavailable at this time."

Scratch that; it sounds like something *trying* to sound like Prophet. You can recognize the impression, but it's not gonna fool anyone.

I look around for another gun, a knife. A board with a nail in it. My surroundings sink in for the first time: some kind of dockside warehouse. I'm in an aisle formed by two rows of big green shipping containers, stacked to each side, unmarked except for the red cross decaled across the door of each. No weapons. The floor's littered with spent casings, so there could be fresh ammo nearby at least. The aisle dead-ends against a wall about ten meters in front of me. There's a little fire flickering down there, a pile of smashed wooden shipping flats that's just about burned itself out. Filtered sunlight spills over the top of the cargo pods to my left. It looks like there's a way out down at the other end of the aisle, a gap between the pods and a stack of big wire cages that look like giant mutant shopping carts stuffed with rags. There's a bad transformer or breaker box down there, too, judging by the buzzing.

I start moving. The thing on the roof starts moving, too.

I think it's tracking me. I think—

I think those aren't rags.

I don't think that's a bad transformer.

Fuck.

There are feet sticking out of those cages. Arms. Some look almost normal, some are wormy with rootlets and tumors. Something glistens from the shadows in all that clothing; before I'm close enough to make it out I already know it's looking at me. And it is. There's a nice clean bullet hole in the forehead right above it. Flies crawl and buzz and do little joyous loop-the-loops around the windfall.

I look down at casings scattered around the floor like leaves in fucking autumn. Standard military issue.

Not one of these people is in uniform. At least two are wearing surgical scrubs.

I'm running so short of headspace to process all the nightmares—hostile aliens, savior suicide, the Thing On The Roof, and now a massacre of goddamn *civilians?*—that I almost don't notice the bright new icon blinking upper-left. All that registers at first is a sense of minor irritation, some vague tugging at the back of my mind. I stand there like a moron for a good five seconds before I notice the damn thing flashing at the corner of my eye. But the moment I focus, it jumps front-and-center and starts talking:

"Find Gould. Nathan Gould. It's all I can do now, *you're* all I can do. I'm sorry, man. I'm so fucking sorry. It's all on you now."

Text crawls across my eyeball—

Gould, Nathan.
89 South St #17, New York, NY

—and my first reaction is *Are you fucking KIDDING? Who GIVES a shit?*

But Prophet has charged me with a sacred quest, and maybe I *can* just turn around and walk away from that. But then again, maybe I can't. The only reason I'm alive now is because of the man lying dead at my back; and my life came with a price tag attached. Besides. I'm cut off from my chain of command, my squad's been exterminated, and I have no fucking clue why any of this is happening. Nathan Gould is a place to start, at least. He's bound to have some answers. Let's go talk to nice Mr. Gould.

What else am I going to do? Count the dead?

Except it turns out I'm locked in. The windows are barred and out of reach, way up near the ceiling. Every door's been welded shut and backed up with weighted cargo containers. Some of the blockage is pure battlefield entropy but most of it's been deliberately barricaded against whatever's got the high ground outside. I climb over sandbags and body bags, I kick open shipping crates and rummage through lockers. I find two bodies in hazmat suits, I find overturned tables, I find microscopes and thermocyclers and those spinning things, what do you call them, *centrifuges* smashed and scattered across the fractured cement. I even find a couple of usable ammo clips, but wherever I go those scary metal footsteps seem to follow me around up there. Although they're not *exactly* footsteps. It sinks in after a while; the rhythm's all wrong.

But there has to be some kind of way out of here because after all, Prophet brought me *in*, right? Only I'm not finding it. And whatever cocktail the N2 fed into my brain is not all it could be, because the obvious answer has been stomping around over my head for the past twenty minutes and I was either too stupid or too chickenshit to see it.

But yeah. Eventually I figure it out.

And I swear to God, I can hear the bogeyman dancing an eager little jig of joy as I start climbing the stairs.

Broadcast Intercept (decrypted): 23/08/2023 09:35
39.5 MHz (gov/nongov shared, land mobile)
Apparent signal source: CELL Field Command, Battery Park
Interceptor: Anonymous (via Edward "Eddie" Newton,
Radio Free Manhattan)

Voice 1:   —is Cobalt Seven. Think he came this way.
                    Spreading to search.

Voice 2:	Yeah, uh, this is Cobalt Four. We got camera footage from the containment fence. Moving fast, man. Never saw anything like that before.
Voice 3:	Fuck are we fighting here? Is he one of *them*?
Voice 4:	That's need-to-know, soldier. All *you* need to know is don't take any chances. Lethal force, soon as you get eyes on.
Cobalt 4-A:	You believe this mess, man? They took out everything: the EMAT teams, the doctors, our guys. There's nothing left.
Voice 4:	Stay sharp, people. Quarantine protocols. You see anything move in there, you kill it.

Dead Air—47 seconds. Following exchange appears to have been broadcast accidentally, possibly due to a jammed transmit switch.

Cobalt 4-B:	So you think he took down that Ceph ship?
Cobalt 4-A:	How the fuck should I know, man? I look like a Squid to you?
C4-B:	I'm just saying, it wasn't us. And if he *did* shoot it down, well . . .
C4-A:	Well what?
C4-B:	You know. The enemy of my enemy and all that.
C4-A:	The enemy of *my* enemy doesn't go around blowing the shit out of *his own guys*.
C4-B:	There is that.
C4-A:	Shit, man. Past few days, there's lots of enemies to go around for every—hey, is that—?

C4-B:	What?
C4-A:	Over there, on the waterfront up on the roof. That a Squid?
C4-B:	Yeah, one of those fuckers—
C4-A:	*grunts,* or—
C4-B:	No, look, there's *two* of them.
C4-A:	You sure? Looks—
C4-B:	No, man, look, there's definitely two. They just look like one big motherfucker because they're in close like—
C4-A:	What are they doing up there?
C4-B:	They're *fighting,* man. They're fighting *each other . . .*
C4-A:	What the fuck. Why would—
C4-B:	Dude, the smaller one. I think it's human.
C4-A:	That's just exoskel. They're all blobs inside.
C4-B:	No, man, I've got him scoped, he's definitely—
C4-A:	Holy shit, that's our guy! That's *Proph*—
C4-B:	Cobalt Oversight! Cobalt Oversight! We have eyes on Primary! Repeat, *we have eyes on*—

Signal squelched at source.
Transmission ends 23/08/2023 09:38.

So this is how it is. No cutesy musical sign language, no guys with bumpy foreheads saying *Resistance Is Futile* or *Kneel Before Zod,* no sexy alien hive queens keeping our hero busy with butt sex while her minions turn our children into veal cutlets. No small talk at all, unless you count the sound it makes when it sees me:

kind of a stuttering hollow croak, like a cheap voice synthesizer trying to gargle.

And then ET *brings* it, motherfucker.

In that first second I'm surprised by how human it looks. Sure, the legs have too many joints and the arms don't have any—more like segmented tentacles with hands, like Doc Ock from Spider-Man—but there's two of each, right where they're supposed to be. Kind of a helmet on top with two compound clusters of orange lights where you'd expect eyes. It's all metal, though, so I'm thinking either *robot* or *armor*.

And then it fires, point-blank, and I'm flat on my back and I should be dead but I'm not. In the next second it's on me like a fucking panther and I can see the meat *inside* all that metal: grayish, translucent, like a jellyfish. Dim brownish orange blobs deep inside that have to be organs, four thick fleshy tentacles flailing out the back. And one part of me's thinking *What the hell kind of armor leaves your guts exposed*, but another part's thinking *Those guts are the last thing you're ever gonna see, asshole*—because I'm already *down*, man, without firing a shot, it caught me flat-footed and flipped me like a bug on its back. And it should be game over right there, but then it just—

Hesitates. Bobs its head, or whatever you call that wedge-shaped thing with the lights. We almost get the sense it's sniffing the air, trying to get a fix on some strange new smell. And that little hesitation, that one or two seconds' grace—that's enough for a comeback. We grab that fucker by the horns, we jam—

I, of course. I mean *I*.

I grab that fucker by the horns, I jam my pistol into the gray goo and start firing. The thing pulls away, makes this *whistling* sound—cold, winter-wind sound—and I'm back up just like *that*, the alien brings its weapon up again but I block, I jab, I don't even think about it. The suit's got its own reflexes, force multipliers, *motion* multipliers. Turns a flinch into a right hook. It barely waits for me to move before responding, I could almost swear it's moving *me*. I lift that alien motherfucker over my head and pitch it off the roof like I was throwing a Hacky Sack.

So much for the bogeyman, bitch. So much for the monster under the bed. So much for the thing in the closet.

I don't know what Prophet was going on about. This suit is fucking *awesome*.

PERFECTION²

When we released the first CryNet Nanosuit four years ago, we described it as "battle armor perfected." That wasn't just our opinion: In a scant two months the N1 had become *the* armor of choice for military and paramilitary forces around the globe, winning an unprecedented 9.8 rating from *Urban Pacifier* and taking home Jane's prestigious Platinum Award for Infantry Support Technology. All of which left we at CryNet with a bit of a problem: How do you improve on perfection?

This time, we perfected the soldier.

Not that we've ignored the hardware, mind you. Our latest offering comes with all the bleeding-edge features you'd expect from CryNet: rad-hardened ceramic epidermis, dynamic Faraday mesh for unsurpassed EMP shielding, state-of-the-art countercurrent heat-exchangers for thermoneutrality in firestorms and LOx spills alike. CryNet remains at the forefront of Moore's law—and maybe a little bit beyond.

But anyone can engineer machinery. It is the soldier *within* that remains the heart of CryNet's products and our highest priority.

The human mind has always been the greatest strength of an augmented infantry—and also its greatest weakness. For no matter how sharp the intellect, no matter how great the courage, the men and women in these chassis are only flesh and blood. They can grow tired. They can quail in the face of overwhelming odds—and even the most dedicated can hesitate for that crucial half second that makes the difference between victory and defeat. They are human. Our technology shields them from outside threats, but it cannot protect them from their own frailty.

Until now.

For the first time, combat armor not only protects your soldiers but also *improves* them: immunizes them against fear and fatigue, keeps them razor-sharp around the clock, feeds real-time tactical telemetry from a thousand sources directly into the brain. CryNet has created something that is more than man, more than machine: something that shares the strengths of both and the weaknesses of neither.

Introducing the CryNet Nanosuit $^{2.0}$.

Perfection squared.

Of course, if I'd known what the suit could do up front I wouldn't have bothered going upstairs in the first place. I would've just punched my way through a wall. Live and learn.

So now I'm alone on the roof. Sun's high, midmorning. The clouds have blown away but the world smolders and flickers around me like fucking Gehenna; I can see little fires guttering all over the lawn. I can see a couple of tanks, too, neither in what you'd call pristine condition. One's burning; the other's been flipped on its back. Some green statue of a horse-mounted soldier surveys the wreckage, one of those memorials they always put up after we've kicked ass in someone else's backyard.

No sign of the bogeyman. Which means it walked away from my bullets, the beating I laid on it, and a three-story fall. Tough little fucker after all, gelatin constitution notwithstanding.

And of course there's still that glowing little To-Do list hanging in the air off my left eye, 89 SOUTH ST #17, NEW YORK, NY. A little blue hexagon floats in front of me, a magic compass that always seems to points to SOUTH ST no matter where I turn. Even gives me a range to go with the bearing. I saccade the icon.

Manhattan glows in blocky top-down Mercator over in the lower-left corner of the BUD. I'm still in Battery Park. Hell, I'm *barely* in Battery Park, I'm still on the waterfront. Old customs warehouse, according to the database. Just to the east the park ends and the city begins; someone's put up a big wall keeping one from the other, massive interlocking dominoes of raw cement topped with razor wire. On the other side, halfway up a thirty-floor apartment building, someone's strung graffitied sheets between two balconies: HELP US.

I head down.

A lot to learn about this second skin. Fortunately it comes with a default training-wheels mode, shows me dropdown menus, nifty little options for maxing armor or boosting speed. I make my way through a wasteland ravaged by an enemy that travels among the fucking *stars*, learning to crawl. Waypoint icons and luminous threads guide me through all the craters and corpses.

More icons flicker at the corner of my eye: comm interface, if I'm reading them right. Sure enough, False Prophet pipes up a moment later: The whole park's been locked down, he tells me. High-voltage perimeter, limited access, unmanned smart guns at every gate programmed to shoot first and never ask questions.

Even in these nanothreads I might not make it through, not in my current—*suboptimal condition,* is the way he puts it.

The waypoints shake themselves into a new configuration, detour me through an ancient circular structure across the park. Castle Clinton, the database says. The only way out. I've never heard of the place. I barely even remember the president.

Remember, I'm still a virgin when it comes to the local politics. I know things are fucked generally, but I still don't know how completely fucked things are for me personally. I'm still living in some cozy little fantasy world where I show up at the nearest checkpoint, write my serial number on the wall with a grease pencil, and get an escort to Nathan Gould's front door by way of a Mobile Infirmary. I'm still thinking these aliens—wherever they're from, whatever they're here for—have at least inspired us to forget our petty differences and unite against the common enemy. Surely we're all allies now, if not bosom buddies.

But the N2's got its own comm center, and it's not only smart enough to decrypt your freqs, but also smart enough to figure out which specific chatter is mission-relevant. I'm really impressed when it first starts doing that—I had no idea our voice-rec tech was anywhere *near* that good—but my waregasm evaporates the moment I realize that you're all trying to kill me.

Actually you're all trying to kill Prophet, but you don't know that he's saved you the trouble and the hit is out on anyone in a high-tech muscle suit. Apparently it's a "biohazard." Lockhart says so. I've never heard of this Lockhart but he seems to be calling the shots. It sounds like most of the grunts on the ground would be gunning for me anyway; judging by the chatter, Prophet's taken out more of them than the aliens have.

I don't know how much of this is gospel and how much is bullshit. It would be nice if False Prophet's eavesdropping skills were up to providing a little context, but it just routes me the raw feeds without comment. All I know is, I'm not going to be shaking hands with any of these guys on the way out. Maybe I can hole up somewhere, call in, try and work things out from a safe distance. I clear my throat experimentally; I try a few words. Nothing comes out. Oh. Right.

I wonder how you say *don't shoot* in Semaphore.

Cobalt Four isn't calling in. They're blaming that on Prophet, too. Cobalt Seven calls in fresh bodies from the waterline: More of those marine special ops, they say. No more survivors. That would be my squad, you assholes, and I know for a fact that whatever else Prophet may have done before we traded lives, he had nothing to do with—

Wait a second: No *more* survivors.

If someone else from my squad made it out we could get this straightened out in no time. Castle Clinton it is.

There are pieces on the ground. Oh, look: a Jackal semi-auto, barely used. That could come in handy. Oh, look: the arm and torso of the guy who barely used it. It is not wearing an army uniform. Not real army, anyway.

CELL. CryNet Enforcement and Local Logistics.

I know these guys. Psychopathic mall cops with a bigger weapons allowance than most medium-sized countries. They make Xi look downright patriotic. Who the fuck put *them* in charge?

By now I'm picking my way through a field of flattened tents and plastic urine-colored Quonset huts, EMAC logos and red crosses stenciled onto their sides. I poke my head into one: a few stripped cots, a toppled IV pole. Sheets balled up in a corner, stained with blood and snot.

Castle Clinton squats just past the ghost camp like a red-brick mesa. It's ancient and it's seen better days, but for the time being it's still standing. I approach from behind. A woman talks somewhere in the distance—the kind of soothing vacuous voice you hear over PA systems in shopping malls—but I can't hear what she's saying over all the comm chatter about how everyone's going to frag the shit out of me the moment I show my face.

Bootsteps, crunching just around the bend. I duck behind another war memorial—big granite cookie-cutter, this time—a moment before he comes into view. He's got the head of a spider with glowing orange eyes, one of those full-face helmets with the quadroptic lenses and the built-in respirator. He obviously thinks he's some serious lethal hotshot, but he's got so many belts of flashbangs and bullets wrapped around him he looks more like a vending machine than a killing machine. He unbuckles the gear around his waist and unzips for a piss against the wall. I figure now might be a good time to try out the N2's cloaking option. I sacc' the icon and watch my hands melt away into the background.

Not just my hands. Not just me. The shotgun I just scavenged melts away as well.

It takes a moment for that to sink in. I haven't worn a cloak since Annapolis but I know the tech: fast-fractal pattern-matching, Bayesian wraparounds. Same basic thing an octopus does when it wants to blend in. But this Jackal doesn't pack a cloak, and neither do the ammo and supply clips I've scrounged, and *all* of that's just turned clearer than glass. The only thing I know that could do that even in theory would be some kind of lensing field, and anything that could bend light around *that* much volume would need the magnets from a cyclotron to shape the field and a CAESAR reactor to power it.

What the *fuck* kind of secret lab did this suit come out of?

I step out from behind the memorial (UNIVERSAL SOLDIER, the plaque says; Hey Roger, what are the odds?) just as the merc zips up and turns around. He looks right through me, turns on his heel, and ambles innocently back the way he came.

I almost let it go to my head. I almost miss the little shrinking bar down in the lower-right corner of my eye, don't notice it at all until the whole readout goes red. By the time I clue in I'm already starting to cast a shadow. I barely get back behind the cookie-cutter in time.

The Urinating Soldier hesitates, looks back over his shoulder. Grunts. Keeps going.

So. How long did that last: twenty seconds, thirty? No such thing as a free lunch. The power bar's creeping back, though. The cloak recharges.

Someone screams.

No: *Parchman* screams. My squadmate screams. And then he stops. And in between there's a gunshot.

From inside the castle.

The cloak's not quite recharged yet but I'm moving anyway, hugging that curved brick wall, closing on the main gate. But it's the flatbed parked in front that catches my eye; it's the bodies piled on top of it.

Some of them are in camo.

Heavy doors clank open around the curve; I flatten back against the wall as a couple of spider-headed mercs carry Parchman down the steps and sling him onto the flatbed like a fucking sandbag. The N2's got a zoom option but I don't need it to see the burns on Parchman's arms, or the cuts on the soles of his bare feet. I've seen those marks before. Those are the marks of special rendition. Those are the marks of interrogations that might not fit comfortably under the rubric of international law. No biggie, they told us in basic. Everyone does it.

They never said anything about the neat little hole in Parchman's temple, though.

The mercs head back into the building, swapping stories about *pukeheads* and Susie Rottencrotch. They leave the gate open: doubled iron doors set into a stone arch, big square columns on each side like something out of a gladiator game. Their own personal coliseum.

If that's how they want it . . .

I cloak again. I walk right through the gates of Castle Clinton, through an outer ring of trashed offices and gift shops. I find myself in an open circular compound full of crates and supplies, a ring of eighteenth-century cannons left over from the tourist season, and a couple of bloodstained plywood pallets outfitted with leather straps where arms and legs might go. And a bunch of CELLulites swapping bets on who's going to take this Prophet asshole down.

And then the power bar goes red and my suit goes *zzzzt* and everyone falls silent as snow.

I look down at myself. There I am.

I don't how many there are. A dozen. Two. It doesn't matter. There could be a fucking regiment and they *still* wouldn't stand a chance. I am the reaper, man, I am all four Horsemen, I am unstoppable. I spent my whole damn career training for toe-to-toe with the enemy and here they are: these paramilitary fuckwits, these *mercenaries,* these washed-out border guards and wannabes who never swore allegiance to any country or any cause or any *thing* but the highest fucking bidder. I remember the trampled tents, the broken stretchers, the dumpsters full of dead civilians. I remember the beaten corpses of my brothers-in-arms and it is not only my sacred *duty* to take these assholes out; it is my *pleasure.* I could fight them all day and be ready to dance all night. I am—

I am *into* it.

And to think that I might have missed it all if I'd let the cloak recharge just a little longer, or if the circuits had drawn just a little less power, or if I'd moved just a wee bit faster. I could have snuck through the Castle and made my way out of the park without any bloodshed at all. What a pity, huh?

I blame the suit.

SANTA'S LITTLE HELPER

When adapting to changing battlefield conditions, when improvising in the face of the unknown and the unknowable, the human brain is still the best computer on the planet. When it comes to the instantaneous processing and integration of thousands of simultaneous streams of data, however, it could use a bit of help.

That's where the N2's *Semi-Autonomous NeuroTactical Augmentation* AI comes in. Powered by a parasitic blood-glucose infusion and our optional electrolytic Ballard microstack, this tenth-generation nonsentient biochip is built around a 10^{13}-synapse core that runs at a blazing 1.5 BIPS. SANTA* instantly integrates remote telemetry and first-person input from up to six thousand distinct channels—ranging from full-spectrum EM to acoustic, barometric, and pheromonal—presenting clear, concise tactical summaries and recommendations via an interface integrated directly into the visual cortex. It can also assume the Nanosuit's purely autonomic and regulatory functions in the event of somatic damage, or should mission priorities call for operations not consistent with the normal reflexes of the N2.

SANTA's most truly innovative feature, however, is its ability to not only monitor the physical and emotional states of the soldier, but to actually *optimize* those states for mission success. SANTA continuously regulates dopamine, lactate, and corticosteroid levels, anticipates debilitating stress and fatigue reactions,

---

Phil: Marketing has serious doubts about this acronym. Worried that irony might not appeal to target demographic. Suggest something less "edgy"—how about *Semi-autonomous Enhanced Combat Ops: Neurointegration and Delivery (SECOND)* instead? Might be less offensive to the Christian community as well, since as I understand it Santa is one of their prophets or something.—*Tom* :) PS: We might also have to lose that *ho-ho-ho* effect on boot-up.

and counteracts them before your troops even feel the urge to yawn.

Nor does SANTA stop at the mitigation of debilitating reactions; it actively augments beneficial ones. Adrenaline, GABA, and tricyclics are all maintained at optimal levels for lightning reflexes, maximal sensory acuity, and positive emotional state. Your forces will pursue their objectives with tireless and unswerving dedication for days on end.*

With SANTA in the battlefield, it's like every day is Christmas!

---

*Extended operation in battlefield-optimization mode is not recommended. Prolonged exposure to agonistic neuroinhibitors can result in long-term damage to metabolic systems. Soldiers should be regularly fed and rested for best long-term performance.

Leaving Battery Park is like crawling through the guts of a whale.

First there are cattle runs, four or five of them, to herd docile civilians in parallel streams for processing. Soothing pastel signage promises quick and imminent evacuation to those who are patient and wait their turn. The looped female voice I heard earlier—just as calm, just as reassuring, even more fucking irritating—says essentially the same thing for the benefit of the blind, the illiterate, and the voice actors guild. *If you feel unwell, please make yourself known to medical staff immediately. Successful treatment of the Manhattan pathogen depends on early diagnosis. Martial law is for your protection. CryNet Security forces operate within a full federal mandate. Do not be alarmed. Do not be alarmed. Do not be alarmed.*

Of course, if any civilian should be any *less* than docile there's always the fallback solution they went with back at the waterfront. I encounter a few straggling CELLulites en route, running late to join the festivities at the castle; they seem more than willing to explore that alternative.

I help them.

At the end of the cattle run a workstation sparks intermittently on a table, too far gone to process my paperwork even if I had any, even if anyone was around to hand it to. Lightsticks and smart-painted arrows point me to a yellow hatch with a tiny window at eye level and a biohazard decal plastered underneath. I look through into a tunnel of shiny plastic, blown taut and puffy like one of those inflatable playrooms rich parents buy for four-year-old larvae.

A keypad glows on the wall to my right. I have no idea what the code is but the CRYNET NANOSUIT 2.0 encourages brute force on those awkward occasions when going through proper channels is not an option. The hatch rips free: Pressurized air sighs past and the tunnel beyond starts to sag.

Bad sign. I know something about these inflatable decon tunnels: the positive pressure in the passageway is supposed to only push back unruly microbes, not hold up the whole structure. It's the higher-pressure air between the inner and outer walls that keeps the tunnel up. If opening the door is enough to cause a slump, the walls themselves must be leaking.

Like I said: the guts of a whale. The light shining through the walls is blood orange, like looking at the sun through closed eyelids. The walls themselves almost seem to breathe around you: air seeps from one bladder to the next, one segment of intestine still taut enough to stand in while the next is so flaccid you have to get down on hands and knees and push through curtains of billowing PVC. Disinfectant sprays like digestive juice from hidden nozzles; it condenses on my faceplate and fucks with my vision. The Reassuring Voice has a different routine in here, urges me to *move to the next chamber when you hear the chime*, tells me to *remain calm and go with the doctors* if the alarm sounds, hints at dire consequences for anyone who might *obstruct medical or security personnel*.

No alarms go off. No chimes sound. The only noises I hear are the endless maddening voice of Loop Lady, the soft wheezing of the tunnel between her announcements, and the scuttling of—

Wait a second: *scuttling?*

Something runs over my boot. Something the size of a sour-dough loaf drops onto my face. I get a split-second glimpse of a very small fire hose nozzle or a very large hypodermic needle; things like gleaming scalpels *rat-tat-tat* against my helmet. I bring my fist up—pure defensive reflex—and I swear I nearly punch myself in the face before remembering the age-old question, *Who wins when the awesome power of the Nanosuit 2.0's artificial muscles meet the awesome protective shielding of the Nanosuit 2.0's armored faceplate?* I don't know who wins but it's pretty obvious that the loser is whoever's *wearing* the Nanosuit 2.0 when we find out. Best-case scenario I end up with bug guts all over my windshield, and I haven't seen any wipers on this thing. Worst-case, I punch right through the faceplate and smash my own brains against the back of the helmet.

So I deflect the swing at the last microsecond, pull off to the left, and however many thousand g's these carbon-nanomyofibrils pull just kinda glance off the respirator and the momentum spins me around like I was sideswiped by a semi and I am going *down,* man, I am spinning like a ballet dancer into all that flaccid plastic and I can hear bladders popping and tearing all along the tunnel, wrapping around me and I am on the floor, gift-wrapped for the delectation of some giant mutant flea out of an old Bowie album.

Whatever it is, I land on it. It bursts under my ass like a burrito.

I buckle down and tear myself free and bull my way through the rest of the sequence. Maybe I see shadows moving behind the plastic, vague shapes the size of softballs and cocker spaniels. Maybe it's my imagination. Valium Girl keeps urging me to remain calm, to be patient, to move forward when I hear the chime. Somehow she sounds a bit testier now. And when I hear for the hundredth time that *Successful treatment of the Manhattan pathogen depends on early diagnosis* I want to break out laughing—because nothing says *medical competence* and *effective quarantine* like a bunch of Mutant Chernobyl Bloodsuckers living in the heart of your decon facility.

It's not working, Roger. Nice try, though.

Actually, I believe you. I'd know if you were lying, and even if I didn't they'd probably leave you in the dark just on general principles. So let me fill you in: Your bosses just tried an emergency remote-shutdown through a backdoor optical channel in the twenty-thousand-angstrom range. Didn't you see that little laser light winking in the air duct back there?

Oh, that's right. You can't see infrared.

The thing about radio, see, is you can always jam the signal. Optics are a *lot* tougher to hack. Pass a light beam through a cyclotron and it barely bends, you're not gonna scramble *that* signal until the day we start building black holes for the battlefield. As long as your target's line-of-sight, you're golden.

So that's the route CryNet went when they built in their kill switch—in case one of their Nanosuits fell into the wrong hands, you know, got used for good instead of evil. It's wired into the saggital lens, and they just used it to try and shut me down.

I don't think so. The only one I can hurt right now is you, and if they cared about dear old Roger Gillis they wouldn't have sent you in here. They're just trying to get back in control, but that's the thing about heuristic battlefield systems: They're built to adapt, so they adapt. Develop countermeasures to your countermeasures.

Hey, don't look so worried. I don't blame you; you didn't even know. Hell, I don't even blame them. I know the drill, I haven't changed that much. If I was in their shoes I'd probably do the same thing.

Let's see if they learn from their mistakes, hmm?

* * *

Anyway. The rest of Manhattan makes Battery Park look pristine.

You can't look anywhere without seeing fire: writhing from abandoned cars, burning in oily rivulets along the gutters, licking out from shattered glass façades on the fifteenth floor. Scorched black trees creak and crackle in neat rows along the sidewalks; one topples across the street, sends a shower of sparks whirling into the air. The goddamn *asphalt* is smoldering. I leave footprints behind on State Street as though I were strolling along the fucking beach.

Oh, and there are the bodies.

I've seen some action overseas, you know. Barely signed up before Ling Shan went down, they had us over in Sri Lanka trying to clean up after the riots. I've seen bodies piled higher than you could reach on tiptoe, I've seen bodies so far gone you couldn't see half a meter through the flies. Back at home I knew this guy, Nickle his name was, saw some action during the Arizona Uprising. He went all post-traumatic every time you zipped up your fly because the sound reminded him of body bags being sealed. And I was like, you fucking girlyman, they gave you body bags? You got to bag 'em *one at a time*? We had to burn whole *villages* just to stay ahead of the cholera. You couldn't even use hazmat filters half the time, the smell was so bad. You had go in like a fucking astronaut, hump your own air supply on your back.

You know what, Roger? This was worse.

Yeah, I know. You wouldn't think so from the footage. I didn't think so, either, at first. The corpses were—scattered around like leaves, like driftwood. The smell wasn't especially overpowering; you knew you were breathing in the dead mind you, no mistaking *that*, but this wasn't Sri Lanka by any stretch. Less heat, less humidity, the corpses were spread thin enough on the ground to let you keep your lunch down most of the time. None of that all-piled-in-one-place critical-biomass bullshit.

Let me tell you, though. It sneaks up on you.

It was the spore, man. Manhattan Path, Softball Syndrome, any of a dozen names I must've heard down there. It seemed to like mouths and eyes and open wounds, any wet tissue. I saw one poor fucker who'd literally been ripped in half, right down the middle; those buboes and filaments—*mycelia,* is that the word?—they were just boiling out of him in a kind of avalanche, right about where his lungs would've been. And I remember thinking, *Brother, I hope that shit got into you* after *you died, because slow suffocation cannot be a fun way to go.*

And of course not all of them were dead, not completely, not yet. Some of them still moved a little; a twitching leg, a muscle tic tugging pulling at the fingers. Or maybe they weren't alive, either, maybe I wasn't seeing anything more than the kick of a dead frog's leg when you hook it up to a battery. Maybe the spore just short-circuited their motor nerves and left them twitching and jiggling until the last cell ran out of juice. I can hope, right? Anyway, I'm a tough boy. I can take it.

But you want to know what I almost *couldn't* take, what fucked me up even worse than Sri Lanka? It was their faces. The ones that still had faces, anyway.

So many of them were smiling.

Yeah. Sorry. Kind of faded out there. What do you call it? Fugue state.

You get used to it.

Anyway, I'm only out of Battery Park for a few minutes before I hear this voice in my head: "Hey, Prophet? You there, bra? Come back." And my first instinct is to duck and cover because all the comm I've intercepted up to this point has been decidedly unfuckingfriendly, if you know what I mean. So it takes a second before I realize that this isn't someone talking about fragging my ass, this is someone *hailing* me. "Hey, Prophet? You there, bra? Come back."

—but it's loud enough to bring me back to the tumbledown canyons of Manhattan, which is just as well because this is no place to be lost in a psychotic hallucination even if you *are* wearing NANOSUIT 2.0 FROM CN COMBAT SOLUTIONS. A shout and a blink and I'm back in the here-and-now.

"Prophet? It's Gould, man. Come *back.*"

Gould? Gould! Hey, man, I'm looking for you. Got a message for you from—

"The whole damn link went down, man, you were completely off the grid for almost four hours. I don't know if the prototype's glitching out or if someone blocked the freq. Any signal-jamming going on in your neighborhood?" I can't answer. I don't have to: "Never mind, just get to the lab as fast as you can, man, things are *seriously* turning to shit up here. Infected all over the place, poor bastards. CryNet are out on the cull. I even saw a couple of Ceph on the way over here. Look, if you're anyplace in the downtown, stick to the subways. It's gotta be safer than the streets. Hope you brought those marines."

And maybe someone *is* jamming the spectrum, because Gould's icon stutters to DISCONNECT and disappears. That magical hexagon compass is still hanging there in v-space, though, and as I watch it shakes itself free of whatever South Street tree fort it was reeling me toward and locks onto a new destination a few klicks to the northwest. Converted warehouse, judging from the wireframe. Must be Gould's lab. He mentions it with a wave of the hand, and SECOND updates its waypoints.

I'm a little bit scared at how *smart* this thing seems to be. This thing I'm inside. That's inside me.

I don't make it more than a couple of blocks before I run into another batch of infectees. These ones are definitely alive; they're walking, or trying to. Half a dozen of them. One's crawling on all fours, barely keeping up. Another's still on two legs, but one of her feet's been blown off and she's hobbling along on the stump of an ankle. Somehow they know where they're going, somehow they've agreed on a direction. I don't know how some of them can even *see* with those tapioca tumors eating out their eyes.

And some of them are freaking out, I hear one chick muttering about bad drugs and some other guy's screaming *this isn't me this isn't me this isn't me* but so many of the others are *smiling* again, those crazy fucking smiles, sometimes they just grin but sometimes their lips split wide open in this kind of obscene ecstatic *laugh* and you can't even see their teeth for all the squirming rot in their mouths. They're murmuring to each other, or to God or something, they're talking about *the light, the light,* and *Lord, take me.* The suit's got this heuristic threat-recognition software but it's not lighting them up. I keep my shotgun raised anyway, just in case. False Prophet pipes up with some shit about *stage-four infection* and *cellular autolysis* and I almost blow them away anyhow—not out of fear you understand, not because they're a threat, but as an act of *mercy* because sweet smoking Jesus, no one should have to go out like that. But then again, they don't *seem* to be suffering, and something's telling me I should probably conserve my ammo.

That was probably just me. Might've been the suit, I suppose. Back then, it was a lot easier to tell the difference.

Executive Summary UNPS-25B/23: Charybdis Epidemiological Agent 01

Timestamp:	1501 23/08/2023
Authorship:	UNPS
Distribution:	CSIRA, FEMA, UN (HoD: Eyes Only)
Key Phrases:	EID, "Extinction Level Event," "God Module," "Green Death," Charybdis, pilgrim, "Religious Impulse," Wanderlust
Jurisdiction:	US/WestHem Economic Alliance

Threat ID: GrEp Ag-01 (UNPS designation: common names
                  inc. "spore," "God Bug," "Softball Syndrome,"
                  "RapCer," others)
Threat Category: Weaponised Biological
Threat Summary:
    Taxonomy: Awaiting classification.
    Origin: Unknown (extrasolar):
                   see UNPS-25A/23: "Charybdis,"
    Description: Engineered agenetic bioweapon,
    monogenerational saprophyte.

Tentative Life Cycle and Epidemiology: Dispersal phase resembles a radially ridged spore 0.1–1.5mm in diameter; released by "Charybdis Spires" common throughout the MIZ. Initial dispersal is ballistic/explosive with an effective launch radius of 50–60m. Subsequent dispersal is passive/windborne, and of limited range: the spore becomes biologically inert and noninfectious within three to five hours of release, effectively restricting its range to New York and its immediate environs.

Infectious spores settle and sprout on animal tissue, preferring moist membranes (eyes, respiratory tract) or open wounds. While they show at least some level of metabolic activity on all animal species tested to date, active proliferation appears limited to hominoid hosts. Humans, chimpanzees and gorillas are most vulnerable; the spore is debilitating but apparently nonlethal to orangutans, gibbons and Old World monkeys, although it may simply take longer for the agent to reach lethal levels in these taxa.* Tarsids, Omomyids and Old World monkeys appear to be relatively immune.

---

* In vitro testing is ongoing. Dr. Strahan has submitted an expedited request for additional live specimens across a range of primate species, and for a temporary waiver of the board's Experimental Ethics rules.

Upon taking root in a suitable host, the spore germinates into a filamentous mass that proliferates throughout the body and shows a special affinity for the myelinated cells of the central nervous system. Superficial physical symptoms during this phase are obvious and grotesquely disfiguring: The lymph nodes grow hyperbubonic, and abscesses erupt across the skin (white cell counts from extracted pus range as high as 200,000). These abscesses frequently present a slight greenish tinge due to the presence of pyocyanine (a pigment evidently introduced by the spore itself). A variety of fleshy protuberances also sprout from the body during this phase, preferentially but not exclusively from the body orifices; these range from filamentous rootlets of <1mm diameter to ropy tumourous structures several centimeters thick. These are chaotically vascularised, and consist of hypertrophied columnar cells. (The precise mechanisms underlying their metastasis are currently being explored.) While the breakdown of host tissue would prove ultimately fatal in any event, death usually results from more proximate causes such as physical constriction and/or occlusion of vital organs, or suffocation.

At no point in this process does GrEp-Ag01 appear to be contagious: No fruiting bodies or other reproductive structures have been observed. However, the agent does rewire the behavior of its victims at the neurological level, inducing the so-called Wanderlust that draws the infected toward Charybdis aggregations. In approximately 70% of cases it also hijacks the religious-impulse circuitry in the temporal lobe (hence the term "pilgrim"); we speculate that it is also responsible for the self-mutilation behavior among some infectees. While victims sometimes refer to the resulting injuries as "stigmata," the behavior is thought to function as a means of increasing exposure to further spore infection.

While the neurological reprogramming of complex behavior is well documented even among earthly parasites (see *Dicrocoelium; Entomophthora; Holy See; Sacculina; Toxoplasma;* others), it should be emphasized that the cognitive abilities of infected "pilgrims" do not appear to be significantly impaired until infection renders them effectively immobile. Victims remain capable of intelligent conversation, complex problem-solving, and other hallmarks of legally competent adults. Areas in which mental faculties *are* impaired—unsupported beliefs in mystical spirits, cryptic behaviors such as "speaking in tongues," and even self-destructive acts born of a desire to give up their lives for their "god"—are well within the pale of mainstream religious practices around the world. While the agent does proliferate throughout the brain and central nervous system, its impact on CNS function is remarkably subtle until the tertiary stage.

Prognosis: Ultimate mortality rate among infected human hosts is believed to be 100%; while not all known victims have yet died, none are known to have recovered. We are unable to provide a cure at this time. The relative resistance of related primate species does, however, suggest that some form of gene therapy may prove effective. This avenue is under intense investigation, although it is currently hampered by a lack of funding and personnel.

Conclusions: GrEp Ag-01 presents a paradox. Its extreme host specificity points inevitably to an engineered bioweapon specifically intended for human targets. However, it is not contagious among humans; to date, the only observed means of infection is via direct contact with a viable spore. This is a profoundly ineffective strategy for wide-scale attack, one which limits human casualties to within a few kilometers of the spires themselves.

It is not plausible that a species with Charybdis's obvious capabilities would commit such an elementary oversight. We propose two hypotheses to account for this discrepancy:

1. The enemy is solely interested in establishing local control, and has no interest in expanding beyond Manhattan (and perhaps its immediate environs);

2. The bioweapon is still under development, and the enemy is not yet ready for a wide-scale release. This would suggest that the Ceph are practitioners of the "Precautionary Principle," and do not wish to globally release an agent that has not been thoroughly field-tested. In this case the limitations we have thus far observed would only be temporary, and the appearance of a truly infectious variant would herald the end of the prototyping stage.

It is our opinion that the second hypothesis is the more plausible of the two. We note, however, that our opinions arise from a distinctly human perspective, while the beings we are trying to second-guess are anything but. Perhaps this offers some grounds for hope.

Oh, Roger, the things I have seen.

Cities turned into swamps. Oceans on fire. Mobs so desperate to get out of the zone they barely even notice the razor wire slicing them open, so desperate for even a *chance* at clean water or a mouthful of freeze-dried *Spirulina* they'll scale livewire fences, jerking like marionettes. I saw a woman's hair catch fire halfway up and she just kept going because really, what did she have to lose? I've fed mass graves so big you could barely see the other side, so big you could see them from fucking orbit.

And then they sent me to Manhattan.

In one way, you know, it was almost a relief. To be picking on something your own size for a change, you know? Something that could fight back. *We* were the underdogs. We'd probably all end up dead or worse, but if we *didn't*—if we actually survived, or even *won*—well, maybe for the first time in our lives we could feel *good* about winning. We were fighting a superior force for a change. We weren't mowing down refugees.

Except when we were.

I remember running across my first—mop-up. Containment. Whatever word they used to whitewash the whole *massacre* thing. I'm climbing down off the rooftops, coming down a fire escape into this little cul-de-sac off William Street and there's a pit dug into the road, lined with PVC. A couple of mercs are standing there shooting random civilians, and the cloak gets me close enough to hear them talking. They're yucking it up because they don't even have to go out hunting, you know, the civvies come to *them*, all of 'em heading the same way like salmon swimming upstream to sp—

What?

I don't give a flying fuck if they were infected. They were *civilians*.

Yeah, that's how they always justify it, isn't it? Quarantine, protecting the population, the needs of the many outweigh the needs of the few. All that shit. Let me tell you, these assholes were not racked by remorse over the *necessary evil* they were committing. They were *laughing*. They were using those poor bastards for *target practice*.

'Course, you're trained that way. It's an old trick. Never call them *civilians*, never learn their names. It's tough to kill a fellow human being. In fact we make it a point to *never* kill human beings. We kill *niggers* and *ragheads* and *terrorists* instead. You know what they call infected civilians down in the zone, Roger? Pizza Pockets. Pukeheads. Because of the way they explode when you shoot them. Their insides are all pulpy, like rotten fruit.

When I saw those first few victims I assumed it was just some random alien fungus or something, you know, like that flesh-eating disease. But it's more than that. It doesn't just eat you, it doesn't *just* turn you into a walking mass of tumors. First it *reprograms* you. It gives you purpose. Something to live for, something to die for. Some of those guys, you'd swear that getting raptured was the best thing that ever happened to them.

Sometimes I almost found myself feeling envious.

Not everyone down there was CELL, of course. There were some good guys as well. Every now and then I'd see MPs or medics from the Red Cross trying to intervene, *Dude, it's a meat-grinder in there, you keep going that way Squiddie will have you for appetizers.* But the infectees, they didn't *care.* They *wanted* to meet the Squids, they *wanted* to be consumed, it was like their own personal ticket to sit at the right hand of Jesus H. Christ in the Great Hereafter. I even saw a couple of Bible-thumpers, they snuck into the zone on some kind of self-appointed missionary patrol. It was almost funny, watching them try to *un*save all these poor doomed bastards who'd got to "Heaven" before them. But those CELL goons, man, they weren't interested in saving souls. All they were after was something to kill that wouldn't fight back.

What do you think I did? We're supposed to *protect* civilians, right? That's the official job description at least. So I did my job. I blew those assholes away with extreme fucking prejudice, and I'd do it again.

Chain of command, huh?

Is that the best you've got?

Anyway I keep on keeping on, closing on Gould, closing on Gould. He says it's safer in the subway so I give it a shot, but it does not go well. Not all of the infected are pilgrims, you know, not all of them have seen the light. Some of them are sane enough to be scared shitless by what's happening to them, some of them just need a dark place to hide and rot away. The subways are full of them: sobbing, suffering, telling anyone who'll listen that it's not that bad, they're getting better, that they'll be right as rain this time tomorrow. Some of them look almost as healthy as you; some aren't much more than gurgling puddles of slime. And those scuttling things are everywhere, those tick-things I ran into back in the decon tunnel. They clatter around on jointed silver legs and jab those needle snouts into the bodies. They must inject some kind of acid or digestive enzyme because the stuff they suck back out looks more like pus and semen than blood and guts. It splatters like pus when you squash them. They're easy enough to kill, the repulsive little fuckers. You crush them with your bare hands but there are so *many* of them. There's just no point.

I've had enough of that after about five minutes, take the next exit, climb back into the first daylight I can find. I end up on a pedestrian skywalk connecting a couple of office towers at the second floor. I'm about halfway across when I see a squad of CELLulites charging up the street below, waving their guns; I'm cloaked and down on my belly by the time they open fire; I've backed off a good ten meters before I realize they're not even shooting at *me*.

And then something smashes through the walkway and I'm down on the street just like *that* and I stop worrying about the fucking mercs altogether.

My whole BUD's flashing red. I'm flat on my back and the whole damn suit's seized up. I've taken some kind of hit but nobody's bothering to close for the kill; I'm nothing but collateral. The actual *target* screams past not ten meters overhead and I'd know what it was even if I wasn't staring right up at it, even if I was *blind,* because I've only heard that sound once before: not eight hours ago, swimming for my life while my whole squad got cut down around me.

Same two glowing hoops sticking out the sides. Must be some kind of antigravity thing, lift elements. Two rows of modules in between, about the size and shape of industrial cement mixers. Cylinder-cone things, lined up like eggs in a carton. The ship's staggering through the airspace, weaving and wobbling, and part of that might be evasive maneuvers but I don't care how *alien* this bird is, you can tell it's wounded. It might as well be skywriting HOLY SHIT I'M FUCKED in black smoke.

And here comes the mofo that's kicked its ass and its one of *ours,* it's a goddamn *Apache.* A 64D, I think, not even bleeding-edge. I mean, this is a flying saucer we're talking about—built by creatures from *another fucking solar system*—and it's getting its ass handed to it by a bunch of apes in a ten-year-old helicopter. Fuck yeah. Somehow it's got its nose back up, it's climbing again, it *almost* clears the building down the street but not quite: skips off the edge like a stone on water, bounces back into the sky, but there are *three* Apaches on its tail now and they're not giving up. One scores a direct hit just as the alien arcs away behind an office tower and I think that's it, end of show—but a few seconds later it punches back into view, *right through the building*, leaves a glowing hole four stories high. I can see right through it to the cloud bank on the other side. This ship's not going anywhere but *down*. It exits stage left, down some city canyon a few blocks ahead. Big orange flash. Smoke billows around the corner.

It's like watching someone shoot down an X-35 with a slingshot.

Gould's voice comes back to me as my suit reboots. "Did you fucking *see* that? I swear, it came down not five blocks from you!" He sounds like an eight-year-old girl who's just gotten a pony for her birthday. "Dude, you *do* realize what this means, right? No one ever shot one of these things down before! This is our chance! This is it! There'll be—I mean—let me think, just let me think . . ."

I do a little thinking myself. According to GPS, Gould's in a warehouse all the way over on the East River. It's just barely possible that he might have looked out his window and seen a tiny distant dot fall out of the sky—but how the hell does he know where I am in relation to it?

This isn't just a comm link. Either this Gould fucker has access to high-rez realtime satcam surveillance, or the N2's putting out some kind of homing signal. I wonder if it's encrypted. I wonder if Lockhart knows the key.

"—to jump on this," Gould's saying. "Extraction can wait—go get me some samples. This could be *it*, man: a shot at rolling back the spore, maybe even the whole invasion. I'll hold for you here. But move your ass. Lockhart's going to have CELL swarming all over that crash site in nothing flat."

I can still hear helicopters buzzing from somewhere in the streets ahead. That little blue hexagon that was pointing the way to Gould's lab jumps west, miraculously recalibrated to the bearing of the crash site. I couldn't find Gould now if my life depended on it; it was so easy just following the waypoints I never bothered to memorize the route.

I may be the one moving these arms and legs, but somehow Gould and the N2 are the ones deciding where they take me. And I'm starting to feel a little like a passenger in my own skin, if you know what I mean.

But you bounce pretty high after cheating death, Roger. Just a few hours back I *knew* I was dying, I could feel myself dying down to the last cell: no denials, no reprieve, this is *it,* dude. And when you come to those kind of terms and then come out the other side—look death in the face and *beat* the fucker against impossible odds, you feel—

Invulnerable. That's the word. Invulnerable.

After all, Prophet took a shell to the chest wearing these threads, and he stayed standing. So yeah, I'm feeling like the last son of Krypton, and there's a *crashed alien ship* just a few blocks away. Who wouldn't want to check that out?

I know I'm being led by the nose. But the truth is I'd have probably headed over to take a look anyway.

Manhattan's been carved into a jigsaw.

It's not the aliens' doing. It's not even the random chaos of collapsing buildings and seismic tremors. It's *us.* Ten thousand slabs of concrete have been slotted together and laid across the cityscape like interlocking dominoes ten meters high, and every last one has CELL stamped across it in big black letters. The whole zone's been partitioned into a hundred irregular cookie-cutter shapes. The last time I saw this much cement in such a small area, it was being used to keep Israelis and Palestinians from tearing each other's throats out.

This particular barricade cuts right across the middle of Broad Street. The nearest storm-sewer grating is about twenty meters back from a massive corrugated gate topped by a scrolling marquee that endlessly repeats LOWER MANHATTAN SEALED OFF in block capitals. I pry off the grille and drop below the street; five minutes later I'm cloaked and flattened against a savings and loan on East Houston, leaning around the corner into the sound of helicopters and idling APCs.

Way to go on the whole partitioned-containment thing, guys.

I think this used to be some kind of open-air plaza. Right now it's a smoking hole, a ragged cutaway model ripped open to show the cracked stacked levels of an underground parking garage. If there's a ship buried down there under all those cement floes, it's too deep for me to make out. I can see three of those cylindrical pods scattered around, though: half buried in the street, face-planted in an urban flower patch, taking the absolute piss out of a dozen tables on a café patio. Strip away some of that weird Ceph chrome and they almost *could* have come off the backs of cement trucks.

A helicopter drifts back and forth over the center of the tableau. I see a couple of APCs parked in front of a deli, and over across the crater half a dozen ammo and supply crates have been stacked along the wall of the elevator hutch that must have been the main pedestrian parkade access before the Ceph pioneered the whole open-access approach. Maybe a dozen CELLulites wander the perimeter. A few more hump kit from the APCs to the elevator cache.

My cloak's almost drained. I pull back around the corner as Gould natters on about checking the pods. "We're looking for tissue samples, dead crew."

Yeah, and the couple of dozen assorted mercs over there are looking for *me*, even with a flying saucer buried under their feet: "Keep your eyes peeled for that Nanosuit asshole. The way they're talking, he's more trouble than the Ceph."

I cloak up, cross the ten meters to the OVERPRICED PARKING: IN ONLY ramp, hop the guardrail, and drop down behind the interlocked front ends of a Taurus and a Malibu that couldn't seem to agree on traffic flow. I risk decloaking, let the charge rebuild while unsuspecting uniforms above my head fill the air with chatter.

"You picking anything up on the scanner?"

"Nah, looks like they ejected before impact. We're just waiting for the cleanup crew."

"If they ejected, where the hell did they go?"

"Good question."

It is, too. I add it to the list as I recloak and start down the ramp; if the pods are a bust, maybe I can sneak into the crater from one of the garage levels. By the time the money shot comes I'm so far down that I almost miss it:

"Christ, that thing's buried deep. Only way down is through the elevator shaft."

Oh.

So the good news is, there may be a way to get Gould his samples: *Could be it, man, a shot at rolling back the spore, maybe even the whole invasion.* Rah.

Bad news is, it's on the far side of the plaza in the middle of a crowd of trigger-happy mercs stationed right next to a fresh stock of ammunition, who have orders to shoot me on sight.

Worst news, though, is that I'm hearing at least four sets of boots approaching the bottom of the ramp ahead of me, and there's no fucking way I can get all the way back up before my cloak runs dry.

I love it when the number of options dwindles to one. Really speeds up the decision-making process.

They hear me before they see me; the cloak is good, but it doesn't mask the sound of boots charging down a concrete ramp at thirty klicks an hour. They stop talking, their guns come up, and suddenly I'm *right there,* laying shotgun blasts into all that Kevlar, bringing the Marshal down like a club on those shiny gray helmets, grabbing one of them by the throat and watching her sail through space until a convenient support pylon takes her from sixty to zero in no seconds.

Shouts from deeper within the garage. Panicked calls for back-up on comm. I'm coming for them. They know it.

But I'm not. I recloak, swap the Marshal out for a recently orphaned assault rifle and head back up the ramp. Strength is amped so I'm moving *fast,* but between that and the cloak every capacitor in the suit's gonna run dry in about three seconds. Make that two: I pull a boosted jump over the reinforcements clattering down the ramp, six eager little sociopaths don't see me coming and don't see me go but that last mighty leap took me down to the fumes and I materialize from thin air as I pass above their heads. I don't think they saw that I hope they didn't see that, their eyes were down and focused on the forward charge, but no time to look it's all in the past and I'm rising up to ground level now, I've got a chopper overhead and a whole shitload of hostiles coming around that crater (two, four, seven, eight, *nine targets* SECOND tells me, and lays neat little ranges and targeting triangles over each). I deke and I duck but it's not enough to keep me from taking hits; and even though the suit can handle them it just *kills* the capacitor feed, the power bar stutters to a crawl on its way up the recharge trail.

HMG fire from the chopper. I lob a grenade into the sky and the pilot pulls back—an unnecessary reflex, that little pineapple doesn't even come close, but it's enough to throw the gunner off his aim. I hit the deck and roll behind a waist-high concrete planter holding a row of spindly stunted trees. The grenade bounces and rolls and blows out the windows of the deli.

Eight seconds, tops, before they flank me.

The charge bar tops up at six. I fade, roll away from the planter, get to my feet. I've noticed that the cloak lasts a lot longer when the suit isn't pulling power for a lot of other things. I can stay invisible for forty-five seconds, maybe a whole minute if I just stand still.

Maybe almost as long if I just move very, *very* . . . slowly.

I amble sideways while the air fills with shouts of *Lost the target* and *Shit he's cloaked again.* I line up my approach: five long steps to the edge of the crater on turbo, then maybe fifteen meters to cross the gap near the left edge. I amp strength to max and *move.*

I nail the launch: solid traction, boots leave the ground maybe twenty centimeters from the edge, and the moment I'm airborne I drop strength right back to baseline. I sail over that gap like a ghost.

And nearly blow the landing. My feet come down with no room to spare. I land just past the lip of the hole and *wobble* back and forth, windmilling my arms to keep from falling over. No time to worry about the sound of my boots on the pavement; if the rotors and the shouts and the random suppressing fire didn't mask it I'm probably fucked.

But here I am, ten meters from the elevators, and all that stands in my way are three CELLulites left to guard the supplies. That running jump burned through two-thirds of my charge, but for the moment I'm still stealthed.

These boys are not convinced. Last time they saw me I was

on the other side of the plaza, but I could be anywhere by now. I could be *right in front of them*. How would they know?

They'll know soon enough. They'll know in about three seconds, because the charge bar's just started flashing red. I bring up the Grendel: not the best accuracy and a downright shitty clip size, but these tungsten rounds would stop a rhino and my targets are almost close enough to touch.

They see my face, and blow apart.

It's not completely clear sailing after that. Their buddies can't wait to lay down the law now that I'm back in their worldview, and the elevator doors are jammed. I have to finesse my way in, and it seems like I have to fend off a whole fucking platoon in the process. By the time I get those doors jimmied open, drop the twenty meters to the bottom of the shaft, and take care of anyone who tries to follow little Timmy down the well—we're looking at a final score of somewhere around seventeen–zip.

Like I said before. That's what you get when you work nine-to-five.

The bottom of the shaft is chest-deep in scummy water; a service crawlway leads off to the north, a half-flooded mess of ruptured plumbing, soggy cardboard crates, and the occasional pulpy corpse. Dim lights glow here and there in rusty little cages, antique bulbs with actual filaments inside. I bet they've been down here since the twentieth century.

There's brighter light farther down the passage, though. I follow it to a hole torn in the ceiling, duck under an exposed I-beam, and climb a pile of cinder blocks and shattered tiles to another Ceph pod; it rammed down into this space at a forty-five-degree angle, and is half buried by collapsed ceiling and uprooted floor.

And it's—bleeding, or something.

The pod's ruptured in several spots. The stuff oozing from

those wounds is the color of snot or old candle wax, and it's *everywhere:* running in ropy strings along the hull, pooling on the screen, hanging in thick gooey stalactites from the breached ceiling. It *moves.* It—undulates. Or maybe that's just the light: I look around for the first time and see the far end of the room, relatively unscathed behind me. A floor lamp, knocked on its side, throws light across the space at a low angle, full of contrast and long shadows. So, yeah: probably just a trick of the light. But I can't shake the feeling that those giant hanging boogers *squirm* just the slightest bit, as if I'm looking at a thin-walled brood sac with some kind of half-seen larva incubating inside.

"That's it," Gould says on comm. "You gotta scan that stuff."

Scan? But SECOND's training wheels take their own initiative: broad-spectrum chemical sensors built into the fingertips, according to the graphical thumbnails popping up on BUD. I saccade the right dropdowns, switch to tactical—remind myself it won't actually be *me* touching this shit—and lay on the hands.

The N2's fingertips leave soft depressions in the alien snot. Almost instantly lists of ingredients start scrolling down my brain: chemical formulae I somehow recognize as organic even though I can barely remember high school chemistry. Amine groups. Polysaccharides. Glycolipids.

Why is this ringing so many bells?

It's ringing bells for Gould, too. I hear him trying to keep his lunch down across a whole borough and a shitload of static. "Jesus, man, that's—that's *people.* Just melted down, just—just *lysed.* What the fuck is this?"

I remember pus spurting from squashed ticks. Odd that Gould doesn't seem to know about that.

"I can't do anything with this. We struck out. You better get out of there before CELL shows up. Back to Plan A."

He doesn't even say *lab*. Waypoints and objectives reset themselves anyway. God*damn* this suit is smart.

Going back up the elevator shaft is a nonstarter. I climb over the wreckage into the other end of the room: some kind of security or janitorial office, judging by the desk and the filing cabinets. A row of windows on the opposite wall looks out into what used to be the lower parking level; now it looks onto a slope of collapsed concrete, sloping up toward a thin slice of sky. The glass is caged behind one of those antiburglary grilles.

Yeah. Right.

I start up the slope. No comm chatter: That's odd. Maybe CELL's figured out that I'm hacking into their frequencies.

No rotor noise, either. That's odder.

Almost there.

I stop. Look right. Nothing. Left. Nothing. Up: just sky.

Forward.

Oh *shi*—

It jumps down on me from nowhere, slams me facedown into the rubble, flips me over onto my back and pins me there. It's a nest of naked black backbones spliced together into something that almost looks humanoid. It's got backbones for arms, spiky segmented things that end in—hands, I guess you'd call them. Claws. I can't get a good look at them, they're pressed down against my shoulders but they seem way too big, like catcher's mitts on a stick man. There's another backbone where a backbone *should* be, connecting those arms to a set of armored robodog legs with too many joints. There's something on top, a helmet for a head like the front of a bullet train with clusters of orange eyes on each side. There's a blob of boneless gray tissue in the middle of it all.

It's like my bogeyman from the roof, but different. *Meaner.*

I try to move but the fucker's *strong*, man, I can't throw it off and my gun's been knocked halfway across the rubble. One backbone-arm pulls back like it's winding up for a punch, and that long metal mitt just *splits open* to reveal more drills and needles and probes than a goddamn dentist's chair on steroids. Something whirls from the middle of that cluster and spears me in the chest. The BUD jumps; my icons scramble; my eyeballs fill with static.

The N2 starts *talking*.

It's not False Prophet. It's not English. It's not even human, it's just—gibberish. Clicks, hiccups, these weird *hooting* sounds. And the shit I'm suddenly seeing on tactical isn't making any more sense, green pastel suddenly flickering into orange and purple, alphanumerics turning into hieroglyphics, and what do you call those blobs you headshrinkers used to use before we laughed you out of town?—Rorschach blots. That's it. The whole interface is fried and I'm stuck there for I don't know how long, can't be more than a few seconds but it seems like forfucking*ever*.

And then False Prophet *does* speak up, and at least he's speaking human even though I don't know exactly what he's talking about. He says:

> *Interface attempted. Tissue vector 11 percent.*
> *Insufficient common code. Rejecting.*

And the alien leaps off me and darts away like *I* was the bogeyman.

Gould comes back to me as the BUD sobers up: "You had it, man! You triggered sampling mode, but it didn't—listen, Prophet, whatever you just did: Do it again!"

Right. Chase down the nice monster and sweet-talk it into skewering me a second time. That's gonna happen.

"Come *on,* man, quit messing around! We don't have time!"

Who am I kidding.

I grab my weapon and take up the chase. I put everything the suit's got into speed; I sprint in turbocharged bursts, huff and puff in between with my own measly muscles while the charge builds back. And wouldn't you know the alien's back in my sights: now leaping along on two legs, now running like a cheetah on four, sometimes keeping to the street, sometimes scrambling up sheer walls like a caffeinated gecko. This thing isn't biped or quad, it's not a runner or a climber; it's *all* of those things, it's fluid, it morphs between modes as easily as I put one foot after the other. It's almost beautiful, the way it moves. It *is* beautiful, and fast, but you know what? This fuck-ugly Nanosuit, this bulky pile of cords and chrome—it's keeping up, it's one step forward and three steps back but that forward step is a *doozie* and suddenly I'm close enough to bring the fucker down. I'm twenty meters back when it pulls a sudden right-angle turn up off the street and starts climbing the walls. I fire on the run, thank whatever gearhead designed the N2's motion stabilizers, and I don't know if it's a lucky shot or old cement but suddenly the bricks are crumbling under the Ceph's claws and it falls backward off the wall, live parts and machine parts both grabbing at the air, both coming up empty, and the whole bastard meat–machine hybrid crashes down on the asphalt not five steps from where I'm waiting. It springs back up almost immediately but I'm already blasting away at the soft parts inside the hard ones and I don't care *how* fast your spaceships go, if you're made out of meat you are *not* coming back from a point-blank encounter with a Grendel heavy assault rifle.

There's enough Squid splattered across my front that I don't even need to punch through the exoskeleton; all I have to do is wipe my hand across my chest and False Prophet pipes up,

"Sample absorbed. Processing." I watch the N2's fingertips slurp up that alien gore like a sponge drinks a coffee spill. I can't tell you how creepy I find this.

I find it so creepy I don't even notice the other stalkers coming down the walls at me.

FAMILY VALUES

Leap Taller Buildings in a Single Bound

Start with a honeycombed coltan/titanium exoskeleton, for 32% greater strength than the N1 at half the weight. Wrap it in CryNet's patented artificial muscle: an armored carbon-nanofiber composite storing elastic energies of up to 20 J/cm^3, with electromechanical coupling that exceeds 70% under most battlefield conditions. Sheathe it all in a flexible doped-ceramic epidermis and a Faraday weave that shields against EMPs while still supporting telemetric throughput of up to 15 TB/sec. Put it all together and you have a combat chassis that laughs at almost anything short of a direct hit with a battlefield nuke. (In fact, in three out of five simulations, the Nanosuit 2.0 even withstood the point-blank detonation of a Lockheed AAF 212 Circuit-Breaker™!*)

And what fuels this unmatched combination of power and protection? Virtually anything. While the N2's primary coupling is compatible with any BVN-series hydrogen cell, the suit also acquires and stores energy automatically from a wide range of ambient sources: kinetic motion, passive solar/thermal, and atmospheric microwave to name but a few. The standard-issue universal adapter allows recharging from virtually any hardline electrical source, domestic or military—and with CryNet's optional Necro-Organic Metabolites plug-in (NOM), the N2 can even extract usable energy from battlefield carrion!

Was I just on too many hit lists? Were CELL and Ceph both gunning for me and it was just my great luck that both happened to

*Results may vary during actual combat.

track me down at the same time? Or were they dusting it up with each other, street-to-street, and I just got caught in the crossfire? I don't suppose you'd care to enlighten me?

'Course not. You're here to *ask* the questions.

That first wave of Ceph, though, I could swear they're running from *something*. They scramble down the walls and the street in a wave—mean-ass stalkers, baseline bogeymen. I open fire out of pure reflex, take a few down, and they're shooting back with those big fucking gunhands of theirs, but they seem to have other things on their minds. And now here comes CELL screaming around the corner in their Humvees, and all I'm hearing is *It's that suit guy, suit guy's right here!* and *Blue Command, engaging target!* and then I'm hitting the fucking *ground,* man, because suddenly the air is a shitstorm of bullets and RPGs. I don't think they even notice the Ceph at first.

They see 'em soon enough, though. One of the Humvees goes up and suddenly the Ceph are getting *lots* of attention.

I'm on the ground, under cover, pinned down but not in anybody's direct line of fire unless they've got a micronuke to take out the collapsed wall I'm hiding under. I cloak up and peek around a pile of cinder blocks; I'll get shredded above the knees if I try standing, but at least both sides seem to be too busy shooting at each other to wonder where I've gone. I keep low to the ground, crawl for an H&M with its doors conveniently pre-blown off.

The suit continues to relay inspirational messages over comm: "Blue eighteen, this is Lockhart. Please confirm kill."

Lockhart.

"Blue Eighteen. I said *report.*"

I make it to Lingerie. There's an employees-only entrance beside the crotchless panties. Elvis leaves the building.

"Can you confirm your kill?"

He's all over the channel, my nemesis, the voice of my destruction—but right now he sounds more like a distraught mother who's lost her child in the playground.

"I'd say that's a no, Lockhart," and that snide dry delivery is such a close echo of what I was just thinking that I wonder for just a moment if False Prophet isn't reading my mind. But no: It's a woman's voice, coming over the comm. A rotor keeps time behind her.

"Strickland, get off the comms. Blue Eighteen, do you—"

"They're *down*, Lockhart. I warned you not to do this by squads. Prophet's suited up, probably not even sane anymore. Anything less than a platoon, he's going to go through them like a grizzly through Boy Scouts."

I'm liking this *Strickland* chick's attitude. I like the imagery, too.

Lockhart doesn't. "You're easily impressed, Strickland. Why don't you go back to running around after Hargreave and let me do my job."

"I *am* running around after Hargreave. He sent me down here to oversee retrieval of the suit. And I gotta say, so far it looks like your boys are falling down on the job."

"We'll get this sonofabitch. And we'll do it without your help."

"Hargreave doesn't see it that way anymore."

"Then the hell with Hargreave, too. He's got no idea what we're dealing with here."

BUD feeds me a bearing: Strickland's chopper is at ten and eleven.

"I'm not going to argue this with you on air, Lockhart. I'll see you down there. Strickland out."

Ten and ten. She's going down. And now that I'm a solid city block from the latest Ceph-CELL dustup, I can hear that descending *whupwhupwhup* bouncing off the walls to my left. My nemesis and his nemesis are headed for a meet-up just a couple of blocks away. If I hustle I might just be able to learn something useful.

What? Oh. Yeah, it is kind of amazing how well I can remember all these details, isn't it? But you know what really sticks in my memory? Just last week I remember not having anywhere *near* this good a memory.

I find a ringside seat behind a second-story window in a bombed-out brownstone. Lockhart's Humvee is parked down the alley behind a Shoppers Drug Mart, like he's run in for a pack of Trojans but is too embarrassed to go in the front door. Strickland's chopper idles front-and-center in an empty lot behind a $uper$ave, sharing space with a carpet of weeds and a couple of porta-potties. The way its rotor slashes the air makes me think of a pissed-off cat, kind of lazy and lethal at the same time.

They face off in the no-man's-land between, bracketed by a couple of CELLulites on perimeter watch. Lockhart's maybe 190 centimeters, your standard flat-topped, bullet-headed, walking military cliché except for the fact that so many of us actually *are* flat-topped bullet-heads.

Strickland is a walking wet dream: mocha skin, half a head shorter than the man she's going up against, dark hair pulled back into a ponytail. But it's pretty clear from the body language that Lockhart's not in the mood to appreciate any of Strickland's finer aesthetic qualities. I crank my audio on a bitchfest already in progress.

"—is to take him alive," Strickland's saying.

"The order is to bring him down," Lockhart spits back. "I'll argue the civil rights details when we've done that."

"Alive is more useful."

"Yeah? To who? The guy just massacred a couple of dozen of

my men, *Ms.* Strickland. I'm taking no more chances. Prophet dies. Hargreave can have his corpse to play with."

"Hargreave wants—"

"Hargreave wants the suit. He'll get it."

"He isn't going to like this. And last time I checked, we both worked for him." I get the sense of a high card being played.

He doesn't even blink. "That's where you're wrong, Ms. Strickland. *You* work for him. I answer to the CELL Executive Board and the DoD. I don't give a shit what some senile old shareholder like Hargreave may or may not like."

"That's *majority* shareholder. *And* former president of the CryNet board. You want to be careful what enemies you make here, Lockhart."

He doesn't answer for a moment. I wonder if maybe Strickland's finally found a way in; enemies, after all, are something Lockhart must know a lot about. I bet he's made more than his share over the years. And maybe he doesn't have to think twice about pissing off Strickland—what could some uppity bitch do to an alpha dog like him, right? But somebody higher up is holding *her* leash. How many enemies can he afford to make, how many fronts can he wage war on at once?

"This conversation is over," Lockhart says, and pisses all over Strickland's territory by climbing into her chopper.

Come on, Strickland. You don't have to put up with this shit. You can take him. You can. I know this territory, I've seen it before, you had to be twice as good to get half as far because of assholes like him. Go in there, throw that fucker out of *your* helicopter, bitch-slap him all the way back to that candy-ass Humvee of his and show him who's boss. You've got *Hargreave* backing you up.

I mean, for fuck's sake. You can stop this asshole, you can stop his whole private army.

You can.

Strickland shakes her head and climbs meekly into the cabin. The chopper lifts off.

That's a very good question. I've asked it myself, more times than you know. I could have blown his head off then and there. Hers, too. Want to know why I didn't?

I didn't want to prove him right.

It's what he told Strickland, you know? *That guy just massacred a couple of dozen of my men.* And I just about went off the deep end because *I'm not fucking Prophet.* I mean, Lockhart's a complete asshole but I have to admit he's got a point. I heard the comm chatter. Cobalt and Blue and Azure—Prophet took out half the goddamn rainbow before he and I ever crossed paths. Lockhart's got every right to be pissed—just *not at me.* This whole thing's a huge case of mistaken identity, and if I can somehow make everyone understand that I'm not Prophet, that all I did was inherit the man's threads, then maybe we could all be on the same side again.

But while I'm feeling all outraged and hard-done-by, this voice in my head tries to tally up all the corpses *I've* made since I put on those threads, and it loses count.

The thing is, that's not really me any more than Prophet is. Not that there aren't a shitload of folks in this line of work who *do* fit that profile. You know that. Any job that gives you rank and a gun is going to attract its share of psychos and assholes who get off on throwing their weight around. But that's not me, that—wasn't me. I didn't sign up to kill things, I signed up to *fix* them. I never—got off on this stuff before.

It's the N2. It gets inside you. It changes the way you think, it turns you into—

Fuck, listen to me. I sound like some wife-beating drunk, making excuses: *It's not me, honey, it's the suit talking* . . .

Do me a favor. If I bring you flowers and promise never to do it again, just shoot me.

Testimony of Cmdr. Dominic Lockhart before the Senate Subcommittee Hearings on the Use of Military Nanotechnology, 18/02/2019, Sen. Meghan McCain presiding.

Excerpt begins:

Sen. Preteela M'Benga: Cmdr. Lockhart, on behalf of this subcommittee I would like to thank you for being here today.

Cmdr. Dominic Lockhart: Happy to be here, ma'am.

M'Benga: Commander, how long have you been an employee of Hargreave-Rasch?

Lockhart: I've been chief of CELL's Urban Pacification Division for four years. Prior to that I was USMC.

M'Benga: And what is your current status?

Lockhart: In addition to my UPD duties I serve as a liaison to the US military when necessary. In those cases I report jointly to CELL and to the Department of Defense.

M'Benga: And this doesn't present a conflict of interest?

Lockhart: With all due respect, Senator, the fact that I am testifying here today proves that it does not.

M'Benga: Aren't you afraid of repercussions?

Lockhart: Repercussions, Senator?

M'Benga: If I've been correctly informed about the testimony you've prepared, you are about

to do what we in the Senate call *biting the
hand that feeds*. Aren't you concerned that
hand might bite back, if you'll forgive the
mangled metaphor?

Lockhart: No, ma'am.

M'Benga: May I ask why?

Lockhart: Without going into details, Senator, let's
just say that knowledge is power. I am in
possession of certain knowledge concerning
Hargreave-Rasch.

M'Benga: Knowledge beyond that you will be sharing
with us today?

Lockhart: Yes, ma'am.

M'Benga: Moving on, then. The report you've
presented is quite, er, comprehensive.
For those of us who have not yet made
it through the entire 864 pages, I wonder
if you could distill the essence of your
objection down to a concise sentence or
two.

Lockhart: Gladly, Senator. I believe this country needs
real soldiers. Not corpses in tin suits.

M'Benga: Excuse me, Commander. "Corpses in tin
suits"?

Lockhart: You wanted concise, ma'am.

M'Benga: I did. Perhaps we're not talking about the
same project here. My understanding of
CryNet's program is that it involves placing
live soldiers into battlefield prostheses, not
the reanimation of corpses.

Lockhart: Senator M'Benga, if you examine the
technical specs that follow the executive
summary, you'll see that central to CryNet's

second-generation proposals is a system that can—and I'm quoting here—"assume autonomic, regulatory, and motor functions in the event of somatic damage or operator incapacity." In other words, the system can run itself just fine when the person inside is dead.

M'Benga: Ummm, yes. But I look at those exact same words and I see a suit of armor that can carry its occupant to safety even if that occupant is injured or unconscious. I don't see—

Lockhart: With all due respect, Senator, what you are *not* seeing is that CryNet's next-generation Nanosuit essentially reduces the soldier to ballast—almost literally to dead meat.

M'Benga: Then why include the soldier at all? Why not simply market this device as a battlefield robot? I'm certain that many on this subcommittee would leap at the prospect of a machine that could take the place of our brave men and women on the battlefield, keep them out of harm's way.

Lockhart: I believe that an autonomous battlefield robot is CryNet's ultimate goal, sir. The model currently under development is merely a foot in the door.

M'Benga: But why not—

Lockhart: *Again,* ma'am, if you read the technical details of this proposal you will see that there are certain—neurocognitive elements that do not yet have a technological solution. Hargreave-Rasch does not say as much publicly, but I believe the only real use they see for our soldiers is as wetware. The system uses the human nervous system to do what it cannot yet do by itself. Jacob Hargreave is asking the American people to fund the development of a machine that would quite literally be a parasite on US soldiers.

M'Benga: Commander Lockhart, assuming that everything you've said today is true, would that not be a powerful argument in *favor* of funding?

Lockhart: I'm not following, ma'am.

M'Benga: Hargreave-Rasch and its subsidiary, CryNet Systems—these are independent corporations with their own very lucrative revenue streams. If we were to deny funding, they would in all likelihood just go ahead and develop this device privately, under no obligation to share any details with us. If we enter into the partnership currently on the table, however, we become—as representatives of the American people—privy to every stage of development. We gain a say in *how* it will be developed. Was it not Patton who said "Keep your friends close, and your enemies closer"?

Lockhart: No, ma'am.

M'Benga: Really? I could have sworn—

Lockhart: It was Sun Tzu, ma'am. Believe me, CryNet would not have approached the government if they didn't have to. If they don't need government funding, they need something else from you and you just don't know what it is yet. We have—*you* have the power to stop this abomination in its tracks.

M'Benga: Commander Lockhart, *we* approached *them*.

Lockhart: Excuse me?

M'Benga: My understanding is that the Pentagon got wind of CryNet's research and felt that such a project might prove useful in fulfilling their own strategic objectives. They *asked* CryNet to submit this proposal.

Lockhart: If the Pentagon approached Jacob Hargreave, then it was because Jacob Hargreave manipulated them into doing so.

Sen. Bradley Dubain: Excuse me, but I believe I might be able to cast some light on . . . ?

M'Benga: I yield the remainder of my time to Senator Dubain.

Dubain: Thank you. Commander Lockhart.

Lockhart: Senator.

Dubain: Please understand, I hold you and your service to the country in the highest respect. It is not my intention to question either your integrity or your experience.

Lockhart: I appreciate that, sir. Did you have a question?

Dubain: It is true, is it not, that you have suffered a personal loss as a result of the Nanosuit program?

Lockhart: (inaudible)

Dubain: I'm sorry, I didn't hear—

Lockhart:	The Nanosuit program does not yet exist, sir. I am here to try and ensure that it never does.
Dubain:	The Nanosuit 2 is still under development, yes. I was speaking of the earlier version, the one that was deployed—
Lockhart:	That is neither here nor there, Senator. I am not talking about the past, I am concerned about how we move forward.
Dubain:	I appreciate that, Commander. That is what we are *all* concerned about. And I'm sure you'll agree that moving forward, we must base our decisions on the available facts, not merely feelings and opinions.
Lockhart:	I am trying to keep my testimony limited to the available facts, sir. It was you who introduced the subject of personal—
Dubain:	But isn't it true that your nephew lost his—
Lockhart:	*Keep your fucking hands off my family, Senator.*
Dubain:	Uh—Commander Lock—
McCain:	I'm going to call a brief recess. We are adjourned until fourteen hundred.

Excerpt ends.

And we're *off,* running on goddamned foot along the Franklin Delano Roosevelt Expressway, doing our best to get to Nathan Gould before Lockhart's minions get to us.

Early betting favors the CELLulites but the Propheteers have pulled it out of the fire before, ladies and gentlemen, the Propheteers should be dead a dozen times over but they're still in there kicking. And don't we all love cheering for the underdog?

Not so much, apparently. Not when CryNet Enforcement and Local Logistics cuts your paycheck. One of the players on the opposing team puts it pretty succinctly over a channel he doesn't think I can access: "That piece of shit took out half of Cobalt Section. That piece of shit is toast."

Which should make me hungry—I haven't had a bite to eat all day, and even toast sounds like a treat—but for some reason I haven't felt hungry *or* tired since the N2 took me in its embrace. I don't know how long I can keep going on adrenaline, or whatever else it's pumping me full of, but I have to admit: This nanotech miracle goes a long way toward leveling the field.

A couple of other variables may actually tilt things in my favor. For one thing, private industry pays a lot better than the feds—and while this does let them buy the pick of the graduating litter, it also tends to attract folks whose primary interests are money, benefits, and no fucking overtime. There's a reason they call these guys *mercenaries*. You don't level up nearly as fast doing nine-to-five as you do pulling twenty-four-seven. So even without the N2 I am a harder dude than 90 percent of these fuckwits, and a lot more experienced.

The other thing is, the upper echelons are bickering again, and the boots on the ground are getting confused.

It starts when Drab Seven helpfully broadcasts the location they expect to take me out at. A familiar voice cuts him off: "This is Tara Strickland on oversight. Our objective for this target is capture and interrogate; I'm placing the kill order on indefinite hold."

Drab Section is not too happy about this. Seems they had friends in Cobalt and do not like *Special Adviser* Strickland reining them in. She keeps trying, though. She tries when a CELL Apache pins me down just south of Fulton, brings the whole damn freeway down on my head. She tries as Lockhart's troops chase me through the sewers under South Street. She tries when Drab tries to take me down with a tame EMP.

That one might have worked, if they'd been smart enough to boost their amps. The N2's coated in a bleeding-edge Faraday weave, specs say you can throw a Lockheed Circuit-Breaker at it and it'll keep on ticking. But nothing's absolutely pulse-*proof;* the only way to keep all EM *out* is to not let any *in,* and then you're deaf dumb and blind. So there's a chink in the armor there. They could have pulled it off if they'd gone all-out.

But they might as well have used a Taser for all the good that sparkler of theirs did. Fuzzed my tacticals for maybe half a second, put a bit of a jitter into the haptics. Barely even noticed.

Drab Section noticed, though. I sent half those assholes off to party with their friends from Cobalt.

But it's still no night in Reno, let me tell you. It's one nasty evil-smelling pile of shit after another. They're throwing every-thing at me from bricks to bombs, and the Ceph are all over the map; they're tying up CELL, which is good, but they're not going out of their way to make my life any easier, either. And through all of this Strickland keeps shouting *Belay that!* And *Shoot to disable!* And Lockhart's cutting in with *Kill order confirmed* and *Disregard further orders from Special Adviser Strickland* and *Someone kill that tin fuck for me.* I gotta hope that at least they've gone their separate ways by now, because I do not envy their pilot if they're still riding in the same chopper.

And of course I don't have enough to worry about already so Nathan Gould pops in on his own channel, gives me the breath-less breaking news that Lockhart's people are swarming over the whole Lower East Side looking for me. No shit, Sherlock. And then they're coming after *him,* I hear them kicking in the door when I'm still six blocks out and somehow Gould gets away, makes it down a fire escape or something, so now Gould's ware-house is enemy territory and he's on the run to an ex-girlfriend's place where he's stashed some surplus hardware that might do in a pinch. He sends me the new address and then he realizes that he also left it back at the warehouse—you know, the lab that's now swarming with CELLulites—and we are totally fucked the moment one of them sits down at the terminal and checks his address book. One guess who gets to storm the warehouse and make sure *that* doesn't happen.

At least this chapter has a happy ending, though, right? How many of those boys did I take out when the chopper crashed? Beautiful, beautiful sight, man. Came right down through the skylights, all that glass sparkling and tinkling like winter snow before the Meltdown. And you know, at least one of them was still alive on impact. I could see her mouth move through the bubble as she came down. I could see her screaming. Thank the good Lord for grenade launchers, eh Roger?

You should probably tell those guys to keep better tabs on them, though. They can be holy hell in the wrong hands.

Manhattan Triage Preprocessing Transcript,
Subject 429–10024-DR
Priority: High (Operation Martyr)
Interviewer: Cpl. Lansing, Analee (CELL HumIntel
Acquisition)
Subject: Sweet, Caitlin (Female, Divorced, 38yrs. Term.)
Subject #: 429–10024-DR (biog. database extract
appended)
Date of Interview: 23/08/2023 19:25
Date of Report: 24/08/2023 04:45

Subject dosed prior to interview with 130mg chlorproma-
zine to mitigate onset of Rapture and 65mg GABAbarbitol
to ensure compliance. Meds administered via isotonic Glu-
cose IV drip (standard rehydration protocols).

Sweet:	Is my daughter all right? Can I see her?
Lansing:	Emma's fine. She's sleeping.
Sweet:	And that—that man, is he—?
Lansing:	That's actually what I'd like to talk to you about, ma'am.
Sweet:	Caitlin's fine.
Lansing:	Yes ma—Caitlin. Now—
Sweet:	Please, can I just see Emma? Just for a mo—
Lansing:	I told you, Caitlin, Emma's sleeping now. She's fine.
Sweet:	I wouldn't disturb her, I just want to *see*—
Lansing:	Maybe in a little while. Ma'am, we really need this information.
Sweet:	(inaudible)
Lansing:	Perhaps you could start by telling me what you were doing in that part of Manhattan.
Sweet:	We—we used to live there, you know, before. Last week. We kind of hunkered down when it all started—that's what they told us to do, right? Stay calm, stay in your homes, let the authorities do their jobs. So that's what we did, we holed up in the apartment for three days before Mike— that's my husband—he decided to head out and try to find some food. We were supposed to go grocery shopping, you know, the day it started. We didn't really have much on hand.
	So Mike's gone for six, seven hours— there's no cell phone coverage, right, there hasn't been since everything fell apart, and I start to—is that my . . . that's my *daughter* screaming, that's—*Emma!*—

Lansing: No, ma'am, that's not Emma. I told you,
              Emma's sleeping.

MedTel Annotation: IV GABAbarbitol increased to
85 ml/l 19:26

Sweet: But . . . who is it, who's *screaming*, who's—
Lansing: It's not Emma, Caitlin. I promise. Honestly,
              it's nothing to concern you. If we can get
              back to your story . . .
Sweet: It's—it's a bit bright in here . . .
Lansing: I can turn down the lights if you like.
Sweet: No, actually the light's . . . nice . . .
Lansing: So your husband's been gone for six or
              seven hours . . .
Sweet: Yes. And the cell phones aren't working,
              and there's this, I don't know, this muffled
              whump from outside. Like an explosion, but
              far away. So I go out onto the balcony, you
              know, just to look around, just to maybe
              see what's happening. And about three
              blocks down along 15th there's one of those
              spires, you know. Just sticking up out of the
              road, four, five stories high, glowing around
              the base with this banner of thick smoke
              streaming out the top. The smoke's blowing
              my way and before I know it it's in my eyes.
              It's not like regular smoke, it's—gritty. So
              I turn my face away, you know, look away
              in the other direction and—and I see him,
              down there in the street.
Lansing: Prophet.

Sweet:	Who? Oh, you mean—no. Mike. Facedown. He never even got half a block. He . . .
Lansing:	Would you like a moment?
Sweet:	No, it's okay. That screaming's a bit distracting though, you know? Anyway, that's when I decided to leave. The neighborhood just wasn't safe, and Mike was—gone, and Emma and I were on our own. But my folks live in Brooklyn, and MacroNet's been saying there was this evacuation site downtown, so Emma and I just picked up and left.
Lansing:	Just so I understand: A spire's just detonated three blocks from your apartment. Your husband didn't make it half a block down the avenue. And you decide to take your child outside.
Sweet:	Yes.
	What?
Lansing:	Nothing. Please go on.
Sweet:	So I take Emma down the stairwell and we head out the back way because I don't want her to see her daddy like that. And I've got my iBall out but the realtime updates aren't working so we're basically going by memory. And the farther uptown we get, the more dead soldiers we see. Or at least, you know, they had uniforms. Like yours. Not regular army or anything. Are you real soldiers? Armed forces? CSIRA?
Lansing:	Yes, ma'am. We're—for all intents and purposes, we are the armed forces.

Sweet:	Well I didn't see any *regular* army, but there were a *lot* of bodies that looked like you. They were burned, and blown apart—
Lansing:	Yes, ma'am.
Sweet:	Some of them were in *pieces,* just *scattered around—*
Lansing:	*Yes,* ma'am. I get the picture.
Sweet:	And then we turned a corner and we ran into what was killing them. They were these—machines. These walking machines. Like, you know, that old invaders-from-Mars book they made us read back in high school, Walls or Wells or something. There were soldiers fighting back but they weren't doing well, I mean, no offense but you guys were getting your asses handed to you—
Lansing:	Why did you keep going?
Sweet:	What do you mean?
Lansing:	You have your eleven-year-old daughter with you, you're walking through a war zone, and the farther you go the more bodies you see. Why didn't you turn around, go in another direction?
Sweet:	We were trying to find the evacuation site.
Lansing:	Uptown.
Sweet:	Yes.
Lansing:	MacroNet said the evac site was *down*town. That's what you said.
Sweet:	Did I?
Lansing:	You did.
Sweet:	Well, it—it just seemed like the right way to go, I guess.
Lansing:	I see.

Sweet: Could we take a break? I could use some fresh air, stretch my legs a little.

Lansing: It's not really safe outside. Besides, wouldn't you rather stay close to Emma?

Sweet: She'll be okay. I don't think she likes the light as much as I do.

Lansing: I'll see what I can do. Just as soon as we finish here. It won't be long.

Sweet: Easy for you to say. You're not trapped in a glass box.

Lansing: That's just a precaution, ma'am. Honestly. Now: You had encountered one of our detachments in a combat situation, is that right?

Sweet: Combat situation? Oh, yes. And that was when we *ran*. Emma was pulling at my hand and I was just standing there, I don't know, stunned I guess, but my little girl's screaming and so I snap out of it and we just *run* back the way we came, as fast as we can. And there are things skittering along in the wreckage after us, not like those war machines, not big, but—fast. We could never really get a good look, we were too busy running but you could hear them gaining, they made these little *clattering* sounds as they moved, like, like big spider crabs or something. And Emma was pulling me to the side, she's going *Mommy, Mommy in here!* because she's seen this little hidey-hole she thinks we'll be safe in and I'm not so sure but she breaks away from me and dives into this wrecked storefront, right through the display window—well it was already shattered of course but there was glass everywhere, it's amazing she didn't open an artery—and I go in after her and the whole second floor has come down, there's concrete and those twisted wires everywhere and some of those collapsed slabs, they've formed this little cave. And Emma dives right into it. And I dive after her.

And I know we're going to die then, because we're snug and secure in this little lean-to of collapsed concrete, we're completely protected except for that open part at the front we came in through, it's the only way in or out. And there's something there, something—bloated. And spiky.

You know what a tick looks like? Mean little front end with needles and teeth for digging into you, and a kind of bulbous inflatable back end that swells up when it feeds? This was like that. Except it had these wavy metal antennae or tentacles or something, like the hoses off one of those old-style vacuum cleaners you had to run yourself. And it was half as big as *Emma*! It made this hungry little *clicking* noise, and its antennae were waving around in our direction and it was climbing over the rubble toward us blocking the only way out and we were dead, I just knew right then that we were both dead.

Except something shifted in the building then, something just *gave way,* and instead of squashing Emma and me it landed on this tick-thing and squashed it instead. This big slab of concrete, and dust everywhere, and these antennae-tentacles sticking out from underneath, whipping back and forth. That's were I got this cut on my face; those things were *sharp,* like needles.

And Emma's screaming even louder now, she's calling out for help and those little lungs of hers are amazing, if there's anyone within ten blocks I figure they have to hear her. But I don't know whether to curse or pray, because that big pile of cement did save us from the tick, but now we're trapped. There are gaps—there's about four or five places where you can see into the rest of the store, even all the way onto the street—but there's no way even skinny little Emma can fit through any of them. And the chittering hasn't stopped. It's only getting louder. I can see things moving out there, the shadows of monster ticks and other things too, I think.

And that's when he shows up. That *Prophet* you're interested in.

Lansing: Yes. Tell me about him.

Sweet: I guess he must have heard Emma. He was just *there,* all of a sudden. He dropped down into sight from somewhere overhead, and he was—I thought he was some kind of robot at first, you know? You see those things on National Geographic and the Discovery Channel, they've got those soft-bodied humanoids over in Japan? Acto, actino-something. Soft muscles, almost like ours. That's what I thought this was at first. Except he wasn't built like any of those nursemaid robots you see in the retirement homes, he looked like he was built for—heavy construction, or something. And Emma's shouting *Over here! Over here!* and I'm right there with her, bellowing my lungs out, and this *Prophet* of yours, big as one of those museum statues, he just turns toward us—slow, almost lazy, like he's got all the time in the world—and without a word he just stares through this visor the color of dried blood. Emma and I both shut right up then and there and he didn't move for a bit, he just stood there cradling this big gun the size of a fire hydrant, sizing us up like he was deciding whether to rescue us or—I dunno—cook us for dinner.

And Emma says in this very scared quiet voice, *He's one of them.* And I knew just what she meant, somehow, but you know what? I was okay with that.

Lansing: Excuse me?

Sweet: Weird, isn't it? It's hard to explain, he just seemed to—not *look like*, exactly, it was more—almost as if he *smelled* like one of them, if that makes any sense. And it scared the hell out of poor Emma, but to me it was

	almost—comforting. I forgot to be afraid for a little while.
Lansing:	Mmmm.
Sweet:	And he saved us. He started tearing through that concrete as if it were cat litter. And the ticks were all over him, he spent more time blasting those vicious little things than he spent digging us out. A couple of times I thought *This is it, they're going to tear him apart* but they never did. And he got us out. He rescued us. I told him what we'd seen, where the bodies were, where the machines were fighting, but he seemed—distracted. Put his hand up to his helmet once, you know, as though he was trying to hear a very faint radio station. I wanted to go with him, I almost asked him to take us to the refugee camp, but Emma just didn't like him at all, Emma never stopped being afraid of him even after he'd saved our lives. So he went on his way, and we went on ours, and that's when you picked us up. And there's really nothing more I can tell you so if you don't mind I'd really like to get out of here now. I'd really like to follow the light.
Lansing:	Just one more thing. Why did you tell him those things?
Sweet:	What things?
Lansing:	Where the bodies were. Where the machines were fighting.
Sweet:	He asked.
Lansing:	How did he—did he *speak* to you?

Sweet: Of course.

Lansing: With his *voice*?

Sweet: How else would he speak to me?

Lansing: Did he sound—was there anything
             distinctive about the way he spoke?

Sweet: Not really. I mean, his voice was a bit
             buzzy. But that's just the suit, right? The
             microphone.

Lansing: Yes, of course. The microphone.

Sweet: I really have to be on my way, now. I have
             to, to . . .

Lansing: Follow the light?

Sweet: Yes.

Lansing: Follow it *where*, Caitlin?

Sweet: I don't know. Wherever. I'll know when I get
             outside.

Lansing: Uptown. Toward the aliens.

Sweet: You don't really *get* it, do you Corporal?
             You don't get it, because you don't *got* it.

Lansing: Got what, Caitlin?

Sweet: This. In my eyes. On my hands. I can even
             feel it in my head, somehow, it's growing
             but it's not—not evil. It's all good.

             That's why you've got me in this cube,
             isn't it? You don't want to catch it.

MedTel Annotation: Halothane introduced into Quar.
Cube 19:36

Lansing: We don't really know what it is yet, ma'am.
             It just seems prudent to get all the facts
             before exposing ourselves.

Sweet:	Well, then, you'll never get anywhere, will you? You'll never have all the facts until you know what it *feels* like. And you'll never know what it feels like until you're exposed. And you won't expose yourself until you've got all the facts ...
Lansing:	Yes, ma'am.
Sweet:	It's just a funny little circle. You're running around and around ...
Lansing:	Yes, ma'am. Would you like to see Emma now?
Sweet:	... Emm ... ?
Lansing:	Your daughter, ma'am. Would you like to see her?
Sweet:	Oh, isn't that nice ...
Lansing:	Ma'am?
Sweet:	The screaming ... stopped ...

MedTel Annotation: Subject loses consciousness 19:37

Subject Disposition: Routine. Transferred to Trinity Center for culture/autopsy. Custody transferred 22:34 (S. M. Samenski receiving).

Notes & Comments: Subject presented mild physical symptoms of early infection (acidosis, mild vitreous turbidity) but no obvious signs of Rapture during initial processing (note, however, that her self-reported, almost unconscious movement toward centers of high Charybdis density is consistent with incipient Wanderlust). Rapid onset of more obvious behavioral changes was apparent during the course of this interview, a period of only 12 minutes; this is significantly faster than preliminary results led us to expect. Changes in speech patterns suggest elevated metabolism in the religious circuitry of the temporal lobe, but we are still awaiting Trinity's galvanic-necropsy results.

Subject's daughter (SWEET, EMMA, SUBJ. #430–10024-DR) showed no signs of infection at autopsy despite extended close proximity to infected subject post-infection. We have yet to encounter an instance of person-to-person transmission.

Flag D. Lockhart/L. Aiyeola/L. Lutterodt: Subject claims Prophet spoke to her, contradicting telemetry intercepts suggesting that his injuries had rendered him effectively mute. It is possible that Prophet's injuries are not as severe as we've been led to believe; this also raises obvious information-management concerns, should Prophet engage in conversation with other civilians.

Corporal Analee Lansing,
24/08/2023 04:45

Motherhood issues. That's what you guys live for, isn't it?

Shrinks, of course. Neuromechanics. Psychiatrists. Therapists. What, you thought I didn't know? You thought I didn't have you pegged the moment you opened your mouth? I don't care how many stripes you're wearing, Roger; you ain't no soldier. And who else would they send in to talk to a suit full of bad wiring?

Anyway, it's what you guys live for. That and sexual dysfunction. They haven't outfitted the N2 with a hydraulic dick, more's the pity. I do have this rubberized nozzle rammed up my ass so I don't soil the suit; I suppose that might come in handy for giggles as well as shits if you swing that way, which I don't.

But yeah, I've racked up such a rep for killing things that it actually makes you *suspicious* when I take a moment to help out a mom and her little girl. Maybe you think there's a bit of a weird vibe there and that's all you need to go to town, right? Shrinks and mommy issues.

Okay, then. Let me tell you about my mother.

She was a cunt.

Not always, mind you. Not at first. She was never Parent of the Year material—bit on the judgmental side, that just goes with the whole Bible Belt mind-set—but at least she wasn't a drunk or a methhead. Never hit me. Never forgot me on the luggage carousel. Perfectly decent woman, you know? No complaints, all while I was growing up.

Then the dementia hit, and holy fucking Christ.

She'd turn into a monster. Not full-time, not in the early stages anyway, but sometimes she'd just—snap. Turn into this rabid snarling animal. 'Course she was getting on by then, and times weren't great generally. My folks lost most of their savings in the Double Dip, which meant they couldn't replace those fancy antique plates we had after she threw them at me during one of her *episodes.* All we had left was that cheap plastic shit that would barely dent if you dropped it from orbit. And I wasn't around much by then, for obvious reasons, so she started whaling on Dad instead. Poor bastard never fought back—some Twen-Cen bullshit about *not supposed to hit a lady,* he wouldn't last a day in today's armed forces let me tell you. I came home on furlough one weekend and he'd locked himself in the bathroom and she was stabbing at the door with a goddamn screwdriver. He was one big fucking bruise, all purple and yellow, this gentle old fart who never hurt anyone. I mean, he was seventy-five years old! And that was when I decided, *enough.* I gave the old cunt a choice between the police station and the psych ward. I never saw her again after I got her institutionalized. Not once.

But what really pissed me off was the way people kept making *excuses* for her.

Nobody saw a monster. All anybody saw was a victim of the disease. That's why Dad never hit back, *It's not her fault, it's the dementia*. People would visit her in the home and she'd rant and spit and say all these vile things about Dad and everyone would just sadly shake their heads and say, "It's the Alzheimer's speaking, how can you cut her off like that, she's your *mother*."

But the thing was, they couldn't have it both ways. If this *was* the disease, then it wasn't my mother at all; my mother had died years ago, she died when the dementia undid all the circuits that made her what she was and rewired her into this vicious twisted body-snatcher thing made out of recycled meat. In which case I owed it nothing. And if she *was* my mother, well, then my mother was a rabid dog that needed to be put down if you ask me, and I didn't owe *that* thing any special breaks, either.

No matter how you looked at it, I was off the hook. Switch the wiring, pimp the neurotransmitters, and *mother* turns into *other*. There's nothing fixed about who or what we are, Roger. Even if it looks the same, it's *not*. It's all just wetware to be wiped, rewritten, rebooted. I learned that when I was just a kid, I learned that without any of your fancy degrees or candy-colored MRI readouts.

And that's why I have to laugh every time you sneak a peek at your reader, there. Because you're a *mechanic,* dude. You should know this shit better than I do. You fumble around using words and drugs when you really should be getting in there with a very tiny soldering gun, but when it comes right down to it you've spent your whole damn career trying to change the circuitry in people's heads. So why do you keep looking for answers in my *file,* Roger? I'm not that person anymore. I'm something new.

And believe me. The thing that's talking to you now has no mommy issues whatsoever.

The elevator slides open on a man in combat fatigues who obviously never pulled a day of combat in his life. Glasses, salt-and-pepper goatee, middle-aged paunch pushing out over his belt. Stupid little ponytail, probably meant as some kind of diversionary tactic to draw attention from his hairline. I've never seen him before, of course; but the sight of me lights his face up with such obvious joy I wonder for a second if he's going to kiss me.

"*Dude,*" he says. "You made it."

Nathan Gould is a slob with a paper fetish. The apartment is piled floor-to-ceiling with all manner of shit: filing cabinets, drawers hanging half open like extruded tongues, piles of newspapers (where the hell did he get *newspapers* in Manhattan?), stacks of old optical ROM. Old paper maps spread out across one of those tilted architect's tables you see in TwenCen movies, you know, before computers. Topographic, geological, architectural. It's like Gould's hardcopied every overlay anyone's ever dumped into the Manhattan database. I don't know what he's using them for, other than to mop up coffee spills and snort the occasional line of grimwire (I can see the crystal residue from across the room; the eyes in this suit don't miss a thing).

"Man, you wouldn't believe the shit that's gone down in the last twenty-four hours. Barclay's guys are getting creamed uptown. CryNet are falling the fuck apart everywhere else. Chaos, man."

The walls—those bits of them that peek through between the mountains of dead trees, anyway—are a mix of smart paint, cork-board, and old 2-D monitors. One wall's three layers deep in pushpins and pictures, everything from false-color satcam shots to coupons for 20 percent off tampons at PharMart. An ancient mini fridge squats in one corner; it doesn't even have an online connection but someone called *Angie* has scribbled *Nate, When are you going to get your shit out of my place?! I'm back for good on the 28th* on the dry-erase board stuck to the door.

Gould leads me through all this chaos like a guide through the jungle, talking nonstop: "That shit you absorbed at the crash site, it's lit up the suit systems like a pinball, man," and "Definitely viral, same base structure as the nano-weave," and "Hargreave must be nuts, playing with that shit like it was Kevlar." I'm not really paying attention. I've just caught sight of an aquarium be-hind a stack of old hardcovers, a big hundred-gallon job, and something's *squirming* in it: something with arms and suckers. For a moment I think Gould's caught himself a baby Ceph, but no; it's just an octopus. Looks as alien as anything else I've run into these past few hours, but at least it's from around here.

Somehow that makes all the difference. I almost feel, I don't know, *affection* for the spineless crawly thing. We're all in the same tank now, right?

Gould leads me down the hall—"Right down here, same basic setup as back on the island, just not as many bells and whistles"—into a room that's at least empty enough to really appreciate how dingy the wallpaper is. Backed up against the far wall is a cross between a recliner and a crucifix. Or maybe a crucifix and a den-tist's chair. Definitely a crucifixion subtext, though: It's a molded recliner with outstretched arms, a socket for the suit. You sit back and—judging by those circular little receptacles along the arms and legs and spine—it plugs right into you. A loose coil of black umbilicals connects it to a server stack in the corner.

"So come on, let's get you checked out."

I lower myself into the cradle, and *whump* I'm stuck in stone. I don't know if it's the damn suit or Gould's setup but here I am again, paralyzed while this middle-aged geek rolls around on his desk chair and fiddles with controls I can't understand.

"Some fucked-up shit, right?" He ends up at an old scuffed desk against the wall, playing with the laptop there. "And Hargreave, well, who knows what's going on in *his* head . . . So let's see what we—

"Wait a second, that's odd—"

And suddenly, whatever welcome I saw in Nathan Gould's face is nowhere to be seen. What I see instead is shock, and anger, and fear. I see the beginnings of a killing rage; I know what those look like.

I see the gun in Gould's hand, pointed at my face.

"You're not Prophet," he hisses.

I still can't move.

"Who are you? What did you do to him?" He leans in close. "Hargreave, right? Just another loose end. Hargreave sent you to kill me."

I wonder how much this suit can take, immobilized. I wonder what kinds of tools Gould has at his disposal. I wonder how long it'll take him to crack me open like a clam, get at the soft squishy parts inside. Just calm down, Nathan. You have the upper hand. No need to panic, no need to be hasty. Just—

That's right. Back to your keyboard. Access the black box. There's gotta be one in here somewhere. Play back the log. Get the facts.

He gets them. Seems to sink into himself a little. After a few moments he remembers me, and frees me with the flip of a switch. He turns without a word and disappears up the hallway.

I find him back in the living room. Somehow, against all odds, he's found a chair that isn't half a meter deep in ancient hardcopy. He sits with his head in his hands.

"I can't do this anymore," he says to the carpet. "I'm not a fucking stormtrooper, I'm not some spec ops hard case like y—like Prophet . . . was. A conspiracy geek with a grudge. That's all I fucking am."

Motion from the corner of my eye: Over by the wall the octopus writhes in its tank. Its arms coil, uncoil, beckon me from across the room.

"Prophet was supposed to get us out. The marines were coming for us. Now . . ."

Suckers attach themselves deliberately to the glass, one after another after another, an endless procession of circular footsteps. The body of the thing *inflates* as I watch, swells up like a great fleshy balloon, then slowly collapses; I get the sense of a weary, resigned sigh. One gold unblinking eye regards me through a horizontal bar of pupil.

"That's Houdini," Gould says, behind me. "Know anything about cephalopods?" He sounds almost hopeful, but it doesn't last: "No, of course you don't."

Houdini and I watch each other through the glass.

"Smartest inver—smartest *earthly* invertebrate that ever lived," Gould remarks. "Astonishing problem-solving abilities, deep memory, physical dexterity an order of magnitude greater than anything we vertebrates ever managed. You know, they have individual motor control over every one of those suckers? Pass a pebble from one sucker to the next: down from the tip of one arm, across the beak, back up to the tip of another arm, do it a hundred times and never drop the damn thing once.

"Imagine what they could do with a clitoris."

I turn, and catch the ghost of a smile fading on his face.

"Half his nervous system's in the arms, you know? You could say those things literally *think* with their tentacles."

Houdini retreats to a pile of fake rocks, pours himself into those cracks and crevices like epoxy. He disappears before my eyes, his boneless body mimicking not just the color but the *texture* of the rock pile. Gould grunts softly.

He's wrong, though. I may just be a dumb jarhead but I knew a thing or two about those crawly beasts even before Gould's little tutorial. When I was a kid there was this public aquarium down by the waterfront, had an octopus in a tank. Big triangular Plexi column backed onto a rock wall full of little caves and crannies. No matter how many times you paid to get in, the fucking octopus was always hiding in that rock wall; you'd see maybe an eye, a little patch of suckers, and a whole lot of empty tank. It was pathetic.

But then one night me and a couple of the guys broke into the place on a dare—it was pretty easy actually, the security guard was a bit of a stoner and kept forgetting to turn the alarm back on after he did his rounds—and my buddies went straight to the shark tank but for some reason I decided to check out the octopus. And the whole gallery was dim and green and deserted, it was great, and wouldn't you know it the fucking thing was out and about. Right there in the open. Turns out octopuses are nocturnal. It would swell up and then *phoomph*—jet its way into the deep blue sea, but of course it's in a fucking tank, right? So it just slammed into the Plexiglas like a limp water balloon. And you could just *see* it deflating, sinking down to the bottom all depressed, but then it would change its mind and gear up for another run, puff itself up, *phoomph* out into the deep blue sea—and *thump* into the glass and it would get all depressed and sink back down again. I watched it for a good ten minutes and it never seemed to learn. So let's just say I'm a little skeptical of the Gospel According to Gould when it comes to cephalopod intelligence.

But the thing is, it never learned but it never gave up, either. I couldn't help feeling sorry for the little fucker. It had needs and wants, it valued its freedom, you never saw it during the day but at night you'd have to be blind not to see how much it *hated* being in that tank. And now I'm looking at Houdini, and I'm thinking about the Ceph, and you know, there's a part of me thinking maybe we just haven't seen these things at night yet. I mean, if an ignorant asshole like me can drum up sympathy for an overgrown garden slug at the tender age of fourteen, who's to say we can't come to terms with these aliens somehow, right?

Nah. Of course not.

Had you going for a moment though, didn't I?

Gould's going on about ancient history. Houdini has retired under a rock so I start paying attention: something about smallpox and the Aztecs.

"Ever wonder how they felt when they saw those pustules popping up for the first time, when they saw what it was *doing* to them? One of the most culturally dynamic civilizations on the planet, wiped out by a bug less than half a micron across. You might be surprised how often that kind of thing happens.

"Ever wonder how history might have turned out if they'd had vaccine technology?"

I can't say I have. It doesn't take a gene genie to see where he's going with this, though.

"Prophet said there might be one. For the spore." Gould nods in my direction. "I think the data's in that suit you're wearing, somehow. It was the only reason he came back in, he sure as fuck doesn't—*didn't* trust Hargreave. I gotta say, even I wondered if he was getting a bit paranoid. Wear that suit long enough, you start to—anyway. If your field trip to the crash site proved anything, it proved that Prophet was right about Hargreave. Your suit, the alien tech—no way independent evolutionary tracks give you that kind of similarity down on the molecular level. Whoever you are, you're pretty much wearing a Ceph exoskeleton. All we did was file off the serial numbers, change the chrome, and slap a dozen CryNet patents onto a black box."

He sighs, and shakes his head.

"Let me tell you a story."

It's more of a conspiracy theory, actually. I would've rolled my eyes if Leavenworth had fed it to me a week ago. After today, though, I'm wondering if it's paranoid *enough*.

There's this company, Hargreave-Rasch. It's over a hundred years old, even though I've never heard of it before. Apparently that's the way they like it; H-R is the company *behind* the companies, the dark force pulling the strings behind the smiling beneficent Monsantos and the Halliburtons and the General Technics of the world.

Think about that. Think about a company that makes Halliburton look socially progressive. Think about a company that uses Monsanto as its *happy* face.

Hargreave-Rasch didn't *have* to hide. It was so fucking scary that anyone in the know was afraid to look it in the eye.

They ran a big honking radio-telescope array out of a chunk of Arizona they'd owned since before Hiroshima. Added some outgrouped satellites up in geosync to widen the aperture, just as soon as the tech was available.

All that time they were looking for space aliens.

We're not talking your average high school SETI project here.

This was no shoestring operation put together by the tinfoil-hat crowd, nobody was holding bake sales or begging spare CPU cycles on peoples' iBalls to crunch space static. This one project had the budget of a good-sized third-world puppet regime.

Also, according to Gould, they had a pretty good idea of where to look. Not that he ever told me how they came by that information.

They went at it for the better part of a century. They strained the whole fucking sky, squeezed every gamma burst and every X-ray and every burp of static through all the filters and algorithms that money could buy, and they came up with bupkis. They must have lost billions over the years, but they kept at it. They didn't quit. This wasn't a gamble, you see. Hargreave was no visionary, he wasn't just playing the odds. He wasn't *hoping* there was something out there. He *knew*.

Six months ago they caught something out past the orbit of Mars. Gould doesn't know what it was—apparently he used to work for H-R himself but by then he'd left over, well, he called them "creative differences." But something. And now, all of a sudden, we've got aliens invading Manhattan.

"Does that make any fucking sense to you at all?" Gould asks me.

And if I could talk I'd have to say, well, sure. It makes perfect sense. I'm a soldier, for chrissake. There wouldn't be a need for people like me if life was all flowers and fluffy kittens. But this is *Darwin's* universe, *Dr.* Gould. There's never enough to go around—and if there is, you gobble it up until there isn't, and then you fight over what's left. You'd think a scientist would know this shit.

What did Hargreave *think* would happen when he went out looking for giants? Did he think they'd invite us into some big shiny galactic federation, cure cancer, and give us the secret of immortality? Of course they're gonna kick our ass. Any soldier worth his shit will tell you: You think there's something bigger than you out there, you fucking well keep your head down and hope it doesn't notice.

I mean, if we're dealing with actual goddamn space aliens here—things that travel among the *stars*—then Gould's wrong: We're not the Aztecs to their Europeans, we're the whales to their factory ships. We're the palm trees to their fucking napalm. What I can't figure out is why we're getting in any licks at all.

"We still don't even know where they're coming from," he says. "If they've got a ship in orbit, it's cloaked against anything we've got. If they've landed already, nobody saw them come down. And God help us if they're teleporting their troops in from out past Mars." He snorts softly, a hollow chuckle, a gallows laugh. "However they're doing it, they're going by the book. First send the pox to soften us up, then send the conquistadores. At least the Mayans could see the damn galleons coming over the horizon . . ."

Houdini waves a listless tentacle at me from across the room. A glossy hardcopy catches my eye just to the left of his tank, a satcam enhance of a fractal coastline stripped of cloud cover: the eastern Chinese seaboard, stippled with text and contour lines. One of the labels is oddly familiar.

LING SHAN.

"Of course." Gould's noticed my interest. "I keep forgetting. Manhattan wasn't *exactly* the first stop on the tour."

There've been rumors. Some kind of covert op that went bad back at the start of the decade, just before the climate jumped the rails and turned the whole fucking planet upside down. You hear things, some of them pretty wild—but I don't remember anything about space aliens.

"They had a—I suppose you'd call it a *skirmish*," Gould tells me. "We're assuming they encountered the Ceph. We're *hoping* they encountered the Ceph; otherwise we've run into two hostile alien species within three years, and how do you like *those* odds? But Prophet—well, you met him. He was top-of-the-line, he wouldn't have been running that team otherwise, but Ling Shan—changed him."

He looks away for a moment.

"No," he says at last. "I'm bullshitting you. The *suit* changed him. Your suit, now." His shoulders rise, fall. "Prophet wasn't—he may not have been entirely sane, there at the end. There's a degree of integration that not everyone can handle. Probably nothing for you to worry about, not over the short term, but Prophet was hooked into that thing for—I don't know how long, actually. He dropped right off the map after Ling Shan. Stopped trusting Hargreave entirely, figured out how to disable the tracking chip, and just—"

Gould kisses the tips of his fingers, spreads them as if blowing smoke to the wind.

"They sent a team in afterward, of course. No trace of any aliens, no trace of our guys, no trace of Prophet. The whole playing field had been slagged to glass." He laughs a sad little laugh. "I was never able to find out which side did that, actually.

"I think Hargreave blamed me, in a way, even then. I mean I wasn't Prophet's *handler*, exactly, but I was there. Doesn't matter how many lab tests you run, your prototype's always gonna fuck up in the field, right? First rule of product testing. So there I was, in the same room with all those black ops need-to-know heavyweights, just a geek to keep an eye on the suit feeds and work out the bugs. When the suit goes dark, who else you gonna blame? I was the guy supposed to make sure that *didn't* happen.

"It was bad enough we all thought he was dead, but then I started getting these messages. A vcard or a voicemail, totally untraceable, just out of the blue every two or three months: *Having a blast, wish you were here,* that kind of thing. I have no fucking clue why he reached out to me of all people. Nobody else heard squat from the man as far as I know, not even his handler.

"But now Hargreave's thinking I was in on it somehow. Prophet was a top-of-the-line field man but there's no way he had the chops to hack that suit on his own, right? I managed to convince him I hadn't conspired to steal his secret technology—it wasn't all that hard, actually, Hargreave-Rasch has machines that can sniff out a little white lie from your *blink rate,* among other things—but that still pretty much wrapped it up as far as the whole Prism gig was concerned.

"Anyway, at least we knew Prophet wasn't dead at the bottom of a jungle canyon somewhere. But we never saw him, and he never came in, and I don't know how much of these past three years he spent in that suit and how much he spent out of it. For all I know he never took the damn thing off, and that would be . . . well."

Outside, the faint faraway sound of something colossal, falling over.

Gould shakes his head, gets back on message. "The point is, he wanted to come in *now.* After all this time. And I'm not working at H-R anymore but I guess I'm the only one he trusts. So he reaches out. Going to bring me something, he says, something to save the goddamn world. And here you are. You're not carrying any gift-wrapped packages. You're not handing me the key to some safe-deposit box. All you've brought me is that fucking suit."

Find Gould. Nathan Gould. I'm so fucking sorry.

It's all on you now.

The Geek from Prism hauls himself to his feet. It seems to take all the strength in the world.

"So," he says. "Shall we get started?"

*   *   *

It's something in the Nanosuit, of course. *Deep-layer package in the memory substrate,* is the way Gould puts it. He puts me back in the cradle, pokes and prods every interface the suit has to offer and probably punches in a couple of new ones for good measure.

"Fuck," he says at last.

I'm impressed by how concise his executive summary is. I wait for a bit more detail.

"I can see it in there," he says. "It's a black fucking box is what it is. Classical electronic I can do. Quantum I can do. This molecular format, though—it's unique to the Nanosuit, it's proprietary. Maybe Prophet didn't realize I'd parted ways with Hargreave-Rasch when he made the recording. Or maybe he just grabbed it in its native format. Either way, I can't decode it here.

"We need to get you to an H-R lab. Prism's over on Roosevelt Island, but it's miles away. Plus they revoked my access when I got sack—"

An alarm goes off, right over my head.

When I peel myself off the ceiling I follow Gould's wilder-than-usual stare to a monitor teetering on a pile of file folders: a compound-eye matrix of in-house securicam feeds. A column of Darth Vader wannabes creeps down a stairwell in one of those facets: they pile up stage left, bleed out of one window, spill across the hallway in the next one.

"Shit," Gould hisses. "CELL."

They carefully test each door along the hallway, leaning back against the wall, reaching out with one arm, placing limpets for maximum sensitivity. Occasionally trying a doorknob for tradition's sake.

Gould spins me around; I'm surprised by the strength in that scrawny body. "They're coming for me. They're coming for *us.* Hargreave wants us dead." Which isn't exactly true. I seem to remember some fairly explicit orders that I be brought in alive.

But I can't begrudge Gould his ongoing attempts at motivational speaking.

Besides, it's pretty obvious by now that being *brought in alive* is not going to lead to an especially happy ending, either.

Gould pushes me back toward the door, indifferent to the teetering piles of crap we're knocking over en route. "You gotta keep them out. You gotta *take* them out." And I'm back in the hall, staring at a closed door, listening to half a dozen locks and deadbolts clicking into place on the other side.

Brave, brave man, Nathan Gould.

But he hasn't abandoned me. A moment later he's back on comm, my own personal Seeing Eye dog: "The stairwell's blocked at this end of the hall, they're gonna have to come out on the other side of the atrium. They're still six floors up, you've got a few minutes . . ."

I call the elevator and jam a potted plant between the doors; if they're dumb enough to try that approach they'll have to rappel down the shaft. The hall opens out on the upper rim of a mezzanine, gloomy as a cave and with almost as many places to hide. But if Gould's right, that door across the atrium is the only access point from the enemy's approach. Good bottleneck, clear line-of-sight. This could be easy if I can just nail them before they have a chance to fan out.

Gould crackles in my ear: "Hey, I hacked their freq. The idiots are recycling their initialization vectors. They're CELL, all right."

I center my sights on the closed door across the space, hold my fire, crank the acoustic gain: sure enough I can hear quiet movement on the other side. I pan back and forth a bit, and double-take: soft sounds whispering at closer range, too, through the nearer walls of the atrium itself. CELL's trying to flank me. I can hear footsteps, and whispers, and

—slithering—

And Gould in my ear breathing "Ohhh, no . . . oh, *shit* . . ."

And you don't need volume enhance at all, to hear the screaming.

They hit CELL first. Even on the other side of that closed and distant door I hear them come through the walls. I hear the gunfire, and that otherworldly *chittering;* I hear shouts and panicked orders and the wet tearing sounds of bones being pulled from their sockets. Then the door bursts open on the far balcony, and all that blood and biosteel tumbles into view like a gory mudslide.

But by that time I've got my hands full with the Ceph that have come through the walls on my own side of the playground.

I don't know how they got in here. I don't know why they didn't show up on Gould's cameras. Maybe they've got cloaks. Maybe they just punched through floors and ceilings to get around, bypassed the halls and stairwells entirely. Brave, brave Sir Nathan isn't any help—"Fuck man I'm *outta* here!"—and I'm not making it back to his girlfriend's place anyway, not without a hell of a firefight. Squiddie *owns* this floor.

The cloak is my only edge. I *think* the Ceph might be able to see though it, but not very well; their aim is wild, and CELL targets are so very much easier to get a lock on. I'm not a big fan of unnecessary heroics. If the enemy of my enemy is my friend, then two families of very dear friends are busy beating the shit out of each other, and I'm not about to get involved in a domestic squabble. So I hide in plain sight. I slip from pillar to post. Sometimes one or two of the grunts turn my way, suspiciously sniff the air with those banana-slug tentacles, then return to the fray.

But just because I'm not an active participant in this melee doesn't mean I can't rack up a few experience points. You can learn a lot by watching. So I take a few notes as I sneak out the back way. I watch one merc shoot the leg off an exoskeleton and the squirming slimy thing inside launches itself right out of the harness and comes at her stark naked, flailing its tentacles like clubs. I watch another take out a monster from the stars with a shotgun, seconds before a different monster blows him away in turn. But most of all I see a fight that's way more even than it has any right to be: creatures smart enough to hop among solar systems, duking it out with us backboned primitives in a dingy hallway like this was some kind of sock hop between the Bloods and the Crips. I see *them* fighting like *us,* and I don't know why they'd do that. I see combat exoskeletons that leave the meat exposed, tentacles or antennae or fucking *penises* for all I know, flailing around completely unprotected.

Know what I see, Roger?

There's got to be something I'm not seeing.

What do *you* think about that, Roger? You must have an opinion.

I wondered for a while if maybe those tentacle thingies were gills or lungs or something, had to stay exposed to the air to let them breathe. But that still doesn't explain why you'd expose them to *bullets;* Jesus Christ, these guys hop among stars and they can't invent chain mail? Countercurrent air pumps are too complicated for them? Doesn't make any goddamn sense, running into battle with your junk hanging out.

But then I thought, maybe that's the whole point.

You know about the Celts, right? The Gaesatae? There were these tribes back in ancient times, took on the Romans, might have even been mercs. And I shit you not, these guys literally ran into battle *naked*. Painted themselves up, spiked their hair to make them look all badass, but they'd leave their dicks flapping in plain sight. It was an intimidation tactic. Made the enemy feel all insecure or something I guess, you know, *Holy shit these guys are so tough they don't even need* armor, *we'd better just run away now.* And there were even armor-using cultures back then that would deliberately leave their backs exposed, even if they loaded up their fronts with enough shielding to stop a battering ram. To keep you fighting on the battlefield, you know? You're less likely to turn tail if it leaves you open for an easy kill. And Squiddie, well, most of that exposed meat is definitely dorsal, am I right?

Sorry, what did you call—*Handicap Principle.* Can't say I ever heard of it.

Oh, right. You mean, like a peacock tail. *Look at me, I'm so fit I can afford to drag all this dead weight around just to look impressive.* Same basic thing, I guess. Except your peacocks are trying to impress their mates, and the Celts were trying to impress their enemies. I mean, it's not very smart, but then again it's a brain-stem thing, right? And I don't have to tell you about the stupid shit our brain stems get us up to.

Maybe Squiddie's not so different after all.

What? Oh, no: They ended up getting their asses handed to them. Scared the shit out of the Romans on first sight, but in the end it doesn't matter how big your dick is: A javelin's always gonna be bigger. So the moment someone stopped running and put them to the test it was all *Hey, the Gaesatae have no clothes!* Game over.

A shame we can't repeat that bit of history, huh?

You know. Because I *am* remembering it.

Dear Neville,

I hope our Lord is keeping you safe in these most trying
of times. I have tried to contact you through more
conventional means but the network has been down
for some time in Manhattan and now my batteries have
died. I have resorted to the old-fashioned methods
our ancient brethren used, in the days before the
technophiles and idolaters seduced us with their global
networks and their Internet pornography (although I
must admit that I find myself missing the satellite feed
and Prayer Line that funds our ministry. Praise the Lord,
who turns the Devil's own tools to such righteous ends!).

It is day four and our mission here is beginning to make
progress, although perhaps more slowly than I would
have hoped. New York was full of wickedness even
before the End Days began, which is of course why Satan
chose it as his first stronghold (though I admit I would
have expected him to start with Los Angeles or Fergus).
Communists and sodomites are almost as thick upon
the ground here as demons, and while recent events
have caused many of the locals to repent, others even

now resist our attempts to lead them to salvation (none so blind as those who will not see). Those damnable Anglicans, sensing an opportunity to spread their particular brand of liberalism, have also set up shop on the other side of the borough; many survivors encounter them first, and desperate for even the appearance of redemption, are fooled by their use of Christian props. I hear that even the ragheads have regrouped at a mosque over in Hamilton Heights! Fortunately they are wasting their time by launching jihad against Satan's armies instead of converting souls (they know the easier enemy to beat when they see it, ha ha!), and we have had no direct encounters with them so far.

Our greatest enemy, of course, is Satan himself. You may have heard mention of "the Rapture" on the mainstream feeds; do not be fooled. It is anything but. I have seen these so-called Raptured with my own eyes. They are *infested,* brother. They seek the light, but it is not the light of our Lord (you may remember that *Lucifer* means "bringer of light"). Some kind of demonic tumors grow in their eyes, in their mouths, in their open wounds. It steals away their souls. They are *already* saved, they say. They have *already* found redemption. And they are gripped by some evil wanderlust that draws them to wherever Satan's spawn gather in the greatest numbers.

And there is something else, Neville, something new. You may have heard of the "pingers" and the "stalkers" and the other abominations that walk these streets, preying on sinners and saved alike. I have seen them with my own eyes; they are half flesh and half machine and not remotely human. But just today I saw something that looked and moved like a man, yet was as depraved as any demon. I saw a ghoul, feeding on the flesh of the dead.

It was the color of stone, or clay. For a few moments I thought it might be one of those golems the Jews go on about—they do figure prominently in Revelation, even though they have spurned Christ—but it had metal seams and joints, and a head like a helmet. And its *body*, Neville, it had such muscles, they shone and rippled and flexed with every movement. I swear, were it not the color of slate it might almost have been you standing there, in the shower at the seminary after practice. But it acted nothing like you, Neville. It was crouched over a pile of corpses and it *fed* on them through some kind of fang or needle that sprouted from its wrist. I did not get close enough to see the details, but those penetrated bodies—they shriveled up as I watched, Neville. This monster sucked them dry and left nothing but husks of skin draped over bone, like one of the steel vermin that scuttle about these streets draining the dead.

I was transfixed. And before I could recover my wits, this thing turned and looked straight at me. Its face—the air was full of smoke and there was maybe half a city block between us, but I could see that it had red eyes, or maybe just a single great eye. It stood up, still facing me; it must have been nine or ten feet tall. It took a step toward me. I held up my Bible, Neville, I was terrified but I had faith in Our Lord, I held up the Bible to this abomination and it stopped! It just stood there for a moment, watching me, and then—

And then it *laughed*.

It had the strangest laugh, Neville. It didn't sound anything like a real voice, it sounded like some kind of primitive machine from the last century.

And it began to move again, toward me.

I confess my faith failed me then. I turned and fled. I must have run for blocks, and when I finally stopped and looked behind me it was nowhere to be seen.

Perhaps it was a golem after all. Perhaps it was the Beast himself that I saw, feasting on fallen souls. I do not know. But it had the shape of a man and the aspect of the Enemy; and while I've seen the Devil's other soldiers wreak much greater destruction, there was something especially *intimate* about the evil this thing wrought in the streets of this accursed place. Don't ask me how I know, but I feel in my soul that this ghoul was the most wicked, the most evil of all the satanic forces I have seen here. I pray I never encounter its like again.

But enough darkness! There is so much comfort to be had even in the face of these abominations—for they prove, once and for all, that we were right and the atheist liberals were wrong. The Devil's minions are everywhere, just as the Scriptures foretold. It is truly a joyous time (perhaps not for the abortionists and the unbelievers— who's laughing *now,* Dr. Meyers? ha ha!). The coming of our Lord is at hand.

One of CELL's Christian soldiers has promised to scan this letter to you as soon as he is able. God bless CELL; they are truly doing the Lord's work. Perhaps once they

vanquish the Devil's Armies they can do something about
the homosexuals, ha ha!

Be well, and rejoice. The Lord is with us always.

Yours in Christ,
Franklin

What? You think this thing powers *itself*?

You think I can leap between rooftops, roll Bulldogs
single-handed, throw CELL drones around like kittens without
draining the batteries? Have you even read the damn *specs*?

Everything about this suit is a trade-off. You can crank the
armor so tight you're pretty much invincible, but only for a few
seconds and you cut your speed in half. You can disappear entirely, just fade right out of the visible spectrum, but the lensing
field sucks so much juice the capacitors run dry before you're
halfway down the block. And don't even *talk* to me about trying
to do any of those things at the same time.

They don't mention any of that in the ad copy, of course.
To hear the brochure tell it, you just put on the N2 and hit the
ground at sixty, invisible and invulnerable, world without end
a-fucking-men. But all those bells and whistles take *power*—and
the suit may be a hundred years ahead of its time, but the batteries? Let me tell you, sometimes it feels like this thing's running
on a couple of triple-A's.

They say it keeps you going under normal conditions for almost
a week without a recharge. I don't have to tell you conditions are
anything but *normal* out there. I tapped into the grid on those rare
occasions when I could find a grid to tap into. Even then, it was
even money whether I'd be able to suck up a decent charge before
the extra load blew the breakers over ten city blocks.

The suit's got a NOM option to metabolize carrion on the battlefield. Cellular ATP gives you almost sixty kilojoules per mole, and that's not even counting bomb-cal content of the raw meat. So, yeah. I used it once or twice, to keep myself going. I fed off the dead like a fucking tick, and I'm not proud of it.

Still, you can't deny it makes sense. The grid may go down, clouds may cut you off from your solar sats—but the one thing you'll never run out of down here is bodies.

Gould isn't gone. I'm starting to get the sense that Gould is never gone, not really. He's like one of those mutant unkillable STDs you pick up out in the Gene Zone: Just when you think you're finally free of it, your dick starts oozing again.

He pops back onto my comm channel as if the dustup at his apartment had never happened, bursting with good news he's skimmed from forbidden frequencies: some kind of field hospital set up at Trinity. He figures that was where CELL planned to "debrief" Prophet. The good news is that hardware designed to interface with all the suit's black boxes is pretty much a given.

"The bad news," he says, "is that we're going to have to storm the post."

He actually says *we*.

"I'm already halfway there," he tells me. "The Harley doesn't give a flying fuck about rocks in the road, I can thread this thing through a gutter pipe if I have to. I'll wait for you there, but you gotta haul ass."

I went to church religiously until I was fourteen. Never liked it much. Don't expect to like it much now but I make the trip, find a decent vantage point to scope out the territory: a midrise apartment complex that looks like it's been derelict since the Double Dip. The top floor gives me a perfect vantage point: Trinity's steeple reaches up from across Broadway, a great stone dildo with a thousand ribs and projections urging the Incredible Fifty-Foot Woman to let go. The main entrance is a two-story arch, deep in shadow; but I have no trouble making out the two CELL grunts slouching in the shade.

I zoom the view and pan the terrain. Gould guesses the entrance is going to be rotten with motion sensors and smart guns and he's right about that: I make three autosnipes in addition to the two hamburgers at the front before someone emerges from inside. The hamburgers jump instantly to attention. I prick up my ears, too: It's—

"Sweet smoking Jesus, that's Tara Strickland," Gould says. "Used to be a Navy SEAL, went over to CELL after her father died. Try not to get killed by her. Try not to kill her, either; she's big fish, she's the goddamn Rosetta Stone if we can get her to talk."

She's talking now, tearing a strip off the grunts for slouching in a war zone. Then she disappears back inside, leaving her minions standing a lot straighter.

"Now, *those* assholes?" Gould says. "You can kill 'em all you want."

So I do. Three shots total. Then I take out the smart guns. Two other hamburgers come charging out of the shadows and decide, too late, that discretion is sometimes the better part of valor. I take one of them out with a single shot; the other gets to cover behind a Ford pickup whose front bumper is festooned with the smiling face of Osama bin Laden and the words I'M STILL FREE: HOW ABOUT YOU? He knows he can't get back to sanctuary without taking a bullet; he knows, as my grenade arcs down on top of him, that he can't stay where he is. He bolts at the last second for an ad-infested bus stop shelter, manages one panicked yelp before the grenade goes off. He dies by the light of a flaming advertisement for Carmat Artificial Kidneys (ISN'T YOUR LIFE WORTH THE PRICE?).

I hit the stairwell and take the stairs ten at a time, make ground level in thirty seconds flat without hearing any rotors overhead, any boots below. I'm not quite sure I believe it; shouldn't there be an assault helicopter coming over the rooftops by now? Shouldn't someone be wondering why Asswipe Seven hasn't called in? I can't hear anything except this little voice in my head chuckling over the fact that we can't even stop killing each other when we're being invaded by space aliens.

It's funny, you know, because it's true.

I peek out, pan on zoom, again on thermal. I pull up my cloak and cross the street; I'm still half expecting a hail of heavenly lead but I don't run into so much as a stop sign. I reach the bodies I've laid out across the asphalt, rob them of firepower and ammo that did them no fucking good whatsoever. I take some comfort in the knowledge that I will put it all to better use. I decloak in the shadows, let the charge build back up, fade again. Push one of those massive doors open just a little—solid bronze, I think, they looked like they were a couple of hundred years old—and sneak into God's House like a shadow on its stomach.

And still nobody's drawn any kind of bead on me. There's nobody even here as far as I can tell. So I stand up and I look around, and—

And holy shit, Roger. It's *beautiful.* It's the most beautiful thing I've ever seen.

I don't know if I can even describe it. One second you're in the middle of a post-apocalyptic wasteland and the next you're on the floor of this great golden cavern, it's dimly lit but somehow you can see everything even without the augments. You'd swear the ceiling reaches halfway to the stars; it rests on massive arches topped by these glorious stained-glass windows and they aren't even broken, Roger, I swear not a single one of them is even *scratched*. The seats, the benches, what do they call those—yeah, the pews. Those have been ripped out. And sure enough a field hospital's been set up in their place but even that's gone now, nothing left but a few rows of stripped cots and a pile of empty crates with red crosses on them. The arches tower over everything like redwood trunks from the eighteen hundreds, you know, you see pictures online sometimes. And way off at the front behind the pulpit, about halfway up the wall are rows of life-sized statues in little alcoves, saints or martyrs or something. And towering over *that* there's this enormous mother of all stained-glass windows: wide as any church I've ever seen, and twice as high, a great arch that's *all one window* full of a hundred colors and a thousand facets. Must be five, six stories high and the colors are so rich they almost hurt my eyes, I almost forgot we *had* colors like that in the world. The light's almost—I don't know. Divine.

I feel like an ant in a kaleidoscope. I swear to God, Roger, that church was so much bigger on the inside, we could pack the whole city in there if we tried. And there's more than enough room, because I'm the only one there. No CELL grunts, no whitecoats running around with beeping boxes, no hard-ass ex-navy bitches waiting to feed me my balls on a platter. I pump up the acoustics, I zoom every shadow, and there's nothing but this insane, beautiful pocket universe I've stumbled into. I just want to stay there and let Armageddon go on without me.

No chance of that, of course. Because here comes Nathan Gould roaring up outside on his motorbike and he comes stomping into the place like a fucking barbarian. I don't think he even *notices* the windows. He looks around and sees nothing, kicks one of the cots. "Shit. We're too late."

But he gives it the once-over anyway, starts poking around the desks and the tables up front, and the spell's broken so I figure I might as well join him. After a few minutes he lets loose a whoop and holds up a sheaf of papers like it was the head of a vanquished enemy.

"They've relocated!" he says. "Moved across the way to Wall Street, looks like. Closer to the trunk line." He jerks his chin at that magnificent windowed wall. "Down in the basement, under the stairwell. There's an access tunnel, goes under the street. I can hack the security codes, but there's bound to be muscle. What we need—"

He looks around, and nods to himself.

"—is a diversion."

CELL Internal Security
Incident Report
Time/Date of Incident: 23/08/2023
Nature of Incident: Security Breach
Location: Field Interrogation Facility, Wall Street,
   Manhattan
CELL Personnel Present: C. Abao, S.-H. Chen, H. Kumala,
   D. Lockhart, M. Parpek, B. Rawles, T. Strickland,
   L. deWinter
Others Present: N. Gould, Unknown
Reporting Participant: deWinter

Account of Incident:

I was carrying out duties assigned by CO Lockhart (installing/ prepping NODAR interface for debriefing incoming rogue agent) along with Chen, Lieutenant Kumala, Parpek, and Dr. Rawles, when the incident occurred. We were operating in an active combat zone but we were guarded by at least 14 active CELL paramilitary both during initial deployment at Trinity and subsequent relocation. At approximately 1300 I overheard Kumala speaking to Special Adviser Strickland on encrypted channel. SA Strickland reported that the rogue operative had been sighted in the area and would be in custody soon. We therefore booted up NODAR and began ground-truthing sims. (We had to do this three times because of intermittent power failures during the first sequences, before Chen got a generator from the trailers.)

Shortly after this SA Strickland entered the facility via the underground entrance and had words with Lt. Kumala. She seemed to be angrier than usual (I think she was unhappy with the soldiers guarding the facility but I did not hear any details). SA Strickland stayed on-site for perhaps five minutes, during which time she approached me and asked if the equipment was ready. I told her that we would be ready shortly (we were still running the third ground-truthing sequence). This did not seem to be the answer SA Strickland was hoping for. At this point Lt. Kumala approached SA Strickland and reported that there appeared to be "a problem" with the guards stationed at Trinity. SA Strickland then assembled a small force (maybe 3 or 4 soldiers) and left through the Trinity tunnel. Before she left she told Lt. Kumala to reassign snipers to the roof because "Prophet won't be thinking as two-dimensionally as you lot."

Parpek and I completed the ground-truthing sequences during this time but then Dr. Rawles tripped over the power cord so we had to start again. While we were reinitializing the NODAR the ground began to shake and I heard what sounded like a muffled explosion in the distance. (I believe this was the ammo dump going up in the churchyard.) I noticed Lt. Kumala becoming agitated over at his command post. He then approached the technical team and said something like "He's here. He's right outside. Get that f_____g machine working already or I'll feed your nads to Hargreave myself." Lt. Kumala then took the rest of his forces and left via the main entrance.

At this point only Abao, Chen, Parpek, Dr. Rawles, and myself were in the room and none of us were armed. We could hear gunfire and shouting from outside. Dr. Rawles suggested that we might be safer if we moved up the tunnel into Trinity but Abao pointed out that the trouble seemed to have started at Trinity so we decided we would be better off where we were. Chen locked the tunnel door.

The gunfire and the shouting trailed off while we were talking. I heard someone crying, and a single shot, and then two sets of footsteps coming up the tunnel. I heard a voice on the other side of the door but I couldn't hear the words. Then the door unlocked from the other side and a male civilian weelding [*sic*] a gun entered from the tunnel (I learned later that this was Nathan Gould, an ex-employee of CryNet). Abao asked the civilian not to shoot and the civilian said he wanted to do a suit scan. Parpek was at the telemetry panel and I saw him mouth the word *cloak* but then there was a gunshot and Parpek was hit in the chest. At this point a second intruder became visible and I could see he was wearing a CryNet Systems Nanosuit either 2.0 or 2.2, it's hard to tell without checking the neuropticals. (I learned later that this was "Prophet," the rogue we were supposed to be debriefing.) He was also holding some kind of pistol, I think maybe an M12, and he had a machine gun strapped to his belt, too, although it was not deployed. Chen promised we would not make any trouble, but Dr. Rawles had been standing behind the door and he came at

"Prophet" from behind. (He had a dynaport multitool in his hand, so he may have been trying to short out the Nanosuit through the cervical interface.) "Prophet" pointed the gun in Dr. Rawles's face and Dr. Rawles backed away. Dr. Gould said something like "I asked you not to shoot the geeks" but "Prophet" had stopped shooting by this point anyway. I thought I saw a tic in the forearm musculature so it could have just been temporary spindle lock.

Gould then directed us at gunpoint to hook the rogue up to the NODAR, which we did. Chen handled biotelemetry and I ran the suit diagnostics. I was parsing the twitch protocols when Chen said "F__k, he's *dead.*"

Gould threatened Chen and told her not to make threats she couldn't back up, but Chen explained that the rogue was actually, literally *dead.* I accessed his vitals myself at that point and confirmed this. The right ventricle and left lung were gone and his right lung was relatively intact but nonfunctional due to pneumothorax. I could see that the right lung might be salvageable (the diaphragm had been perforated but the N2 had infiltrated the injuries with a synthomyosin mesh that was restoring some integrity), but the rest of the thoracic cluster was just gone. The N2 had bypassed the pulmonary system entirely and was infusing O_2 directly into the aortic arch. I also noticed that it had extruded synthomyosin around the shrapnel and it had coated all the torn internal surfaces with anafibrin, but none of these were stand-alone modifications. The N2 extended into its wearer at the molecular level and had taken over most of the vital processes, so Chen was medically right. The undamaged tissues left inside the suit did not meet the definition of a complete viable organism

as defined by National Health Industry Standards. "Prophet"
was legally dead.

I watched for some kind of reaction to that news, but he
kept his visor locked the whole time and I could not see his
face. I did not notice any obvious change in body language.
I think maybe he knew already.

How did I feel? How did I *feel*? How do you *think* I fucking felt?
Betrayed. That's how.

I knew it was bad, of course. I knew I was dead the moment
that gunship hit me on Battery Park. But then, Prophet, yo? My
hope and my salvation. This Lazarus suit, this second chance. I
didn't know if it was actually fixing me or just keeping me going
until the guys at Syracuse could put me back together but I always thought that if I made it out of the battle zone alive I'd
at least get a chance to step out in my own skin, you know? I
thought, somewhere down the road, I'd be human again.

But all the suicidal thoughts and the despair over my lost humanity, none of that really gets a chance to sink in at first—because
I'm still trying to parse the fact that the N2 just mutinied on
me, that it actually froze my goddamn finger on the trigger and
scolded me for killing "mission-critical collaborators." I've already taken out the lab rat who tried to hack me on remote but
there are still four other *potential enemy combatants* in the room,
as they say. And the suit—the fucking *suit*—is telling me I can't
eliminate those threats.

But then I hear what one of those techs has just told Gould—
I'm dead.

I'm *dead*.

—and suddenly, crazily, I actually *feel* dead. I could swear that
up until this very moment I've felt the air flowing in and out

of my chest; when those Ceph came through the wall, when I tangled with the mercs outside, I felt my pulse pound. It's not something you think about consciously but it's damn well the kind of thing you notice when it's gone, right? And I haven't noticed anything missing until right now, until the moment that tech with the V-gloves says, "No, he's *literally dead*," and just like that all those comforting biorhythms I thought had been keeping me company all this time, they just drain away. I reach for a pulse and find nothing. I try to catch my breath and I can't. And all I feel in that instant is this crazy gobsmacked astonishment that all those things have gone and left nothing behind and I *never even noticed*.

And the next thing I feel is a rising, murderous fury at Nathan fucking Gould.

Because Gould scanned me, just a couple of hours ago. Sure his rig didn't come with all the latest bells and whistles but it sure as shit should've been able to tell when someone's *dead*, you know? It sure as shit should be able to tell you when your goddamn *heart* is missing.

Gould, you fucker. You slimy, sorry sack of shit. You *knew*. You knew all along, and you let me do your dirty work, and you never even *told* me, Gould, you never even—

I swear I'm going to break his scrawny pencil neck but I'm locked down in the cradle. I can't do anything but listen to the lab rats talking over me like I'm fungus in a petri dish. Gould couldn't give two shits about my injuries, he just wants to know what the N2's holding in its deep-layer substrate. The technician tells him they're uploading it as fast as they can, and they're all pointedly ignoring the body twitching at the corner of my eye. And that twitching, it doesn't stop. It actually gets worse over time and its not just the body anymore it's the things around it, it's the very *air* and I'm trying to turn my head for a better look and no dice—I'm still wired into the harness—but that's okay because that weird shimmery twitchiness is spreading across my visual field like water spilled across the floor, like the ground racing up at you when your stabilizers are down and you're coming in too fast—

I think it short-circuits me, somehow. The cradle. Knocks me right out of the here-and-now and right into some, some—I don't know. Some schizophrenic's nightmare. I can hardly see anything, just shapes and silhouettes stuck in shades of blue and black like I'm in some kind of subterranean grotto. Giant machines everywhere. At least I think they're machines, judging by their outlines. And there are things all over them, crawling down the walls, slithering along the floor. Coming for me. The monsters are coming and I'm stuck in molasses, I've got a gun but I barely even have the strength to bring it up much less defend myself.

Pretty classic nightmare scenario, right? Looking back now I figure maybe some kind of voltage spike when the cradle linked in, maybe it kick-started that part of the brain that lights up when you're scared shitless. Limbic system, I think they call it. The amygdala. But I'm not thinking about any of that in the moment, I'm just terrified, and then—you're not gonna believe it, but suddenly, just like that, I'm *happy*. You know why?

Because I can feel my heart beating again. I can hear my breath, harsh and ragged and *fast* because I'm scared, man, I'm still so scared but there's also this huge sense of relief, of *joy* almost. I'm real again, I'm alive. I *feel* alive. As if this is the world and I've just awakened from the nightmare.

And then this nasty little voice in the back of my head says, *No, soldier, that's not your pulse. That's not your breath. These aren't even your eyes, you corpse, you meat sack, you miserable rotting zombie. They're Prophet's. Everything's Prophet's.*

You stole it all.

And then some other voice says *It's spiking* and someone else says *lookit those fucking delta waves* and now the nightmare's leaking back into the dream, the monsters are fading and real people are yelling in the distance, spoiling everything. The world turns back to shit and I can feel my breath disappearing, my arms and legs turning to dead meat, and all I can think of as I fall back to earth is Prophet, poor ol' Prophet, and the last thing he said before he blew his brains out: *Remember me.*

Remember you?

It's not like I have a fucking choice.

And here I am again, dead, paralyzed, surrounded by lab rats and liars arguing over how best to carve me up for the data in my guts.

Except things seem to be going a lot worse for them than last time I checked in.

The light's gone longwave. Sparks pop like fireworks. Half the boxes hooked into my cradle are smoking; the other half are alive with machine code. I can see the script scrolling up across techie faces, I can zoom in and see warning icons reflected in their eyes. And those eye are wide, lemme tell you. Those eyes are scared shitless.

Someone shouts "Overload!" and a very calm machine voice answers *Uncalibrated nano-routines detected. Alien tissue vector. Thirty-three percent.*

"It's online," bleats the rat who pronounced me dead. "It's *transmitting . . .*"

Gould: "Shut it down!"

"I'm *trying . . .*"

In the distance, the sound of rotors beating the air. The sound of boots moving with *authority.* Suddenly someone else is in the room, scaring back the lab rats, grabbing Gould by the scruff of the neck and smashing his face into the wall. Gould goes down like a priest on a choirboy; the intruder turns to me and smiles.

Lockhart.

Suddenly things are very quiet. The rotors outside have spun down. The local hardware has stopped sizzling; one of the techs must have succeeded in shutting it off before Lockhart scared them all into the corner. None of the usual trash talk from the mercs who've flooded the room in their master's wake. The room pulses with dim red emergency lighting, but the alarms have fallen silent.

But there's Lockhart, with a gun in his hand. Smiling through the glass.

Fuckfuckfuckfuckfuck.

I try to move; no dice. I'm Christ on the cross in this thing. I can't even access my tacticals.

Lockhart moseys past the observation port, steps into my cage. His sleeves are rolled halfway up the biceps. The camo pattern on his CELL fatigues is a mesh of hexagons, blue-gray, green-gray, brown-gray. Honeycomb, like Prophet's tattoo. You notice these things at the weirdest times.

"Nice," he says.

Just a light pistol, the M12 Nova. You never really appreciate how big it is until you have one jammed in your face.

I'm going to die, I think, and then, *No.* Gould's going to die, maybe. Maybe even the lab techs, if Lockhart's a stickler for loose ends. But not me.

I'm already dead. I'm already dead. I've been dead all day.

Lockhart leans in close. "Got men all over the downtown looking for your ass, tin man. And here you are, trussed and tied."

"Which takes his threat potential down to zero, I'm thinking. Which means that pulling that trigger makes you a murderer. Not to mention a war criminal."

Tara Strickland, in the flesh and the nick of time. She gestures at the floor: a couple of CELLulites haul Nathan Gould to his feet.

I can't help noticing that Lockhart's gun is still in my face. Tara Strickland, no slouch herself, notices, too. "Commander Lockhart. *You will stand down.*"

He doesn't want to. He hates this uppity bitch who thinks she can order him around, he hates the fucking Rules of Engagement, he hates me most of all.

But he stands down.

Strickland's already moved on to other things. "Nathan Gould. Always a pleasure."

"Jesus, Tara." Gould shakes his head and sighs. "Working with these assholes? If your father could see you now."

"My father's dead, Nathan," she says mildly, and graces him with a gentle smile: "Now why don't you shut the fuck up before I change my mind and send you after him?" She nods at one of the goons holding him up. "If he gives you trouble, don't do too much damage. We'll need to interrogate him later." Back to Lockhart: "Power him down."

She tosses him a matte-black gizmo the size of a sixty-round casket box. The moment he slaps it against my helmet, I see double: two fuzzy overlapping Lockharts snarling at my side, two Stricklands leading two Goulds out through two sets of security doors. The world slides in and out of focus. A swarm of bees buzzes in my right ear.

"Get up."

The cradle releases me. I stand, or try to; I almost go over with the first step. I force my eyes to focus, and after a moment my worlds converge. Everything's still—muted, though. Almost colorless. I feel as weak as a Democrat.

"Don't *fuck* with me, Prophet. *Move.*"

CryNet built this thing, after all. Only makes sense they'd have some kind of off-switch.

We are the Odd Couple, Gould and I. We move side by side up the hallway, guns in our faces, guns at our backs: one of us built like Atlas, one like Charlie Brown; one of us probably good as dead, one dead already.

Only one of us is silent. Gould mutters as we move forward—I catch snatches of Tara, her father, lousy career choices, but after one abortive attempt to strike up a dialogue with Strickland—

"You think you're so smart, Tara? You realize this isn't even Prophet, it's just some *grun*—"

"*Jesus*, Nathan, give it a fucking rest."

—he stops talking to anyone but himself.

I'm still unsteady on my feet. The floor seems to shift under me with every step, and it's only when Strickland hisses "Seismic tremor!" that I realize this is bigger than me. We move into a broad lobby just in time to see a ceiling full of decorative masonry shake loose eight meters overhead.

That speeds things up.

Suddenly the goons are bursting with really useful information like *The fucking ceiling!* and *It's coming down!* and Strickland's ordering everyone out *now* as if we needed the encouragement. One of the decorative coliseum-style pillars flanking the door *craaacks* down the middle like a split log and I'm outside again, Lockhart still holding the suit-sapper against my skull, a squad of mercs lighting me up with little red dots, the whole pack of us moving in a clump toward an Apache spinning up across the street. Gould's disappeared—no, there he is, they've bundled him into a double-parked Humvee down the street. Bye-bye Gould. Sorry it didn't work out. Glad you found some balls there at the end.

You asshole.

The whole street's vibrating. They bundle me into the chopper. Lockhart hands the suit-sapper to the nearest merc, yells "Get him to Prism!" and exits stage left. The chopper climbs into the air.

And the very fucking ground reaches out after it to smash us back to earth.

I don't know what I'm seeing in those moments. Suddenly the building we've just left is shedding windowpanes like fish scales. Earthquake, I think, but in the next second something explodes out of it, just punches through all that steel and concrete like it was cardboard and keeps coming and it's after us, I could swear it's reaching right for the chopper and no matter how high we go it just keeps coming. And then it's *past* us, I can see the sides of the fucking thing sliding by like one of those antique moon rockets from the museums, you know, the Saturn V's. Except it's not all shiny and white and tricked out with stars-and-stripes. It's *black,* it's black as fucking coal and it's *bony,* I don't know how else to describe it, it's like ammo belts and the tire treads off a strip-mine harvester all twisted into a tight spiral. Something glows deep inside, shining through the cracks and seams like lava. And it's *still* spearing up out of that building, out of the ground, it's streaking up so fast you'd swear it wasn't moving at all, that *we* were falling down past *it.* Something bitch-slaps us hard to port and it's no fucking illusion anymore: We're falling. The engine's deader than I am, the blades are still beating the air but it's all just wishes and inertia now. Pilot's doing his best. He's in full autorotation mode and it must be doing some good because the ground comes spinning up and the tail rotor snaps like a twig and the cabin spins and bounces along the ground—but when I'm thrown clear I'm still in one piece, man. I'm shaken and stirred but I'm still breathing—

I mean—

You know what I mean.

So I'm flat on my back looking up at this spire, this giant twisted tower of backbones and machinery that's just rammed its way out of the earth and I do not know what to make of this at all. These are supposed to be *space* aliens, right? Not Mole Men. Because seriously, you want me to believe that aliens from out past Mars have been planting these goddamn things under Manhattan and *nobody ever noticed . . . ?*

And that's when I hear it.

It sounds like the spear's revving up: that special creepy hiss that only Cephtech seems to make. There's a kind of grillwork assembly around the base, these flaps or fins or something that fold up and you can see something behind, starting to glow like the coils of a space heater, but that's not where the sound is coming from. It's coming from higher up. I try to get back on my feet but the haptics are fratzing out, must be an aftereffect of the suit-sapper; I can stand but when I try to put one foot ahead of the other it's all staggers and error icons. Mercs are pouring from the skewered building and I'm looking around for a bazooka or semiautomatic or a goddamn rock to throw, if and when my joints reboot; but CELL isn't paying much attention to me anyway. They're all looking up at that big ugly earth-raping spear, they're looking up trying to get a fix on that sound, and suddenly I realize it isn't coming from the spear at all. It's coming from *way* higher up, from this little flock of beetles dropping down from the sky. They're dropping *fast:* It's only about two seconds before they're big enough to not be beetles anymore. Now they're big fucking dragonflies with glowing crescent scythes for wings. They're flying wedges of metal shot through with pipes and armatures and big honking cement mixers. And those cement mixers might have been slop-full of digested human remains in the ship that came down this morning but I'm betting that's not all the Ceph use them for. I'd bet Lockhart's miserable life that these are dropships.

They are. They're still ten meters off the ground when they drop those pods like giant eggs, and the things that come out of them are a lot nastier than any newborn hatchling has any right to be. The bogeymen I've seen before, but some of these fuckers are *huge:* three times the size of a man, like—like tanks on legs. Their arms don't *hold* guns and don't *end* in guns: their arms *are* guns, big fucking cannons bolted to the torso, bores the size of manholes. The ground shivers with every step they take.

I gotta hand it to CELL. They stand their ground, they fight back. I don't know if I'd call it courage. Maybe. But by the time my joints unlock I'm in the middle of another massacre and the only decision I've got to make is whether to die with my fellow backbones or just fade to black and hope the Ceph forget about me while they kick the shit out of black ops over there.

And then the spear starts hooting. Something *snaps,* way overhead. I look up and the tip of the spire has opened like the petals of a big black flower; and the thing those petals have folded back to expose is full of vents.

I take half a second to scoop up a carbine from a mall cop who won't be needing it anymore. Then I run like hell.

Before I've even turned tail I can see the smoke belching out overhead, black stuff, darker than oil and coarser, somehow. It reaches for me. That's not a metaphor. This shit doesn't disperse, it *hunts.* I can see cords of it, big ropy tentacles of smoke thick as telephone poles, reaching around in huge sweeping arcs and circles. It looks a lot like what they always said battlefield nanotech would look like, if we could ever get it to work.

These aliens, they've got it working just fine. The suit's finally back up to full strength and I'm driving it as fast as I can, don't even dare look back, but I can feel the sky going dark behind me. I can see my shadow fading against the pavement and just like *that* it's got me, it's like being caught in a goddamn tornado. It lifts me right off my feet; it slams me onto the pavement. I can see little black particles sleeting across my faceplate. It's like being sandblasted with pepper. I try to get back up but my joints are seizing again, tactical's sprouting error icons like hyperherpes and just *dies*. BUD disappears; the world follows a moment later. I'm blind, my motor systems are spazzing out, and the last thing I hear is False Prophet telling me there's been a systems breach, that the N2 is *infested*—that's the word he uses, *infested*—and that we're initiating a total core-systems downboot to protect life support.

He's still calculating the odds of pulling that off when I black out.

EYES ONLY

This media will autowipe if moved more than 2m from
an authorized courier

Case Study on the Integration of SECOND (CryNet Systems Nanosuit 2.0) with
the Human Central Nervous System: Insights from Interrogative Interactions

Executive Summary

Lindsey Aiyeola (PhD),[1] Komala Smith (PhD, MD),
and Leona Lutterodt (DPhil)
Directorate of Science and Technology
Central Intelligence Agency

Context:

The manner and degree to which CryNet Systems Semi-autonomous Enhanced Combat Ops: Neurointegration and Delivery (SECOND™) biochip integrates with the wearer of the CN Combat Solutions Nanosuit 2.0™ is a matter of intense interest from scientific, military, and national-security perspectives. The Hargreave-Rasch Corporation, staunchly asserting the proprietary nature of this and related technology, has been reluctant to cooperate in our investigations to date.[2] However, it has become increasingly apparent that while HRC could no doubt provide valuable insights into the design and manufacture of the Nanosuit, they might have much less to offer our investigation than was originally thought. Put simply, we believe that both the degree and the nature of the observed human/artifact integra-

---

[1] To whom correspondence should be directed.
[2] While the committee could classify the Nanosuit and its associated technologies as an asset vital to national security—opening the door to outright expropriation—we have been advised to proceed cautiously on this front. HRC will have certainly anticipated such a move and is likely to have put countermeasures in place. It would be unproductive to put these to the test under current circumstances.

tion was as unexpected to HRC as it was to us; and while we did not design this technology, we are currently in possession of it. Hargreave-Rasch knows only what the Nanosuit was designed to be; we are in possession of what it has *become,* and HRC is unlikely to launch any legal proceedings so long as they need our cooperation in managing the PR aftermath of the recent fiasco at their Prism facility. We would therefore advise against making any unnecessary concessions in exchange for technical data we can probably derive ourselves using the materials at hand, and which may prove to be largely irrelevant in any event.

Methodology and Results:

The Nanosuit 2 (hence, *N2*), following a long-term but ultimately unsuccessful symbiosis with Commander Laurence Barnes, is now integrated with Patient A^3 of the USMC. P*A* alleges that he suffered terminal injuries during the Manhattan Incursion, dying on the battlefield, and was subsequently installed in the N2 on the initiative of Cmdr. Barnes (who then took his own life). This story remains unverified, and is inconsistent with independent observations;[4] we are currently seeking corroboration from other sources, but advise that at least some of P*A*'s allegations cannot be considered reliable at this time.

P*A* was successfully extracted from Manhattan in the wake of the Incursion and taken to a secure location for protective debriefing. During this time we were able to establish an interface

---

[3]See DHS Bio-23A-USMC/4497C-4014 for biographical and medical background on this individual.

[4]For example, *A* reports an extended period of intermittent consciousness—we estimate no less than two hours—between the time he was injured and the time of his integration with the N2. NODAR analysis undertaken later the same day, however, shows conclusively that *A*'s heart had been effectively destroyed, presumably as a result of enemy fire on the battlefield. It is medically impossible for him to have survived for more than a few minutes, even on a tissue-metabolic level, in that condition.

with the N2 via its optical interface, using an infrared laser link. P*A* detected the handshaking protocols but misinterpreted them as a failed shutdown command; we were therefore able to monitor the internal states of both he and the N2 during interrogation, without P*A* ever being aware of this fact. The N2's biotelemetry capabilities proved far beyond what we had expected, providing fine-grained cortical synaptic maps at a resolution of 1–2 voxels (comparable to that of fixed-location scanners that occupy entire rooms; the integration of such technology into battlefield prostheses is at least 20 years ahead of our current state-of-the-art).

A relatively inexperienced and low-ranking individual was selected to interview P*A*, and was provided the minimum necessary information prior to debriefing. This was intended to increase P*A*'s confidence during interrogation, and to encourage him to talk at length about his experiences.[5] By asking wide-ranging questions beyond the pale of a conventional debrief—and by encouraging digressions and lengthy responses—we were able to isolate the functional clusters involved in various cognitive processes, and compare them with baseline norms. We were also able to influence the direction of the exchange by periodically exposing P*A* to subliminal images projected onto the facing wall (duration <20msec to allow for the subject's increased visual acuity), which were designed to provoke a range of emotional responses.

Some of our more significant findings are as follows:

1. P*A* did not "speak" in the conventional sense throughout the entire interview. On its face this might seem obvious—since his vocal cords had been extensively damaged, P*A* was forced to rely on the N2's onboard

---

[5]The alternative use of a more experienced interrogator who would merely *pose* as a low-status, nonthreatening individual was rejected since *A*'s enhanced perceptions might have been able to detect the subtle behavioral and physiological cues that inevitably accompany any staged performance.

speech synthesizer throughout—but it goes much farther than this. P*A* generally spoke without invoking the saccadal text interface that should have been necessary for such communication. Furthermore, his speech centers (notably Broca's and Wernicke's areas) were often relatively inactive during conversation. We did, however, note increased activity in the nanoneural mesh that connected P*A*'s nervous system to SECOND at these times.

2. P*A*'s ability to recollect the details of specific events borders on savantism. During our interviews he often recited overheard conversations verbatim, in their entirety. We have managed to acquire independent records of two of these conversations (from streamed security surveillance of Central Station); P*A*'s recollection of these exchanges proved accurate, and we have no reason to doubt his account of the others. There is, however, no record of eidetic memory in his USMC personnel file.

3. When discussing events that took place prior to his integration with the N2 (childhood memories, or reminiscence about previous tours of duty), P*A*'s hippocampus and prefrontal cortex lit up in a manner consistent with the activation of long-term memories. However, when discussing events that occurred during the Manhattan Incursion, activity in these areas declined, and throughput between SECOND and its associative coelomic meshes increased significantly.

4. When P*A* considered theoretical or tactical problems (such as the most efficient route through complex topography or the assessment of local cover), activity in the prefrontal cortex increased only marginally. How-

ever, when considering problems with a significant moral or ethical component (*e.g.,* lethal containment of infected civilians), P*A*'s anterior cingulate gyrus lit up as it would in any normal human. (SECOND's input channels also became more active at these times, although outgoing signals did not increase; this is consistent with the "passive monitoring" profile of heuristic biochips when in learning mode.)

5. P*A*'s speech patterns tended to vary with the type of experience he was describing at any given time. He spoke of interactions with his fellow marines and "conventional" battlefield events (whether against the Ceph or human paramilitary) using the familiar argot of the typical foot soldier, and while P*A* did evince an interest in science not often found in his demographic, he showed no great expertise beyond what one might acquire from a healthy dose of nature documentaries. However, when describing radically *atypical* experiences—his journeys through landscapes heavily modified by Ceph technology, for example, or the visions he attributed to the N2's previous host—his vocabulary improved and his sentence construction formalized somewhat. In other words, P*A* proved to be most articulate under circumstances where someone of his educational background would normally be most *lost* for words; this coincided with increased activity levels throughout the SECOND-Neurosomatic Complex (see #6, below). This is reminiscent of the serial manifestation of "alters" reported in cases of multiple personality disorder, albeit far less extreme; it was merely P*A*'s linguistic skills that changed, not his fundamental personality.

6. Distribution of processing workload changed over time across the SECOND-Neurosomatic Complex (SNC). On some occasions activity would be centered in P*A*'s brain, on others in SECOND and its associated meshes, on still others distributed relatively evenly across the entire metasystem. There exists a weak but significant correlation between these distributions and the subject's vocabulary and speech patterns. P*A* was most articulate when processing activity was evenly distributed throughout the SNC, or when concentrated in the architecture of the N2. He was least articulate (and most given to the casual use of slang and profanity) when his own brain was the primary locus of activity. While these properties fluctuated from moment to moment, P*A*'s overall mean eloquence and articulations scores increased by 7% and 9% (respectively) over the course of the interrogation. This suggests an ongoing off-load of cognitive processes from organic to artificial system elements.

7. At a more fine-grained scale, on several occasions as many as two (possibly three) loci of high cognitive activity were simultaneously present across the SECOND-mesh elements of the system (in addition to the locus more consistently discernible within P*A*'s brain itself). The signatures of these loci were similar to those of standard functional clusters, but were of far greater magnitude. The significance of these "islands of cognition" remains unclear: They could be artifacts of a background autoarchiving subroutine, or an emergent property of SECOND's parallel-processing architecture. We are continuing to explore these possibilities.

Preliminary Conclusions:

A significant proportion of P*A*'s cognition is being "outsourced" to the SECOND biochip and the associated networks proliferating throughout the N2. While this level of integration is certainly unprecedented in magnitude, we all do something similar every time we let our iBalls plan our daily schedules, or use the Cloud to store our vital information. The difference is that we maintain volitional control over our activities, using our "virtual exocrania" as essentially glorified secretaries. In the case of Patient *A* it is difficult to establish where the centers of volition even *are* from one moment to the next, or even if they still reside exclusively within his biological brain. It is almost as though P*A*'s consciousness has become detached from its own substrate; during the course of this interrogation all three investigators had the experience of hunting down a cognitive locus, only to find nothing but baseline activity when the relevant clusters came into focus—as if the system had rerouted itself in response to our investigations, abandoning each set of coordinates a moment before we got there.

There is no known mechanism to explain how any mind could perform such a feat; it is more likely that Subject *A*'s mental processes have simply become less constrained by virtue of the greater computational volume available to them. (Put crudely, they simply have more room to move around.) What does seem certain, however, is that much of what we regard as the "person" that is Subject *A* now resides outside his own head. We are no longer justified in regarding the Nanosuit and its wearer as separate entities.

Not really sure what's real here, and what's the spawn of my fevered, fetid, infested imagination. I see Ling Shan, although I've never been. I see constellations in an alien junkyard, spinning slowly on the surface of an invisible globe. A voice threads through it all, a voice that talks as though we're old friends although I can't quite make out the words. I've never heard it before.

SYSTEM START flickers at the corner of my eye.

CN COMBAT SOLUTIONS.

SYNAPSE CHECKSUM . . .

The boot crawl scrolls over my visions, eats them away like acid. By the time it's gone through its song and dance there's nothing left to see but two words: PHAGE ISOLATED.

I can make out what the voice is saying, now. It's telling me to wake up. It sounds worried.

It calls me *son*.

I open my eyes and look up at the dome of smoke covering Manhattan. There's something up there that doesn't belong somehow, bright threads of blue and yellow lacerating the overcast like veins of quartz. It takes me a moment to remember what it is.

Oh, right. Sunlight. Sky. It jerks for a moment, as if someone just fucked with the vertical hold in my eyes.

"Come back, son. Focus."

Tactical returns, slow and halting. Icons flicker on and off and on again, as if not quite sure they're in the right place. The sky jerks again, but this time I realize it's not just my eyesight: Something's—tugging at me. I lift my head.

Those fucking ticks. Those bloodsuckers. One of them has its hooks into the N2. It's pretty much all the wake-up call I need: I *hate* those things. I kick the little fucker and am back on my feet in a second, reaching for a gun that isn't there, looking up and down a street that seems to be hosting a goddamn tick *parade*. Some of them carry nothing but the swollen bladders on their own backs. One or two are actually dragging body parts, like ants taking crumbs to the nest.

My own personal chaperone is back, trying to take me down by the ankle. My gun lies a dozen meters away: Golem Boy don't need no goddamn carbine to stomp it like a big ugly zit. None of the others seem to notice. They don't seem interested in anything that moves under its own steam.

"I'm getting a limited feed from your suit, but for now it'll have to do." A little window opens up in my visual field and there he is, standard old white dude, maybe midsixties, looks like he was cut-and-pasted out of some black-and-white video from a hundred years ago. "I don't believe we've been introduced. Jack Hargreave, at your service. Nathan Gould might have mentioned my name, although I don't imagine he had much good to say about me."

Actually, old man, Nathan says you want me dead.

On the other hand, Tara Strickland says you want me alive. It's *Lockhart* who wants me dead, and I know for a fact that Lockhart has an absolute fucking *hate-on* for Jack Hargreave.

"I have to ask you to take Nathan's opinions with a grain of salt. He's a fine man, I think the world of him personally, wouldn't have kept him on so long if I didn't. But he's also something of a fuckup, pardon my French. All those psychotropics he dropped out on the left coast—they've dulled his edge a bit. Not quite the clear thinker he once—well, we could spend hours on the long and sordid relationship between Nathan Gould and Jack Hargreave, but right now there are far more pressing concerns.

"You are standing not far from the diseased bureaucratic heart of this city. And while you'd think that airlifting all the politicians out of the place should have had a cleansing effect, sadly, what's replaced them isn't a lot better. Go on, see for yourself. Follow the parade."

He does not pat me on the head or offer me a Milk-Bone. Probably only because the N2 doesn't come with those options.

"By the way," Hargreave adds after a couple of seconds have passed and I still haven't saluted. "I'm given to understand someone may have told you you're dead. I would urge you not to put too much faith in definitions designed primarily to allow the health insurance industry to cut benefits at the first appearance of a hangnail. Life and death are far more malleable than most people imagine, as you are finding out for yourself; and while, yes, you may technically fall into the latter category at the moment, I have access to certain—remedies—denied most policy-holders. Don't you worry, son. I'll be right there with you, and if you do this for me—for the *planet*—we'll get you patched right up. After all, it's my technology that's already made you such an active corpse."

He has a point. This, this high-tech infestation wrapped around me—it's Hargreave's property. He built the damn thing, or pirated it at least. He designed the people-friendly interface that papers over all those scary alien guts that I hope to Christ someone understands. And he'll *be right here with me.* Of course you will, Jack. You are my Lord and my Shepherd, and you've probably been walking with me since the moment I died. A comm link without an off-switch is the least of your divine powers: I bet you've built overrides and remotes into every fucking circuit in this thing.

Still, that whole not-being-dead thing. That would be really nice.

Hargreave wants me to follow the parade? I follow the parade.

I'm in a shallow depression of cracked asphalt, a street collapsed into some hollow space below, ankle-deep in wastewater from half a dozen broken mains. Hargreave leads me from the valley of the shadow. He leads me through half-assed barricades, past schools of dead yellow cabs and burning police cars. Something bleats from the rooftops; I look up in time to see a blur of pink flannel before the baby bursts like a grapefruit against the pavement. Its mother hits a second later without a sound.

Infected. Infected.

"Stay the course, son," Hargreave says sadly. "There's nothing you can do for them."

A woman cries out from a shattered window twelve stories above Liberty Street; a man and his daughter call for help from a balcony over Fulton. Sometimes I see them before they see me; I cloak, and creep past without ever raising their hopes.

He tries to distract me with tales of our mutual acquaintance. "Don't get me wrong about Nathan; his heart is definitely in the right place, he's the same humanitarian he ever was. He's just—lost that edge that once made him so brilliant. That ability to make intuitive leaps, *counterintuitive* leaps, that distinguish the great minds from the merely competent. Case in point: He finds the black box in that second skin of yours and he just assumes it's some kind of blueprint: the genspecs to fight the spore."

Three stories' worth of old iron fire escapes lie smashed on the sidewalk; someone's hung a bedsheet from the railing of the fourth, painted a slapdash NEED FOOD & WATER for any Meals On Wheels truck that might be cruising past.

"Ten years ago Nathan would have seen the truth instantly.

The suit doesn't contain the specs for a weapon. The suit *is* the weapon. It just needs to be activated."

He takes me through an abandoned field hospital: Quonset huts lined up in an underground parkade, all cots empty, body bags stacked in neat virgin piles. Down in some subterranean food court I pass through an improvised checkpoint blocked out in chain link and razor wire: rows of tables, suitcases and backpacks with their contents turned out and spread under racks of purple UV. Ticks clatter past, draining the dead while Hargreave natters like a Discovery Channel voice-over: "Think of the Argentine Cattle Crisis two years ago, or the British BSE outbreak in the last century. The issue was not slaughtering the animals, the problem was *disposal*. What do you do with millions of rotting corpses? Here you see the Ceph's answer. They wipe us out, they break us down, they reduce the environmental impact almost to zero. Exemplary, really."

The ticks have spilled onto Dutch Avenue. I'm starting to see that this isn't a parade after all. It's a *drainage basin*, full of little tick streams that join up to form mighty tick rivers that converge on—

I turn the corner at Spruce.

I have no idea what happened here. I think this used to be City Hall—three stories of arched windows, topped by a domed tower almost as high again—and I think the space in front of it used to be a park. But some giant has jammed a spade into the crust of the planet and just *twisted*. There's a rift in front of me, a *canyon* where the ground has opened up. The road runs off its edge and ends in tatters like a hacked-off limb. An eighteen-wheeler leans over the break, cab dangling in midair; it looks almost curious, craning its neck to see down into the pit. Broken sewer pipes jut from the cliff face. There used to be a subway line down there, too; it's been chopped in half like a worm by a shovel, the track line pulled into daylight and torn apart, subway cars scattered around the gap like cheap-ass Chinese toys. There are outfalls everywhere, and fires, and down through the mist and the smoke I see the vague shapes of uprooted trees and fractured asphalt.

There's something else down there, too, something deeper than the merely human wreckage. I can only catch glimpses through the pieces of rock and road blocking the way, but that segmented bony aesthetic is almost familiar by now. Way down deep, built into bedrock under one of the most densely populated cities in the world: an architecture that couldn't have been put together by anything we'd think of as *hands*.

Way off on the far side of City Hall I see a silhouette in the smoke; it looms maybe twice as high as the dome that foregrounds it. Another Ceph spire, and I'm praying to fucking Allah it's already shot its load.

This is Tick Mecca. This is the point of their pilgrimage, this is where they bring the liquefied dead of Manhattan: a clacking, clicking river flowing down into the center of the earth.

"You have to go down there, son," Hargreave says solemnly

I'm not your fucking son, Jack.

But I go down anyway.

What happens if I just say *no*? Good question.

I was keeping an eye out, you know. Ever since the suit mutinied at Trinity. That was a kick in the throat, man—kinda paled next to being dead, but it added insult to injury. Like I'd been on a leash all that time and just hadn't known it, because SECOND'd never yanked me to heel before.

It never tried to pull that shit again. Of course, I never tried to cross it again. It fed me objectives and I pretty much went along with them. And most of the time, why wouldn't I? BUD points out the most likely local spots for cached ammo and I'm *not* going to weapon up? Hargreave offers my life back if I follow the parade and I'm going to go in the opposite direction? Why? Just to prove I can?

Still, what if I *tried*?

Of course, those were early days, before the N2 really got to know me. We have a much better relationship now. Now it would never lock me down against my will. It just makes sure I'm always willing.

You do know how this thing works, right? They've told you that much, at least?

We're not talking about a meatport here, I'm not one of those new cybersoldiers with the spinal jacks. We're talking about carbon nanotubes and room-temp superconductors. Synthetic myelin. Tendrils finer than human hairs burrowing into me, sniffing their way up and down my backbone, twisting up through that hole where the spine enters the skull.

You don't wear the N2, you *mate* with it. You *fuse*. And it feels pretty good at first, let me tell you. It feels great—and after a while you start wondering *why* it feels so great. A neuron's a neuron, right? When you get right down to it, what's the difference between sending signals to my visual cortex and sending signals to any other part of my brain? BUD shows me unreal images; who's to say SECOND doesn't give me unreal thoughts, unreal feelings? A bit of icy calm to help you figure the angles before a big dustup? A bit of extra hate to help you mow the motherfuckers down in the crunch?

Dude. Spare me your pitying looks. You think you're any better off than me? Did *you* get any say in how your brain was wired up? You think all that sticky circuitry you call *thought* just makes itself? Every effect has a cause, man: You can believe in physics or you can believe in free will, but you can't have it both ways. The only difference between you and me is, I'm part of something bigger now. We've got a *purpose*, Roger, bigger than yours, bigger than your bosses', so much bigger than you. So you might want to start asking yourself if the people behind those cameras are the sort of folks to whom you really want to pledge your allegiance.

Because there are other sides to be on, you know. And maybe it's not too late to get on the right one.

You have to go down there, son.

Turns out I'm not the first guy he told that to.

There were these tremors, apparently. A dozen seismographs grumbling about something under City Hall, even before the ground opened up. So just a couple of days ago, Jack Hargreave sent a squad down into the subway. Their signals garbled. Their signals stopped. They haven't come back.

Hargreave sends me down the same tunnel: a long dirty intestine lined with train tracks, torqued and twisted and torn open enough to let in occasional shafts of dirty gray light from overhead. I share the passageway with occasional ticks, but they're headed the other way and they don't bother me; their bladders are already filled to bursting. I imagine stomping on them and watching them go *splat*. Once or twice I indulge the fantasy.

Fifty meters in, the tunnel opens into a subway station. The walls are cracked and oozing, the overhead pipes burst. Puddles on the floor. Most of the lights have been smashed; a few hang from the wires at one end, sparking and flickering. There's graffiti all over the walls, FUCK YOU and EAT THE RICH and THANK YOU LORD. Trash bins kicked over. Shotgun blasts and little high-caliber divots scattered like terminal acne over every surface.

Actually, it probably doesn't look much different than it did *before* the invasion.

There's a blood trail smeared across the tiles, around the corner, into a crumbling backstage service area. I find three bodies at the end of it: CELL, but not the usual mall-cop colors. Better armor, for one thing. Different insignia. More—understated.

"My men," Hargreave murmurs. "I'd hoped . . ."

He sounds almost choked up. Almost *sincere*.

I give him a moment, scavenge the remains: frag grenades, laser scope, ammo clips. A scarab with a cracked handguard. One of those nice big L-TAG smart grenade launchers that grunts like me never seem to get their hands on.

"Casualties of war, I suppose. We all make sacrifices." Hargreave has come to terms with his grief. I never knew the traditional *minute of silence* could be so therapeutic. "I don't see Reeves here, though. Don't see the scanning gear, either. See if you can find it; it might give us a little advance warning on what we're heading into."

I find him through a rusted fire exit, halfway down another tunnel where the loading platform is high and dry and the tracks themselves are knee-deep in the water table. Derelict train cars, knocked off their rails, sit in the water like gondolas in the world's most butt-ugly Tunnel of Love.

Mitchell Reeves lies dead on the loading platform with two of his homeys, twitching under the ministrations of a pair of ticks. I waste some ammo on a bit of cheap visceral satisfaction, pry Reeves's field laptop from his cold dead fingers. The tech's proprietary from boards to buttons, but the I/O's standard WiFi.

Hargreave delivers the eulogy as SECOND builds the connection. "Best I had, aside from Tara Strickland. What a waste."

Reeves stares through me while his machine shakes hands. At least he still has eyes.

At least the spore left him with that much.

I'm heading for something Hargreave calls "the Hive." Doesn't that sound like fun. According to Reeves's laptop it's almost dead north. This subway tunnel curves northeast.

Close enough.

The tunnels arched and ancient and lined with patterned tiles that wouldn't look half bad if someone stripped off about a hundred years of grease and black mold. Some stretches have grimy skylights behind ornate iron grilles, and the dim dirty light that filters down might even be natural. Others are lit by yellow bulbs in cheap tin chandeliers. I slosh past cracks and cave-ins and zigzag chains of derailed cars as Hargreave checks out Reeves's data. I climb along tracks that used to be flat; now they've been wrenched into roller coasters. Sparking fluorescents and brain-dead signal lights flash at random, filling the passages with brightness and shadow and flickering bloody twilight.

I never walk alone. Hargreave whispers in my ear. Ceph infantry stalk along the tunnels and shoot on sight, hooting and chittering and clicking. I must be on the right track; their numbers climb the farther I go. Too many to take on at once; the suit isn't flooding me with bloodlust so I guess it agrees. We cloak in fits and starts, and try to pass unseen.

It works for a while.

Something crashes down into the tunnel just ahead: a steel fist, a battering ram, a subway car punching through from an overhead line like Thor's Hammer through a leaky condom. I don't know what sent it down here, I don't know if it's accident or assault, I don't know what set the fucking thing on fire. But there it is, forty meters dead ahead, a few hundred tons of torqued and screaming metal, belching flames and smoke. It spits pieces everywhere: shards of glass, ragged little shurikens of flaming metal, chunks of concrete ricocheting from the shattered wall. One of them must have hit me, because suddenly I can see my shadow dancing in the firelight like a big fucking arrowhead.

And all these armed and armored garden slugs see it, too.

They're on me from angles I didn't even know they had: from

behind, from around the corner of the burning train, but from above, too, from overhead service catwalks I've been too fucking stupid to even notice all this time. They fire through grilles and gratings way too narrow for a clean return shot—and man, even the grunts I *can* get a bead on are way tougher than they have any right to be. I'm pumping off shots that blow good-sized divots out of reinforced concrete, and these fuckers just *take* it. Four, five shots to bring them down sometimes—even with all that unprotected meat showing—and I don't have nearly enough ammo to go around.

There's a service closet at my back, heavy door, double-locked, but a few wild shots from the Ceph take care of that before I even get there. I manage to duck back inside an instant before the armor setting bleeds out the cells. It gives me some cover, buys the suit a bit of recharge time. I fire around the corner often enough to keep the Squids from advancing too quickly, but they're out there and I'm in here and this is not what you'd call a sustainable situation.

I switch to StarlAmp—light flickers in through the doorway but the corners of this little cave are still deep in shadow—and I spare a moment to survey the digs. There's a pail in here, and a mop. A fuse box on the wall, jammed with breakers and switches and high-voltage cables. There's a bloated corpse squirming with spore, some poor bastard who found a dark place to die. I flash back to all the other poor bastards before him, the Rapture-heads, the suicidal mothers, the bodies twitching in the street like frog's legs jumping to an electric current—

And suddenly I see something else in here, too. I see a way out.

I duck back around the corner and hand out way more ammo than I should. Ceph scatter before my suppressing fire; I catch at least two of them right in the dorsal tentacles, blow a couple of those waving wormy things right the fuck *off*, leave them flapping on the ground while their owners dive for cover. Doesn't even slow them down. Gotta hand it to the slugs; if someone blew off one of *my* limbs I don't think I'd be quite so blasé about it.

And then I think: *Predator–prey*. And then I think: *Nature documentaries.*

And suddenly, for just that one brief instant, Ceph battle armor—the sheer idiocy of leaving all that meat exposed to enemy fire—almost makes a kind of sense.

Maybe it's like those reef fish that have the big fake eyespots down near the tail, to trick predators into going for the wrong end. Maybe those big wavy tentacles are vulnerable by *design,* maybe they're not gills or penises but *cannon fodder.* Maybe the whole *point* is to look vulnerable, to draw enemy fire to something that can be dropped and discarded the way a lizard sheds its tail, leaves the predator chewing on some scaly scrap while the primary target skitters away unharmed.

Now I'm not saying that kind of Animal Planet shit would necessarily work when you graduate to dustups that use actual honest-to-God technology. Any enemy smart enough to lob a flashbang or build an SMG is gonna figure that trick out pretty quick. But so what? Why go out of your way to shield something that only exists to be blown off in the first place? You don't need it for anything, so you might as well allocate your resources to something that matters.

Apropos of nothing, of course. Just a friendly pointer in case you ever find yourself face-to-phallus with those slimy little fuckers in the near future.

But it's just a flash, really, a little chunk of insight crammed into the space of an eyeblink. The brain plays with the theory but the body keeps the plan in motion. My suppressing fire has got the Ceph to back off a bit, given me a few extra seconds to put the pieces into place. I rip open that switch box, I rip out those cables, I loop them up and tie them together. And when I cloak at last, fully charged, and sneak back out into the tunnel, the

Ceph don't even notice—because they still hear me, trapped in that little room. They can still see my shadow moving in there, framed by the flickering blue light of shorted circuits. And by the time they get their nerve back and rush my defenses—by the time they discover that corpse wired up like a marionette, live cables under its arms, dancing a fifty-thousand-volt jig against the wall—I'm already behind enemy lines.

Galvanic reflexes.

I bet I'm the only one in my whole fucking squad who would've thought of that.

The ghost of Mitchell Reeves leads me on to an impassable cave-in where his living body planted canisters of C-4 before turning back to die a thousand meters farther upstream. I don't know why he never detonated them: But I do, and when the dust and the wreckage have settled I crawl from the tunnel we made into one we didn't: a place full of shadows and segmented machines and dim, sickly gray light.

I think it's a cave at first, carved from the bedrock beneath Manhattan and almost as large. Great curving spinal columns of dark gunmetal arc across the vast space, orange eyespots glimmering from each vertebra. Massive towers of wheels and gears and sawtooth machinery loom ahead. A cave, a subterranean city. But then something rises out of a fissure ahead—a floating cannon, a flying abortion put together from gun belts and engine blocks, all its viscera welded to the outside of its hull. The usual flickering red levitators push it into the sky, and as I watch it rise I see there *is* a sky up there, grim and gloomy, but that is not the roof of a cave and this is no hollow beneath Manhattan. This is an open pit, and up around its edges I can see the towers of New York.

Then I'm flat on my back, and a horse has just kicked me in the chest.

A horse, or a high-caliber armor-piercing round. Tactical vectors back and highlights a target halfway up a faraway cliff face, too hidden in the local cover for a make. Not human, though.

"Ah," Hargreave murmurs. "That's interesting."

No warnings on tactical.

"Stay absolutely still. If its dealings so far have been with ordinary soldiers, it thinks you're dead. Act like it."

I sacc' suit diagnostics just to be sure. No redlights.

SECOND keeps a targeting triangle on the sniper as it emerges from cover. A single impossible bound and it's covered half the distance. Another jump; it's on the ledge with me, not ten steps away. It steps forward with that strange half-upright-half-panther gait. I swear it's cocking its headpiece at me.

It was mainly grunts in the subway. I wonder how this carbine works point-blank against stalkers.

It actually works pretty well. But I'm guessing this means they know I'm coming.

Jack Hargreave fills my helmet with waypoints and mission objectives. I descend into the pit and he talks about ecology, and insect societies. I look up at a murky yellow sky and he rhapsodizes about evolution and coral reefs. He warns me that I am in a hive, that the level of infestation is high, that I have to be *careful*.

But all I can see are the thousands of infected rotting on the streets behind me, and I don't *want* to be careful. I don't give a flying fuck about *infestation*. There can't ever be *enough* of these fuckers in my sights, not as long as I've got a weapon in my hands and ammo to feed it.

And oh, Roger, it's as though all of fucking Cephdom has gathered here to grant that very wish.

I'm not crazy enough to take them all on head-to-head; there are stalkers here that jump like fleas and shoot like snipers, Heavies that barely feel a direct hit with a fragmentation grenade. I cloak and cover, I hide, I fight on the run and never in a straight line. But there are times. Times a bogeyman falls injured in front of me and instead of finishing the job with a burst of firepower I lift the fucker over my head and smash it against one of its own machines. There are time when I find cracks in the armor, and pry them open, and rip out that translucent gray Spam by the fistful. There are times I shoot to kill, and times I flip that gun around and use it as a fucking club.

They're all the same to me, every stalker like every other, each grunt as faceless as the last. I don't know if they're clones or assembly-line robots, I don't know if the suit's just filtering out their distinguishing traits to keep my conscience dead, and I don't care. But there's one Heavy down here who doesn't line up with the others. It doesn't go down, it doesn't give up, it doesn't stop moving. It lumbers like a fucking cow but somehow it always manages to get out of the way of my grenades, somehow my armor-piercing rounds just never seem to get through.

And I swear, Roger, Ceiling Cat as my witness, this thing has as big a grudge as I do. It sees me airing out its buddies, sees the ranks thinning down, and it doesn't chitter or burble like the other Ceph: it *roars*. I can outrun it easily enough—I'm the hare to its tortoise, and yes I am painfully aware of who won *that* particular contest, thank you very much—but somehow it always manages to get ahead of me after I leave it behind, always manages to rise up between me and my waypoints. It comes after me like a runaway semi, like I'd raped its mother, and it's smart enough to play to my weaknesses. I could stay ahead of the fucking thing if I didn't have to deal with some grunt or stalker on the side every time I turned around. But the Heavy keeps coming, runs me down, forces me to drain my suit. Then, once I'm bled down to moving at pathetic baseline human speeds—*then* those cannon arms shoot out missiles from an endless ammo belt that must reach into another fucking dimension, the damn thing never runs dry. I try to keep to the high ground and some stalker sails higher, raining down plasma and lightning. I take cover behind rockfalls and overturned dumpsters and grunts swarm me like giant lethal gnats.

I don't know how it happens but it catches me in the open. A missile slams into the rock face just a few meters to my left—not a direct hit but close enough, close enough. The blast kicks me into the air like a tumbleweed in a windstorm; half a dozen redlights bloom on BUD. The world spins and then stops with a jolt, way too soon, way too high. I'm back on the ground but not *that* ground. I'm higher up. I'm on a ledge, an uplifted chunk of asphalt. There's a car behind me. Yellow cab. More cabs than cockroaches in this burg.

From just out of sight, past the lip of the ledge, the sound of something pounding the ground.

Carbine's gone. The scarab won't do shit against this thing. I've got grenades but the Heavy just—

Oh, wait . . .

The charge level's barely grazing 50 percent but it'll have to do. I slap two stickies onto the front of the cab, set the timers so they don't blow up in my face. Whatever the suit's got to give, it gives now. Lord: Give me Strength.

I *kick*. The cab skids off the ledge and sails down in a beautiful arc that ends right on the head of that missile-spitting motherfucker. The sound of massive metal objects smashing together: just beautiful, Roger. Just fucking beautiful.

It doesn't die. But it goes down, pinned under two thousand kilograms of Chevrolet's finest alloys. I can hear the roars of my vanquished enemy, I can see the car swaying and rocking as the thing underneath struggles to free itself before the timers run down.

Doesn't take much to set off a sticky. Even a footstep within a couple of meters is enough if you crank the sensitivity. And this bruiser, it's moving that cab around like a goddamn seesaw. It's half a second, tops, between the timers zeroing out and the whole damn vehicle going up in a ball of fire, HE, and gasoline. It's almost too long. The Heavy's actually tipping the cab up on its side by the time the stickies detonate, actually getting back to its feet when its feet get blown out from under it.

But you know what they say. Close only counts in horseshoes and hand grenades.

After a while they stop coming for me. After a while they get harder to find. But Jacob Hargreave is still there, telling me what I have to do.

A riot of alien machinery sits in the center of the pit like some kind of nerve ganglion, radiating those massive spokes in all directions. The base of a Ceph spire rises from its center: the same spire I saw past City Hall. Most of the spokes look like the backbones of some colossal cyborg; three sprout a pair of leg-like spines from each segment. They look like the bodies of monstrous centipedes.

"Ah," Hargreave says. "Yes. Well."

I wait for something a bit more helpful. I wait for more Ceph to come pouring through the walls and tear me apart. All I see are spines, and pipes, and see-through panels here and there—portholes, almost—behind which clouds of spore swirl and seethe like coffee grounds. They're not going anywhere, though. The flow is random, chaotic, like boiling water trapped in a pot: all wired up and no place to go.

"From the look of this feed, the spore loop's running near dormant levels," Hargreave says at last. "We'll need to fix that. There must be triggers around here, but what they look like is anyone's guess . . ."

Turns out those centipede spokes are key. So I follow one of them out of the spear, across the pit, back down to earth where it plunges into some terminal structure of plates and spines and glowing orange slots. I find the interfaces, I go through the motions. The plumbing trembles under my hand; the spore in the nearest porthole begins to surge back up the conduit, toward the machinery at center stage. One down, two to—

What?

Uh, Hargreave must've—Yeah, that's right. Hargreave told me. I mean, how else would I know? It's not like those controls looked like anything *I'd* ever seen before.

Damn good question. You should ask him.

Oh. Right.

Emergency Forensic Session on the Manhattan Incursion
CSIRA Blackbody Council
Pre-Testimony Interview, Partial Transcript, 27/08/2023
Subject: Nathan Gould

Excerpt begins:

You know how dreams work, right? Our brains are full of static; neurons just fire off at random sometimes, not thoughts or anything, just—background noise. The visual cortex gets its share, but normally you don't notice 'cause the signals coming in over your optic nerves are so much stronger, they just swamp everything else.

When you're asleep, though, there's nothing coming in through the main cables. Nothing to drown out the static. And the brain—notices. It's got these pattern-matching circuits and when static's all they've got to work with, they'll find signal in that noise even if there isn't any signal to find. They try and shoehorn these random flickers into the experiential database. Same reason we see faces in clouds.

That's what I thought those visions were, when they first started coming over the feeds. Just static. So I laid some dynamic filters over them, just to try and clean up the signal, and wouldn't you know the residuals weren't random. There was a whole other AV track embedded in there, and holy shit the things it showed.

Fragments, mainly. A few seconds, maybe the longest was getting up around a minute. Glimpses of the inside of some weird gloomy structure, blue end of the spectrum, like it was deep underwater or way out around Neptune or something. Architecture. Machinery. Some kind of twisted plumbing everywhere, all tangled and messed up. Not human, though. Not even close.

One fragment looked like a cross between a junkyard and a museum, full of things that had to be vehicles. Another looked like some kind of lab, Ceph running around everywhere, operating various bits of equipment. Not your usual Ceph, though, nothing we've seen in Manhattan. Some new geek caste, maybe. I saw a magic mirror once, a swirly portal that looked like some kind of teleportation device. Oh, and I kept seeing constellations: a cluster of blue stars, little sapphire pinpricks connected by a network of dim glowing filaments, rotating in midair. Arranged along the surface of an invisible sphere, you know, like a star globe. Ceph planetarium or something, I thought at first. Saw that track a few times, the suit must've had it listed as a favorite. Anyway, you've got the files. You must have turned my place inside out by now.

No comment. Right.

At first I thought this was all just a contaminant from the suit's camera feed, right? Quantum echo of old footage, something from archival storage seeping into the signal. You could hardly blame the N2 for springing a leak or two after all the shit it had been through. And it was pretty fucking creepy, I mean finally I'm getting a glimpse of where Prophet's actually *been* all those months, and wouldn't you know he didn't spend all that time getting pissed in some Taiwanese dive.

It never occurred to me that Alcatraz would even be aware of it. Even if he called up the cam feed, I'd had to squeeze the signal through a whole shitload of amps and filters to find the embed. Even if he had the wherewithal to do that from his end—which he does not—why would he? I didn't even mention anything to him at the time. Poor fucker already had his hands full, he didn't need me freaking him out with the news that his suit was haunted by the previous owner.

But once I figured out what was going on, I went back and looked at all those other burps and hiccups I'd written off as static the first time around. If there *was* anything useful in there, I figured I could pass it on. And then I run into that hive sequence, you know, the logs from when Hargreave was leading him around by the nose, and the only way that makes any sense at all is if Alcatraz *already knows* this shit. I mean, you must've seen the feed, right? He plays those Ceph controls like a fucking maestro, things I'd never have even tagged *as* controls. And sure enough, just before he pulls those moves out of his ass there's static on the line, and when I squeeze out the signal it's Prophet doing the same thing. Alcatraz was just going thou and doing likewise, bra.

So the suit isn't just leaking these signals into the camera feed. It must be laying those images right across Alky's visual cortex, poking those voxels the way you'd light up an LED. Far as I can figure the brain feed was the main feed; what I was getting off the camera was just an induction leak or something.

Now, I'm not saying Alcatraz is hiding anything, you understand? I know you fuckers, I know that's the first place you're gonna go with this, but most of the inputs our brains operate on are subconscious. You're thinking *Oooh, Alcatraz was seeing movies in his brain* but for all we know he's not even aware of the stimulus. It might all operate below the level of conscious perception, he could just get a *feeling* that this is how you're supposed to work this or that control. So you might want to go easy on the poor bastard, unless you've started beating the shit out of people for having flashes of intuition.

You want something to blame, blame the N2. But really, it was only doing what it was supposed to. It's programmed for mission success, right? It's designed to analyze data from a thousand sources, figure out what's most mission-relevant, serve up the intel most vital to current objectives. That's all it was doing. That's all it's ever done.

We just had no idea it was going to be so goddamn *good* at it.

You ever have any direct dealings with Jack Hargreave, Roger?

Well of course you wouldn't have actually *met*. I'm asking if you ever got into a conversation with the man: text chat, Third Life, online chess club. That sort of thing.

Ah. Then you may not know that he liked to play things *really* close to the chest.

I was halfway through the sequence before I knew what I was actually doing, and even then it wasn't because Hargreave let me in on his master plan. I was just kick-starting these damn spokes, one after another, fighting off grunts and stalkers every goddamn step of the way, and I basically put it together myself. We're priming the pump, right? We're booting up this spire to shoot a huge wadge of spore all over central Manhattan, which on the face of it doesn't make a lot of sense if you're actually fighting for the home team. But I remember what Hargreave said, that one insight Nathan Gould's synapses were too drug-addled to parse: The suit doesn't contain the specs for a weapon, the suit *is* the weapon. And the suit, it's pirated, right? It's Cephtech on a leash. And I'm remembering that first stalker, my hand going into whatever goo those fuckers use for blood, and the N2 trying to *interface* with it . . .

So finally I figure it out. The suit is a weapon. The suit is a *virus*—Prophet said as much before he blew his brains out and left me holding the bag. And Jack Hargreave, he's the tenth-degree goddamn black belt in battlefield judo, he's the absolute master at using your opponent's strength against him. So I'm wearing a virus, and all this spore, and the spear over my head—that's the *delivery platform*.

Simple, huh?

But you're not gonna get a tight-ass like Hargreave to just come right out and *explain* it like that, are you? No sirree. That dude learned decades before you and I were even born that Knowledge Is Power. He's been keeping his cards facedown for so long that I bet even spilling the time of day would make his shriveled little testicles crawl back up into his body.

Still. I figured it out, in between fighting off aliens and fucking with the plumbing. And now I'm standing there with Ceph bodies bleeding out all around me, spore flowing full-bore from all three substations, and Hargreave says: "Now we need to get you inside the central structure."

It's not like there's a door in the base of the spear with a neon sign saying THIS WAY TO THE INNER WORKINGS. Hargreave suggests that I just blow the shit out of it—"Try to blast loose one of the spoke seals and use the resulting rupture to effect entry" is the way he puts it—and that seems kind of ham-fisted even to me, but I don't have a better idea. So I line up an overhead joint that's bleeding steam where spear meets spoke—must have taken a hit during the fighting—and I force-feed it a couple of sticky grenades from the L-TAG, praying to the goddamn Spaghetti Monster I'm not punching through a motherboard.

Boom.

The dust clears instantly, sucked into the hole I've just blown. Huh. Negative-pressure differential. This thing *breathes*. The tracheotomy wound is just big enough to let me squeeze inside, where I find—

—well, *tentacles* is what they look like.

It's a kind of silo. Curved glassy panels on all sides, arteries of orange lava-light running vertically between them. I follow those arteries up along a vertical shaft ribbed with cross-bracing every ten or fifteen meters, like hoops of cartilage around a trachea. High up in that space lightning flickers: some kind of static discharge. Even higher: daylight.

But down here in the basement, spore seethes behind those transparent panels as if it were alive. As if it were really pissed off.

Hargreave says I have to get it from *in there* to *out here*. No obvious controls, no obvious hatches or access ports. No way through except, well, *through*.

Hey, it worked last time.

So I proceed to shoot the shit out of those panels, and the machinery—*screams* . . .

I don't know how else to describe it. Maybe it's an alarm, maybe it's just the equivalent of metal fatigue, some kind of mechanical stress. Or maybe Ceph machinery *is* alive somehow, maybe I'm *hurting* it. Anyhow, it works: The air around me is thick with spore, I can barely see my hand in front of my face. Hargreave makes approving noises from the ass end of nowhere.

SECOND writes across my eyeballs—

Incoming Protocols Detected
Handshaking . . .
Handshaking . . .
Connected.
Compiling Interface.

—and even throws up a little progress bar so I can see Hargreave's science fair project edging toward the blue ribbon. Little patches of orange light flicker across my forearms—some kind of photic interface—and for a moment there it almost looks as though we're going to pull it off.

But then I guess the spore remembers: It eats backbones like me for lunch. And if we're a little too tough to chew, it spits us out.

Something throws me against the wall. I rattle around on the floor for a moment like a pebble in a pickup; then the spire opens its throat and shoots me halfway to the goddamn jet stream. Suddenly my guts are in my boots; all I see is orange streaks and dark blurs. And then I'm *out,* the human spitball, shot into the sky like a watermelon seed. I hang there in midair for a moment, a tabletop Manhattan turning on all sides, God's own middle finger jabbing up at me from a dark gray pit dead below. Then I'm coming back to earth and one hard fucking landing. I land back on the spire ass-first and off-center, like dropping onto a free-fall waterslide. I roll, bounce off into space again, grab some bit of alien corkscrew plumbing my body somehow knew was there even though my brain didn't see it. I hang on for dear life: bait on a hook, thirty stories up. One precious handhold away from street pizza.

"Ah," Hargreave says with mild disappointment. "More resistance than I expected."

You've got to be fucking kidding.

"An immune reaction, I suppose you could call it. You'd better—uh—

"Just hang on a sec," he says, and drops off the channel. He's probably not even being ironic. Either way, fuck *that* advice: I haul myself back up onto the rim that bounced my ass off the spire, climb back up the vent as far as the slope will let me, scope out the angles. Just off to the left a twisted strip of some avenue ramps up from the ground like a ski jump, a tangle of I-beams and blacktop pushed into space by the erupting spear. It's close enough to make a jump, if I can get a running start.

I make it, barely. Lose my footing on the very first step, stumble, keep going three long loping steps down a forty-degree angle and push off into space, flailing like an idiot. But I make the jump and land on solid asphalt, in no more pieces than I was before.

I start down the road to ground level. I'm almost there when static cackles in my ear and Hargreave's back. There's nothing fake about his tone this time. I can tell with his first word that he's stressed; I can tell by the second that he's scared shitless.

He tells me the Pentagon has decided on drastic measures. He tells me bombers are inbound from McGuire.

He tells me they're going to put all of Lower Manhattan underwater.

AQUARIUM

Ever seen a sweeper in the field, Roger?

Street-Sweeper. No, not the trucks that clear out the gutters. The basic theory's chimp-simple: Drop a bomb into a body of water offshore from your target, blow it up, let the wave do the dirty work. Cleaner than an airborne nuke, more devastating than a neutron bomb—UniSec even tried to sell it as *environmentally friendly*, if you can believe it. It's only water, after all—with a few rads mixed in, sure, but at least there's no aerial fallout. Pure, clean, *natural* water.

A twenty-meter wall of it moving at two hundred klicks an hour. Mother Nature's Doomsday Machine.

That's what your bosses set on us, Roger. That's what we had to deal with.

I didn't believe it at first. Thought there was something wrong with the comm link—I mean, the ol' N2 can certainly be forgiven for losing a little EM gain after all we've been through together, right? So when I get comm back and the first thing I hear is Hargreave shouting about tidal waves I thought I must've misheard, you know, a fucking *tidal wave*? Are you *joking*, Jack? But the dude's never been more serious about anything in his life. Because Manhattan has not been dealt enough shit yet, no Roger, it has not. And so there is a cleansing tsunami coming to *flood out the aliens*. Anything with a backbone that doesn't have access to a pair of industrial-strength water wings has just been written off as collateral.

What do we know about the Ceph, Roger? I don't mean whatever secret genetic insights the black labs have under wraps; what does every sad-sack sonofabitch on the street know about the Ceph? Well, we know that they need those exoskels to ride around in, which suggests they're not great in earth-type gravity situations. We know that when you peel them out of those skels they really look a lot more like boneless sea creatures than like anything that ever walked on land. We call them Ceph because, you know, *they remind us an awful lot of cephalopods.* All of which strongly suggests a native lifestyle that's at the very least amphibious, if not aquatic. So what secret weapon does the Pentagon use to take them out?

Seawater.

Let me repeat that, Roger, for the benefit of your chickenshit bosses behind the mirror. The Pentagon. Decided. That the best way. To take out. Super-advanced. *Aquatic.* Aliens.

Was to *drown* them.

Oh, and did I tell you I've got this phobia about water? I swear, sometimes I feel like cheering for the other side.

So I hear the jet streak by overhead and I don't even waste time looking up; I've got maybe twenty seconds before it's far enough offshore to deploy, maybe ten minutes—if I'm lucky—for the wave to drive back through the bottleneck and put us all in hot water. Hargreave's yelling about getting to higher ground, but what's higher ground in downtown Manhattan?

I run like hell up Broadway.

Of *course* it was a bad choice. There weren't any good ones. What would you have done, hide in a dumpster? Run up fifty floors of some office tower that's already been so torqued it might go over if you kick it in the shins? Fuck that noise. The farther you get from the waterfront, the higher the ground; the more buildings you've got between you and that big fucking flyswatter heading for the coast. Office tower doesn't do you much good if it comes down around you, but even in a million pieces all that mass is gonna act like *some* kind of breakwater.

So I'm burning up the boulevard as fast as the N2's mighty little nanofibrils can move me, and neither CELL nor Ceph nor civilian get in my way. Maybe they didn't happen to be hanging around on that street, maybe they were and I didn't notice, maybe the word's gone out and *everyone's* just running for cover; but all I see is cars and corpses, and all I hear is a low steady rumble rising behind me. I know I can't outrun it—not even NANOSUIT 2.0 can win a race against a tsunami—but maybe it'll be worn out by the time it catches me, maybe it won't be a flyswatter so much as a plain old flood. Maybe it'll just lift me up and carry me along and it'll be just like river rafting, just a day at the water park.

Right.

That rumbling's pretty loud by now, and *deep*, almost subsonic; you hear it with your bones more than your ears. The ground won't stop shaking. I can feel it under my boots, I can see windowpanes bursting over the street, I can hear car alarms going off. And there are these other sounds too, little metallic *popping* noises, and I don't turn around to see what they are because I don't *dare*, I can hear the whole Atlantic roaring at my back and no *way* am I going to break my stride for even a second. But I don't have to look behind because a manhole cover blasts out of the street right in front of me, and farther ahead, and all the way down the street like a row of space shuttles blasting off on columns of white water. I run through an intersection and something's blocked off the street to my left and it's *moving* and holy Mother of Muhammad the goddamn ocean *flanked* me, it's coming at me from all sides now, these huge motherfucking gray-green *mountains* of water and I barely have time to look up and take one last look at the sky—just this tiny strip of brightness *way* off overhead, disappearing between two dark heaving walls. It's like being swallowed whole, it's like taking one last look at the world through closing jaws.

And I'm squashed like a bug at the bottom of the Mariana Trench.

> To: Site Commander D. Lockhart, Manhattan Crisis Zone
> From: CryNet Executive Board
> Date: 23/08/2023, 16:05
> CC: CELL Oversight Secretariat; Jacob Hargreave
>
> Commander Lockhart,
>
> We reluctantly conclude that your assessment of Jacob Hargreave's mental competence is correct at this time, and we herewith relieve him of all board-related duties and shareholder privileges. He is to be contained within the environs of the Prism building until a medical team can assess his mental health. Operating mandate is also revoked in the case of Special Adviser Tara Strickland, pending further investigation. She is to be detained for questioning.
>
> Your request for overall authority in the Manhattan Crisis Zone is herewith granted.

I wake up to a soft distant roar, like the sound of a seashell held to your ear. I hear a river chuckling away somewhere nearby, a seagull squawking *Don't fuck with me,* and False Prophet mumbling something about resequencing vectors. I hear other voices, too: *Must be around here somewhere,* and *Yeah, if Gould's tracking gizmo actually works worth shit,* and *If the wave didn't get him. Fucking Pentagon* . . .

That last sentiment of which, I gotta say, I'm finding myself more and more in sympathy with. But these guys sound friendly for a change—even familiar—so it is with something close to a sense of hope that I open my eyes.

And what should greet me but a blue sunlit sky full of puffy white clouds. And a giant green fist the size of a bus, ready to punch my lights back out.

I think Jolly Green Giant. I think Incredible Hulk. Statue of Liberty comes a distant third, but that's what it turns out to be when my eyes finally focus. Big green disembodied fist in a river that used to be a street, still bravely holding aloft the Torch of Freedom or whatever the fuck it's supposed to symbolize. Too bad statues don't come with a sense of irony.

Oh, and here comes the gunfire. Naturally.

Regular army, this time. Camo fatigues, no insectile body armor, just a bunch of jarheads and Squids shooting at each other. The Ceph seem awfully undrowned, but maybe they have been rocked back on their heels a bit because our boys don't seem to be having too much trouble mopping them up.

It's a nice sight to wake up to, even though I can't join in the festivities because my suit is still rebooting along with my brain (I swear, Roger, the way this thing crashes I'd swear the OS was written by Microsoft). By the time I can do anything more productive than twitching and rolling around there's nothing left but backbones. And the best sight I've seen all fucking day is the guy who reaches down to help me to my feet.

"Alcatraz. Nice suit, man. Fifth Avenue? You been shopping without me?"

Chino, back from the dead. I thought he went down with the Swordfish, I thought he was rotting on the bottom of the Hudson. I'd hug the dude if I could do it without crushing him to jelly.

"You *do* remember me, right? Gould said they'd knocked your voice box out, but he didn't say anything about brain damage." He leans in, squints through the faceplate, doesn't see anything but his own reflection. "What the hell happened to you?"

He's fallen in with some kinda ad-hoc mash-up of marines and airborne and regular army, the closest thing left to a chain of command in this shitstorm. The man who's holding it all together is one Colonel Barclay—"I served under him once, good man," Chino says. "Anyone can pull a winning hand out of this pile of shit, he can." The colonel's set up a field command at Central Station, way above the high-water line, and he's keeping the Ceph hordes at bay while the evacuation kicks into gear.

Barclay. I know that name. I heard it a hundred meters under the surface of the Atlantic, back in those innocent days of childhood when we thought gengineered Ebola or a dirty nuke was the worst that could happen, when we thought we were Lords of fucking Creation, when we thought we were such incomparable badasses that we had to make enemies of one another because no one else was up to the job. I heard it a hundred years ago, back when I still thought there was some kind of *line* between life and death.

I heard it this morning.

There is a chain of command. There are still backbones out here who know which side they're on. There is a CO to report to, there is a higher purpose. His name is Barclay, and these are his men, and they have come to take me home.

And since Jacob Hargreave's grand viral counterattack seems to be on hold, I have nowhere else to be. I saddle up and join the posse. I lost pretty much everything I was packing when the wave hit, but Chino's new friends came prepared. I rearm and reload and help hold back the tide as we head for higher ground.

But oh, Roger, what thy masters have wrought.

There are no streets left, only rivers. Half the storefronts are still underwater. Streets have split down the middle; foundations, turned to quicksand, have given way and dropped whole neighborhoods into the earth. Ceph conduits lie exposed in the fissures, emerging from *these* masses of bedrock, disappearing into *those:* They're everywhere under the city, like sewers beneath the sewers. We walk along the edges of newborn cliffs and see streetlights and shredded leafless treetops, more like roots than branches, barely breaking the surface. The buildings across the park are walls of pigeonholes, all torn open on this side. Anything more than five or six stories up seems dry. Everything else is draining; trickles from the upper reaches, cascades from lower floors that only just got back above the waterline. It's actually kind of scenic: a great majestic matrix of waterfalls, tinkling and roaring and filling the air with glittering mist. The wave did absolutely nothing to stop the Ceph but it seems to have scoured the battlefield, left all the wreckage squeaky-clean. I see rainbows everywhere I look. Rainbows, Roger. Even nature's part of the spin machine.

"Maybe it took care of the bedbugs, at least," Chino says.

We fight north while the city drains around us. We evict Squiddie from a flooded Coffee Stop and make it safe for Free Enterprise again. We help out some marines getting their asses kicked by a Ceph gunship in Madison Square. Sometimes we go together, sometimes separately, but we always leave Ceph blood in our wake, pooling like mercury in the wetlands.

Good times, Roger, good times. Once or twice I even remember that I'm dead and it almost doesn't matter; I'm doing more good now than I ever did when I had a heart. Not even Hargreave can spoil the party. He comes back online once or twice to complain about the dents and scratches I'm putting on his suit, but it turns out even a rich tourist like him has his own problems. He tells me events are *escalating beyond his control.* Welcome to the human race, Jack. But apparently he and the suit are already busy cooking up Hargreave's new-and-improved Countermeasures Interface Soufflé, and that's not gonna change whether I'm fighting Squids or surfing porn. Hargreave spells it out himself: What we need now is *time*, and if Barclay's Badasses can buy us a bit of it, maybe I can help them get a better rate of return.

For once, everyone seems to be on the same page. Not sure how I feel about that. I guess you could call me *ambivalent*.

Now, there's one of those words I never used when I was alive.

There's a whole lot to feel ambivalent about these days. I'm sure you appreciate that. But you know what really strikes home when I think of that word? You know what picture illustrates *ambivalent* in this souped-up superconductor that used to be my brain?

My own guys. The backbones I fought side by side with. Grunts, regular army types. Even Chino, although he'd never admit it.

Some of the shit they say, when they think I can't hear them:

I dunno, man, looks to me like something they'd build.

You think there's anything inside at all? Anything human, I mean?

That suit guy. I mean yeah, he saved our asses but Christ he creeps me out.

Chino had to keep telling them not to shoot at me. Had to keep reminding everyone whose side I was on. Even my kill card didn't help. The more Ceph scalps I collected the scarier I became, somehow. Golem Boy, The Unkillable Monster That Even The Ceph Can't Vanquish. If I'd been a little *less* good at my job—got an arm blown off or something—maybe they would've trusted me more.

Of course, if I'd really wanted to prove that I wasn't unkillable, I suppose I could've let them know that I was already dead. Probably just as well I didn't, though.

Oh, you think my feelings are hurt. That's not it at all. I suppose there's some little module down in my midbrain that's feeling wounded and alone, but it doesn't call the shots anymore. No, what I am is *concerned*. Because I really *don't* look like *one of them*. The tech may be Ceph down in the molecules, but the morphology is all human. I don't look like *one of them* at all; I look like one of *us* in weird-ass body armor.

But these guys, they see through that somehow. Maybe it's pheromonal, maybe I smell wrong or something, but they sense a truth their eyes can't possibly detect. They know who I am, they know we all wear the same dog tags. But something about me still freaks them out, right down in the brain stem. Even though they can't put their fingers on it. And that, to me, is cause for concern.

Why, Roger, because we have things to do. And it's going to be a lot tougher to do them if we can't get people like you to trust us.

Not to worry, though. We're working on it.

The good times don't last forever. The party screeches to a halt when Hargreave comes out of the closet.

"Hopefully I'm reaching your comrades, too, with this," he says when he comes back online. "I've bounced this signal off your suit to their comms."

He's reaching them all right. Chino's tapping his earpiece like he's trying to dislodge a bug. "Who the fuck is that?"

"My name is Jacob Hargreave. You may or may not be aware that Alcatraz's suit is evolving into a powerful bioweapon against the aliens you face. But in order to complete that process, a stabilizing agent is required. Ideally I would ask you to come to Roosevelt Island, but clearly that is impossible now."

Chino looks at me. "Is this a joke?"

I'm feeling like my mom just showed up on the LAN in

front of all the cool kids and asked me if I remembered to clean my room. But Mom is completely fucking oblivious; he announces that there's an early prototype of said agent over at the Hargreave-Rasch building, right here in Midtown. He squirts coordinates: the familiar red line zigzags down wireframe canyons and comes to rest somewhere on East 36th.

"Take your colleagues with you; you will need their support. Please make haste, all of you. The Ceph will not wait on us."

Nobody moves for a moment. Then someone says, "Did that civilian fuck just give us an *order?*"

Chino looks around at the congregation. "Actually, I'm gonna read that as more of a *request*. And we *are* talking about something that'll kill the Ceph." Now he's looking at no one but me. "Aren't we?"

Ah, shit.

I nod. I don't know how well it comes across from the outside, but Chino takes it as a yes.

We head out. Hargreave helps me pass the time, fills my eyes and ears with tactical intel on our destination. The main entrance to Hargreave-Rasch is blocked solid with rubble; the building itself is in lockdown. We might be able to get in through the parking garage, but the research wing is up on the eleventh floor and the stairwells and elevators are all locked out.

No problem, Hargreave says cheerily. The security console in the lobby's still hot. Should be able to manage a systems reboot from there.

All things considered, we make good time. The wave may have smashed half of Manhattan down to the bricks, but it also pushed a lot of that wreckage into nice convenient moraines: a real cocksucker if they happen to be in your way, but if they're not the streets are cleaner than they ever were when we backbones were running things. At least most of the bodies have been flushed out of sight. And those few corpses still tangled in trees, or skewered so far down signposts that not even a twenty-meter tidal wave could wash out the stain—even those are being taken care of. Ticks never sleep.

We come up from the south. I don't know if our route has been uplifted or the Hargreave-Rasch block has dropped, but we've definitely got the high ground on approach: There's a tumbledown escarpment of broken streets and buildings leading down to the south face. Hargreave wasn't kidding when he said the entrance was blocked: collapsed and pulverized office towers jam the streets to either side and spill around into the space in front. You can barely see the tops of the southern doors under all that shit. The tactical wireframe shows another way in on the north side—at the bottom of a big cylindrical silo, like a castle turret, half embedded in the middle of the façade—and I think that's actually the main entrance, but there's no way we're gonna get there from here.

There's the parking ramp, though, off to the right, sloping down and out of sight right where it's supposed to be. The only thing between it and us is about fifty Ceph on the ground and a dropship hanging overhead like a giant black scorpion.

"Oh, *fuck*," Chino grumbles.

Even as we watch that scorpion drops another egg onto the playing field, shoots it into the ground like a meteorite. Any one of us earthlings would have turned to jelly on impact. The Heavy that emerges from that shell doesn't look anything but eager.

I remember enemy combatants, hesitating at my scent. I remember a stalker trying to shake my hand at the crash site, I remember a horde of Ceph waiting in ambush at Gould's apartment. And now here they are again, waiting.

Are they really just swarming through the city like rats, or is it me?

"Fine." Chino heaves a theatrical sigh. "We'll cover your approach. Go in and get your fix, man. But make it fast.

"And if you *do* get out of there alive, drinks are on you for the rest of your fucking life."

Broadcast Intercept (decrypted): 23/08/2023, 16:32
37.7 MHz (gov/nongov shared, land mobile).
Source unknown (.mp6 transmitted anonymously to
Cpl. Edward "Truth" Newton, USMC [ret.]). Identities
of JACOB HARGREAVE and DOMINIC LOCKHART confirmed via
voiceprint comparison with public archives.

Hargreave:	Hazel section—what the hell do you think you're doing? This is Jacob Hargreave! I order you to cease fire!
Voice (presumed Hazel Sec.):	Blow it out your ass, old man! Tin man dies here!
Hargreave:	You idiot! The suit, you idiot! You'll destroy our only hope! *Cease fire!*
Lockhart:	Take him down, gentlemen. Maximum force. I want this abomination ended *now*.
Hargreave:	What are you doing, Lockhart?
Lockhart:	I'm doing what the CryNet board should have done three years ago, old man. I'm pulling the plug on your obscene cyborg dreams.
Hargreave:	You fool—you think you can hide from the future? We have no choice in this!
Lockhart:	That dog won't hunt now, Hargreave. The board sides with me this time—they're not buying your bullshit anymore. I am in command here. Now *you will stand down*.

Chino and chums are as good as their word. They take the heat and I slip from cinder block to sewer pipe: cloaking as I cross the open spaces, uncloaking behind the shelter of a bakery truck or a pile of concrete, fading to black and sneaking to the next blind spot. Occasionally I pass too close to a grunt and it hesitates, sniffs, stutters trains of soft clicks into the air. I never let them see me, though, and they never press the issue. They're too busy trying to kill my friends.

The ramp drops me below line-of-sight in an instant. I'm up to my knees in scummy water by the time I reach the corrugated door at the bottom. It's jammed half open. I duck down and under. I'm up to my waist. The ramp continues down. I take another step. I'm up to my chest. The ceiling slopes down ahead of me, mindlessly parallel to the ramp beneath, and cuts off the airspace.

I wonder if maybe I'd be better off lending Chino a hand against the Ceph.

Jesus Christ, you fucking girlyman. It was twenty years ago. Get *over* it.

I dive under, and push forward. The water pushes back, dark and dirty and full of swirling shit. The harder I stroke the thicker it gets; it kills my momentum, turns my reflexes to tar. I look up but there's no surface overhead, just pipes and cement cross-beams and a few silvery bubbles sliding around like mercury. My inner eight-year-old is shitting bricks; the rest of me just hopes we make it through before I hit the rebreather's immersion limit.

After about two hundred years the water starts to brighten up ahead; shafts of dirty gray light stab down onto two-lane as-phalt, finally sloping back up. Now the surface is back; now the water's low enough to stand in. It never recedes entirely—this whole level's flooded—but it's only up to my knees. I stand and my inner eight-year-old goes back to sleep. Suit clock tells me the whole trip took forty-five seconds but I guarantee, Roger, at least five minutes went by every time that second counter ticked over.

Pylons and parking spots to one side; the cinder-block wall of a service closet to the other. Maybe sixty meters past that wall is a stairwell that should take me straight to the lobby.

I hear voices.

What the fuck. Hargreave said this place was *sealed*.

Can't hear the words. The voices float around the corner, low and easy, clarifying as I approach: the usual idle bullshit about hardware and poon. Maybe Hargreave sent a couple of grunts to meet me.

"You hear that?"

I freeze. I cloak.

"I'll check it out. Hold your position."

Good plan. Split the party. Go off on your own.

Gotta be CELL.

It is. He sloshes around the corner, the muzzle of his MP5 waving around like a stoned bumblebee. He pans toward me, through me, past me—

—stops, and looks again.

I've noticed by now: The cloak isn't perfect. It turns you to something clearer than glass, but if you keep an eye out you can see the occasional refraction artifact in bright light. Even in semi-darkness there's the barest bit of motion shimmer you might be able to pick out. If you know what to look for.

Let me tell you, this goon is looking *hard,* and I see it just before he does: the wake I've been kicking up as I move, that insignificant little bow ripple still playing itself out across the water's surface.

But by then he's opened fire, and lensing artifacts are the least of my worries.

I'm hit, he's dead, the echoes of our conversation are still ringing off the walls and I hear bodies churning through the water just around the corner. Can't count on the cloak down here.

There's a big box of circuit breakers hanging on the wall beside an abandoned Prius. I put out the lights. Someone yells "Switch to thermal!" and SECOND ccs me some local comm: "He's in the building. Repeat: Prophet is in the building."

Game on.

I can see the stairwell. At least I can see a bunch of body-temp false-color heat prints clustered around the exact spot where the stairwell's supposed to be. They had me pegged, they knew just where I was going. Fuck, did Hargreave set me up? Who else, this is his building after all, he lured me in here, he's got eyes on—

"Roger that. Kill order is in effect."

Not Hargreave.

Lockhart.

He got in here somehow, snuck his people right under Hargreave's nose. Hacked the telemetry or something. Lockhart, you stupid asshole, not Hargreave.

I circle away from the stairwell. Not nearly as many CELL-ulites guarding the elevator, and a couple of those fan out into the level as I watch: They know that only an idiot would use an *elevator* under these conditions.

I'm too smart to be as smart as they expect; but I still leave two of them bleeding out in the disabled-parking zone. By the time I'm in the elevator and punching L, hostilities have spread beyond the local airwaves: Hargreave has broken into the freq, and he and Lockhart are having a slapfight all over the thirty-eight-megahertz band. Hargreave's ordering Lockhart to stand down, Lockhart's telling him to get stuffed. Lockhart says some not-very-nice things about me, too: *abomination* is the word he uses, I think. No big deal. Words will never hurt me.

Sticks and stones, on the other hand. Not to mention our old friends Heckler and Koch . . .

The elevator decelerates smoothly to a stop at the lobby level.

I kick the cloak back into gear and boost armor, flatten myself against the side of the car, crouch down.

They almost take me out anyway, the moment the doors open. It's the view that does me in.

I'm underwater. The whole damn building is. I look out into that lobby, that turret, that grain silo I saw in the wireframes: It's *glass*, the whole thing's glass, a single vast cylindrical space ten stories tall. I look past a great sweeping arc of windowpanes onto the bottom of a lake: wrecked cars, sluggish clouds of suspended sediment, dim shapes in murky green water. I look up, up; wave-bottoms slop against the panes thirty meters above me. There's all sorts of shit floating around up there: office furniture and cardboard boxes and big wooden telephone poles snapped like toothpicks.

This whole damn building—and the buildings beside it, and the chunks of buildings jammed up in the streets between—it's a big piecemeal dam, holding back a deep pocket of floodwaters north of 36th. We came in from the downstream side, and it was just our good luck that the whole pile of junk didn't give way and wash us out to sea like logs down the crapper before we even got here.

I can't help but wonder how long that luck is going to last. How long those *windowpanes* are going to last. Something creaks, way overhead: a billion tonnes of water looking for a way in.

And in those instants I've wasted staring like an idiot, they hose down the elevator with so much lead I take five random hits to the chest.

They don't get through. They *do* knock me back against the wall of the elevator, though, and my head back into the game. Hazel Six has obviously called ahead for reservations, and invisibility isn't much of an edge when every gun in the place knows you're somewhere in a box two meters square. I crank the N2's strength setting and jump into the lobby like a frog on a trampoline.

I take out two of those CELLulite fuckwits before I even hit the floor. But there are six left, my cloak is down, and public lobbies are not what you would call *rich in available cover*.

I bounce off the wall, make it to the back side of the security desk, come down hard on some merc who evidently thought he had dibs on the spot. The air is fucking *incandescent* with crossfire, and I'm almost wishing that these guys were better shots because half the rounds that don't hit me are smacking into the windows. Spiderwebs are cracking through the glass everywhere I look. I can't believe the windows haven't shattered yet.

Fortunately, fragging CELL asses and covering my own is a full-time job. My inner eight-year-old can take a number. And believe it or not, when the dust finally settles and I am the Last Corpse Standing, that whole round wall of windows is *still* keeping the water at bay. Half a dozen panes are almost opaque, they're so shot through with cracks; there are more trickles and rivulets and needles of spray than I can count. But there's a whole orphaned chunk of the Atlantic leaning against those windows, and goddamn it, they're *holding*.

Lockhart's gone offline. Or maybe he's just sulking because I wiped the floor with his toy soldiers. Hargreave keeps the flame alive, though, riding my ass to reboot the upper-level elevators from the main desk. I still can't take my eyes off the windows, off all that dark heavy water piled up on the other side, but Hargreave nags reassuringly in my ear: No need for concern, supernanoglass, guaranteed floodproof. Go on, get over to the desk, reboot the system. What could possibly go wrong?

I go over to the desk. A couple of brain-dead monitors flash test patterns at me.

Something goes wrong.

I hear it before I see it. Glass against metal; ice cracking on the surface of a frozen lake. A sharp, cutting sound, halfway between a crack and a *ping*.

Half a dozen windowpanes split from side to side. Water sprays in fine sheets of mist.

Something's moving out there in the murk, something *big*. I can't even make out a silhouette; it's hidden behind the mud and shit swirling up off the street.

Just past the front doors, three cars lift majestically off the bottom, turn slowly end-over-end, then settle back down in billowing clouds of mud.

More windows crack. Two trickles upgrade to *small waterfall* status. Inner eight-year-old's eyes go wide, watching the water run down the inside of the panes; but then motion catches my eye again and drags it back down to street level.

Something's standing on the bottom, just the other side of the glass. It towers over the muddy cumulus boiling around its legs. It looks in at me—*down* at me—with one glowing vertical slit of an eye.

It *crouches*.

Every pane in front of the thing shatters in an instant. The ocean reaches in with big battering fists and takes me away.

The impact doesn't knock me out this time. I wish it had.

I am deadwood, man. I am flotsam *and* jetsam. I am a fly on the goddamn jet stream, and I have no say at all in where I'm going.

Maybe that saves my ass, I don't know. Maybe if I *had* managed to fight the current I would've ended up skewered on rebar or wedged under a bus until my rebreather gave out. But I'm just a speck in the current, carried by a million tonnes of water following the path of least resistance; and water tends to flow *around* the rocks in the road, not *into* them. It fires me through doorways already smashed open, shoots me down halls and out broken windows, swings me around corners like a rag doll but it doesn't smash me *into* anything. Way down in some sub-basement it finds a hole in the floor, slings me around it like a turd in a toilet bowl, flushes me down into a breached sewer pipe. Corrugated steel blurs past on all sides, and it goes on forever before spitting me out into—

—I don't know where, exactly. Water spills over my shoulders in a brown cascade, loses steam, subsides to a trickle. There's a strip of sky overhead, fractured walls of dirt and gravel and bed-rock looming on either side. Now that the deluge has tapered off I hear water running in rivulets down a thousand cracks and crevices. I'm at the bottom of a tiny canyon, a rift in yet another Manhattan street that's buckled and split and left me exposed like a grub dug out from under a rotten stump.

And all I can think is I made it, I made it. Dragged under-water, underground, away from air and sunlight, that stupid eight-year-old whiner inside trying to scream his fucking head off but I gagged him, I kept him down, I held it together. Not so scary this time; not fun by any stretch but at least I didn't panic, didn't even verge on it.

The whole fear-of-drowning thing. I'm almost getting used to it.

I listen to water lapping against concrete. I hear gulls scream-ing at one another. It's almost peaceful. I close my eyes.

"What a goddamn mess. Now of all times; those boardroom idiots."

I keep my eyes closed. Maybe it'll go away if I ignore it.

"Alcatraz, it seems I am facing a boardroom coup at the worst possible time. I can no longer control Lockhart or his forces. I am effectively under house arrest. And the Ceph are deploying in force. Until I can find some way to reverse this . . . palace revolution, our objectives are blocked. You must attempt to hold back the Ceph until I can stabilize the situation."

Oh, must I now.

"Good luck, son—I will be in touch."

Take your time, old man. Don't hurry on my account.

Wait: Chino.

If he got caught in that flood he could be nothing but teeth and strawberry jam by now. I wonder if—

An icon pops up center-right on the BUD: comm log from a restricted band. I sacc' PLAY.

"Alcatraz, if you can hear me—listen, man, I'm sorry. We can't hold here. Repeat, cannot hold here. The Squids are just *hammering* us. I'm pulling the squad back to Central Station. Get there if you can, man—we're going to need you."

I check the timestamp: ten minutes before the dam broke. If they were lucky, they got clear in time. Weird, though. I didn't know the N2 did voicemail. I wonder why I didn't hear it live.

Wait a second: I didn't say anything. I didn't even sacc' anything. All I did vis-à-vis Chino was *think* about the dude.

And you know, by this point I'm not even surprised anymore.

PILGRIMAGE

"This is Delta Six to base, we . . . backup now! . . . *civilians in tow, wounded . . . engaging . . . some kind of alien armored . . . sonic . . .*"

Rebar. Power lines. I-beams and buildings blocking the signal. Wherever Delta Six is holed up, I can't hear shit down here.

I get off my ass and start climbing.

"Delta Six, this is Echo Ten."

Echo's coming through clear, at least. Bad news for Delta; huge difference in signal strength probably means huge difference in location.

"We are en route to your position, but the streets are blocked. It's gonna take time to . . ."

I poke my head back above ground level. Delta Six's signal firms up:

"*We don't have time, Echo Ten!*"

Delta Six is losing it. Delta Six is screaming. And something else is screaming in the background, too, something that sounds a little like glass cracking on metal . . .

"You get here *now* or you're just gonna be counting our fucking *corpses!*"

SECOND serves up waypoints and sat fixes and triangulated guesswork. Echo Ten is still out in the boonies. I might just make it, though.

Shit.

I check what's left of my gear, ditch the scarab; the seawater's fucked the firing mechanism. Everything else seems good to go. GPS puts me about three or four klicks from the action, depending on the waypoints.

I start running. The farther uptown the higher the ground: I wade the occasional stretch but when my feet hit solid ground they burn city blocks like firewood. The topography's been radicalized up here: Buildings lean into one another, flat streets shaken into corduroy, whole blocks just kind of *pushed back* and piled up against the terrain behind. Madison Square Park is a steaming swamp—the tops of cabs and SUVs rise above the water like sunroofed boulders. One of the Staten Island ferries is jammed up at a crazy-ass angle against the buildings on the northern perimeter; I never realized before how huge those things are. You gotta wonder how many buildings *that* bad boy took out on its way uptown.

I keep moving as north as the terrain will let me. Delta Six fades in and out at the whim of whatever obstacles happen to be fucking with the freq at any given moment. Bad news from Central; something's going on there and it's not going well, but I can't tell any more than that. Some kind of running battle seems to be moving east, and the news from that quarter is no cause for joy, either. But I still take heart because hey, at least the battle's still *on*, right? They haven't been squashed like bugs yet; at least some of them are still kicking after being in the thick of it for half an hour or more, and I'm thinking that's no small accomplishment. I know what these guys are up against.

Thought I did, anyway.

Something's making the ground shake, just a little. I see it more than feel it: ripples in puddles, like a stone's been dropped when no stone has. My reflection shivering in some miracle windowpane that hasn't shattered yet. Aftershocks, I think. I'm moving too fast to feel anything through my boots, so I stop for a few moments to get a sense of the seismo. Nothing. The ground's rock-solid under my feet—which is, now that I think of it, even weirder.

Bompf.

Now that I *did* feel, just barely: a single pulse through the asphalt. A short sharp shock; not like any seismic rebound *I've* ever felt, and I pulled the Ring of Fire tour for a solid year. This felt more like an impact tremor.

An impact of steel against glass.

Delta Six isn't talking. Or at least I'm not hearing them. I hope it's just another radio shadow, but I pick up the pace anyway. GPS leads me up Fifth, around a corner, and smack-fucking-dab into a dead end.

Can't really blame the system for not knowing a building had collapsed across the alley. The realtime updates haven't refreshed since the wave—it takes a lot to swamp the GoogleSat servers but I'm guessing a sudden massive rewrite of the whole lower mainland's geography might do it—and even plain old GPS gets iffy with all these leaning towers blocking out the sky. Nav's been falling back on OLR and inertia for hours now, to take up the slack. But there it is: a pile of rubble that used to be an office tower, right between me and where I have to be.

The building it's fallen against is still standing, though. There's a loading dock off to one side that I don't even have to force my way into; any one of a thousand shocks has blown the door off its rollers and halfway into the street. I'm up on the dock with a single bound.

A glassy *ping.*

Even louder, this time. And not an impact tremor, not the usual kind. If I was underwater I'd compare it to high-freq sonar, you know, like those tests that drove all the whales crazy a few years back. I'm not underwater, and air isn't *nearly* dense enough to conduct a p-wave that intense anyway, but still: Whatever's making that noise sounds like a submarine on steroids.

Or maybe like some kind of one-eyed monstrosity striding across the bottom of a flood zone.

I'm in the loading bay. I'm in the shipping manager's office; just like the one I worked in back during my school days except the Golden Showers centerfold is full-motion 3-D now (the whole damn building's dark but that golden girl keeps glowing and spreading her legs every time you walk past, and she'll probably be doing it for the Ceph a year from now if those flatcells are as good as everyone says). I'm in some kind of dark hallway, a tunnel; maybe I hear the scuttling of little tick feet but nothing jumps out at me. Three lefts, two rights, one wrong turn into the ladies' room and there's an emergency exit sign shining in my eyes like a beacon of blood-red hope. I should be three blocks from the action, four at the outside. I kick out the door.

And wouldn't you know it, the action has come to me.

You know that poem. *Give me your tired, your poor. Your homeless, your wretched refuse. Give me your junkies, your yuppies, your headbangers, your white-collar tapeworms, your priests and your pedophiles.*

Yeah, I may be taking a few liberties. But there they all are, a whole fucking avalanche of humanity, pouring around the corner from the Avenue of the Americas. A lot of them are bleeding—from the ears, the nose, some of them are even bleeding from the *eyes*. Almost all of them are screaming. And you know what my first reaction is?

Relief.

None of them are infected, you see. They're scared out of

their fucking minds, every last one of them is injured in one way or another—but behind the blood and the noise they all look *human*. No lumpy potato sacks full of tumors, no eye sockets jam-packed with squirming hamburger, no crazy-ass religious ecstasy or hallelujahs for the corruption of the flesh. The spore hasn't got this far yet. These are just regular run-of-the-mill victims of war, scared to death and probably dead inside the hour, but next to what I've seen today this is *nothing*. I can deal with this. I'm *glad* to deal with this. This panicked endless mob washes around me, running, staggering, falling, and it's all so familiar it's almost like being *home*.

And then that *sound* hits again, that Crystal-Godzilla sonar, and even inside the suit I go deaf in the aftermath. People are still screaming, I can still see their mouths making the right shapes, but all I can hear is this weird low-pressure *trough* in the soundscape, this kind of dull roar sucking up every other sound in the wake of that single earsplitting *PING*.

A little girl's eyes explode right in front of me. She can't be more than eight. She doesn't even stop running; she's past me and gone in a gory New York second and I don't even turn around because what kind of sick fuck would go out of his way to watch a blind girl get trampled to death?

This wicked little part of me that never seemed to exist before today, this curious little psycho that doesn't feel and can't stop thinking, wonders why just this one little girl and no one else. Figures it must be the size of the head, the diameter of the eyeball in relation to the wavelength or something. Harmonic resonance. But it also figures that pulse is gonna be taking out more than little girls at close range. I'm betting anybody within fifty meters is lying in the street with their skulls blown apart.

A Bulldog comes screeching around the corner on two wheels, the grunt on the roof gun hanging on for dear life and firing back at something farther up the avenue. He can't keep it up; the vehicle crashes back down on all fours and he goes flying. The driver does his best to keep from collateraling the crowd but the Bulldog still manages to sideswipe half a dozen civilians on its way into the jewelry store across the street.

Something stalks into view around the corner. It stands eight meters tall if it's an inch.

I've seen it before. But this is the first time I've *seen* it.

Three legs, double-jointed things with clawed metal feet; just one of those *talons* is almost as big as a man. The carapace is a cross between a cockroach and a B-2; a wedge, a great fucking arrowhead with cannons sticking out the front end like fangs.

Doesn't use those big guns, though. Not at first. It *crouches* and this, this *column* rises out of its back: a red glowing cylinder, vertically segmented, like a space heater the size of a gazebo. It rises slowly, almost lazily. Think of someone pulling back on a crossbow before releasing the string.

PING.

Every window with so much as a splinter in the frame explodes. Cars and storefronts shriek for blocks in every direction. A blizzard of glass rains down on the street, dust and daggers and great jagged sheets; it skewers the living and the dead, takes off hands and limbs neat as a laser. It seems like hours before all that slicing and dicing tapers off; the towers of Sixth Avenue still have a *lot* of windows. By the time it's over the living have fled; the dead are dismembered; and I'm the only one left in between.

The monster twists on those giant tripod legs and bends down to look at me.

It's a smart motherfucker. It sees through my best tricks. I wrap myself in my cloak of invisibility and somehow it knows just where to fire. I hide behind pillars and billboards and it lobs some kind of plasma grenade into its blind spots, coolly flushes its quarry instead of stomping down streets and alleyways in hot pursuit.

It turns into a game of tag. I can take maybe a hit or two from that acoustic death ray without bursting like a grape—we share common ancestry, this pinger and I, and maybe we're a little bit immune to each other's venom—but I'm pretty sure that three blasts would lay me out and a fourth would kill me, assuming this monster didn't just decide to squash me flat with one of those big clawed feet instead. And nothing I've got up my sleeve seems to do more than scratch the paint on its hood ornament. So I lob a sticky mine and fade back around the corner before I even see if I scored. I drop a proximity mine and dive through a manhole while three floors of office crumble to dust on the other side of the street. I start to see patterns: The pinger has a habit of strafing the air with high-frequency click bursts, especially when it can't see me.

It's *echolocating*. No wonder the damn cloak doesn't work.

It's not cat-and-mouse: it's saber-toothed-tiger-and-mouse, it's *T.-fucking-rex-*and-mouse. And that dinosaur may have me outgunned a hundred times over, and it may be able to beat my ass on the straightaway, but it's a big fucking ship and those things turn *slowly*. It's got cannons that even CELL would trade half its annual profit margin for, but it can only fire them *forward*. I can't outrun the monster but I can outmaneuver it, dip and weave and jump from ground to rooftop and back again. It would have slaughtered me a dozen times if I hadn't gotten out of the way a split second before it let loose.

And all the time I'm bobbing and dodging and running between its legs, I'm scratching the paint on the hood ornament. After a while the hood ornament falls off.

I start scratching other parts.

Now some of the other mice start poking their heads up, make the most of the diversion. The pinger charges down the street with its sights fixed firmly on my retreating ass, and a line of flechettes hemstitches across its flank from the carpet store across the street. Some brazen glorious asshole with nothing to save his balls but standard-issue camo and a pair of mirrorshades jumps down from the second floor and gives this felching tripod the *finger*, I shit you not, and takes off around the corner. The pinger takes the bait and chases that beautiful bastard onto the biggest spread of proximity mines you ever saw outside an Israeli payback party.

You know what happens when all those scratches finally strip paint down to the primer? You start scratching the *metal*.

It's a running battle, man, it's a long fucking battle, all of us mice against one big metal dinosaur, and it may be death by a thousand cuts but it's the JAW that finally brings it down. A single rocket, right under the carapace where the legs plug in. It *blooms*, Roger, like a flower opening in the morning, it blooms into this great ball of crimson electricity like someone red-shifted the northern lights. The pinger *groans*, it staggers; it starts to fall, puts out one leg to brace itself and the leg just snaps clean off. That big metal mother goes down like a mountain sliding into the sea.

Delta Six love me to death. I'm the guy who scored the winning touchdown. They slap my back. They like my moves. They say they could really use me back at Central. They call me *suit guy*, and we shoot some well-deserved shit at those fucking Pentagon brass: *Hey, lucky for us the flood wiped the Ceph off the board, yeah, things could be really nasty if those mofos were still around.*

And then we hear something.

I don't know quite how to describe it. A kind of breathy sound, a *hooting* sound, drifting over the rooftops and down through skyscraper canyons. It seems to come from everywhere and nowhere, an icy, undead whisper. I tell myself that all the hairs on my forearms have not just stood up.

Everyone falls silent as hunted rabbits.

"Dear God," someone whispers when the sound has stopped. "What *is* that?"

The CO steps in before that shit can spread: "Stop standing there with your dicks in your hands, people! Sweep for survivors! Fifteen minutes, tops! Then we go find out what's making that noise, and kick its ass!"

It's gotta be a joke, of course. But the delivery's so deadpan you'd never know it.

Broadcast intercept: "Radio Free Manhattan," Pirate signal, 23/08/2023 17:52
1610 kHz (unsecured AM)
Source: CPL. EDWARD "TRUTH" NEWTON, USMC (RET.)
(confirmed via voiceprint comparison with public archives)

Newton:	Oh, man—this, you gotta hear. Remember that little wave swept on through the downtown a few hours back? All the work of those pesky tentacular invaders from another star? Well, we're getting calls in from civilians across Midtown now, and what they got to say, you got to hear:
Voice #1:	Jets, man! I heard jets! Saw the vapor trails. I been hiding out in this city for a solid week now, I know what the Squid airborne sound like. This wasn't no alien aircraft, man, our own bombers did this to us!
Voice #2:	Saw them for sure, Eddie. Air force jets, clear as day. Operational height, 'bout a minute before we heard the blast. It had to be them.

Newton: You getting this, people? That's—midway through a marine evac operation, some pencil-neck at the DoD decides, just fucking decides, that we are all, from 16th Street on down, expendable assets or hey, just very good swimmers. Well, hell, yeah—why not? All the rich folks? They choppered out of here last week with the mayor and the DA. So what's left that matters? Just us, people, the dregs and the working stiffs. Well, I got a message for all you dregs still alive out there. Remember this—and stay alive to tell the tale. And—hey, we got a call coming in hot off the grid. Hello caller—who we got here?

Williams: Yeah, Eddie, this is Wayne Williams again.

Newton: Hey, Wayne. Welcome back. How you doin', man?

Williams: Yeah, we made it into Midtown. And, listen, there's marines here, just like you said. I got one right here, and get this, Eddie—he wants to talk to you.

O'Brian: This is Gunnery Sergeant O'Brian, US Marines. You that Radio Free Manhattan asshole?

Williams: Sir, yes sir—I am exactly that asshole.

O'Brian: Then I got a job for you. Get this message out, stat. Colonel Barclay's evacuation will still proceed, despite the flood. Repeat, the evacuation will proceed. Anyone wanting to get out of this city had better haul ass to Central Station. We have outlying squads

	across Midtown—make yourselves known to them, and they will help as much as they can. That is all. O'Brian out.
Williams:	Holy fucking shit! Got that, people? Evac ongoing! Get your asses in gear. Now, we got reports earlier from Wayne and other witnesses up that way saying all this water shallows out around 23rd Street. Ain't gonna be easy, the ground is seriously fucked up, but it's the only way you got, so take a marine vet's advice here—improvise, adapt, overcome. Get to Central Station however you can! And do not stop to shop for shoes. This is your ticket out of here, people. Don't lose it!

Transcript ends.

Of course, getting there is half the fun.

I listen to my new friends as we head out, pick up a few in-sights. The local chain of command is down to a few rusty links by now. Army, airborne, USMC—hell, even the NYPD and the fire department have gone seriously entropic from the top down. What's left is a mash-up of half a dozen uniforms and half a dozen jurisdictions, deserters and rogues and decent shits who would still do the right thing if only they could get a straight answer from an authorized CO. But over the past few days these lost souls have found their center, their father figure, their beacon of command in the Shitstorm of the Apocalypse.

I hear him on the ether as we slog past 29th and Broadway: "This is Colonel Barclay to all marine fire teams at the primary and secondary perimeters! I want a controlled fallback to the terminus by stages, regrouping as you go! Our objective is full evac of civilians and wounded, and we will hold this station until it's done! You have at most one hour to make your way back here; after that you're going to be walking home."

He doesn't sound like the Second Coming. He sounds like he thinks the world's going to lie down on the job the moment he drops his voice below fifty decibels. But Chino's vouched for the man, and every surviving jarhead and gravel-pounder seems to back him up: Sherman Barclay is the only reason the Ceph are still facing any organized resistance at all. Without him, we'd all be Lord of the Flies by now.

Central Station is well above the flood zone; everything north of 26th stayed high and dry. *Too* dry, actually: Carbon and clouds water down what's left of the late-afternoon sun, and coming up Sixth we can see the storefronts glowing from five blocks away. A couple of the guys start coughing as we cross 36th—

"Smell that? What the fuck *is* that?"

—and I crank open my hepafilter to get a whiff for myself. Not the usual taste of a city on fire; I've smelled that a hundred times since I joined up, it sits in the back of your throat and stings your eyes like an old friend. The smell of *this* great burning is different, somehow. More—acrid. It's not completely unfamiliar, though. I've smelled it once before, down in Texas during the Secession Riots. Mob was torching a publisher's warehouse full of science texts.

Oh, yes. I know that smell.

"This is Charlie Seven. The western approach is compromised. We are pinned down at the library on Fifth and West 42nd. We've got dozens of civilians here. Requesting fire support to get 'em through to the station."

The smell of burning books.

We cross East 40th and into the ragged remains of a green

space. GPS serves up BRYANT PARK: in better days a broad perimeter of trees around a central lawn. Kindling, now, and a trampled kill zone with no cover at all. The New York Library looms on the other side, a great stone edifice slotted with narrow windows fifteen meters high; a whole other set of windows, glassed arches eight meters tall, sits on top of those. I can see the faces jammed in behind them.

In the background, Barclay's deploying reinforcements to our location.

Closer to home, the Ceph are doing the same.

It's a mess. The library's full of soldiers and civilians but we can't even get across the goddamn street without some dropship raining Squids and hellfire onto our heads. We take cover in a converted apartment complex across the street and even in there I get my ass shot at, by fellow *backbones* no less: the requisite asshole from Retard Six thinks I look like *one of them.*

I don't know how many got out of the library before the dropship bombs the shit out of it. I don't know if *any* did; we're coming in from the back, don't have any kind of bead on the main entrance. But suddenly the whole place just goes up. The windows blow out, the ceiling crashes in, fire everywhere.

I didn't even know stone *could* burn like that.

It doesn't kill everyone inside, not immediately. You can hear faint screaming over the flames. We're supposed to have cover by now—Charlie Company's got a missile battery across the park but the guy manning it is either dead or taking a bathroom break, and whenever anyone tries to cut across the park they get mowed down from on high. We finally make it, get the turret back online, even take down that motherfucking dropship, but by then the voices have long since lost out to the flames.

We push on anyway, partly because Hey, there's always a

chance, but also because we're taking heavy ground fire from behind and we're literally being driven forward. We fight rearguard
across the park, and a few marines—that guy from Retard Six, for
one—even make it to the back steps with me. But the place is a
fucking inferno; they'd be toast two steps past the threshold. I
leave them to find their own way around.

First time I've ever been in a library in my life. I gotta say,
Roger, I really don't see the appeal.

There are places even I can't go: stone glowing red, smoke so
thick there just isn't any point. I try thermal but it's even worse,
like being caught in a false-color blizzard. Lots of bodies, black
no matter *what* wavelength you use to look at them. Steam rises
from some of those mouths, from corpses still wet enough to
boil inside. They sizzle on the floor like bacon. Some are charcoal
already. They break and crumble and burst into pieces when you
trip over them.

I hear voices. At first I think I'm hallucinating. But I follow
them anyway, to some shattered stairwell where a freak cross-draft
blows away enough of the smoke and the heat to keep the people
huddled there from dying quite as fast. I turn a small hole in the
wall into a bigger one and they stagger outside, coughing, to take
their chances with the Ceph.

But it gives me an idea: Forget the people. Key on the *habi-
tat*. Don't waste time looking for life signs, look for those few,
far-between places where life signs are possible. I toggle back to
thermal and yeah, the psychedelic hurricane is still distracting as
hell, but now that I know what to look for I can see dark patches
here and there in the static, little sunspots of less-than-killing heat.

Roger, I got some of them out. Four marines, a few firefight-
ers, maybe half a dozen civilians. Less than twenty all told, next
to Christ knows how many who burned to death. I lost count of
the corpses I passed in there, and I only covered a fraction of the
floor space.

But I got them out. I got them out.

And for a little while, being dead isn't so bad.

But only for a little while. Because yes, it's nice to save lives for a change instead of ending them—but even that doesn't really fill the emptiness inside.

And no, I'm not being maudlin. I mean that literally.

You think I don't know? I'll grant you I was a bit slow on the uptake back at Trinity, but I've had a lot of time to think since then. Hell, I've grown a lot more of whatever it is I think *with,* and you know what I remember? I remember those med techs in the basement saying I didn't have a heart.

That hurt.

I'll tell you what else I remember. Squiddie laying a bull's-eye on my chest the moment I crawled up onto Battery Park. I remember knowing beyond any shadow of a doubt that I was dying. I remember Prophet dragging me across the battlefield, stashing me in that warehouse, stripping himself out of this suit and bolting me into it. That took *time.* It wasn't even dawn when I got hit; when I woke up it was midmorning.

Tell me, Roger, do you think *you* could hang in that long without a functioning heart? I know I couldn't. So however shredded up I was back then, the ol' ticker was still beating. Had to be. And then just a few hours later they scan me outside Trinity and it's nowhere to be found.

Maybe it doesn't even stop with the heart. Maybe my lungs are gone, too, by now. My liver? My guts? How much of me's actually *left*—am I just a shell of bone and muscle around a whole lotta empty space? Put a zipper in front and I'd have one big honking extra allowance for carry-on, hmm?

You know what happened to them, Roger? (Ah, I see you don't. Something else your masters didn't tell you.) They got *recycled.* Because even this magical suit can't do everything. It's a nanotech miracle, it can turn blood into bone and water into wine, but it's gotta start with something, *capiche?* Needs raw material. Can't magic up mass out of nothing.

So the way I figure it, it had a *lot* of shit to fix and not enough bricks and mortar to go around, so it—triaged. Robbed Peter's heart to pay Peter's spinal cord. It can fill in for the plumbing, that's dead easy. Alcatraz doesn't need a bunch of pipes and pumps when CryNet Systems Nanosuit 2.0 is taking up the slack. But the central nervous system, now; that's a whole different pile of pigeons. You take away *that* stuff and there's no Alcatraz left to interface with. So this magic suit's been hollowing me out all this time, *mining* my expendable biomass to repair the more important systems. Maybe it's still at it, for all I know. Maybe it won't stop until there's nothing left but a brain and a couple of eyeballs and a mess of nerves hanging off the bottom.

Yes, I suppose that *would* be excessive. But maybe it's got other reasons, maybe physical repair is just part of what it's doing. It is a jealous skin, Roger, and it's already been dumped once. Prophet had to literally rip it from his flesh and blow his own brains out to be free of the fucking thing. Maybe the suit doesn't want to go through that again. Maybe it's whittling me down so I won't be able to—leave . . .

Just a machine, eh? *Just* a machine. Tell me, Roger, have you ever seen a *machine* that can do what this baby does? Do you know how it works? Because I can guarantee you that even Jacob Hargreave has only the vaguest goddamn clue, and he stole the damn thing.

Angry?

Not really, now that you mention it. I'm alive, after all—or at least, I'm not as dead as I would've been otherwise. On balance, it was a good trade. But it's a stupid question, Roger, a meaningless question. You should know that by now.

Editing anger out of the equation is dead simple for something that can turn hearts into minds.

After all this I get to Central Station. I just don't get to *stay*.

There's a makeshift convoy outside the front entrance to the library. There are Ceph, too, but there are always Ceph. We've learned to deal. We shoot at each other all the way along 42nd, but for once the backbones have the edge; we're closing on Central, we've got mines set up all over the place and defensive perimeters behind them, we *own* this neighborhood.

Except when we don't.

Turns out the Ceph have artillery, or something like it. The western approaches are a gauntlet of mortar fire raining all around the station. Once we get inside—after we've dodged the shells, and shouted down the usual friendly fire from paranoid trigger fingers, once we convince them we're all on the same side and get under cover and make it to the decon tunnel—before I can even sit down, a staff sergeant name of Ranier appears at my side and politely asks me to leave the premises again. Turns out Barclay's laid down some countermeasures to take out the Ceph bombardment. He's going to drop a building on them, or at least block their line of fire with one. But the plan's gone off the rails; something tripped the safety breakers, the demolition charges need to be reset manually, and the guy Echo Fifteen sent to do the job is trapped across the street with half his leg blown away. Ranier doesn't suppose that maybe *I'd* be willing to . . . ?

He's not quite that polite, of course. He's just firm enough to make sure I can't possibly interpret it as a request.

You know that line they feed you in boot camp, *You can relax when you're dead*? Complete bullshit.

So now I'm back outside and by now the day is done and the night is young. Ranier's considerate enough to call ahead and tell

Echo Fifteen to expect me; he even asks them not to shoot at me by mistake.

You're not going to believe this, but the hike down Park Avenue is almost—beautiful. The sky is a luminous orangey brown, big half-moon hanging over the skyline. I'm moving along one of those elevated rail lines where the subways break surface now and then, and I've got a great view. Ceph artillery arcs majestically overhead like comets in formation. They light up the whole zone, blue-white, radiant. A couple of them smack into the MetLife Building behind the station, and the electric ripples pulsing out from those hits look like fifty thousand volts of Saint Elmo's fire.

The only real drawback is, if the Ceph got Ranier's memo about not shooting at me, they've definitely circular-filed it. They've got their own turf right next door, their own perimeter, and it is sewn up so tight it squeaks. By the time I get through I've got a whole lot more respect for Echo Fifteen; there's no goddamn way I would've made it that far without a cloak.

I find them a dozen dead Squids later, in a shot-up diner a few blocks down Park Avenue. They point me to their point man, Torres, stuck in a hotel three buildings farther down and five floors up. Torres is still clutching the detonator when I get to him, sprawled on the floor with ammo and blasting caps and a couple of Bren guns scattered around like empties. He looks like the lone survivor of a high-octane frat party.

"Hey, man, good to see you. Help yourself to some gear." He's in pretty good spirits for a guy trapped behind enemy lines with one leg out of commission. Must have been some primo shit in the empty hypo sticking out of his thigh.

We're hunkered down in a corridor that runs around the edge of the floor, shot-up drywall at our backs, shot-out windows in front of us, and perfect line-of-sight to the target: ONYX Electronics, a twelve-story brownstone with a gaping four-story bite already taken out of it halfway up. It's kitty-corner to our position, and the intersection between is a ninja's wet dream: cover everywhere, cars, upended slabs of roadway, even a couple of subway cars teetering on rails hacked off at the edge of an overpass.

Torres takes it in with a wave of his hand: "As you can see, I have got myself a ringside seat. And I am well and truly pissed that the main event canceled after I went to all this trouble to get tickets. I think all the seismic activity must've tripped the breakers or something. I'd go back and reset 'em myself, but—" He pulls the hypo out of his leg, grins at me with a row of bleached teeth and one very stylish gold incisor. Little gemstone or optical circuit or something embedded in there. "We set three charges down in the parking garage. Once I get a green on all three, you've got a New York minute to get yourself clear, but man, just *look* at all the cover I made for you."

He knuckle-bumps me. Must be older than he looks. "You can thank me later. Getting in should be easy."

It is. So's getting out again afterward.

Sitting on the fifth floor of a bombed-out Hilton, waiting for the guy in the magic suit to come back? Not so much.

Maybe one of the reasons I got in and out so easy is because every damn Squid in the neighborhood was gunning for Torres.

It makes sense. I mean, who knows how those spineless bastards think, but Torres was the one who planted the charges. Torres was the one with the detonator. Anyone—any*thing* with a set of eyes on the ground could have figured he was the linchpin. Not to mention the weak link.

All I know is, about two seconds after Torres radios, "That's it, man! Green across!" Echo Fifteen starts taking fire.

Torres calls back to Barclay: He's arming the detonators but he's under attack and needs covering fire. But the rest of Fifteen's already gone rearguard under the Ceph assault. Barclay calls me up: Tag, you're it.

'Sokay. I was in the neighborhood anyhow.

I'm barely out of the ONYX before I know how it's going to end, how *Torres* is going to end. Right now he's scared shitless because he's still afraid to die, and he's afraid to die because he still thinks he might live: "Ah fuck, they're flooding the building! Covering fire, *I need covering*—"

But the only cover he's got is me, and I'm down on ground level with my back to a shot-up taxi while Squiddie shoots at me along three separate vectors. By the time I take two of them out Torres has learned the facts of life, swallowed them whole, and processed them in what, thirty seconds? A minute?

He's not calling for backup anymore. He's not talking to us at all. He's talking to *them*—

"Come on, you motherfuckers! *Come on!*"

—and *fuck it*, I don't care what the odds are and I don't care if there's still something out there with a bead on me, I'm up and running, zig and zag and *jump* while Study's ammo streaks past and Torres rages in my headset, one-legged Torres, Torres the gimp, and his last furious act of defiance and that *rage*, man, that absolute blood-boiling rage when you know you've done every last thing any soldier could and it's *not enough,* the fuckers just keep coming and the most you can do is check out with your teeth buried in something's throat.

I'm almost back at the building when I see him coming down to meet me.

He hits the pavement—I hear every bone shatter from ten meters away—and he *bounces*. He flips in midair, flops like a rag doll, comes down again, smears blood and guts across the asphalt as a fire hydrant catches him in the spine. It stops him dead, folds him in half like a broken branch.

Suddenly the freq is jammed with fucktards specializing in the blindingly goddamn obvious, *Torres is down* and *We lost Torres* and I *know* assholes, I saw him die, he's right here in front of me. Even Barclay gets in on the chorus, *We lost Torres, Alcatraz, you need to find that detonator.*

But he's wrong about that. I know exactly where the detonator is. I'm looking right at it. It's clenched in Torres's left fist. He hung on to it right down into hell and gone.

He brought it to me.

I pry his fingers open. I pull it free: the size of a staple gun, a pack of smokes. Torres died with his thumb pressed on the stud; ONYX stays standing across the street, even though all three lights are green. I squeeze the trigger the way a man would; nothing happens. Something's jammed in there.

I squeeze the trigger the way Golem Boy, the way False Prophet would. Something snaps. I hear a *click.*

Across the square, ONYX *rumbles.*

It lights up at its base, flickers like sheet lightning. It *shivers,* from street level all the way up to that blue neon logo on the roof; it slumps in on itself. Sparks explode at its crown: ONYX Electronics shatters into three neon scribbles and goes dark. The whole damn building splits down the middle as it falls; light fixtures and torn wiring light it up from the inside.

And back on this side of the street, something's following Torres down from the fifth floor.

It shatters the pavement in front of me as it lands: a tank on legs, cannons for arms, compound eyes like clusters of sodium spotlights. A Ceph Heavy, and if these garden slugs are even capable of anything approaching human emotion, this one is *pissed.* It doesn't even bother shooting at me with those cannons; it *backhands* me with them instead, knocks me halfway across the street as ONYX collapses in a heap over its shoulder. I reach for my weapon but there's a couple of tonnes of angry mechanized jelly in the way. The Ceph raises one of its cannons, aims. I stare down a muzzle big enough to fit my head into.

And one of those teetering subway cars, dislodged by the death throes of the building across the way, lurches down off its embankment and squashes my nemesis like a bug.

The Echoes give me a victory lap with pom-poms and cheerleaders all the way back to Central, cover my ass against the vindictive sniping of a bunch of Squids whose biggest gun has just lost line-of-sight. But when they send me around to the back entrance I get the usual grief from the usual hopped-up goon: the spotlight in the face, the gun barrel, the usual *looks like them* bullshit. I almost dance with the fucker on general principles—show him firsthand how much ice his yapping-poodle act cuts against a dead man wired into battle tech so far ahead of the curve he couldn't see it with the fucking Hubble—but his CO calls him off. Nathan Gould, apparently, says I'm one of the good guys.

I let the poodle live. You're no Sergeant Torres, asshole.

The wounded are stacked up along the halls before I even make it to the loading bay. Some civilian with more heart than brains—and a stage-one infection to boot—tries to get to his wife through a checkpoint marine and gets thrown back on his ass for his trouble. I hear screaming in the distance; a jarhead faces off against two medics in hazmat suits. *There's nothing wrong with me, man, I feel fine. This is bullshit.* I pass a man on a cot muttering, *Jesus, it's eating me, I can feel it eating me.* He looks fine to me.

I keep walking. The medics have it. The medics have it.

There's that other kind of ambience, too, of course, the kind I've gotten too damn familiar with over the past day or so:

. . . there a man in there?

Sure doesn't move *like a man . . .*

What, we've got robots fighting for us now?

I keep walking.

This is where all roads lead: a decontamination checkpoint manned by more hazmat humanoids, razor wire strung out across the bars and turnstiles that herded commuters back in better days. A couple of CELLulites cool their heels in a holding cage off to the left, arguing with the marine on the other side of the bars. I listen in while a med tech passes some kind of UV wand over the N2: used to be army, one of the mercs is saying. Nine years. Just like you. But the guard isn't buying it: Whatever you were in the good ol' days, you're private now. RHIP *revoked*, assholes.

You tell 'em, Sergeant.

Interesting that CELL's been reclassified to arrest-on-sight, though. Maybe Hargreave's got his groove back.

Dr. Hazmat waves me through; the gate swings open behind him. Decon air lock on the other side sprays me with disinfectant and Christ knows what else. The far hatch hisses open a crack; I recognize the voice that wafts through. A little rougher, perhaps. A little more worn-out.

I push the hatch open and run smack into Chino—"Hey man, glad you made it!"—but he's not the man I'm looking for. Colonel Sherman Barclay stands in a basement grotto of cracked marble and cement, surrounded by cots and supply crates and jacked vending machines. His eyes flicker in my direction, but he doesn't miss a beat; he's in the middle of instructing one Nathan Gould on the subtleties of civilian status in a city under martial law. From the set of Barclay's jaw I'd have to say that Gould is proving to be a slow learner.

They both turn to me at the same time. Gould's all hail-fellow-well-met; I think he's just glad to have an excuse to get out of remedial class. Barclay's a little more restrained. "Good to have you aboard, marine. My men speak highly of you." He pauses, almost smiling. "Shit, most of 'em are downright *scared* of you."

Really. I hadn't noticed.

Colonel Sherman Barclay in one word: *tired.*

He hides it well enough from the troops. Turns that bone-deep weariness around and serves it up as the eye of the storm, the deep pool of calm in the middle of Armageddon. His men swarm around him like ants on uppers; he fields their questions and feeds them commands and he never breaks character once. Maybe one of the reasons he's so exhausted is because of all the needy terrified grunts feeding off him.

It's a good act, and it keeps his troops together in a cesspool that should by rights have us all shitting our pants and heading for the hills, but you can see the signs if you've got the right accessories. You can see the stress lines crinkling the eyes. You can thermal past the three-day growth of stubble and catch that involuntary tic at the corner of his mouth, that nervous little spasm nobody else seems to notice. He's good, he's very good, but he doesn't fool Alky, False Prophet, and the Holy Ghost. We see right through him.

It's okay, though. He's holding it together, one weary-ass cocksucker outmatched and outgunned by monsters from the stars, and he doesn't bitch about the fates or complain about his bosses, he just buckles down and does the fucking job as best he can. And after the Nathan Goulds and the Jacob Hargreaves and the Commander fucking Lockharts, it is a nice goddamn change.

And God bless him, he doesn't even break character for Gould, although nobody here would blame him if he just hauled loose and belted the little geek into next Tuesday. No, he listens as we follow him through the huddled knots of refugees, down the endless rows of makeshift cots for the wounded, past the doors of prefab refrigerators and crematoriums waiting for the turnover. He listens as Gould tells him how to do his job: Gotta find Hargreave. Hargreave has the answers. Go to Roosevelt Island, bring him out, by any means necessary. Hargreave Hargreave Hargreave.

Barclay shakes his head, and continues his rounds, and says nothing. Gould raises his hands, exasperated. I brush past him.

He pokes me from behind.

Suddenly I'm facing him; suddenly my fists are clenched. I can feel synthetic muscles cording up my forearms. Gould doesn't even notice. He's plugged something into my spinal socket, and he's only got eyes for the readout: "Fucking military mind-set, man. If I can't tell him, maybe I can *show* him."

Yes, Gould, show him. Show him my black box and my deep-layer protocols, show him my secret antidote to the spore.

"I scammed this little reader out of the CELL lab when no one was looking. It's not much, but at least we can access the op logs . . ."

And why don't you show him what's left of my heart while you're at it. Why don't you show him the great fucking hole where my left lung used to be.

"Wait a minute, that's not right . . ."

Why don't you show him that I'm fucking *dead*, Gould, since you couldn't be bothered to fill *me* in on that little detail when you had the chance. Why don't you—

"Holy shit. Holy *fucking shit.*"

Finally he looks up, but he still doesn't see what's in front of him. He doesn't see my face through the visor, he doesn't see how close I am to putting his head through the wall. I don't know what he sees, exactly.

But whatever it is, it's bright enough to leave him blind.

"Man, what have *you* been up to today?" he murmurs, and there's something like awe in his voice.

He grabs Barclay coming back the other way. "You *have* to go to Prism."

"No."

"I know how to beat the Ceph!"

That gets Barclay's attention.

"I've been a complete idiot," Gould says.

Barclay does not argue the point. "*How*, exactly, can we beat the Ceph?"

"Give 'em AIDS!"

"That's not funny, Dr. Gould."

"Lupus, then. Rheumatoid arthritis. That's what this damn suit is—or at least, that's what it's turning into: an *autoimmune disease!*"

Barclay doesn't speak for a moment. Then: "Uh-huh."

"Dude, I am *serious*. I'm looking at the op logs right now, and you wouldn't *believe* the places Alcatraz has been hanging out over the past few hours. I don't have the equipment here to confirm this directly, but the only way this telemetry makes sense is if the whole damn suit is studded with receptor sites! I never even looked for them before, I mean why would I, why would you expect a battlefield prosthesis to—"

Barclay cuts in and to the chase: "Dr. Gould. So *what?*"

"The *spore*, Colonel! Didn't I say that? This artifact"—he jerks his thumb in my direction, a gesture that takes in the N2 but somehow excludes the meat sitting inside—"can interface with the spore!"

There are wounded, there are dead on all sides. There are orders to be given to those still standing. But Gould has ignited the dimmest spark of hope in Barclay's eyes. Barclay lets him run with it.

"The spore might not be a bioweapon after all," Gould continues. "At least, not *just* a bioweapon, not the way we'd understand it. If these readings are right it might almost be a kind of, of portable ecosystem. No, scratch that: more of an *external immune system*. It basically retcons the local environment to make it Ceph-friendly. That means taking out potentially dangerous macrofauna, of course—"

"Us, you mean," Barclay murmurs.

"—but I think it also filters out any microbes that might be incompatible with Ceph biology."

Barclay grunts softly. *"War of the Worlds."*

Gould blinks. "Huh?"

"Nineteenth-century novel," Barclay says. "Martians invade Earth, kick our asses, but then they all die of the common cold. No immunity. The Ceph have been around a lot longer than we thought; who knows, maybe the bastards read it."

"Uh, right." Gould hesitates; lifers who read ancient science fiction don't fit comfortably into his worldview. But he's back up and running in the next second: "Anyway, the spore's part of a synthetic metasystem, and the N2's derived from technology designed to interface with that metasystem, so we can, we can—" He snaps his fingers, suddenly inspired: "It's like gay rape in hanging flies!"

That shuts down conversation for about ten meters in all directions. Even the wounded stop moaning.

"Excuse me," Barclay says after a moment, "I must have misheard. I thought you said—"

But Gould's on a roll: "There are these insects, hanging flies. And sometimes a male will rape another male; just punch a hole right through the abdomen and ejaculate inside, you know? It's called traumatic insemination."

I don't know what parts of me the Ceph have blown away and I don't know how much else has been broken down to keep the rest of me going, but I know that at least my balls are still intact.

I know this because I can feel them crawling back up into my abdomen.

"But the *really* cool thing is, this is actually a viable reproductive strategy! Because the invading sperm doesn't just float around once it's in there, it *seeks out the gonads of the victim*! It infiltrates the testes so that when that victimized fly goes out and inseminates a female, he's actually *injecting someone else's sperm* into his mate! It's reproduction by proxy. You use someone else's delivery platform to spread *your* genetic code!"

Barclay purses his lips. "Get the spires working for us instead of them."

"Why not? When you come right down to it, we're all made out of meat."

Barclay looks at me, and looks away.

"But look, Colonel," Gould says, "the thing is, the system's nowhere near field-ready. According to the diagnostic logs, Pro—*Alcatraz* here tried to interface with some Cephtech earlier today and all the protocols locked up. The suit's trying to resequence on its own the best it can, but it needs help. It needs Hargreave, *we* need Hargreave. He's been three steps ahead of us the whole way. *This*"—Gould waves his stolen scanner—"this is basically a rectal thermometer. Prism's a state-of-the-art *hospital*. It's got hardware you won't find anywhere else on the planet, stuff built specifically for the N2. We need to take Prism, by force if necessary, and if Jack won't cooperate—well, that's what you have interrogators for."

It's a thread thrown to a drowning man. It's an oasis shimmering in the distance. Barclay is not the kind of man to let wishful thinking trump the facts on the ground, but we are all in such desperate need of good news.

For a moment or two I almost think he's going to go for it.

But then he looks around at the huddled civilians under his

protection, at the ragtag soldiers under his command, at the duct tape and chewing gum he's using to keep it all together, and I know exactly what lesson from Strategy 101 is going through his head: *Never* fight a war on two fronts. The oasis is a mirage.

Barclay shakes his head.

Gould won't let it go. "Colonel, listen—"

"I *have* been listening, Doctor. I can't spare the resources for an assault against a fortified paramilitary installation, not under these circumstances."

"But you have to—"

Barclay wheels on him, and the light in his eyes now is anything *but* hopeful. "What I *have to do*, Dr. Gould, is hold this location against a superior force that is perhaps ten minutes away from bringing the place down around our ears. What I have to do is keep a thousand civilians alive—including *you*, I might add—long enough to get them to safety. What I do *not* have to do is leave these people unprotected on the chance that your scientific theorizing isn't just a clever dive down the wrong alley."

His voice is dead level and cold as fucking Pluto. It doesn't rise a decibel. Gould steps back as though he's been slapped in the face.

Barclay turns to me. "I need you on defense. Put that suit to some *practical* use for a change. And *you*"—turning back to Gould—"are shipping out with the rest of the civilians."

Gould's still got some spine left: "You need me here, Colonel—I'm the only one who knows what you're up ag—"

Barclay waves Chino over from down the row. "Escort Dr. Gould downstairs. See that he gets away safely." He walks away, tapping his tacpad.

Gould grabs my arm as Chino grabs his: "He's wrong, man. Hargreave's our only hope. You've gotta take it upstairs."

Chino's not a huge guy, but you don't fuck with him. He wants Gould to move; Gould moves. But he manages one final appeal on the way out: "Go over his head if you have to! Tell them about the hanging flies! That'll convince them!"

"*Soldier.*"

I turn at the sound. Barclay stares unwaveringly at me across three rows of collateral damage.

"You're with me," he says.

Emergency Forensic Session on the Manhattan Incursion
CSIRA Blackbody Council
Pre-Testimony Interview, Partial Transcript, 27/08/2023
Subject: Nathan Gould

Excerpt begins:

Well, of course I didn't have the gear to pick up that kind of micro-structure, even when I was working at Prism. I was more of a systems man, right? Leave the nanohisto stuff to the grad students. But even if I had the equipment, I'd never have looked for it. I mean, why would you expect the skin of a battlefield prosthesis to come loaded with receptor proteins? Why the fuck would anybody build something like that?

You know, I don't think Hargreave himself knew what they were at first. That's got to be a problem whenever you reverse-engineer foreign tech. You don't really know *how* it works, you don't know what all the parts do. You can copy it, piece for piece, but you don't really understand it. It's like, Hey, all these parts fit together to make the best artificial muscle we've ever seen! What do these nanohex thingies do? No idea, but when you leave 'em out the damn thing doesn't work, so we better leave 'em in. And because you don't know about Charybdis's shall-we-say *unconventional* approach to microterra-forming, you've got no reason to expect that every piece of tech they ever built is going to have a spore interface right down at the molecular level. You just blindly cut and paste—and sure, you get a kick-ass piece of field armor, but you also get every square millimeter of the thing chock-full of receptor sites and who *knows* what signals they'll send when the wrong enzyme cozies up to their substrate?

It's not just the basic nanochem we're talking about here, either. It's the higher-level stuff, too, the neural meshes. Hargreave laid his own OS over the system, of course, he programmed that suit to his own specs. But you can be damn sure he didn't program it to fry his own machines when they got too intimate with the deep-layer protocols. The N2, it doesn't *like* people poking around down there. Like taking an angry cat to the vet. It hisses, it claws. Shorts out every server in the chain. Weirdest thing I ever saw. Something else Hargreave didn't count on: The thing's got its own agenda.

I pity the poor bastards who end up inside it. I've known two of them now. Decent dudes both, you know, Prophet and I go way back and he's—he *was*—100 percent stand-up. Alcatraz, now, I only just met him. We hung out for maybe two or three days, off and on, seemed like a decent guy. Kind of cryptic. Once or twice I caught him looking at me—I *assume* he was looking at me, you know, I've never even seen his face?—and I got this, this weird bottled-up sense he was going to explode, but—well, you know as well as I do.

The thing is, Alcatraz, Prophet—two more different jarheads you will never meet. Prophet never shut up, he was always joking around, and Alcatraz—well, let's just say, not much in the way of social skills. But put 'em in the N2 and even people that different start to—converge. EEG, voxprints, ACG gates, they all start looking the same after you've been in that suit for a while.

Nothing wrong with that, of course. It's just the system interface, doing what it does. But I'd be lying if I said it didn't bum me out just a little, you know, for the guys inside. You may think the N2 turns you into God's own jihadist, what with the induced bloodlust and the enhanced reflexes and the superconducting cognitive enhancements. But you're just feeling and doing what the damn thing's told you to. From the outside, sure, you look like an absolute ass-kicking wild man, but really you've been—

Tamed, I guess.

Tamed.

I follow Barclay into a service elevator. We go down.

"Your friend," he remarks, "is full of shit."

I haven't said a word all day. Right now it seems especially important to nod.

"He says he 'escaped in the chaos.' From Tara Strickland. I know Strickland, she was a decorated Navy SEAL before she went off the rails. You don't just 'escape' from that woman. I figure she cut him loose."

The cage jerks to a halt. The doors creak open.

"The question is, why?"

I follow Barclay into an observation gallery; it's obviously been a dingy sub-basement hole for decades, but I'm guessing the shattered windowpanes are a recent development. We stand on a carpet of broken glass and look down on one of the loading platforms. Civilians crowd nervously beside a chain of subway cars. A dozen marines stand by just in case, but this crowd looks about as violent as a yard full of field mice.

Of course, that could all change in a split second if Squiddie crashed the party. I've seen little old ladies throw babies to the wolves when their lives were threatened.

"Look at these people," Barclay says, and I'm not even sure he's talking to me. "I grew up in this town. Any one of them down there could be family. And if it boils down here like it did at Ling Shan . . ."

He shakes his head, pushes through a slatted door at the far end of the gallery. We pass into some kind of control room from the last century. A pendant light hangs from the center of the ceiling, a rusted metal cone with a bare bulb shining from its center. A bank of ancient CRTs glows on one wall, serving up securicam images from around the station. Two grunts sit at an antique command console stretching the length of the room, all buttons and manual switches and actual hardwired *lightbulbs* embedded in painted schematics of the New York subway system. One of them slaps the board: "Goddamn it, *nothing* works in this place."

I can sympathize. I thought this place was supposed to be brand new—it's only been, what, eight years since Black Tuesday? And only five since they finished rebuilding the station. But the tech down here is one step away from smoke signals and tin-can telephones. Obviously the reconstruction wasn't the grand and glorious megaproject they led us to believe; looks to me like they just rebuilt from the ground up. These sublevels have to be left over from the original.

"—was at Ling Shan, you know," Barclay's saying. "I saw Strickland—Tara's father—I saw him die. When Tara heard she just . . . cracked. Drink, drugs, a string of—unwise command decisions. Dishonorable discharge. And now she's queen bee at CELL, probably getting five times her old salary. Her father must be turning in his—"

Boom.

Dust drizzles from the ceiling. The overlight swings back and forth on its wire; the room fills with stretching swooping shadows.

"*Shit . . . ,*" someone breathes. Something with claws and cannons lurches across one of the CRTs.

"They're breaching the main hall, sir."

Barclay clicks into overdrive: "Martinez, get down on the platforms and tell Dickerson to roll the first train out. Our clock just stopped."

He turns to me.

"Stations, son. Main hall. Get up there and buy these people some time."

I get. Squiddie's running rampant by the time I get back upstairs. Grunts and Heavies stomp across the floor, shattering marble and mowing down Barclay's men like wheat. Stalkers scramble along the walls and ceiling, gigantic steel roaches, leaping on the unfit and tearing them limb from limb. There are sandbag barricades everywhere—*sandbags*, Roger, can you fucking believe it?—and the guys who take cover behind them do seem to be a bit better at staying alive but it's not because a few burlap sacks full of dirt can stop a Ceph shell worth shit. It's just that the Ceph haven't noticed them yet.

Doesn't take long for that to change, though.

Word from behind: The last of the wounded are out of the mezzanine. We fall back, regroup at the choke points on the stairs, hold fast a bit longer as the trains start to pull out of the tunnels below us. I'm asking myself, Barclay knows about the underground hives, right? He knows which lines are still intact and which ones have been ripped in half, these trains aren't going to barrel off into midair and plunge down into one of those brand-spanking-new rifts that are all the rage these days? And I tell myself not to be an asshole, of *course* they know, just do your fucking job and stop second-guessing the chain of command. But then I keep not running out of ammo, I keep picking up new clips and new scopes and preowned BFGs that hardly even got fired before the Ceph turned their owners into bloody blobs, and maybe I *should* be wondering about whatever tactical genius decided the best resupply strategy was to hope that those few miserable assholes still standing after five minutes have lots of bodies to scavenge.

We fall back.

We fall back.

We fall back.

Most of us have been left behind, by now: on the stairs, in the hall, in pieces. But they bought us the time we needed; we few survivors are at the north end of the loading platform now and there's not a civilian in sight. Squiddie's pressing hard on our ass but down there at the end of the platform there's one last train waiting, already half full, our names on the empty seats. Barclay's back at my side, fighting with the rest of us, and he's even more exhausted but he's not scared anymore. He even sends me a smile, not much, just a half-second curl at the corner of his mouth that says *We did it, son, we saved the civvies.*

I smile back, although of course he can't see it.

And then the ceiling crashes in.

Maybe it's Ceph artillery. Maybe the place has just taken as much abuse as it can, and something gave way. But suddenly there's rock and rebar and concrete everywhere, and anyone who still needs to, you know, *breathe* is coughing up dust and grit out of their lungs, and the viz is down to about three meters of pea soup. Barclay's shouting "Move out, *move out you assholes,* don't wait for us!" and I'm guessing that's the first order in a long time that anyone on that train actually *wants* to obey and there it goes, our lifeline, our ticket home, our reprieve for the days or hours or ten fucking minutes until the *next* assault drops us right back into another no-win scenario.

And behind us, out of the murk, I hear things scuttling and clattering and climbing over all the bodies we left behind.

*   *   *

I don't know how many of us are left. Eight or nine, maybe. Barclay, me, a handful of grunts I've never been formally introduced to. One of them remembers that there's a couple of jeeps parked upstairs in the main hall, if the Ceph haven't smashed them to shit.

All we have to do is waltz back up there and get them.

Sounds like a piss-poor idea to me. I'd rather take my chances in the subway tunnel. It's a safe retreat—or at least if it isn't, the higher-ups have their heads up their asses and we've just fed a thousand civilians to Squiddie—and we'd only be fighting rearguard, not wading back into a Ceph stronghold. But Barclay's leading this charge, and he's leading it back upstairs. Maybe he knows something I don't. Hope so. He doesn't strike me as an idiot. It'd be a drag to be disillusioned after knowing the man for all of an hour.

We lose another one going back up the stairs: Private First Class Andrea Gamji, her midsection shredded by enemy fire. I'm the last thing she ever sees; one second she's staring up into this goddamn faceplate and the next she's just *gone*, nothing at all left behind these dull frosted things she used to look out from. I rob her body and try to think of her as one of the lucky ones, keep my head down and dodge the incoming.

For about thirty seconds it goes better than I'd hoped. The hall isn't swarming; the handful of Ceph in evidence seem to be mopping up, not digging in. Now that the backbones have buggered off, they aren't all that interested in the territory.

They don't seem to be expecting us. We take out two stalkers, three grunts, and a Heavy without losing a man. We don't get cocky, though; the losses from Round One are scattered everywhere. Some of them are still moving.

Sure enough there's a Bulldog parked just outside, visible through one of the holes blasted in the wall. Barclay details a couple of bodies to start it up and back it in, a couple more to check out the wounded, and radios for chopper evac. The rest of us exchange gunfire with the Ceph, and I can't stop thinking about how *thin* their ranks are up here. These fuckers swarmed our position like fire ants not thirty minutes ago. Where are they now?

Easy answer: They've backed off to a safe distance to give their heavy guns a free hand to mop us up.

It comes through one of those three-story windows in the south wall, you know the ones where the glass sits behind a grid of iron bars. It tears through that mesh like it was tissue paper, jumps into the hall in a blizzard of glass, crashes down like some kind of red-eyed three-legged cyclops scanning for prey. Even inside the suit, my eardrums bleed from the sound.

I think: *You again.*

Through the ringing in my ears I can hear the Bulldog cough, start up, choke. I hear faint tinny curses from We Who Are About to Die. I give silent thanks once again to PFC Andrea Gamji, who bequeathed unto me the only weapon I know of that can take this fucker down.

I am Golem Boy, zombie, giant killer. I bring up the JAW and I pray to Allah that I can only die once.

There are details you know already: the body count. The men Barclay got out, the men he had to leave behind. You know that his call for chopper evac was turned down flat—too much traffic in Midtown during rush hour, I guess—or if you don't know you fucking well should.

There are details you don't need to know, details you don't have any *right* to know. I'm not going to tell you what a certain squad member told me before I put a bullet in his brain. I'm not going to tell you what his squadmate told me afterward. Pray to whatever imaginary friends you worship that you never have to find out.

I will tell you it wasn't the pinger that nearly did us in. It wasn't *just* the pinger. It was also the Ceph dropship that kept shooting at us through the roof; fucker zipped around like a moth on uppers, it was almost impossible to hit. But the N2 isn't exactly dog food, either, you know. I dip, I weave. I jump wreckage and piled corpses with a single bound. Somewhere in that shitstorm the pinger goes down in a gout of red fire and I don't even get to do a victory lap because that alien motherfucker up above the skylight is still raining glass and hollow-points down on the zone.

I don't take it out, not directly. I wing it, though, knock it off-kilter, send it skidding sideways into the MetLife Building; and MetLife finishes the job. The ship goes up like the Pickering reactor, it's a beautiful sight, Roger, a glorious sight, but even that doesn't last because now the whole damn skyscraper's leaning over in the wake of the blowout, leaning down over the station, and it's really damn lucky that Barclay's Banditos finally got that truck running because we barely make the running jump onto the tailboards, barely grab the last bus out of town before MetLife just *tips over* onto Central and buries it in glass and steel and concrete. Down for the count, for the second time in eight years.

So now we're flooring it down East 43rd and Central's just a pile of dust and debris in the rearview. I can hear Barclay down in the cab talking to Dispatch; the local airspace is too hot for traffic but they can probably set a VTOL or two down in Times Square so that's where we're headed. But I barely hear that over the other voice in my head, this giddy hysterical voice saying *We made it out we made it out we made it out*. I don't know how many times *that* cycles before *another* little voice cuts it off with: *Whaddya mean, WE?*

And that's the first time I notice. Barclay. The driver. Me. We're the only ones on board.

Nobody else made it.

*   *   *

They give us twenty minutes to get to evac before the VTOLs withdraw. We pick up a few stragglers on the way—a couple of battered jeeps with even more battered-looking grunts inside, the remains of an airborne battalion on West 43rd, pinned down by angry Ceph and feeling very damn lucky we happened by to lend a hand. By the time we run into the wreckage piled across West 43rd it's just this side of midnight, and raining. We ditch the vehicles and crawl through the wall of debris on foot.

I've never been to Times Square before. Supposed to be the heart of the City That Never Sleeps, right?

It's not sleeping now.

The traditional line of cabs is still there, although by now most of them are smoldering shells. Half the surrounding buildings have been skinned in patches, five stories of façade ripped off halfway up one tower, a big smoking hole punched into the top of another. An abandoned NYPD van has taken out the front of the Hard Rock Café, a fire engine's plowed into a USAF recruiting office (not that there'd've been anyone lining up to enlist anyway). I have to laugh; even this deep in Armageddon the billboards and marquees are still lit up, scrolling down, ticking along: DOUBLE TEAM YOUR TASTE BUDS. BROOKLYN BRIDGE: MILITARY TRAFFIC ONLY. THIS APOCALYPSE BROUGHT TO YOU BY NIKE.

The only other sources of light are the lines of halogen floods glaring down from the big prefab barricades that wall the square off from the rest of Manhattan. The cookie-cutters have been especially busy here: Every side street's been sealed off, every avenue blocked by ten-meter walls of interlocked blast-hardened concrete, flat and featureless except for an occasional reinforced hatch to let in the refugees. The barriers even extend *inside* the perimeter, an extra layer of protection between the square at large and the actual evac site at the north end. Like the fortified keep inside a castle, or a cross section of a giant two-chambered fish heart scaled at ten thousand to one.

We make our way through the ventricle: sandbag revetments, blast shields, pillboxes installed along strategic lines of sight. Voices and VTOL sounds drift over the top of the inner wall. Barclay leads me through into the keep and I'm pleased to see that as his official escort, I'm exempt from being threatened by my own side. Over on the other side the VTOL is spinning up, its belly full of civilians pathetically happy at the prospect of dying somewhere else. The ones left behind jostle and cry and push against a line of marines ringing the load zone. The civilians beg to be taken away; the soldiers make promises and deliver warnings and hope like hell the refugees don't realize how easy it is for a mob to swarm a single-file perimeter.

That's about the time the Ceph breach from 42nd and Broadway.

Nothing's linear after that. Everything happens at once: I'm back outside the keep, forming up ranks with a bunch of Echo-Fivers who must've drawn short straws. We man our pillboxes and bring our guns to bear and light up everything down the avenue that walks or squirms. The floodlights at our backs pin the slugs in bright white circles while the Ceph shoot out their reflectors one by one. At least I don't have to scavenge the bodies of dead comrades for ammo; there are caches stashed everywhere and it's even raining down from on high, clips and belts and RPGs delivered by human chains over the top of the inner wall. And all the while the VTOLs come and go, drop down empty at our backs and lift off wallowing and straining against the weight of too much loaded meat. Most of the time those cattle cars disappear over the skyline; sometimes they just crash into it, spewing smoke and fire and burning bodies. Barclay's shouting simultaneous orders in ten different directions. Somehow he manages to keep the fog of war from closing in completely.

Some panicked teenager shouts into his mike with a voice that cracks midsentence, then goes dark: heavy assault units crawling up Broadway. The perimeter is long since breached but so far the walls themselves are holding. That's something. Not enough, not for long: One Ceph gunship comes down over the keep and it's a slaughterhouse back there.

A Pinger steps in from stage left and rattles the rooftops. The lights go out. I mean *everything*: The floodlights on the barricade. The ABC news ticker down the street. The Hard Rock Café. Nike. BMG, Viacom, Planet Hollywood: all dark, all dark.

Madison Avenue has fallen.

We fall back, too. Barclay's orders.

The ground's shaking under my feet when I hit the northern hatch. I risk a look over my shoulder but the pinger's still advancing, not crouched down the way it does when it shits out one of those sonic blasts. I get back through the barrier in time to see a VTOL stagger up into the sky. I look around, do a double take: The place looks downright empty.

No civilians. No lights. The ground shakes again. Someone comms down from the battlements: For some reason the Ceph are pulling out. So are we. The latest incoming VTOL radios in for an update, and Barclay himself lays it down: "Cyclops Four, you'll be the last—going to be cramped but we'll get everyone out this time."

I can hear our getaway softly slashing air in the distance; it drifts into view over the ramparts as I watch. But the tremors haven't stopped. In fact, they're getting worse.

Barclay notices: "Cyclops Four, be advised we have unstable—"

I guess he hasn't been here before.

The ground bucks underneath us; the asphalt splits down Seventh like someone unzipping a duffel bag. A few of the guys yell *incoming!* and look around for airborne bogeys but they're looking in exactly the wrong direction. The spire ruptures the center of the compound and punches into the air like a giant fist; electric auroras writhe along its sides. Humvees, blacktop, shattered sewer pipes—that whole thin crust of shit we call *civilization*—tumble and bounce down its flanks. A jeep flips over and nearly squashes a medic. Cyclops Four rears back, slews to starboard, skids back out of sight like a toy thrown by some spoiled and angry child.

I wait for the impact. It doesn't come. The spire grinds to a halt, steaming.

"Cyclops Four, this is Barclay, can you still land? We are evac-ready, repeat we—"

"Colonel Barclay, I really must advise you against that."

Hargreave.

Nobody speaks for a moment. The spire towers over us like a great twisted backbone: dull orange embers glow in twisted bands along its length. Volcanic DNA.

"Who the hell are you?" Barclay says at last.

"Jack Hargreave. Colonel, there isn't—"

"This is a military channel."

"—really time for introductions. You and all your men—"

"Get off this channel, Hargreave."

"I would love to comply, Colonel, believe me. I have my own problems at the moment and I have no time for this bullshit, but I *promise* that if you let that chopper continue its approach you will be killing everyone aboard. Not to mention whatever remnants of your command remain on the ground. That thing has *reflexes*. You must deal with it first."

Barclay has delivered no commands to Cyclops Four but I can't help noticing that the sound of those engines seems to have faded a bit into the distance; someone up there is taking Hargreave seriously even if Barclay doesn't.

But Barclay does, eventually. He stands there with his hands wrapped around the grip of his Majestic and you just *know* he wishes it was Hargreave's neck. But when he goes back on the air, it's only to say "Cyclops Four. Back off. Return to operational height."

Barclay waits until the sound of the rotors fades away, never taking his eyes off the spire smoldering in our midst. He tweaks his mike. He speaks with slow, deliberate calm.

"So what, exactly, does our resident self-appointed expert suggest?"

"The spires are essentially an area-denial bioweapon," Hargreave tells him. "Their current iteration seems designed to render a given area safe for alien habitation." (A twitch at the edge of Barclay's mouth: point to Nathan Gould.) "They have a baseline activation cycle for routine operations, but they accelerate that process in response to incursions of—well, of pests. Once the spire is up and running, it perceives the approach of any incompatible biosignature as an increased threat, and will discharge preemptively—at the cost of overall coverage, but even premature, er, ejaculation would be more than enough to infect all of your men."

"Recommendations." Barclay's voice would freeze beer in the keg.

"You must neutralize the spire, of course." Hargreave pauses like a stand-up comic timing a punch line. "Fortunately, I've provided you with the means to do just that."

Suddenly everyone's looking at me.

I've been here before. Last time it didn't end so well.

Hargreave is all about climbing the spire and getting in from the top. Fuck that: *I'm* all about not getting shot out of that thing like a spitball if Hargreave's hack goes south again, and that means having an escape hatch right down here at ground level. What's really odd is that I *find* one. I circle the base of the thing, climb across torn-up pavement and plumbing, and of course there's nothing familiar about it at all. It's *alien.*

And yet not, somehow . . .

There's a segment just a little off-kilter from the others, a slipped disk, a fused vertebra: whatever you want to call it. Most people wouldn't even notice it; someone with an eagle eye might see a slight flaw in mass-production, a cosmetic glitch. I look at it and a familiar voice whispers, *Access panel.* I wait a bit but it doesn't tell me anything else: not *combination lock* or *key code* or *press and turn.*

So I blast it open with a sticky grenade.

A stiff breeze tugs at me from the hole: pressure gradient, just like before. I bet these things are pneumatic, I bet they suck in a huge long breath to build up the pressure for the Great Spore Pukefest. Which means we've got time as long as it's still inhaling.

When it stops, boys, head for the hills.

Inside it's the same layout: the silo, the curved panels, the seething currents of spore. The same virtual vulture sitting on my shoulder, reminding me how little time I have, how vital it is that I *compromise the settings for spore dispersal,* how it's *so much more likely to work this time.* I wonder about the hole I've just blown in the side of this thing—an open door between the spore in here and all that unprotected meat outside—but the pressure differential should keep everything contained. Assuming it lasts.

Besides, it's not as though the whole area *won't* be rotten with spore if I just stand back and do nothing.

So: the same smash and grab, the same blood-chilling cries from an alien machine in pain. The same dark blizzard of uncontained spore swirling around me, cutting my viz to zero, clinging to the surface of the Nanosuit like a billion antique keys in search of microscopic keyholes.

The same static discharge. The same tactical countdown:

Incoming Protocols Detected
Handshaking . . .
Handshaking . . .
Connected.
Compiling Interface.

But this time: COMPILED.

RUNNING.

And suddenly, spore sparkles into snow, electric white. The air *hums* around me; it's coming from the suit, it's the sound of a cascade, of a million tiny voices learning a new song and teaching a billion others, of a billion teaching a trillion. It's the sound of mimetic fission.

It's the sound of a process that sucks power like New York on New Year's. It's the sound of an alarm going off in my head, red icons blooming across my sightscape, energy levels dropping like bricks off a cliff.

I've got to get out of here.

I duck down and fall through the hatch; hungry spores swarm after me like a comet's tail, like a cloud of hungry mites. I try to stand; it's *hard*, it's almost impossible, it's like being human again. I stagger against my own weight. Voices spill into my head: groundhogs and chopper jockeys talking over each other. Hargreave. Barclay. My name, over and over. *Alcatraz. No.*

I fall onto broken pavement, stare up at the sky. Cyclops Four is up there, fully loaded, dwindling.

Something else leans in, much closer. Its eyespots glow like suns. It picks me up as if I weigh nothing at all.

It's not alone. The compound's swarming with Ceph.

The spire detonates.

The cloud erupting from the top of that thing doesn't look like anything I've ever seen. It glistens, it *sparkles:* It's just nanites talking to each other, spreading the gospel according to Hargreave all along the visible spectrum, but I don't find that out until later. Right now it just looks as though an evil cancerous monstrosity has vomited a whole galaxy of stars into the sky, and it's so beautiful I forget for a moment that I'm about to die.

And I think, in that same moment, the Ceph realize they *are* about to.

The grunt drops me without a second glance and leaps away at top speed; a white tendril swirls down like God's finger, touches it in flight. The grunt *melts,* just liquefies in its armor. Its exoskeleton face-plants in a pile of joints and plating, bleeding clear viscous fluid from its seams.

Down the street a stalker scrabbles at the barricade, collapses in a puddle. Half a block farther on a pinger staggers, takes a wobbly step toward me, crouches for attack; but the blast never comes. It doesn't give up; it draws itself back up to full height and continues its advance, slowly, deliberately, taking care with every step. There's a kind of desperate dignity to the way it moves; for a second or so I almost feel sorry for it. A shell slams into its side and detonates, knocking it over. Whoops and cheers on comm; I raise my eyes to Heaven and see Cyclops Four coming in for another pass. Her port turbine gouts flames. She slews, wobbles to a stop ten meters ahead, hangs just a couple of meters above the ground and doesn't dare to settle.

I can't stand. I don't have the strength. So I crawl, drag myself along the ground like a paraplegic toward that lowering tailgate, toward the shouting voices and waving arms. Something grabs me, hoists me off the ground as the ground begins to fall away. BUD's charge alert downgrades to yellow; I feel my systems starting to firm up. Cyclops tilts into the sky. Someone passes me a cargo strap: I grab hold and look down across a battlefield of empty machinery, robot bodies dropped and discarded as if the things inside have just been raptured up to Heaven. They haven't, though; I can see what's left of them dribbling through the cracks in all those suits of armor, congealing in sticky puddles on the road.

Explosive catalytic autolysis I think, and somehow I know what that means.

I've seen bioweapons in my time. I was there when Egypt laid that pimped-out necrotizing fasciitis down on the Syrians, back at the start of the Water Wars: You could see it eat the meat right off the bones in realtime, like it was some kind of Discovery Channel time-lapse. Those poor bastards died in minutes; the wounds actually *steamed* because the Strepto's metabolic rate had been cranked so high. They had to retcon a whole new suite of bacterial enzymes just to handle the heat.

Next to this, that was *nothing.* I've never seen *anything* kill this fast.

If this is what Hargreave's capable of when his hands are tied, I say let him off the leash and get the hell out of the way.

Colonel Sherman Barclay in *two* words: Tired.

Scared.

Not of death—you don't wear that many scars without making some kind of peace with mortality—but of failure. Scared because he's presiding over the end of the world, and whole platoons are looking to him, and what if he isn't up for it? We're living through the mother of all doomsday scenarios, you don't expect to win; but there are so many different ways to lose. Here at the end of his career Sherman Barclay has finally seen it all, and accepted that for him there is nothing left to see; and what he's been fearing even since the End Days began—what he's been fearing even more than Squiddie—is a bad death.

But you know what *really* got him scared, Roger? You know what he *really* fears, now that he's just seen a whole platoon of Ceph turn into beef consommé before his eyes? I see it the moment they haul me into the VTOL: I see it in the look on his face as we dust off.

Hope.

Because wouldn't you know it, Gould was right. Barclay knows that now; he doesn't have to weigh the odds of a wild-ass theory against a cost of human lives anymore, he's seen the N2 in action. This suit is a certified Ceph-killer, this suit could be the goddamn Black Death of Cephdom if we knew how to fine-tune the damn thing. This suit could turn the whole war around.

What do you do when you've finally resigned yourself to your own inevitable extermination, and someone offers you a way out? Any hope in a place like this almost *has* to be false; all it can do is shake your determination, tempt you with thoughts of *after this is over* when you should just be thinking about getting the job done *now*. Hope is distraction, hope is fear undercutting resolve, because hope gives you back that most terrible of battlefield commodities: something to lose.

Colonel Sherman Barclay is trying to decide whether he dares to hope.

Times Square dwindles behind us, a new wave of Ceph moving in to take possession. The Rapture doesn't seem to be taking them; I guess Hargreave's turncoat spore is all used up. Too bad he couldn't have programmed it with a longer life span. Too bad he couldn't have programmed them to *replicate*, like any self-respecting doomsday bug. We could've just sat back and watched smallpox take out the Europeans for a change.

But no. We now return you to your apocalypse, already in progress.

I'm not quite as dead as I thought; Hargreave's hack didn't actually need *that* much power but it needed it all at once, and there's a limit to how many joules-per-second the N2 can give up. It didn't faint on me because it was losing blood; it fainted because it stood up too fast. Now that it isn't being suckled by a billion microscopic mouths, its charge level's almost back in the green.

I could still use a top-up, though, and there's a couple of outlets right here by the tailgate. I jack in and let the suit feed while Barclay goes forward. Two dozen haggard faces follow him up the aisle. A few others look back at me.

A couple of them even smile.

By the time I reach the cockpit myself, Barclay's deep in argument with a familiar face on the far end of a video link.

"We *tried* to evacuate," Gould yells on the screen, "you think we didn't try? I told you, they *swarmed* us! Derailed the whole fucking train not halfway to Harlem! Now will you *listen to me?* We have to go to the Prism! It's our only hope. If there are any answers, Hargreave will have them. I worked for that fucker half my life, I know him. He's on top of this for sure. Someone has to go in there and bring him out."

Colonel Barclay does not like civilians. He sure as shit doesn't like this one, and if anything he likes Hargreave even less. But there it is again, whether he likes it or not.

Hope.

So he clenches his jaw, and takes a deep breath, and nods. He tells the pilot to change course for Prism.

The pilot laughs aloud. "Not a chance, sir. We took a lot of damage back there, I got multiple ruptures to the fuel lines, the pods, too—we're bleeding fuel like a stuck pig."

"How close can you get us?"

A couple of seconds, a quick backbrain calculation. "South end of the island. Maybe."

"Do it." Barclay turns to me as we bank to port. "Look at them," he says.

I do: burns, bullet wounds, thousand-yard stares. Half these people should be in therapeutic coma. The rest should be dead.

"You're it," Barclay says.

And you know something, Roger? It's just as well.

I'm sick of wading through infernos wearing this superskin while other soldiers, *better* soldiers probably, burn like moths on all sides. I'm alone in here no matter how many people they send along for the ride.

"We can meet you on the other side," Barclay continues. "Cover your exit. We've got good men and women on that train, they're shepherding the civilians to safety. I'll send a squad to meet you and Hargreave at the Queensboro Bridge." His shoulders rise, fall; I can't hear the sigh over the sound of the engine. "I'll send Gould along, too. I suppose the man might have some—helpful insights."

Something beeps and flashes red on the dash. "That's it," the pilot says. "We don't drop him here, we don't get home. I'll go low as I can, but we're down to fumes."

Back down to the tail. Barclay's ahead of me, slaps a button: the tailgate folds down like a drawbridge in front of me. Streamers of fire dance in and out of view to my left, blown back from the burning engine.

"Good luck, marine. Watch your ass."

The East River rolls by a few meters below—black and oily in visible, a deep peaceful blue on thermal—and for a second I think it's taking heavy fire. But no: Those are only raindrops.

The VTOL's already banking back to shore by the time I jump.

I hit the surface straight vertical, perfect entry. The river closes over my head with barely a splash. Dead of night, pitch-black water, viz so low I can't even see my own hand unless I push it right up against the helmet, and you know what?—

It doesn't bother me a bit. No sign of the fear that's plagued me ever since I was eight years old. Not a *twinge*.

Maybe I'm just getting used to it. Or maybe it's a fringe benefit, courtesy of SECOND and the N2.

For a second that almost scares me more than water used to. Because I've been inside this beast for, what—twelve hours, now? Fifteen? And if it's already got its tentacles buried so deep that it can edit out my *phobias*, what the hell will it have done after a day or two? After a week? I mean, what *are* we, what makes us unique, if not for our own personal fears and quirks? What if some mission algorithm decides that my personality's an operational liability? How many more of these background edits does it take before I don't wake up tomorrow, before something *else* wakes up that just happens to have my memories?

I'm not used to being such an existentialist wanker, you know. But all of this passes through my mind in the two seconds between the time I hit the water and the time I stop sinking. I hang there in that muddy black current for just a moment. Physics weighs buoyancy and momentum and gravity, and as I start to rise the dread just—drains out of me, somehow. The thoughts remain, that scary conclusion is still front and center, but it's colorless. I can look at the prospect of being edited out of my own head and it really should scare the shit out of me, but it doesn't anymore. I'm not even scared by the obvious reason *why* it doesn't.

Because after all, I've got a mission to complete. And by the time I break the surface—ten, twelve seconds after splashdown—that's really all I'm focused on.

> To: Site Commander D. Lockhart. Manhattan Crisis Zone
> From: Jacob Hargreave
> Date: [header corrupted]
> (See attached.)

> Did you *really think* I wouldn't find out about this, Lockhart?! Did you *really think* you could undermine me with the board that easily?!

Your days are numbered, son!

Archive: 28th March 2021
From: CryNet Executive Board
To: Lieutenant Commander D. Lockhart, Seattle
Deployment Team

Lt. Cmdr. Lockhart,

We are in receipt of your opinions in this matter and
have weighed them carefully.

We are also aware of the deeply personal nature of
your grievance against the nano-suit program. We have
no wish to re-open old wounds for you, but must point
out that this personal element forces us to consider the
possibility of your having a "vendetta mentality" where
the new technology is concerned.

At present, although the US military has formally
withdrawn from the N2 program, Pentagon funding
for our research continues in force, and forms part of
a substantial revenue stream for the company. Our
client relationship with the Pentagon remains a cordial
one and in these turbulent times, that is not something
we take lightly. Your concerns notwithstanding, the N2
program will therefore advance (under close security
supervision, you may rest assured) to Stages Seven and
Eight.

We will inform you if this situation changes. Until then,
you will please consider the matter closed.

Archive: 22nd March 2021
From: Lieutenant Commander D. Lockhart, Seattle
Deployment Team
To: CryNet Executive Board

Sirs,

I refer you to my previous correspondence regarding
CryNet's Nanosuit program, and specifically the
continuance of research and funding under the new N2
protocol (Stage Six).

If early reservations among myself and other experienced
military personnel on the original program were not
previously sufficient, then I would have hoped that the
debacle at Ling Shan would prove the validity of our
case. Hargreave-Rasch's proprietary nanotech has failed
so many legal safety requirements now and so badly
that the US military has withdrawn its personnel from all
testing in protest. And our company's success in acquiring
new test subjects for N2 from among the US Supermax
prison population and the troops of our developing
world allies should be no cause for rejoicing.

Sirs, I am an American patriot, and a shareholding
supporter of our corporate values. But what this country
needs (and this company needs to support logistically)
is a culture of well-trained and well-equipped modern
soldiers we can be proud of—not a Frankenstein parade
of psychopaths and dead men walking in tin suits whose
technical systems apparently remain a mystery even to
those who build them.

I respectfully reiterate my request that the N2 program
be formally terminated.

Faithfully
Dominic H. Lockhart (Lt. Cmdr.)

Rain hammers across my helmet. Lightning strobes on the horizon. Off in the middle distance a bright light turns in the sky like the eye of Sauron, sweeping land and sea: lighthouse.

I'm a hundred meters off the southern tip of Roosevelt Island. GPS puts Prism in the shadow of the Queensboro Bridge. A little over one klick northeast.

Hargreave's back in my ear before I even make it ashore. "It's good of you to come for me like this, Alcatraz, but you will need to proceed with caution. Lockhart has deployed his elite forces across the island. I'll guide you as best I can, but my view from here is, shall we say, severely limited."

The lighthouse rises in my sights like a terraced stone birthday cake: wide first layer with guardrail icing; narrower second; one big honking candle rising from the center. A wide stone stairway curves around the outer wall but even before I hit the shore I can see heat prints in the shadows of the first landing. I make three, line of sight; probably more inside the structure itself.

SECOND samples the airwaves: "You see that fly-by? Thought they were going to come in and strafe us."

"Nah. Too shot up. Didn't you see the flames? Be lucky if they manage five more minutes in the air."

"Saffron Three and Eight, *keep your comms clear.* Run silent, perimeter sweep again—that tin fuck is coming, I can feel it."

Daddy Lockhart, breaking in and squelching the signal.

"Yes, sir."

I'm on the stairs now, flattened against the brickwork as Three and Eight clatter innocently past on their perimeter sweep, swinging their dicks. They hope I *do* show up. One of them had friends in Cobalt.

I wait until their voices fade, cloak for as long as it takes me to stick my head above the landing. Nothing but the backs of the Saffron Duo disappearing in the night. I don't believe it. Lockhart's an asshole but he's not an idiot; he won't have left the southern approach unguarded.

Sure enough, other voices slow me to a creep as I circle the first landing. Somebody thinks they should be out fighting the Ceph, not sitting here in the boonies. Someone else would rather be home fucking his boyfriend.

Way overhead, Sauron's eye flickers and goes out. For a moment or two the night belongs to fires burning across the water. I look up at the lantern, catch a bright cloud of heat radiating from the dead lamp and a smaller shadow in front of it, something cooler. I switch to StarlAmp.

Ah yes. An arm. A sniper rifle. Have to remember that.

The lantern reignites. Somewhere behind all that stonework, gears grind faintly back up to speed: The beam resumes its endless track around the horizon.

"Ah, shit. Must be another power surge."

"I swear, Lockhart's losing it, man. He's taking this shit *way* too personal."

"Easy to get personal when some cyborg asshole puts half your friends in body bags. I want that fucker dead as bad as he does."

"There's no way he's coming."

"Maybe he's already here. He's got a cloak, you know . . ."

I do, at that. I bring it up and move along the wall and there they are, just outside the lighthouse door: three beetle suits, blinded by Science.

" . . . he could be watching us right now . . ."

I could reach out and touch her. I am so tempted. I am so tempted.

Right up until a fourth merc comes around the corner and touches me first.

Touches isn't exactly the right word. *Blunders* would be closer. I am cloaked, after all; the dumb fuckwit walks right into me and bounces back on his heels, flailing. His buddies laugh as he goes over. For about half a second.

"He's there! He's *right fucking there!*"

"Well now," Hargreave says softly on the penthouse freq. "That didn't last long, did it?"

I make it easy for them. I jump clear of the blunder zone the moment Fuckwit Four goes over so I'm spared the blizzard of bullets that Swiss-cheeses the spot a heartbeat later, but I'm not especially quiet about it. It's about two seconds before the line of fire veers over to the sound of my boots on cement. Half a second after *that* the cloak runs out of juice and I start taking hits. A couple even get through before I crank the armor setting, but I don't think there's much left inside to hit anymore; for all I know the slug just bounces around in there and rolls down my leg. (Sometimes, Roger, I think I can almost hear it rattle when I walk.)

"Oversight, this is Saffron Two! Enemy contact in Sector Bravo!"

I hit back, of course. I teach Saffron's front line the timely lesson that payback against Cyborg Assholes is a lot harder to do than to brag about, but by then they've called in air support and backup boots. I throw some suppressing fire up the tower on my way; I don't have a hope in hell of hitting that sniper, but at least I've thrown off his aim. I scoop up a Feline submachine gun from one of the fallen (shitty recoil, awesome rate of fire) and head up-island, trying to balance stealth against speed.

Waypoint options, not great. Roosevelt Island's maybe 150 meters across: not many degrees of freedom there, not much cover, and from the look of it those buildings that are still standing were derelict long before Squiddie came calling. Something hulks in the middle distance so that's what I head for, calling up GPS on the fly: RENWICK HOSPITAL, it says, but there's not so much as a streetlight out front. No big surprise; every other hospital in the country went under during the Double Dip. But it's a building, it's cover, it's dark on thermal so there aren't any blue-eyed beetles waiting to light me up from the shadows. I hear shouts and comm traffic behind me; the faint sound of rotors drifting down from up ahead. In between there's crab grass and trampled chain link and no cover at all except for Renwick Hospital. So I charge toward it, weaving and deking because that lighthouse sniper must have got his groove back by now, yes?, and I look up and—

And it's not a hospital.

At least, it doesn't look like one. It's a castle, or something. A dark castle looming in the rain, backlit by lightning, three stories of ancient brickwork and square-toothed battlements, mats of ivy crawling around windows as empty as eye sockets. I stop dead for a second, look up through those gaping holes straight through to smoke and sky. I feel like I've passed through some kind of time machine. Or maybe this place has: a little piece of the eighteenth century that somehow managed to hang on into the twenty-first.

It looks haunted.

And then those old stones splinter with the impact of the .30-caliber present, and I'm diving inside.

Turns out it's a hospital after all. I don't find out until later, but the place was built to hold smallpox patients back in the eighteen-hundreds. The original smallpox, not that Cuban strain—anyway. It was even a historic landmark for a few years, back before Hargreave-Rasch bought the place out.

Originally it was a quarantine site, they stuck it way out on the end of the island because they didn't want all those poor sick bastards laying waste to the healthy population. A place to hold people too dangerous for civilized company. I wish I'd known that at the time. I would've felt so much more at home in the place.

A lot of people died in there, too, of course. Hundreds at least, I'd bet. Maybe thousands.

If Saffron and Hazel had known that, maybe they'd have felt more at home, too.

It's a shell. What's left of the floor is a tangle of dirt and scrub and stunted saplings. Half the second-story floor is missing; beams crisscross the empty spaces overhead. Rusty iron banisters angle up the walls, stairways with no stairs to floors with no floors. The roof has long since caved in but the stone walls are still standing; they might even be thick enough to foil whatever deep-scan thermal the incoming chopper might be packing.

Not too many places to hide once you're inside but you can't *get* inside without going through a bottleneck or two: open door-ways, empty window frames. I plant my last few stickies with as much care as thirty seconds of lead time will give me: just inside the main door, under a few empty windowsills.

Hargreave drops in with a few helpful words: "Lockhart's set an EMP trap for you up ahead."

Good to know. A bit busy right now, Jack.

"Given the way they're rerouting the local grid it's going to be a big one, maybe big enough to get through your Faraday mesh. Might fry the Nanosuit, might even fry your *own* synapses depending on how deep the interface—uh . . ."

Two passageways leading to other parts of the ruin, narrow and relatively intact: my last couple of stickies go there. I just hope the grunts get here before the chopper does. I'm as good as naked to an airborne thermal scan.

"Now there's no way to bypass the trap," Hargreave says, "but why would we even want to when we can we can trick it out?"

I jump up to one of the few spots on the second level with both a floor and a ceiling. Not a bad view of the southern entrance, either.

An icon blooms on GPS: a hydro substation over on the east shore. The tit from which Prism sucks—but there's no time for that now, because—

Saffron is at the door.

Two beetles, flattened to either side of the main door, waving their Scarabs around like magic wands. Something bounces off the stoop, rolls into the middle of the hall. I close my eyes.

My eyelids light up blood orange. Flash grenade. I hear Saffron whoop and come through the door.

I hear the sticky detonate. Saffron turns into a bloody piñata.

I open my eyes. It must have been bright as the sun in here a second ago; now it's all orange flames and black smoke. Hazel Eight and Saffron Five scream news of my treachery back and forth across the channel. A beetle dives in through the window to the left of the main door window and nails the landing, a beautiful roll that brings him back on his feet in a second with his rifle cocked and sweeping. His buddy dives through the right window; another sticky blows his leg off. The acrobat whirls to face the carnage, off-guard. I shoot him.

A muffled *whoompf* from behind; one of my hallway grenades has just brought the walls down on someone approaching from the north (Hazel, that's it. Reinforcements from up-island. The northern claw of an ill-advised pincer movement.) So far no one's even spotted me yet.

Then the chopper heaves in out of the night and lacerates my little attic hideaway with tracer bullets.

I hear it coming, just in time: amp up the armor setting for those few seconds of HMG fire, cloak and hope there's enough charge left to keep me covered as I roll off the platform and fall back to earth. The Feline's in my hand by the time I hit: I spray the room like a water sprinkler and the cloak wears off but that's okay, that's okay, by now there's nobody here but us corpses.

One of them died clutching a Grendel: half the firing rate, but twice the damage. The feline's almost dry anyway. I swap out.

The chopper's hanging just off the parapets up there somewhere, drifting back and forth along the building. Good news, I guess: It doesn't know where I am. Can't see through the walls. Just gotta make sure it doesn't get line of sight on me again.

Here at ground level, the beetles have pulled back for the moment. Only a couple of the stickies are still live but they don't know that, and they've learned their lesson. If I was them I wouldn't risk rushing the place again, either. I'd set up a perimeter, make sure the Cyborg Asshole stayed inside it, and call in something heavy to bring the whole fucking place down on his head. An AGL, maybe. Hell, just call in an air strike and firebomb the place.

Time to be somewhere else.

I work my way sideways, keeping a wall between me and the chopper, keeping an eye out for heat prints and an ear cocked for comm. Can't go this way; I stickied that route. Can't go that way; beetles and choppers and CELL, oh my. There's a window that opens to the northeast, wide-open path to a red-brick building maybe ninety meters away but I'd never get out before—

Something armor-piercing slashes a row of little divots across the stone at my back. I drop barely in time.

Gotta be more careful.

Okay, they know I'm in here. I can either wait to get bombed, or make a break before they bring in their big guns. They know that as well as I do.

Maybe I can use that.

I crawl back to the beetle I just disarmed; he'll do nicely. Too bad I don't have any more sticky grenades; that would be the ribbon on the wrapping. Doesn't matter. I check my levels: Cloak's fully charged. Twenty seconds guaranteed invisibility to beetles *and* choppers, forty if I don't have to do anything fancy. And out there, all those cobalt-eyed cocksuckers just *waiting* for me to make a move . . .

Grendel Boy must weigh 120, 130 with his armor on. With the N2 backing me up I could throw him like a softball.

That's what I do. One armored, badass, humanoid softball, blurring through smoke and rain and leftover flames, barely seen as it flashes past gaping stone windows in the dead of night but man that fucker's moving *fast*, can't get a good look under these conditions but it's *gotta* be Prophet, just gotta be, I said he'd make a break for it and *here he comes, boys, right through the window he's coming right for us,* and it's

"Target in view! Southwest side, southwest side, he's *going for it—"*

And by the time they figure it out—by the time the chopper stops strafing and the beetles stop shooting and everybody settles down enough to realize that the life-sized rag doll they've just reduced to sponge toffee is actually one of their own—I'm halfway to cover in the opposite direction, cloaked and running like stink. Shouts and shots fade behind me; I spare a glance over my shoulder and see the chopper swinging back and forth against the flickering brown sky like a fucking Nazgûl, black and hungry and slashing the air with rage and frustration.

I'm headed for the east side, about seven or eight hundred meters up the island. Nothing I run into on the way gives us very much trouble. Nothing gets a signal out.

The substation itself is almost anticlimactic. I don't have to kick in the door, don't even have to *knock*. The door's wide open, a couple of CELLulites standing off to one side, snorting a bit of dopatrix and complaining about all the brownouts spiking through the grid. Also complaining about Lockhart, who has apparently sent them down here to get it all fixed.

"You wanna go in there and fix it from the console? It's a death trap in there."

"Let's just get it done. Lockhart's pissed enough as it is."

They're right about the death trap part, anyway.

I don't know shit about running a municipal power grid but the monitors I find inside do show a lot of icons changing a lot of different colors over a lot of the board. Hargreave hand-holds me through the protocols, which after all can't be all that difficult if those ropadopas outside were supposed to know them.

"Good. Now, Lockhart doesn't know it, but the power systems he's using for his EMP blast have to route through that station, and they're pushing close to overload."

Line up the red lights. Reroute the yellows.

"If you can trigger the emergency shutdown, it'll kick his loop out, and when the systems come back up, they'll disallow any major power surge. It won't show up on his board—he jerry-rigged the breakers in the first place to get the extra power, so there's no diagnostic circuit on his board—but when he hits the trigger, trust me: It'll fail."

Oh, I trust you, Jack. I trust you as far as I could throw a Bradley.

"Excellent! Now get out of there. CELL will no doubt have spotted the outage, they'll be on their way to investigate."

I wonder if he's dim, or if he just thinks that I am. *He* told *me* about the trap, after all. The great Jack Hargreave steals magic from the stars and can't even put two and two together? Doesn't he *get* it?

They're not *supposed* to kill me, not anymore. Not even the chopper sniffing me out along the rooftops, Azure Seven calling in from behind its eyes, the HMG in its nose twitching in anticipation. Not supposed to kill me, not really, not unless it gets in a really lucky shot. Lockhart has switched strategies—or maybe this was his plan all along. After all, it doesn't take a genius to realize that you don't chase fish around the ocean. You wait until they swim upstream and *ambush* the scaly little fuckers in a bottleneck.

Azure Seven spots me at the substation. Azure Seven can't do a damn thing about it, not without shooting up Prism's power supply. He tries to hem me in and calls up more boots on the ground, but one of the CELLulites on electrical duty brought along an L-TAG he won't be needing anymore.

Azure Seven goes down in fire and rain.

Okay, Lockhart, you miserable sonofabitch. You want to stop chasing me around this goddamn city? You want me to come to you instead?

Let's do this.

Send me your cannon fodder. Send me your second tier. Send me your sad-sacks and your Saffrons, your fresh-faced mall cops who can't shoot straight. Don't make it too easy, though. Gotta keep me thinking it's an uphill battle, can't ever let slip that I'm being lured, directed, *herded.* Don't worry, I'll play along. I'll mow down your boys and girls for you, do my part to keep it real. I'll pretend to fight my way forward and you pretend to try and stop me and all the while that honey pot gets closer and closer and *there it is,* Lockhart, the outer wall, the edge of the kingdom, ten meters high and topped with razor wire. The edge of Jacob Hargreave's Secret Kingdom.

Only one way through: a vehicle air lock big enough to hold two M1 Abramses shoulder-to-shoulder. It's not inside the kingdom, it's not out. It's the gatehouse where all those who'd pass between must wait to be judged. It's Limbo.

And it's open at both ends.

I can look straight through into the outer compound. And why not? Ever since CELL planted its flag all the way down to the lighthouse, the whole damn island is Prism's backyard. Why worry about arbitrary checkpoints inside the green zone?

I make it look good. I lurk out there in the rain, peeking around corners, going through the motions: thermal, StarlAmp, zoom. I step out in the open.

"This should be interesting," Hargreave murmurs.

I go for it.

I dial up a fast sprint—no point making it *too* easy. It doesn't change anything: I'm barely in the tunnel when a few tons of steel and concrete slam down directly in front of me. I skid, turn, bounce off the barricade: another hardened slab of steel and concrete crashes down and blocks my retreat.

I dial back the power, let the charge rebuild. Best-case scenario I'm going to be indulging in a few high-energy maneuvers in the next minute or two. Worst-case scenario I'm dead.

Deader.

Recessed nozzles along the walls, probably loaded with everything from halothane to nerve gas. (Nothing my filters can't handle, worst-case I can always use the rebreather.) Recessed drainage gratings bolted into the floor. I pan the ceiling: a camera in every corner—

Shit. Lockhart's going to know his pulse is a bust the moment he hits the trigger and doesn't lose the video feeds. So much for the element of—

Something goes *ping* in between my ears. I taste copper.

The lights go out.

"Uh—wait a second . . . ," Hargreave says.

No little red LEDs glowing in the darkness past my helmet. The cameras are down. I'm not, though; my eyes are still full of icons and overlays. I can still move.

"Nothing to worry about, son. Just a *small* pulse, built up enough to kill the lights before the circuit blew. Nowhere near strong enough to penetrate your shielding."

I hear voices whispering on comm, faint and riddled with static: Blast confirmed, they say. They've got me.

"There's a drainage gate to your left," Hargreave says. "Smash it out. Follow the pipes to the river. I'll send you Lockhart's location."

They're getting ready.

"Move!"

They're coming in.

The inner door rises just a hair as the bolts unlock. Lockhart's voice channel comes clear and strong through the crack: "Soon as you get line of sight, gentlemen, you hose him down. We're taking no chances this time. I want that suit turned to *scrap*."

But by then I'm already in the sewers.

I can hear them shitting bricks behind me. Their voices bounce down along all this unsecured plumbing, shout back and forth along frequencies they don't know I know: *Fuck he must've cloaked. He's not cloaked he's gone. Drain gate's out. In the pipes. Saffron Ten be advised.*

Tin man is loose. Tin man is inside.

"Flush him out of there! Bring him down!"

That's Lockhart, supervising. Hargreave squirts me a way-point: I squirm left at the next junction.

"Do I have to do everything myself? You are elite soldiers! You are *equipped*!"

That's Lockhart, venting. I see a mesh of light ahead, dim and gray and cold.

"Will somebody grow some balls and kill that tin fuck!"

I'm at the grating. The East River crawls past on the other side, broken into eddies and sluggish backwash by the concrete dock just upstream.

"He's just *one fucking man*! *What the hell am I paying you for?*"

That's Lockhart doing something I've never heard him do before.

That's Lockhart, losing it.

He sees me coming for him, oh yes he sees.

He spies me on the pier and calls in another copter; I send it down to the sea in flames. His cameras catch me on the rooftops and he calls for his mercenaries; after a while there are no mercenaries left to answer. He sees me squirming up from underground like some kind of childhood bogeyman, before I shoot out the lens of his camera. He sees me in the gatehouse and stalking facelessly through the storage bay and by now he's got to know I'm *letting* him see me, I *want* him to see me: each new sighting a little closer to his command, each new tag leaving him a little less room to run.

But he doesn't run. He calls in every man on the chessboard, bishops and castles and Saffron and Hazel, he calls out along all the empty hissing wavelengths at his command. He calls on everyone right up to the sacred whoremother of God's bastard Son but at the end of it all, the only one to answer that call is me: Alcatraz the Invincible, climbing the stairs to this sad and lonely little command center under a downpour of rain and ordnance and lightning bolts.

Behold, motherfucker. I stand at the door and *knock*.

The door blows off its hinges.

Lockhart blows back, Gauss gun cradled against his gut: "Come on. *Come on!* Show me the color of your guts, boy!"

The joke's on him, of course. My insides and outsides are all the same color by now, all honeycombed and striated and gunmetal gray, and they barely feel the impact of Lockhart's sabots.

"Fuck you, Tin Man."

I don't even bring up a weapon. I grab him by the throat and raise him high and I *squeeze*. At first I think *he's* making those sounds, those hacking choking coughs, but no: It's Hargreave, invisible and omnipresent as always. Hargreave, laughing.

I throw Lockhart through the window. He arcs down past two stories, clears the razor wire, hits the gravel road facedown not ten meters from the inner compound.

"Good work, son." Hargreave's voice pats me on the head. Down on the road, Dominic Lockhart drags his broken body by inches through the rain.

"Now let's get you inside."

There's a gun in my hands.

"I'm opening the Prism entrance right now. Head on over here, as fast as you can!"

Part of me wants to shoot Lockhart in the back. Part of me wants me to stop. I don't know which part is which anymore and I don't give a shit. I don't stop squeezing the trigger until the hammer clicks on empty.

I throw down the Grendel, pick up the Gauss. I keep it moving on my way across the inner compound but nobody tries to get in my way. Everything leads to this moment: Battery, Prophet, Gould. The Wave. The fucking suit. Ever since I crawled up on shore I've been stuck in the bleachers; *this* is the end zone. A jumbled pile of multistoried cubes looms up through the rain like giant building blocks; Hargreave waits in the tallest. This is the place where the answers lie. The end of the Yellow Brick Road. The man behind the curtain. Victory over the Ceph. Maybe, if I'm very lucky, my own resurrection from the dead. It's all right in there.

The door is open. The light inside is warm and inviting.

I walk in.

A flash bomb goes off in my head. Electricity *sings*, right down in my bones. I can't feel my skin—no, the suit. We can't feel the suit. We can't move.

"EMP assault." I don't know which one of me is saying that. "Systems shutdown."

"Ah," Hargreave says from the other side of the universe. "That's perfect. Thank you, Ms. Strickland."

I'm blind. I'm blind. The whole world strobes around me in bright jagged flashes. BUD is nothing but tinsel and static.

"Check his vitals, would you? Then have him moved across to the skinning lab. We need to get him prepped as soon as possible."

The bright light fades in time to see the floor come up like a kick in the face.

Outside I see nothing. Inside, my head is full of gibberish: FRDAY_ WV and FLXBL DPED-CRMC EPDRMS and LMU/894411. GPS scribbles idiot wireframes across my brain: Digital Manhattan swings and twists like a tabletop model under an eight-year-old's swing set.

False Prophet reads out omens of doom, incantations full of *critical shutdown modes* and *limbic integration overrides*. Eventually the wireframes go away; something like an EEG takes their place. Falsey's making a little more sense now: We're switching to core function mode, apparently. Life support takes priority. *Deep-layer protocols* are engaging. Some kind of system reroute is under way.

That's nice. Just reroute everything away from me. That'll be perfect.

Footstep echoing against the shitty acoustics of raw cinder block. Vague, fuzzy bars of brightness passing by overhead. I can't squeeze my eyes shut, so I squeeze them into focus: fluorescent lights. The EMP's worn off but I still can't move; I'm strapped to some kind of rolling gurney.

I raise my head in time to see it push through a pair of swinging doors into a cavernous gray room with tiled walls. Big blocks of machinery sit humming in all that empty space; the place reminds me of a furnace room or a physical plant, one of those dull grimy places infested with ducts and piping you find in the sub-basements of office towers.

"Just another grunt, I'm afraid." Hargreave, still hidden behind his curtain, sighs to someone who isn't me. "Prophet could have told us so much more."

It's not a furnace room, though. It's an operating theater. I can tell by the lackey in the blue surgical scrubs playing on the keyboard up ahead, a CELLulite grinning at his elbow. It's a machine shop; I can tell by the gleaming enamel spider bolted to the ceiling, each jointed hydraulic arm tipped with a laser or a scalpel or—

I've never seen a lug wrench with a built-in spinal needle before.

"At least we have the nanogear intact, that's all that really matters. The rest I'll have to improvise once I'm in the suit."

The spider drops with a soft whir, comes to a stop a meter over my chest. It unfolds its legs, flexes each joint as if warming up for a marathon. Bits and pieces click together like chopsticks.

"Let's get started."

The table *flexes* around me, tightens my restraints. Lights wink at the end of those articulated arms; tiny saws whine into the ultrasonic, dip and weave and *plunge*. My bones rattle in their cage. Suddenly I'm seeing the world through blood-colored glasses.

Way over at the corner of my eye, the man in scrubs pays very close attention to the monitor on his desk. His eyes are bright and tiny over his surgical mask. They never look at me.

Just following orders.

"Ah, my young friend."

Hargreave again. Deigning to address me directly. "I had hoped to spare you consciousness at this point, but the nanogear is not proving cooperative. I am truly sorry for this betrayal, but I really have no choice. I need the suit—this particular suit, in fact—if I'm to have any hope at all of stopping the Ceph. A simple soldier will not suffice here."

My body goes numb. The room still rattles in my eyes, but suddenly I can't feel the vibration.

"Don't misunderstand me. You've proven far more resilient than I ever would have expected. You are a soldier, and a damn good one, and you would be an asset in repelling any invasion, alien or otherwise. But allow me to fill you in on a little secret." I can hear the wink in Hargreave's voice, I can hear him leaning in to share his little confidence. "This isn't an invasion, son. It never was."

I wonder if these restraints are even necessary anymore. I bet they've cut my spinal cord.

"It's obvious if you think about it. Why would a race that can terraform worlds, that plans and builds across light-years, across millennia—why would they be interested in anything so vulgar as *territory?*"

My eyes go out. I'm in a black void: blind to the abattoir, numb to my own vivisection, cut off from everything but Hargreave's voice, the snap of lasers, the whine of spinning bone saws.

"There was a time, son, when people tried to save the rain forest. Oh, they were an emotional lot, woolly-minded and disorganized, but a few of them knew that they could never get a shortsighted and indifferent public to care about a bunch of trees half a world away. People don't give a rat's ass about anything unless you can answer the question, *What's in it for me?*"

The saws are gone. The lasers are gone. I'm deaf now, as well as blind and numb and paralyzed. But somehow I can still hear Hargreave here in my head. True to his word he stays at my side, walking with me through the valley of the shadow of death. Jack Hargreave is my universe.

"So the more clever environmentalists came up with an answer: *There's Taxol, there are antioxidants and anti-aging drugs, there are cures for every cancer and filters for all the shit we pump into the air. There are a billion compounds and a million cures, the rain forest might make you immortal someday, but we lose it all if we wipe it out without even knowing what's in there.*"

I know what this is: this cable-cutting, this endless monologue, this pointless fireside chat with the senile old uncle you wish would just shut the fuck up. This is deliberate distraction. This is an attempt to take my mind off what's happening. This is Jack Hargreave being *merciful.*

I wonder if Prophet ever found out what it means, when a man like Hargreave calls you *son.*

"It was a good strategy, and it might have even worked, but then some company—actually, I think it may have been one of mine—synthesized Taxol. And then of course we arrived at the dawn of Synthetic Biology, and why leave all those millions of hectares *undeveloped* on the off-chance of some miracle cure when you can program artificial microbes to shit out whatever you need? The rest was history. As is the rain forest, sadly."

I think he's receding. His voice sounds—fainter, somehow. Hard to tell, with nothing to compare it with. Maybe it's just my imagination.

"But the Ceph are so much smarter than we are. They know we can only see what we look for, we can only make what we can imagine. Nature—four billion years of experimentation, endless mutation and selection, Darwin's tangled bank in all its glorious diversity—Nature creates what we *haven't* imagined, gives us vital gifts we'd never even *think* to look for."

No, his voice is definitely fainter.

"The Ceph understand these things: They come upon life-bearing worlds and they set up their monitoring stations to watch nature grind out its wonders and they *leave it alone.* And every million years or so they drop by to see how their garden grows and let me tell you, my friend, they don't much like the cancer that's infested this place since the last time they were here. Here we are, growing out of control, destroying everything around us and too stupid to see that we're destroying ourselves in the process."

I have to strain to hear him now. He must be light-years away.

"We are metastasis made flesh, my boy. We are pestilence, we are the weeds in the garden, and we are not facing warriors at all. We've never seen their soldiers, and I pray we never do. This is a *pruning* expedition. We are getting our asses whipped by a bunch of *gardeners* who are improvising in the face of the unexpected."

I can barely hear him at all. My whole universe is a whisper.

"And that is the only reason we have a hope in hell of winning."

Gone.

I wonder how many pieces I've been cut into. I wonder how many pieces are thinking this.

(*Cellular force overload,* someone says at the bottom of a very deep well.)

All things considered, I think I'm thankful to be here. To be nowhere. A far cry from my Happy Place, but at least I can't feel the drills and the needles anymore. I can't hear my Creator and my Tormentor. I know I'm being disassembled somewhere, but at least I can't see it happening. You learn to be thankful for what you get.

(*Wake up.*)

That's not Hargreave. That's—

(*Wake up, marine.*)

I know that voice. I shouldn't be hearing it though, not now. Haven't Hargreave's lackeys cut it out of my head yet?

"Wake up, marine! This is no time for dying!"

It's False Prophet. It's False *Prophet,* I can see his face hanging there in the void before me. It's nothing like the original, it's barely even an imitation. Just pixels and polygons. A constellation, a thousand stars that just happen to look like a human face.

It's the goddamn suit. The suit is *shouting* at me.

"Get your ass back in the fight!"

Go away. You're dead. I saw you die.

"Back at you, soldier. You think that's an *excuse?*"

Maybe this is SECOND in denial, just a dumb biochip reliving the good old days in an attempt to rekindle the flame with a partner who dumped it days ago. Or maybe it's pretending to be Prophet because it accessed a psych database somewhere and decided I'd react better to something that sounded like it had a life. Shit, maybe it *is* Prophet—some warped-mirror cartoon of Prophet at least—cobbled together from loose talk and synaptic echoes long after the conscious meat blew itself to kingdom come. Maybe it's insane, maybe it thinks it's real.

Or maybe not. This could just be the oxygen-starved brain of Cyborg Asshole Mk2 making stuff up as it goes along, Tin Man's version of a near-death experience: as meaningless as all those lights and angels the neo-agers go on about during their asphyx parties. Maybe there's not even any brain left to starve, maybe it's been dead for hours and all these thoughts are running along a net of carbon nanotubes. Maybe they've already cut open my helmet and puked their guts out from the stink of all the dead meat that's been rotting inside for fuck knows how long . . .

What *are* you, in here with me? Are you alive? Are you even *real*?

"Enough of this shit, marine!" it bellows. *"Enough!"*

What the fuck are you?

What the fuck am *I*?

I am awake.

Somewhere very close, alarms are singing. Multijointed robot arms quiver spastically overhead. The doctor with the optional Hippocratic Oath is not avoiding my eyes now, no sirree: He's staring right into them, and he looks about ready to piss himself. Flickers of unfocused light and shadow play across him: reflections of outputs changing far, far faster than they have any right to. And although it should be impossible for anyone to retrodict those vague blobs and blips into anything even approaching the original image that cast them, somehow I find it easy. I can see the good doctor's monitor reflected in his scrubs, in his mask, in those dark shiny pupils grown so huge you can barely see the irises around them.

I know it before he says it: "Some kind of overload! The suit's—it's *rejecting* the rip somehow . . ."

"Stop him!" Hargreave's voice rises an octave. "Kill him if you have to, but don't damage the hardware!"

What, no sad farewell? No fond final words for your latest *son*? Doors slam open up past my head. I hear boots on bricks. "Headshots only!" Hargreave cries to the CELLulite leaning over me.

"Got it." The CELLulite slides back the bolt on his pistol, lays the muzzle against my forehead. I keep waiting for SECOND to lay on the tacticals—AY69 AUTO, ENEMY COMBATANT, THREAT LEVEL: HIGH—but I guess they shut it down. I'm alone at last.

My executioner's head explodes.

Then his buddy's.

Then the man in the scrubs, and some hapless med tech I never noticed before now. Four shots, four kills. I turn my head, almost interested, while Hargreave seethes on the radio: "Tara, *no*! Tara, listen to m—"

She kills the channel and goes to work at the doctor's station. Her fingertips come dark and shiny off the keys.

"CIA," she says. "Special ops. Recruited three years ago now."

I wonder what her code name was. Probably *Deus Ex Machina*. Or *Belle*.

"You've got me to thank for this whole shitstorm." She barely glances up; her eyes, her bloody fingers are all about the controls. "I'm the one who ordered your squad in to extract Prophet and Gould in the first place. Best-laid plans, huh?"

My restraints pop open. Up in the left-hand corner of my eye, uplink icons wink back into existence.

Strickland's at my side, her hand at my elbow, urging me to sit. "We've got to get out of here."

I'm a little bit surprised to see that everything's still attached. I swing my legs over the edge of the gurney, roll to a sitting position. GPS and MODE SELECT come back online. A panicky amber light on the ceiling spins in its glass bubble, stabbing my eyes five times a second.

Little crosshairs pan across my field of vision and lock down on the heavy assault rifle one of the CELLulites dropped while he was getting his brains blown out. BUD serves up a subtitle: HEAVY ASSAULT RIFLE: GRENDEL/HOL. PT.

"Let's *go*, man! The Ceph are coming and we've got to get Hargreave out."

And she's right. Suddenly, I'm *there*. All that fatalistic indifference I was feeling just a few minutes ago, that candy-ass *que sera* resignation to my own death? Fuck that. I'm *back*, baby. I'm strong, I'm stoked, I'm ready to kick ass all the way to the next millennium.

Nice to have you back, SECOND. I missed you.

No, I don't think he was right at all. He got maybe halfway there, tops. But the fact is, even *gardeners* would've done a better job.

I mean, try and wrap your head around the magnitude of the imbalance here. Maybe you're imagining us as a bunch of cavemen going up against a Taranis or a T-90 with reactive armor, but that's not even close. Cavemen are people, too, Roger, they've got the same raw brainpower even if their tech is Stone Age. The Ceph are a whole different *species*. So let's say Hargreave's right and we're not facing soldiers. Do you really think the world's lemurs, say, would have a better chance against a bunch of *gardeners*? If a bunch of *gardeners* wanted to take out an anthill, would they attack the ants with formic acid and titanium mandibles? 'Course not. They've got sprays and poisons and traps and guns, things no ant has ever seen, things no ant could possibly defend against.

So why the Ceph gunships, Roger? Why the exoskeletons that walk pretty much like we do, and the guns that fire pretty much like ours, and bloody *artillery* for chrissake that does pretty much what ours does? Why are Ceph weapons and tactics so much like ours, hmm?

I don't think they're gardeners at all. I don't even think they're aliens. Not the *real* aliens, anyway. Not the real gardeners.

I think they're hedge clippers and weed whackers, left in the shed to rust. I think they're the dumbest of the garden tools, programmed to bump around the property mowing the lawn while the owners are away because after all, this place is too far out in Hicksville to waste *real* intelligence on. I think they have basic smarts because where they come from, even the *chairs* are smart to some degree—but nobody ever read them *The Art of War*, because they're goddamn *hedge clippers*. So they've had to learn on the fly. Their tactics and their weaponry look like ours because they're *based* on ours, because we were the only game in town when those cheap-ass learning circuits looked around for something to inspire them. And I think a lemur wouldn't have a hope in hell against a bunch of gardeners, but he just might stand a chance in a war against the Roombas.

Organic? Are you fucking kidding me? Dude, even *we've* got CPUs made out of meat, we had neuron cultures wired into machines back before the turn of the century! Why do you think those blobs in the exoskels are any different? What makes you think the Ceph—whatever made the Ceph—what makes you think they even draw a distinction between meat and machinery?

Because I'm telling you, Roger, that line is not nearly as black-and-white as you seem to think.

Trust me on this.

Strickland sketches out the essentials while we make our escape. Hargreave's a sick twisted motherfucker—"totally insane," she says, "thinks he's the only competent human being on the planet"—but Gould was right: He knows more about the Ceph than any other backbone around. It goes back farther than Ling Shan, farther than Arizona; apparently Hargreave's known about the Ceph ever since he jacked some of their tech out of the Siberian backwoods in 1908. (Which would make Hargreave around 130 years old by now. Kinda surprised *that* didn't prick up any ears over at the Census Department. Of course, Hargreave probably owns the Census Department.)

Tunguska is the word Strickland throws over her shoulder, as if it's supposed to mean something to me. Turns out that was the site of a fifteen-megaton airburst back then, decades before the human race figured out how to make nukes. Two thousand square kilometers of forest flattened just like *that*. Nobody ever figured out for sure what it was: comet fragment, meteorite, microsingularity. Nobody ever found anything definitive, because Jacob Hargreave and Karl Rasch got there first and carted it all away.

And in all the long decades since, Hargreave has been walled away with the fire he stole from the gods, breathing on those dangerous embers all through the twentieth century and into the twenty-first, patiently waiting for our technology to grow into something that could crack the codes and solve the riddles. Sometimes not so patiently; you have to wonder how much of our vaunted human technology really belongs to us and how much we were herded toward by some megalomaniac and his stolen box of miracles, working behind the scenes.

Not enough, judging by the past couple of days.

So three years back Hargreave engineers some ill-fated foray into a Ceph outpost in the South China Sea; the Ceph wake up and Tara Strickland's father doesn't come home. Hargreave's been waiting for the other shoe to drop ever since. He's had a hundred years to get ready and three years early warning and he's got some kind of plan to beat back the invaders; Strickland's masters need to know what it is.

I know what it is. It's a plan to rip me out of the N2 like ripping someone out of their own skin and nerves, throw away the parts you don't need, and graft yourself into the rest. After that I'm not sure; but Strickland's already foiled Part A, so I suppose it can't hurt to find out. It might even save the world.

We rise again. The cargo elevator is a metal cube with a grill-work floor and no walls: I-beams and cable conduits and greasy white cinder blocks scroll sedately past as Strickland talks. "He's holed up in the executive level. You'll be running into heavy resistance. No one gets in to see him face-to-face; believe me, I've tried, and *I'm* his head of security. You're going to have to break in."

She doesn't seem to notice the dead employee sharing the car with us. He's got a very nice silencer screwed onto the end of his M12. He won't be needing it.

The elevator lurches to a halt on some level not meant for open house: server cabinets, ammo crates, lockers. Another one of those rotating amber lights.

Oh, and cameras.

"I've locked down local wireless; you've got maybe five minutes before Hargreave breaks the lock and sets the dogs on you." She snorts softly. "I guess that'd be on *us*, now. I'll get up to the helipad and secure our transport. Bring him out and meet me on the roof. We fly him out, we take him away, we make him talk. Go."

I cloak. I hear the elevator grind back into motion as I run invisibly past the securicams on my way to the stairwell.

No waypoints, this time. No helpful filepics or friendly voices telling me what to do. Just stairs and switchbacks and, two or three landings above me, low worried voices:

"Comms still dead in the skinning lab."

"Where the hell's Strickland?"

"Must be offline, too. I can't get hold of her, anyway."

"Shit. This isn't good."

It isn't good, but it's quick and it's easy. They go down before either of them can draw a weapon or a breath. The silencer works like a charm.

I'm a shark circling a shipwreck. I work my way through befuddled mercenaries torn among so many masters—Lockhart, Strickland, Hargreave—that they were starting to suffer whiplash even *before* Strickland jammed their communications. I move up from spartan basement storage into rows of spotless offices, into conference rooms paneled in oak and leather. Each floor is more opulent than the last, each outfitted with darker grains and older antiques, each more anachronistic. The whole building is a time machine. Waypoints would be redundant here; the path to Jacob Hargreave is obvious. Just follow him back to the Victorian era.

It takes closer to ten minutes for Hargreave to undo Strickland's sabotage; thirty seconds for the kill order to spread. By that time I'm already on the executive level. A tiny knot of armored mercs kills the lights and hunts me on thermal, but they've just spent the last thirty-six hours watching Golem Boy cut their numbers in half. Last night, maybe, they were jonesing for payback; right now I can track them by the sound of their knees knocking together.

I'd put them out of their misery myself, but the Ceph beat me to the punch.

I don't know where they came from. Haven't seen a Squid since I hit the island, but here they are: an intrepid little band of stalkers, eye clusters blazing, dorsal tentacles flailing, crashing through the walls and tearing out human hearts for all the world as though they're on my side. There are only four of them—three after one of the CELLulites gets off a lucky shot—and I manage to take out another before diving into a convenient stairwell and dropping down a level. I back against a corner that offers decent cover and a slitscan view of the door above. I aim the SMG.

They don't come after me.

Not an assault force. Not a measly four stalkers. Recon party at most; but advance scouts implies scouts in advance of something. Strickland was right: The Squids are coming to Roosevelt Island.

It would be a really good idea to get Hargreave out before that happens.

"So. Despite all the betrayals, all the pain, you are coming to get me out. Remarkable. Almost heroic, one might say." No hysteria in that voice, no more anger. Just—weariness. Resignation. Something almost approaching amusement. "But I fear our tentacular friends have formulated a similar plan. You'd better hurry if you hope to beat them to it."

Our tentacular friends are not back in the hall where I left them.

"Come. I won't fight you anymore. I've even rescinded the kill order, for the benefit of any soldiers you may have left alive."

There it is: a golden thread of waypoints. A trail of bread crumbs to the inner sanctum: down the hall, hang a right, hang a left. Knock.

"It is time to admit that loyalties are concentric. It is time to unite against the greater enemy . . ."

For some reason—only SECOND knows why—I finally believe him.

Marble columns. Double doors between them, ornately carved, brass-handled, high enough for a pinger to walk through without stooping.

I don't knock.

The doors *creak* as they swing inward. They *grind*. You'd think that someone of Hargreave's means would have been able to afford a can of WD-40.

Then again, maybe there's no point. Maybe these doors don't get used enough to matter.

Not just a room, through those doors. A cathedral. The great hall of some museum. A library. An endless carpet, three meters wide and red as clay, runs down the center of this vast space. On either side, rows of marble columns hold up dark skylights twenty meters overhead; suits of armor stand between them, mounted in glass cabinets. Massive bookshelves rise along one wall, barely visible in the dim distance; dark draperies go up forever on another.

"Theseus, at last. Welcome."

His voice does not crackle over comm. It *booms*. It fills the room.

Breakers *chunk* overhead. The lights come on. The glowing face of Jacob Hargreave, four meters high, smiles sadly down on me from overtop a wall-sized map of the planet: an old Eckert projection in faded yellow and pale blue.

Not armor in those glass cases, I see now. Nanosuits. Prototypes. Antiques in their own right, even now; Moore's law makes everything new old again.

"Scant reward for so much effort, eh. Crack the labyrinth, and you would at least expect to see the Minotaur before it kills you."

Dwarfed by map and monitor, someone has arranged half a dozen overstuffed antique chairs around a massive wooden desk. Its surface is smooth and polished and utterly empty.

"Ah well, it seems only fair. Come, then. Masks off."

The sound of old machinery, grinding into gear.

"I am here."

The map on the wall splits down the center and pulls apart like drawn curtains. There is only one antique inside, and at first I do not see it.

"Shocked? I would be."

See *him*.

"I'd revel in it, if I were you: that sudden jump of the pulse, the cram of flight-or-fight chemicals into the belly. So sweet while it lasts. But it's been so very long since I felt any of it."

So pristine in there, Roger. So, so *antiseptic*. Past the great chrome bars sliding back into the wall, the enameled walls *gleam;* the concentric tiles on the floor form a spiderweb with Hargreave's capsule at the center. Life-support machinery chirps and hisses around it. Half a dozen umbilicals sprout from its ends and loop up into a low ceiling. Flatscreens scroll nutrient levels and biotelemetry like billboards running stock prices.

There's a window in that capsule. It runs nearly the whole length of the cylinder; it leaves nothing to the imagination. The capsule is full of yellow-green liquid, like a public swimming pool too many six-year-olds have pissed in. The thing looking out from inside does not look like Jacob Hargreave. It barely even looks human.

"A century or more since my pleasures were anything but cerebral. I took the path Karl Rasch refused, the cold road to immortality."

Its lips don't move. The eyes above them are bright and hard as obsidian, and they don't leave me for an instant.

"I can still hear him—cursing Tunguska and what we found there, screaming at me for a coward and a fool. I wonder which of us really was the coward."

You ever see those bog men, Roger? On National Geographic, online, anything? The ones that died hundreds of years ago, somewhere in England or Ireland or something. Whoever killed them threw them into these peat bogs full of tannins, lignins. Natural preservatives. Bodies don't rot in there. They shrink, they shrivel up. They turn brown and wrinkly like baked apples but they don't rot, not for hundreds of years. You could fish them out of those bogs and they'd, they'd—

—They'd look just like Jack Hargreave, floating in his tank.

"And now so little time remaining."

Oh, Jack. You're not going anywhere, are you?

"I'd hoped to wear Prophet's suit myself. Take on the weapons he brought us, wear his armor. Enter the labyrinth and confront the Minotaur. But now . . .”

Hargreave's lips move at last. They tighten, split, pull back over toothless gums. He probably thinks of it as a smile.

"You. You will have to finish what Prophet began."

Something flickers in all this brightness. I can't tell what it is.

"Nathan? Are you there? Are you eavesdropping on my affairs again?"

And he is: There's his filepic, up above my left eye. There's his voice in my ear, faint and grainy and shot through with static: "Get out of there, Alcatraz!"

"No, wait."

That flicker again. A bad fluorescent, maybe.

"Wait," Hargreave repeats. "You need the final piece of the puzzle. There on the desk."

Behind me. I turn and look out into the hall. *That's* where the flicker is coming from. Not in here, not in this bright sterile oasis. Out there, among the towering bookcases and the marble pillars and the caged Nanosuits.

"Go!" the wizard urges from behind his curtain. "Take it!"

The surface of the desk opens as I approach: Panels slide back to reveal a shallow compartment, flat-gray, soft blue light glowing from the rim of a beveled disk in its center. A wooden cigar box waits for me there. I open it.

"This is m—your destiny now, Alcatraz. Use it."

Close, but no cigar. A loaded hypodermic syringe.

"Stick it anywhere! Are you looking for a *vein?* How can you have spent so much time in that armor and still not realize that *it knows*, Alcatraz. It knows what to do."

And Hargreave's right. Because good old Alcatraz would have had serious second thoughts about shooting himself up with a hypo full of Formula X, but the suit knows what it wants. SECOND knows.

We stick the needle in and plunge it down.

"Yes, there." Hargreave's avatar is almost purring. "The Tunguska Iteration."

Everything goes fuzzy.

"The key to all gates . . ."

Everything goes black.

There in the void, Nathan Gould is with me. Whining.

"Here? They were here, in New York, all along?"

"Their dormant systems were, yes, Nathan." Hargreave speaks slowly, patiently, as if explaining the facts of life to a special-needs child. "One of their cottages, and the quantum port facility to transmit themselves aboard. You think I'm based in this cesspit city because I *like* it here?"

Red clay carpet, going in and out of focus. Some weird pattern on it, like birds. Never noticed that before.

"Why didn't you warn someone?"

"Warn whom, Nathan? Humanity at large? The species that has proven so bracingly honest with itself in the face of unpleasant truths? That race so quick to accept the facts about population growth and resource overconsumption and climate change? No, thank you very much, I preferred to trust only myself, and a few handpicked men."

I'm back on my knees. I'm back on my feet.

"A few handpicked men. Right. And look what it's brought us to. Look what you've done, old man. They're *here*, you—"

"That's right, Nathan! The owners are back—"

They are, too. I can see where that flickering is coming from now: the dark sky above those overhead panes, strobing to gray. I can see insectile shapes backlit against the clouds, scampering and leaping across the skylights. I can see the blinding blue sparks of arc-welding torches.

"—waking the systems, firing up the boiler. Back to spring-clean the old family residence, and not much liking what they've found festering behind the fridge."

A Ceph gunship eclipses the moon. It hangs in the sky like a segmented crucifix, lining up the shot.

"And really. Can you blame them?"

The gunship cuts loose. All those superstrong reinforced windowpanes fall to earth in a shower of jagged glass.

Wind and rain and Ceph infantry cascade into Hargreave's inner sanctum. The wizard on the wall welcomes them with a giddy laugh: "Ah, the angels of death at last! My escort back to human frailty! It took you long enough!"

They're not just interested in him, though. Not judging by the fire I'm taking.

The flames are already rising. Stalkers and grunts leap across the chamber toward me like eager Dobermans. I flee up a metal staircase to a catwalk that accesses the upper reaches of all these bookshelves; it's high ground at least, a place to shoot back from, a hill to die on. I don't expect to find a way out but there it is, jammed into the narrow space between two bookcases: a backstage exit, an emergency stairwell, cinder-block walls and concrete steps and ventilation ducts running up the shaft like tendons.

Hargreave's avatar urges me on: "Become Prophet! Take on his armor! Strike for your species, for humanity in all its fumbling, half-made glory! Go, go! Save us all!"

I charge up the stairs past spinning emergency beacons. The building shakes around me.

"This is Jacob Hargreave to all CELL personnel. Commander Lockhart is dead, I will be joining him shortly, and the Prism facility is wired to self-destruct. Subject Prophet is now your only hope of turning back the alien invasion. You will therefore afford him every assistance you can as you evacuate this island."

That's nice of him. I wonder if anyone's listening.

Some machine—some *other* machine—starts a countdown in a cool feminine voice: "All Prism facilities will explosively self-seal in ten minutes. Your employee duties are terminated. Please exit via the indicated channels."

Plenty of time to make it to the helipad, I'm thinking. Right up until Tara Strickland checks in to tell me that the whole damn roof's been trashed. The Ceph have left nothing flyable up there at all. "I'm heading for the Queensboro Bridge," she tells me. "Meet me on the far side if you can."

The Ceph are everywhere. So are CELL, and it really doesn't matter whether they heard Hargreave's last orders or not; we're all just animals in a forest fire now, all just trying to keep ahead of the flames, and there's no predators and no prey when you're all about to be burned alive. We run like hell; we shoot at Squids when they get in our way. Countdown Girl pops onto the channel every now and then with timely updates that *All Prism facilities will explosively self-seal* in eight minutes, seven minutes, six minutes, but it's not like we need to be reminded. We *get* it already.

Someone says something about a service elevator, a way onto the Queensboro Bridge. I don't know where it is and nobody's feeding me waypoints but it's easy enough to follow the herd. A little less easy, maybe, when the herd keeps getting thinned out from above.

The elevator turns out to be right where the bridge crosses the eastern edge of the island. Three CELL are crowded around the lower doors when I arrive, repeatedly stabbing the call button. They bring up their weapons the moment they catch sight of me; I bring up mine. We stand there waving our dicks at each other, wondering about appropriate battlefield etiquette at times like these. Countdown Girl says two minutes.

The elevator arrives. We pile in. Someone pushes UP, again and again and again. Someone else pushes CLOSE DOORS.

We start moving.

There's one of those old speakers bolted to the frame, you know the ones that look like big square megaphones. There's Muzak coming out of it, a Nine Inch Nails cover done entirely with violins and pan flute. Countdown Girl says one minute.

I bring up my Grendel and shoot out the speaker. One of the CELLs says, "Thanks."

Then we're on the bridge, and it's every man for himself.

I've got every goddamn capacitor in the suit dedicated to speed—maybe twenty seconds at maximum sprint before the juice runs out. The bridge is taking fire from below, fire from above. Ceph tracers fill the air with streams of bright hyphens. The bridge is jammed with abandoned vehicles, some gutted, some still burning: cars, cube vans, semis. I think I see a pinger through the struts and girders, stalking down the oncoming lane; I *know* I see a gunship swooping in for another run.

Countdown Girl runs out of things to say.

Turns out the lady was a real mistress of understatement. The Prism facilities do not *explosively self-seal.* They blow sky-fucking-high, and they take the whole damn bridge with them.

It heaves under me, buckles in the middle. Fire boils up from below. All those great iron girders, the arches and trusses and studded yellow I-beams, crumple around me like origami. A tanker truck shoots by like a space shuttle and gets caught up in a web of burning metal. I try to keep running but I can't even *stand,* it's like balancing on the back of a harpooned whale. The bridge tears apart around me and I go over the edge, barely manage to catch myself on an exposed strut while an Airstream trailer sails past on its way to the river. I hang by my fingertips, too drained to haul myself back up, hoping against hope that the N2 manages to build back a charge before the spreading heat turns me to slag. I have a pretty good view of what's left of Roosevelt Island, though. It's hell on earth, it's fire on the water. I can't see a single recognizable feature through all those flames. When they burn down—if they ever do—there won't be anything left but a mound of glass.

Explosive self-sealing. I wonder what the zoning permits look like for that.

I don't wonder for long, though. One of New York's yellow cabs drops from a nest of tangled steel, bounces, rolls down a forty-degree chunk of burning asphalt, and flicks me off the bridge like a gnat.

Will there be an afterlife, I wonder? Choirs of angels? Or a fiery pit? One unlearns these falsehoods over time, but the child who learnt to fear hell is never really gone. To tell the truth, I think I've had quite enough of afterlives as it is—this one has been pretty purgatorial.

Almost fifty years floating in supercooled jelly like some medical specimen, thoughts creeping like rats through the cramped silicon corridors of machines, trapped behind video screens and camera systems. Never sleeping, never resting, never ceasing to think about the world you no longer belong to.

No, if this is a taste of the afterlife, I think oblivion will do nicely.

—Unencrypted signal fragment intercepted at 0450
24/08/2010
37.7 MHz (gov/nongov shared, land mobile)
local source (Manhattan)
No Positive ID.

ERECTION

Viral. That's the way Prophet put it.

I don't know how to put it any better. I can feel it in me now, I can feel it in *us:* seeking out the old code, shaking its hand, seizing control and changing its mind. Spreading the good news, particle by microscopic particle. It's changing me from the inside out: the Tunguska Iteration.

The good plague.

Maybe just a dream. I mean really, even with Cephtech, what are the odds that you can *feel* the reprogramming of individual cells? How is that even possible? Imagination, more likely, fueled by False Prophet murmuring at the back of my head that *Nano-catalyst viability assessment is complete* and the iteration is *ready to deploy.*

All I know is, the feeling fades as I rise from the darkness. I hear other voices, here at the bottom of the river. They're not loud, but they're distinct. I can hear them clearly over the hissing of my respirator.

"You were CIA all along? Why didn't you tell me?"

Gould *again.* I swear, that fucker's got to be my own personal spirit animal.

"Give me a fucking break." Tara Strickland's down here, too.

Pale daylight filters down through the muddy water. Another glorious Manhattan morning has begun.

"You want to help, help me find this guy," Strickland says. "You're so sure he's the key to all this."

"The *suit* is. Alcatraz and the suit, together. *That's* the weapon."

Ah, Nathan. So near, and yet so far. Would you talk about you *and* your right arm? Would you talk about Tara Strickland *and* her spinal cord?

"Uh-huh. Chino—anything?"

"Nothing, ma'am. Sweep complete. We're working our way back along the shore."

Chino. Dude. Good to hear your voice.

I roll over. The riverbed slopes upward, bare gray rock, current-scoured.

"I don't think we—"

"There! That's his signal!"

"We got him, Chino. Back to the vehicles."

"Over here! This way! Over here!"

I crawl across the waterline. Gould and Strickland wave down at me from the edge of a torn-up underpass, fissured and buckled. Grids of rebar show through the gaps like sutures. The Queensboro bridge is a tangle of broken Tinkertoy at my back. Behind it, on the far shore, Roosevelt Island smolders like Pompeii after the fireworks.

So much for getting my life back. So much for rising from the dead. Help me, Obi-Wan Hargreave; you were my only hope.

You fucker.

Strickland's already ringing up the chain of command by the time I jump up to rejoin the home team: Lieutenant Tara Strickland, seconded, special ops. Announcing the Return of the Prodigal Daughter, *sir*. Would like to go partying with the Ceph at their Central Park HQ. Wanna come?

Colonel Barclay is unconvinced. Much talk of foolish heroics and pointless suicide. Strickland counters by saying that Gould

has convinced her we have a real shot at turning this thing around
(I couldn't swear that that was the best approach to take, but at
least Barclay doesn't turn her down flat). Strickland asks for air
support; Barclay says he'll get back to her.

Strickland doesn't wait for that. We move out.

Gould tries to fill me in on the way. It's not the smoothest nar-
rative I've ever heard, punctuated as it is by *uhh*s and *umm*s and
*Get down get down fucking Squids at nine o'clock!*s. But it turns
out the N2's been tightcasting more than basic vitals and GPS
coordinates. It's been reading the voxels in my visual cortex. Or
no, that's not right: It's been *feeding* the voxels in my visual cortex, lighting them up like LEDs on a flatscreen display, and that's
just as true for Prophet's memories as it is for waypoints and
weapons specs. And it's been writing it all to the thirty-gigahertz
band as well.

Nathan Gould has been spying on my dreams.

Prophet's memories have told him more than they've told me.
They've told him that the center of Ceph operations is under the
Central Park Reservoir. *Isn't THAT a coincidence* I think, and
then: *Hargreave.* Hargreave and his corporations within corporations, their tentacles squirming down through the boardrooms
and the back rooms and the generations, the butterfly flaps its
wings in 1912 and a hundred years later neither crime nor depression nor all the developers in the world have managed to
make a dent in that sacred green space.

What was it Hargreave said to Gould, just before the ceiling
crashed in? "You think I'm based in this cesspit city because I *like*
it here?"

Think about it, Roger. Think about how *old* New York is. The
Europeans showed up what, five centuries ago? The Amerinds,
thousand of years before that. All that time the Ceph have been
sleeping under our streets and none of us even knew it. *Almost*

none of us, at least; down through all those ages I bet at least one or two people must've wandered into the wrong cave at the right time, tiptoed among all those sleeping giants, maybe made off with a box of Kleenex or a bedside alarm clock or a fountain of youth.

Hargreave was an adult in 1908. I wonder how old he was then. I wonder if Tunguska was really the first time he stole fire from the gods. I'm thinking, what if Hargreave was around back when New York started clearing the squatters out of central Manhattan? What if Hargreave was there in the fifteen-fucking-*hundreds*, playing his backroom games to make sure that someday the biggest city on the whole damn continent would be sitting on the roof of the Devil's summer cottage?

I have no idea why, Roger. It's all just idle speculation bouncing around in the back of a Bulldog on its way to the final showdown. All I'm saying is, maybe Tunguska wasn't the first time Hargreave got in and got out, and maybe Ling Shan wasn't the second. Maybe Ling Shan was just the first time the owners woke up and found him in their bedroom.

But like I say, I don't really get much chance to follow up on any of this because the Ceph keep distracting me. I've never seen more than one dropship at a time before: *Four* of them do a low-altitude flyby over the water before we're off East River Drive. I'm on the turret but I don't even try to light them up: they're going too fast, the ride's too bumpy for a bead, and I gotta admit a part of me's hoping that if we don't draw attention to ourselves they might not notice us, just head off to wherever they're going and let us get to Central Park in peace.

Then we swing onto 58th and you can see just how fat a chance *that* was ever gonna be.

The whole damn avenue is crisscrossed with Ceph conduits. They jut up out of the road, arc across five or ten floors of airspace, disappear into holes smashed through storefronts and skyscrapers. The street is a tangle of concrete and uplifted bedrock and giant jagged sawtooth alien plumbing, and as we come around the corner you can see the last of the dropships dumping their cargo in a big nasty line all across First Avenue.

They know we're coming.

The first two Bulldogs are already jammed up and taking fire; one of them rolled before we rounded the corner and is over on its back, spinning its wheels. I'm doing what I can but East River Drive was smooth as fucking *glass* next to all this buckled asphalt and my crosshairs are bouncing across ninety degrees of arc until our driver hits the brakes. Except it's not so much hitting the brakes as getting his rib cage blown to matchsticks by the shell the Ceph just lobbed through his windshield. I bail in the split second before it explodes, which isn't nearly enough time to get out of the blast radius. Thank Christ for the armor option.

This is resistance like we've never seen before. The street ahead is crawling with alien grunts; stalkers leap from wall to wall like giant metal grasshoppers, taking their shots and bouncing away before anyone can get a bead. I count at least four Heavies lumbering up the street; their cannons flash like Gatling guns. Our whole damn convoy is scattered to hell and gone: three vehicles out for the count, their occupants either dead or taking cover; no sign of the others. Hopefully they saw the scoring on the walls and took a less scenic route.

I lose the convoy. They lose me: Too many torqued I-beams and shorting electrical networks to keep in touch over more than a block or two, and oh, here come the pingers. Always the life of the party. But somewhere between the blowing-shit-up and the not-being-blown-to-shit I make it to the upper reaches of a trashed office building. I'm not running away: I'm fighting uphill. Half a dozen Ceph drop modules are embedded way up in the executive levels and the grunts that came out are making the most of the high ground.

Half the fucking floor is in flames by the time we finish mixing it up, but it's worth it. The altitude gives me my signal back and Barclay's geek squad has been working overtime: Gould has loaned them my suit freqs and it turns out they can tap into the N2's targeting subsystems to help pinpoint the air strikes the good colonel has managed to coax out of McGuire. Too little, way too late for most of us: Strickland's heroic little convoy has been decimated.

Not exterminated, though. Not extinct, not yet. A few of us make it through all the way to Central Park.

Or as your friends at the Pentagon prefer to call it: Ground Zero.

Now, from the folks who brought you *Swimming with Ceph*, the new off-Broadway smash hit: *New York Nukem*.

The word comes down somewhere between East River Drive and Fifth Avenue. I can't really put my finger on when, because I'm too busy getting shot at. But by the time I finally catch up with what's left of Strickland's convoy just outside Central Park, the news is really sinking in.

Strickland is furious. Barclay fought it tooth and nail. Gould says what do you *expect* when you keep putting psychopathic assholes in charge. (In his own fucked-up Gouldian way, I think he almost feels vindicated. A shame he never got a chance to meet Leavenworth.)

Me? I gotta say, I was kind of on board with it.

Maybe I've lost my sense of empathy. Maybe after a few years in the service you just get used to it, come to terms with the fact that life is cheap. Maybe SECOND's programmed it out of me with all these nanoneurons infiltrating my cortex. Or maybe it's just harder to care about the living when you don't actually have a dog in that race anymore. But I listen to Strickland ticking off the outrages—What about the people? What about the surrounding boroughs? What about the fallout?—and if I had a voice I might shut her down with a question of my own.

What about the *Ceph*?

I mean, it's not as though I've agreed with most of what the Pentagon has been up to lately. That sweeper they set off just about inspired me to resign my commission on general principles. But the fact is, it didn't work. Nothing they've tried so far has worked—and when your back's to the wall, scorched earth is not exactly unprecedented military doctrine. A tactical airburst over Manhattan might be the only way to contain this thing. Probably won't be enough, granted; but if all else fails it's worth a shot.

Of course, all else *hasn't* failed. There's still the Alcatraz Initiative. But the brass aren't boots; they've got reports from the front lines but they haven't seen this apocalypse for themselves. Chances are, all they know about the Tunguska Iteration is that it was invented by a half-crazed recluse pickled in formaldehyde, and Nathan Gould says it has something to do with homosexual rape in hanging flies. If that was all *I* knew, I wouldn't have much faith in it, either.

We haul into Central Park under a yellow sky infested with sheet lightning. Nobody's waiting for us. No reinforcements. No Ceph. No pilgrims.

Nobody.

We park in a field of scrub and crab grass. Dead silence except for the far-off rumble of thunder. "Where the hell is everybody?" someone wonders.

"Maybe they threw everything they had at us back on 58th," Chino suggests. "Maybe they got nothing left." He doesn't even believe it himself.

No birdsong. Not even the crickets are talking.

Strickland looks around grimly. "Something's wrong here."

The birds haven't left, though. We know this in the very next second, when they do. Great clouds of them rise suddenly from the trees in waves, dark as spore, utterly silent. They flap away to the east as the first tremors start to shake the ground.

The tree line—*buckles*. Treetops lash back and forth against a windless sky. They *rise* into the twilight as if on hydraulics; I can see brief explosions of blue sparks in the darkness around their bases. Power lines, I realize. Tearing apart as the ground rises *there* but not *here,* as cliffs grow from the woods as we watch, walls of raw fissured bedrock standing up from the earth, lifting the forest on its back. One of the Bulldogs hops two meters in the air, flips, lands upside down. The nearer copses are leaning toward us now, farther, farther, toppling over. Ridges of rock and earth rise and pile up and slide back down the sides of something very large and very old, waking up after a million years in the ground.

Those of us with vehicles floor them in reverse. Those on foot run like hell. Barclay's in every headset, "Strickland? Strickland? What the hell just happened out there? We're reading massive seismic disturbances, we're reading—"

I can't see the top anymore and the Thing in the Earth still rises smoothly from the ground. It must be halfway to the jet stream by now. A dozen little waterfalls cascade out into space and disintegrate into mist far over our heads.

"Sir, we are going to need an immediate airlift," Tara Strickland calls in with admirable calm. "As well as armed air support. As many aircraft as you can manage. The situation has . . . changed . . ."

It's the mother, the father, the whole damn extended family of all Ceph Spires. It's the last page of the Book of Revelation, the end of the Mayan Calendar, the drowning of the world at Ragnarok, and it's taken half of Central Park along for the ride. There's a mountain towering over the skyline. I bet you can see it all the way to Canada.

The spire holds it up, all that mass stuck to one impossible pylon: a chunk of earth the size of a hundred city blocks, hanging over Manhattan like Everest balanced on a pool cue. The spire itself towers even higher, a dark twisted sculpture skewering the floating island about two-thirds of the way along its length. From down here, through the deepening gloom, it looks a little like the Statue of Liberty with brimstone highlights. If the Statue of Liberty was a couple of kilometers high and had a terminal spore infection.

Whatever chance Barclay may have had to talk the nuclear option off the table with his superiors, it's pretty much vanished now. They do give us a few choppers, though, and all the moral support we can carry.

They also give us thirty minutes before they send in the bombers.

It gets darker as we approach. Water drains from ponds and reservoirs, atomizes as it falls, turns the sky into soupy fog: dark in places, flickering bright where fires have caught, flashing where dismembered fragments of the power grid spit and spark. I can hear the groan and crack of breaking granite over the beating of the rotors. Gas lines and sewer pipes stick into the air like severed veins, gushing flame or wastewater.

I was wrong. This is no island in the sky; this is a tumor. If God had cancer it would look like this: black and lumpy as a miner's lung. On closer approach I can see it's not even a single mass: one foggy silhouette resolves into many, a jumble of boulders: some no bigger than houses, others that could crush city blocks. The cracks and fissures between are infested with black

spinal conduits of Ceph architecture, embedded, a web of liga-
ments holding everything together.

Well, not *everything*. Chunks of granite calve away like ice-
bergs as the pilot looks for a place to land. We're coming in low
from the south, ten meters over the treetops: tiny blue mainte-
nance trailers and miniature statues sit down there like tabletop
ornaments, lit at odd angles by a random handful of streetlamps
still running off stored solar.

The chopper's bucking like a cork in a wind tunnel. The closer
we get to the spire the worse the turbulence becomes; if we keep
on this approach the downdraft's going to slap us into the rocks
before we get another hundred meters. Landing here is out of the
question. Even farther back we can't risk it; the whole thing's a
pile of shifting rubble, loosely bound with alien rebar. The pilot's
willing to push it to eight meters, right at the southern tip; I drop
the rest of the way and he backs right off to a safe distance, whatever the hell *that* means these days. The rotors beat away into the
soupy darkness and suddenly it's—

—Peaceful.

I'm on the grass. There's a constant wind but the sound it
makes is almost comforting. Just five meters behind me the world
drops away, and I can see the dim gray shapes of downtown New
York spread out like chips on a motherboard.

And in the next second the world drops away just *two* meters
behind me, and I'm scrambling back from that edge before this
crumbling rock pile pitches me overboard.

"Oh, man, look at the calving on this thing!" Gould's back
in the chopper with Strickland, but he's riding shotgun through
the suit feed. "Alcatraz, listen, all this bedrock's just hanging off
the structure. It's completely unstable, could go at any time. You
gotta watch for stress fracturing."

You know, Nate, I think I figured that one out.

To the north, the superspire stabs up into the night like a church steeple for Devil-worshippers. Twenty-six minutes to Plan B. The N2 drives me over the ground faster than the ground can open up to swallow me.

And then the chopper pilot blurts out, "Oh shit, they're *everywhere* . . ."

"Alcatraz, listen." Strickland again. "Barclay's expeditionary guys got into the park yesterday before they were driven back. And CELL had an evac base here as well. Look for ammo caches, you're going to—well, you'll need firepower."

And they're on me before she hits the period.

I barely hear her breaking the pilot's balls to get in closer, give me some cover. I barely hear False Prophet announce that he's completed a local scan and nailed some likely ammo dumps. I hear the Ceph, though, stuttering like bullfrogs, lacerating the air with their tracers. I take a couple of hits before cranking armor; a couple more after I leap across a shifting chasm (gray chaos, nothing at all down there) and roll to cover. It's too far for the grunts but a lone stalker sails easily over my hiding place and clamps its talons around the trunk of a tree ten meters past. Then the tree's falling, torn free of the earth by a couple of hundred kilograms of metal and jelly using it for a grab-on at thirty meters a second. And the outcropping it jumps to next, crumbling under its feet. And the pickup truck it tips over the edge of a severed roadway. The stalker leaps from point to point, never missing, never regaining the edge; it disappears into the void, dancing between falling objects.

Far to the north something lashes the sky: The spire has grown *limbs,* segmented tentacles that flail back and forth like whips. A pair of spines extend from each segment. Or legs, maybe. I've seen them before: monstrous metal centipedes writhing in the air.

I see other things, too, smaller but just as monstrous, moving south to welcome me across the shifting landscape. We skirt each other, exchange fire, duck back into hiding. The ground tilts and slides as we dance. Something sets two massive slabs of substrate jostling like continents in collision; downhill and uphill trade places; some pond or wading pool breaks free of containment and floods across the battlefield in a thin sheet, turning earth to mud and making the grass slippery as oil. Sometimes the Ceph nearly take me out. Sometimes I take fire from an unexpected quarter, SECOND backtracks a bearing, but I can't see any targets.

Still, if the point of the exercise is to kill each other, I'm better at it than they are. So far.

In between the skirmishes, though, there are—moments. I almost feel guilty talking about them. Fighting for the survival of a planet, halfway through a thirty-minute nuclear countdown with all objectives yet unmet: How dare I waste a *second* on goddamn *aesthetics?* But there they are, surrealistic and beautiful: a dense blue carpet of tiny, perfect flowers, running down the middle of a pedestrian avenue. An ancient bronze statue standing atop a granite pedestal: long since turned green, its head and shoulders white with pigeon shit. A lone taxicab skewed across the grass, softly spotlit by a single streetlamp in the fog.

I find one of Barclay's caches in the passage under Bethesda Terrace: scuffed plastic crates piled up in a dim grotto full of arches and golden alcoves and polished ceramic tiles that pattern the ceiling like a Persian carpet. There's more than enough canned carnage here to see me through to whatever end awaits me in—yup, twenty minutes and counting. I scrounge one of those new X43 microwave guns. I saw a couple of the guys using them earlier today; not much good on armor but they cook jelly right in the package so long as you remember to squeeze off short shots. Hold the trigger for more than an instant and you'll drain the battery in no time.

Resupply, reload, resume. I cloak at the north end of the underpass, stick my head out. The spire towers into a dead gray sky; the cracked fountain in front of me looks like a bug in its shadow. I think the tarnished thing in its center is supposed to be an angel but it looks more like a zombie with wings.

The centipedes have stopped flailing. They've bitten into the ground and taken root, given up the wild days of their youth and settled down to become great hairy arches looping across the sky. As if the spire has grown legs.

Ah, shit. I know what that means.

Sure enough, here's Nathan: "Dude, it's set up substations. Like back at the hive. Whatever you did back then, you gotta do it again."

The suit serves up new targets and tacticals. At least the Ceph are consistent: either form follows function or the aliens have no fucking imagination whatsoever. Same substation layout, same relative distances, same basic vulnerabilities.

Harder uphill battles.

Heavies guard each substation, slow but almost indestructible. Their missiles are easy enough to dodge a few hundred meters out, but the closer you get the less time there is to get out of the way—and these fuckers are smart enough to play defense. I have to come to them and they know it.

Besides, there are plenty of grunts and stalkers to take the game forward. More than I think, at first. I stealth past choke points and high ground (higher ground) where the enemy should be waiting, find no one there—then get my ass shot at from behind, five seconds later. I hear little rockfalls to my left, the soft chittering of a stalker on my six, turn to track and come up empty—and ordnance lights up my flank where there was nothing but rocks and air a moment before. The rising wind blows the mist off most of the exposed reaches but everywhere there are pits and depressions where the air is stagnant and the fog pools like milk. Naked eyesight is useless in there; StarlAmp and thermal see through the fog but still can't catch the Ceph. They pin me down between the edge of the world and a crumbling cement footbridge, turn the sky into a shooting gallery whenever I so much as peek around the corner.

The ground crumbles to air under my feet and now I've got no choice; it's either an express trip back to earth or a Hail Mary run straight across the kill zone. I lay down suppressing fire as I run, spray an arc as empty as the eye can see—and a grunt materializes from thin air and collapses in a twitching heap in front of me.

Holy shit: The Ceph up here have *cloaks.*

I make it to the safe side of a toppled army barricade, wondering: What took them so long?

Fifteen minutes.

New weapons, new tactics. Two shots with the Mike makes your average grunt pop like a zit windshield—but the substation Heavy on which I try it is still shooting back after I've drained it dry. I ditch the Mike, switch to L-TAG: Two smart grenades finish the job. It takes four to down the Heavy at the second substation, but I get lucky at the third: I miss the target completely but I knock out whatever's holding up the US-ARMY prefab barricade leaning behind it. Ten meters of hardened cement comes down on the Squid like God's own tombstone. Forty seconds later the last substation is down for the count.

The wind's been building with every step I take toward the primary target; now it howls around me like something tortured. But I'm so close, now. The spire isn't even a spire anymore: it's massive, it's city blocks on a side, it's a goddamn cathedral of the underworld. It's every part of every bottom-dweller the earth ever spawned: armored shells and jointed legs and segmented antennae; more sharp-edged mouthparts than you can count;

blood-red gills, pincers and claws all jammed together by some monstrous trash compacter and pressed into a tower that stabs the stratosphere. The cracks between those pieces pulse and dim with orange light, as though someone were blowing on embers.

Bright light ahead, spilling around the rocks of this outcropping. I cringe in the shadows like Adam after the apple, hiding from an angry God. The wind tries to push me into the light. My fingers find cracks in the rock, dig in against the gale; flattened against the granite, I lean forward.

Wheels within wheels: a spoked, segmented disk, at the base of the structure, big enough to plug the Holland Tunnel. It seems to lead into the structure's interior, a great circular portal awash in blinding white radiance. Air intake. Or if you prefer more romantic imagery: a tunnel of light.

It's about fucking time. I've been dead for two days already.

I remember lessons learned at Hargreave's knee: the spore's basically an antibody. It'll swarm to the site of an injury. Nathan Gould, bringer of Bad News, pipes up: "Dude, you gotta get *inside.*" I can barely hear him over the wind.

Tara Strickland, bringer of Much Worse News: "God*damn it.* The STRATCOM order just went thr—Alcatraz, you're out of time! *Go!*"

Shit.

I step out from behind my rock. I don't even have to jump. The Tunnel of Light sucks me up like a bird into a jet engine.

Blizzard doesn't come close. *Hurricane* misses the mark. *Wind tunnel* might catch the nuts and bolts, but it can't convey the gut feeling.

I don't know if anything can.

The spire breathes you in and for the merest instant it almost seems calm: The walls are a blur but there's no resistance as long as you just go with the flow. Then you reach out for a handhold, grab on to the first thing that hits your fingers, and the wind slams down on you like a mountain at Mach Two.

I'd have never even made the catch without the suit; my fingers would have ripped right off my hand. If I had made the catch, I'd never have held on; I would have left my arm hanging against the wall while the rest of me slammed down into—

Where am I now? Far beneath the tumor in the sky, at least. I must have shot out the bottom of that rock pile a split second after the spire sucked me in. Surely I'm back on earth, back *under* it, down in the deep dark levels where extinctions are made. The spore blasts down, around, past me like a storm of needles, like ball bearings from a railgun. BUD strafes my visual cortex with yellow-coded updates on *epidermal integrity* and *maximum armor* settings but it's all just talk; the suit's abrading around me like a heat shield on reentry.

I can't even see where I am. There are flickers of orange light, flickers of blue, everything high-contrast and stroboscopic; I'm blind to anything more than a few centimeters past my faceplate. I realize that whatever I'm hanging off, I'm hanging one-handed: my other hand, miraculously, is still clutching the L-TAG. I cradle that launcher to my chest like a baby, I hold on to it for dear life.

I try to bring it up but the wind resistance is too great; the most I can do is aim down and off-center, toward the wall of the shaft. Could be conduits along this thing, right? Could be power lines and vital circuitry. I fire blind, empty all my grenades into the maelstrom; the wind yanks the empty weapon away. I think I might hear a distant muffled *boom* over the howling of the wind. Maybe not.

There's no doubt about the sudden vibration that shakes the walls, though. It shakes me loose and slams me down another endless tunnel.

Which actually ends.

Maybe the suit keeps the impact from turning me to jelly. Maybe it just keeps the jelly contained in a human-shaped sack. But I'm on the deck now, and the wind screams sideways instead of down, and I can just barely roll into the lee of some protruding piece of machinery half embedded in the wall. It's still not even close to calm air: the back-eddy scouring this little wind-shadow is a gale by any standards—but it's nothing the suit can't handle, assuming it hasn't already been damaged beyond repair.

The nuke could go off, and in here I'd never even notice.

Thoughts occur to me. I don't know if they're mine or SEC-OND's, or even if that's a difference that makes a difference anymore. Something thinks: *Bad vent design: Too much turbulence.* Something thinks: *Maybe this isn't a primary vent. Maybe the primaries are offline, or damaged. Maybe the Ceph just aren't into laminar flow.*

Something thinks: *There's so much spore swirling around this goddamn suit I can barely see my own feet so why isn't it interacting?* and I'm pretty sure that's me. Because the answer's so bleeding obvious:

It's an antibody. It swarms to the site of an injury.

So far I'm just an inert particle in this body. It's time to turn malignant.

I'm all out of fancy firearms but the N2 comes equipped with a pretty good Kung-Fu Grip. And way down here in the basement of the doomsday machine, there just *has* to be something important to tear at. Doesn't have to be vital. You don't have to attack the heart or the brain to get the white blood cells to take notice. Any old chunk of tissue will do.

This outcropping I'm hunkered down against right here, for instance . . .

I raise my fist, bring it down. Nothing.

Again: a dent. Maybe. Maybe just spots in front of my eyes.

I find something that looks like a seam, hook my fingers underneath, pull. It gives a little. I pull again, putting my back into it.

The panel peels back like the zip-top lid on a can of cat food. Blue light sparkles within.

I go to town.

Blue light recedes. Orange is in ascension. Every time I bring down my fist, copper lightning forks and crackles from the breach. It takes thirty seconds for me to bring this whole segment of passageway alive with electricity.

It takes less time than that for the antibodies to pay attention.

They boil out from the main flow as though someone's punched holes in an invisible pipe: black angry thunderclouds in search of a parade to rain on. The wind doesn't seem to bother them; they cut across that howling flow as if the air were dead still. They're more than smoke, more than particles; they're a *collective*, a billion microscopic agents acting in unison. I can see them talk among themselves: I look into that seething darkness and I see a million faint sparks winking back and forth as the nanites trade notes and make plans. Structural damage in sublevel whatsit. Power failure in thingamajig twenty-three.

Invader.

Infection.

There.

They swallow me whole, billow around me like some monster amoeba. The suit catches fire. That's what it looks like, anyway: that orbital time-lapse of burning rain forests where half of SouthAm is sheathed in orange sparkles. Only the smoke isn't *rising* from the tiny fires burning across my body; the smoke is falling *into* them, it's precipitating, it's *condensing* down into the light. It's Brazil, run backward. The suit drinks in the spore; the embers fade along my arms and legs. Nothing else happens for a moment or two.

My fingertips start to tingle. My fingertips start to *glow*.

I begin to brighten from the outside in.

All those black specks, resurrected. All that ash turned back into flame. The particles rise like a blizzard of stars: from my arms, from my chest, from my legs and feet. So much mass, escaping; it seems impossible that any might be left behind. Perhaps my very molecules are flying apart, perhaps my whole body's ablating into luminous mist.

Suddenly I'm as incandescent as a goddamn angel.

The rest, as they say, is history.

The spire vented, of course. That was the whole plan. It went off exactly when it was supposed to, but not before we'd raped its hanging fly ass; and when all that jizz spread out across Manhattan, it was carrying *our* sperm, not the Ceph's. The Tunguska Iteration blew those fuckers apart like maggots in a microwave.

They say it was even closer than we thought. All those other spires popping up across the city, those were just beta releases. Tweaks, test runs, short-lived and self-terminating. That Central Park fucker, though: That was the mass-production model. It would've been shooting *replicators*. And then you're not just talking about Manhattan, or New York, or even the whole tristate area. You're kissing the whole damn planet good-bye. That's what they say, anyhow. Of course, they don't really *know* anything.

Actually, Roger, I don't think they even know that much. I don't think we *have* won. In fact, this is just the beginning. I'm pretty sure your bosses know that, too.

Because Gould had access to Hargreave's feed. Gould knows what I saw, Gould knows stuff I haven't told you here today. And if Gould knows, your bosses do, too.

Personally, I think of it as kind of a group home, a mansion with many rooms. And one of the residents wakes up in the middle of the night—hears a noise upstairs, maybe—and goes to investigate. He doesn't bother waking the others. It's probably just squirrels, or the cat knocked over a lamp or something. No point disturbing anyone else.

But it's not squirrels, and it's not a cat—or if it is, it's a cat that's figured out how to use the shotgun on the mantel, and now a gunshot's gone off in the attic. Maybe there was a scream when the bullet hit, maybe someone shouted out a warning. And all the other gardening tools in all the other rooms, they're waking up now. They want to know what happened. They want to know where their friend is. Maybe they're even putting in a call to their owners to come have a look-see.

Hargreave would probably have some really valuable insights right about now, don't you think?

Well, yes. As far as we know. But come on, Roger; you can't have forgotten that Hargreave was never in it alone. It's right there in the name of his company, for chrissake.

So tell me. What do you know about a dude called Karl Rasch?

Emergency Forensic Session on the Manhattan Incursion
CSIRA BlackBody Council
Pre-Testimony Interview, Partial Transcript, 27/08/2023
Subject: Nathan Gould

Excerpt begins:

You remember those constellations I told you about, the ones that kept showing up in the static: *clusters of blue stars, little sapphire pinpricks connected by a network of dim glowing filaments, rotating slowly in midair.* Ceph starglobe, remember?

I bet your guys are going over it right now. The suit kept playing it so it's gotta be important, right? Some kind of star map. Interstellar trade routes or invasion plans. Maybe the location of the Ceph homeworld. You've been poring over that shit ever since you tossed my place; nine, ten hours now? Trying to line up those sparkles with our own star maps, trying to figure out where a planet would have to be in the Milky Way to have that particular constellation hanging in its sky. How many possible matches you got so far? Few thousand, maybe?

I'll give you a hint. You're looking in the wrong direction.

One of those stars is under New York. Central Park, if you really want to narrow it down. There's another under Ling Shan. And you know there's a shitload more. Dozens more. If you'd waited another ten minutes before kicking in my door—hell, if you'd just asked nicely instead of waving those fucking guns in my face—I could've given you a list.

No big deal, though.

I've got a feeling everyone's gonna know exactly where the rest of those stars are, real soon now.

Excerpt ends.

Emergency Forensic Session on the Manhattan Incursion Excerpted Testimony of Dr. Lindsey Aiyeola Before the CSIRA Blackbody Council, Unknown Location, sometime between September 1 and 6, 2023.
(Names of all BBC members redacted.)

Excerpt Begins:

Aiyeola: Alcatraz—Prophet, whatever he calls himself now—there is nothing in his file to suggest any aptitude or special training in the behavioral sciences. Certainly nothing to suggest he was capable of the sort of psychological insights sprinkled throughout his interview—and yes, some of them were quite astute.

In hindsight, we made the right decision by using an inexperienced and uninformed interviewer. Lieutenant Gillis couldn't give

away much because he didn't know much—
and on those occasions when he *did* bluff
or dissemble, Prophet saw right through
him. In fact, Prophet was in control of a
great deal of the interview process.

BB 1:   And yet according to your own report, *you*
were manipulating *him*. You encouraged
him to ramble, to go off on tangents, not
only to acquire information about brain
function but also in the hope that he'd
inadvertently reveal things he might not be
likely to in a more formal setting.

Aiyeola: That's true. And we believe we obtained a
great deal of useful information, but—well,
we also have to consider the possibility
that we were being played, at least in the
later stages of the process. The subject's
abilities varied throughout the course of
the interviews but the overall trend was
upward. Certainly we weren't slipping
anything past him by the end of the
interrogation. The question is, how much
of the earlier information just "slipped out"
and how much was deliberately fed to us.

BB 2:   Excuse me, but I've only just been brought
into the loop concerning the esteemed Mr.
Alcatraz. Would you be so kind as to give
me some examples of these "abilities"?

Aiyeola: His linguistic skills have improved
significantly over a very short period of
time. His memory has become eidetic.
According to his file he was originally
right-handed; he is now functionally

ambidextrous. Levels of comprehension,
retention, and recall are increasing literally
by the—to make a long story short, he is
simply becoming *smarter*. There's some
indication that the growth in his abilities
is following a sigmoid curve, in which case
they're bound to level off at some point.
At the moment, though, we're not entirely
certain where that might be.

And of course, there is the troubling fact
that he still insists on referring to himself as
"Prophet," although he is fully aware that he
is not Laurence Barnes, and that Laurence
Barnes is dead.

BB 3:   Why would Alcatraz "feed" us anything
that wasn't true? I've seen the man's record:
He wasn't top of his class, but he's a good
marine. I see no reason to question his
loyalty.

Aiyeola: That was a different person, sir. We don't
know who or what Alcatraz is anymore.
We don't know what's going on in there,
beyond the fact that his integration with
alien technology has probably changed
his—well, his outlook. We *do* know, thanks
to Dr. Gould, that he was privy to specific
information about Charybdis technology—
his ability to hack the City Hall hive is
difficult to explain any other way than by
accessing some kind of memory archive
from the N2's previous occupant—and that
he was not as forthcoming on that subject
as he might have been. I will also admit that

I find his remarks to Lieutenant Gillis about having to "choose a side" more than a little worrisome.

BB 1: In light of your position that he may have some special knowledge of the Ceph, what do you think of his take on their motives?

Aiyeola: He made a number of good points, sir. Certainly the Manhattan Incursion doesn't make any tactical sense as a conventional invasion, and even Hargreave's Gardener Hypothesis leaves a number of issues unresolved. Prophet's take makes more sense, but it's all pure conjecture at this point.

BB 1: Do you agree that the Ceph are not primarily interested in invasion?

Aiyeola: I believe that when we are talking about the Ceph the very concept of *invasion* is almost certainly inadequate.

BB 1: Would you care to elaborate on that, please.

Aiyeola: Are we *invading* an anthill when we build a drive-through bank machine on top of it? Probably, from the ants' point of view. And if some small fraction of those ants survive—if they manage to get out of the way and set up a new colony somewhere else—are we incompetent invaders because we haven't exterminated all of them? Have they *beaten* us, if the bulldozers came and went and left some ants alive? No, because we weren't trying to wipe out an anthill. We were putting up an ATM. But you can't explain currency, finance, automated

tellers to an ant. It's impossible for them
to comprehend our acts as anything other
than a devastating attack by a god-like
force that the ants—for some mysterious
reason—were able to fend off.

BB 3: So your opinion is that we're irrelevant to
them.

Aiyeola: I have no idea whether we are or not.
All I'm saying is, given such a vast gulf
in technology and biology, it might well
be physically impossible to ever fully
understand what happened in Manhattan.
What might happen in the future.

BB 2: I think that what Dr. Aiyeola is suggesting
is that we concentrate on the immediate
tactical threat, and not waste valuable
resources on an impossible quest to
comprehend the incomprehensible.

Aiyeola: Excuse me, [REDACTED], that's by no means
what I'm suggesting. I said *might*. I
profoundly hope that someday we are in a
position to understand Ceph motivations.
Unfortunately I can only think of one way
to do that.

BB 3: And that is?

Aiyeola: Become very much smarter.

BB 1: Alcatraz may prove useful in that regard.
Assuming we can crack that particular nut.

BB 2: Well, whatever the Ceph are doing here, we
can safely assume it matters a great deal
to them. They wouldn't have gone to the
enormous cost and trouble of launching
such a large-scale—

Aiyeola: With all due respect, sir, we have no way of knowing what constitutes an "enormous cost" to the Ceph. This is a species with an interstellar reach, a species that can teleport macroscopic objects—including, apparently, living organisms—over interplanetary distances. This whole campaign might have been a trivial investment to them—perhaps no more expensive than bending over to retrieve a dropped set of car keys. All we know for certain is that Hargreave stole their technology.

                    Maybe the Ceph just wanted it back. Maybe they got it.

FORTUNE FAVORS THE BOLD

The N2 is destined to be ubiquitous in theaters of engagement from downtown Johannesburg to the Ross Slush Shelf. Don't let the Red Queen leave you behind: Contact CryNet today for a free on-site demonstration in a combat environment of your choosing.* Mention this brochure and we'll knock 5% off the price of any order for twenty units or more.

The CryNet Nanosuit 2.0. The next generation of combat technology has arrived.

Wouldn't you rather have it on *your* side?

*Some restrictions apply.

ABOUT THE AUTHOR

Biologist, author, and convicted felon, Peter
Watts (author of *Blindsight* and the Rifters tril-
ogy) appears to be especially popular with people who have never met him. At least, pretty
much every award his work has received comes
from overseas (with the exception of a recent
Hugo, which probably won on a sympathy
vote in the wake of recent encounters with the
Department of Homeland Security). His science fiction, oddly enough, has been used as
a core text in science and philosophy courses
as well as the usual gamut of SF electives; he
only wishes his actual science had been taken
half as seriously, back in the day. Both he and
his cat have appeared in the prestigious journal
Nature.

Printed in the United States
by Baker & Taylor Publisher Services